Sara

Thanks again for reading CI. Best of luck – Hope you enjoy the book.

Regards

[signature]

CRIMINAL INTENT

CRIMINAL INTENT

Bruce Marvin

Glenbridge Publishing Ltd.

This novel is based on a true story. Names and
locations have been changed and some
events fictionalized.

Copyright © 1996 by Bruce G. Siminoff and Marvin J. Folkertsma, Jr.

All rights reserved. Except for brief quotations in critical articles or reviews, this book or parts thereof must not be reproduced in any form without permission in writing from the publisher. For further information contact Glenbridge Publishing Ltd., 6010 W. Jewell Ave., Lakewood, Colorado 80232.

Library of Congress Catalog Card Number: LC 95-82058

International Standard Book Number: 0-944435-34-3

Printed in the U. S. A.

PROLOGUE: ENCOUNTERS

Fall, 1965

She knew he lurked outside somewhere, waiting for her to leave, to take that single step out of her office and into the hallway. Then he would appear and confront her, remind her of foolish words that had gushed from her mouth at a particularly vulnerable time in her life, when she was too desperate to refuse his offer. A dread scenario paraded through her mind with devastating clarity. He would follow her, maybe corner her in some remote room, paw her clothing while whispering promises, yet making demands. He would fling an arm across her shoulder, another around her waist, grapple her body, and then . . . *What?* She didn't know. Fear stalked her thoughts as she considered the possibilities. Her stomach churned. Acid crept up her throat, jammed behind what felt like a miniature fist clenched inside her neck, and squirted into her mouth. She gagged, then swallowed hard.

Crackers, I need crackers.

She flung open the top drawer of her desk, thrust her hand inside, grasped a package of saltines, and attacked its noisy cellophane wrapper. Her fingers clawed at the stubborn container like clumsy tentacles mangling a small animal to death. Finally, the wrapper burst open, crackers exploded across her desk, on her lap. She scooped up a handful of crumbs and stuffed them into her mouth. A second package surrendered to her stabbing fingernails, then another. She felt better now, less nauseated. Nothing else changed, though; she still had to face him.

She checked the time. Six-thirty, p.m. Retreating sunlight spilled through the window behind her, hurling yellow beams across her desk and painting the parquet floor with a warm hazy glow. Sounds of rustling trees filtered through cracks in the windows, calming her thoughts, beckoning her outside. *This is ridiculous,* she concluded. *Just get up and leave.* And, who knows? Maybe she had exaggerated the danger, or had imagined it completely. Maybe words he repeated to her earlier that day represented nothing more than empty posturing, vacuous drivel sputtered by a man simply venting fear of his advancing years, declining virility. *He wouldn't really do what he said . . . would he?* She didn't know. Sooner or later, she would find out. But she could not live every day of her life like this.

She cleaned off her desk, tossed a few items into her purse, and snatched the file that had kept her working late this evening. She walked toward her office door, opened it a crack, peered into the hallway. Empty. She stepped outside and closed the door behind her. Folder gripped tightly, purse in hand, she strode across the noisy wooden planks, toward the stairs. *A few more steps,* she thought, *then I'll be down on the first floor, through the offices below, out the side exit, into the parking lot . . .*

"Hey, there!"

She stopped, froze in place. Slowly, she turned around. There he was, standing by his office door. Hands on hips, confident look, arrogant. Like a man who always gets his way.

"I . . . thought you'd left," she stammered.

"Of course not. I've been waiting for you."

She took a deep breath. "I finished what I could on this account." She lifted her folder, as if presenting an offering. "I'll look it over tonight, and . . ."

"That's not what I'm interested in, and you know it," he huffed.

She remained silent. He gestured toward his office. "It's time we talked about our deal."

Run! screamed a voice inside her. *Run away now, while you have the chance!* Still, a spark of rational thought wriggled through her fears, issued a calmer voice. *He wasn't serious, he was just blowing off steam. Probably.*

A hard swallow. "Okay," she said weakly, deciding to get the matter resolved, once and forever. She walked toward him and entered his office. He closed the door behind them. The sound of its bolt clicking shut pierced the room's tense quiet.

A bevy of familiar sights greeted her view, as she stood in place, not yet daring to turn around and face him. She would let him have his say, make the first move. That would give her time to think how to respond. She fixed her gaze on the sofa beneath the window and waited.

The lights clicked off.

Oh my God!

Before she could turn around, a hand rested on her shoulder, another grappled her waist. His body, moist, heavy, pressed against her back . . .

Hot breath hissed in her ears . . . Soft whispers issued promises, reminders . . . And, most important, *obligations.* Obligations encased in threats.

Suddenly, the grip around her waist turned to steel, and he whipped her petite frame around to face him. Eyes ablaze with lust and fury, he grasped her blouse below her neck and ripped it off. Terror raced through her mind. She shrieked with every ounce of breath within her, while helplessly pummeling her assailant's chest as he tore off her clothes, groped every part of her body. She tried to scream again, but he planted his ravenous lips over hers and smothered the sound, suffocating her as his tongue slid into her mouth. He hoisted her up and threw her on the sofa, effortlessly, as though heaving a doll across the room. In furious movements, he shed his own clothes, as she lay there, gasping, stunned.

Then, in that sliver of time permitted by a mind reeling in horror, she spied something across the room that she had never seen before in her life. He descended upon her naked body; she shut her eyes and blotted out the present. While he ravaged her with lecherous ferocity, she escaped to the most private compartment of her soul, where she could be completely alone, and plotted her revenge.

December, 1966

"Justin, go to your room," the woman ordered, keeping an eye on the man who stood before them in their living room.

"But Mommy . . ."

"Do as I say!"

Her four-year-old boy cast a fearful look at the large man hovering above him and reluctantly complied with his mother's wishes. A minute later, she stood alone.

"Cute kid," rumbled the intruder's voice. "Hate to see anything happen to him."

His threat put a tremor in her voice. "What do you want?" she asked.

He stepped closer, a fierce expression glinting from dark, cruel eyes. "I want to know where your husband went."

"I told you," she stated indignantly. "I don't know."

"Not good enough, lady. You *do* know."

"No, I don't! What else can I say if I have no idea . . ."

The crack of his hand across her face snapped her head to the side and sent her teetering across her living room. She crashed into a lamp, tripped over an armchair, and crumpled to the floor. Dazed, terrified, she lifted her eyes toward her attacker and raised her arms to ward off another blow. A futile, pitiful gesture. Her assailant slapped her again, the loud smack of his leathery hand against her helpless skin cut through sounds of her gasping voice like a knife. She screamed. Like lightning, his arm bolted forward, powerful fingers clamped around her throat, squeezed tight. Desperate lungs thumped in her chest, pleading for breath. Nothing. Terror succumbed to invading darkness. She felt faint, went limp, collapsed.

"Where is he, lady? Tell me! Tell me, or I'll twist your head off! Where did he go?"

Sounds of the man's bellowing voice punctuated the din of blood roaring in her ears. She felt the grip on her throat relax. She clawed for oxygen, air shrieked past her lips, filled her lungs, consciousness blossomed once again. She looked up, tried to focus. The man's outline filled her vision, his fearsome countenance locked on her, a wicked sneer angled across his lips.

He bent down, grasped her clothes, pelted her face with his stinking breath. "One more time, lady, I'm asking you. *Where did he go!*"

"I . . . don't know," she stuttered.

"Oh yes you do!" he boomed. "A man don't skip town, leave his family, and not tell his own wife! Now, where did he go? Where?"

She whimpered, then sobbed uncontrollably. "I don't know, I tell you, I don't know! We hadn't been getting along. He came home last night; we argued—he said he had to leave for a while but was going to return." She swept her fingers down her face, collected tears and smears of blood, then wiped her hand on her dress. "Something about owing money to someone. He didn't explain. Then he left. That's all I know, I swear to God!"

The man stood up, glared at her, but seemed to be considering this reply. He bent down again. "You listen to me, lady. You listen good. If you're lying to me . . ."

"I'm not lying!" she croaked.

". . . if you're lying to me," he repeated. "I'll be back. You got that? And next time I won't be so gentle."

She jerked her head to acknowledge this threat and cowered on the floor, trembling. Then she heard his heavy feet thumping away. Front door opened . . . Slammed shut . . . Sounds of footsteps trailing away . . . Car engine revved . . . Tires squealing . . .

Silence.

Heart still pounding, she crawled across the floor, struggled to her feet, and sprawled on a chair. Ten, fifteen minutes passed before she got her breathing under control and settled down. Finally, she collected her thoughts, assessed what had happened and why. Fear subsided; bitterness filled the vacuum.

I hope you do find him, she concluded at length. *Find him, and for all I care, kill him.*

"I tell you, boss, she don't know nothing."

The man in the back seat remained silent.

"You sure about that?" asked the driver, flitting a glance to his companion.

"As sure as anyone can be!" he snapped. "Broads don't usually hold out that long, and I slapped her around pretty good. She said the guy owed money, was going to be gone for a while, but would come back. I think he skipped town for good."

"Brilliant conclusion," uttered a sinister voice from the back seat.

No response was forthcoming; the thug who had beaten a helpless woman had learned to endure his employer's rebukes. "So, now what do we do?" he inquired.

"Find him, of course," snarled his boss, stating the obvious. "No one skips town owing me a hundred grand."

"That ain't going to be easy," observed the driver, taking a turn that put their Cadillac on a highway leading to upstate New York.

"Not as hard as you think," snapped the reply. The two men in the front seat exchanged glances and waited for additional explanation.

"I *know* this man," continued their boss. "I know his *type*. There's only a few places he would go. He'll lie low for a while, give him a few weeks, then you guys start checking out the most likely places."

"Suppose we find him," asked the driver. "Then what? Teach him the usual lesson?"

"No," their boss replied. *"When* you find him"—an evil cackle erupted from his throat—"you phone immediately and leave the rest to *me."*

January, 1967

"Mr. Simon! Oh, Mr. Simon!"

Ted Simon turned around to greet his young hostess, a pleasant woman of immense girth, matched by her agreeable temperament and excessive willingness to please. She plopped another hors d'oeuvre on his plate and turned to her companion standing next to her, a man Simon had never seen before.

"I would like to introduce you to Mr. Stewart Lawrence. He's a friend of Tom's and is visiting Long Island for a spell. He loves harness racing, so you two should have a lot in common!" she announced enthusiastically. Then she scampered away and fluttered about the room, like some mammoth insect, pollinating guests' plates with an ample supply of crackers, cheeses, pickled herring, and assorted other snacks concocted from her private cookbook, all of unknown pedigree and undoubtedly seeking appropriate names.

Simon grinned. He cast a questioning glance at the latest addition to his ensemble of munchies, then looked up to face the person Madam Butterfly had planted before him. A pleasant visage, with a broad forehead, sparkling eyes, and an expansive smile greeted his view.

Lawrence extended his hand. "A pleasure to meet you, Mr. Simon."

"Call me Ted," Simon replied. "What brings you to Long Island?"

"A job, I hope," he chuckled. Lawrence's eyes twinkled when he smiled, and every facial feature sprang to life, radiating charm. Simon immediately took a liking to him.

"Janice told me you've written a few books on harness racing. Maybe we could go to Lakewood Downs together some time, and you could give me some pointers. The science of handicapping intrigues me. A great hobby."

Internal alarms inside Simon's head were normally triggered by a comment like this, but Stewart Lawrence's ingratiating manner rendered them mute. Simon twirled the pink liquid in his punch glass and gave a thoughtful reply. "I think it's more of an art than a science, and it's never as easy as it seems."

"What do you mean?" Lawrence asked, taking a nibble off something that looked like a cheeseball.

"Even the best handicapping efforts can be ruined by what seems the most trivial, accidental thing. I've discovered that you can pour your best analysis into, say, a pacer with an impressive record, one you're convinced will at least show, if not place. Then after it ends up in seventh place, fifteen lengths behind the winner, you find out that some minor discomfort from the complex of leather straps encasing the animal rubbed it the wrong way, distracted its concentration. Even if you guess better than that, a precious fifth of a second can mean the difference between winning and placing fourth by nearly a length. It's not a game of inches. It's a game of millimeters and a host of imponderables."

Lawrence's animated expression indicated he was fixating on Simon's every word. Noting this, and flattered by the attention, Simon continued. "Take a horse I bet on last week," he said. "I did everything a handicapper is supposed to do. I studied the horse's record, its pedigree, the driver, track conditions, competition, weather—all the usual stuff. I even looked at time of the year, continental drift, and phases of the moon.

To make sure I left nothing else out, I gazed at stars the night before the race and slaughtered a duck the morning after, to examine its entrails for hidden messages."

Lawrence chortled in delight. "Sounds pretty scientific to me. Which one of those things proved most accurate."

"Probably the duck. My selection came in fifth. Got boxed in by a horse tiring in front of him at the same time one was passing him on the outside. By the time he could break free, it was too late. And I don't even want to discuss horses that break stride. Breaking horses break my heart. Not to mention my wallet."

"My feelings exactly," Lawrence stated agreeably.

"What do you mean?"

"I don't want to talk about breaking wallets, either, though your duck theory has me intrigued. Let me ask you this. Have you ever bet on a *winning* horse?"

Simon scratched his chin, threw a glance toward the ceiling, in an obvious affectation of deep thinking. "Seems to me I did one time. During the Eisenhower administration, I think. After that, I concluded that writing about the sport was easier on the nerves than actually betting on horses."

More ingratiating laughter. "Again, if you'd like someone to commiserate with at the track now and then, I'd love to join you," Lawrence offered. "Better, if you hear of job opportunities for a top-drawer salesman, let me know. I promise I'd make you look great as a reference."

Simon merely nodded and sipped his drink, regarding Lawrence's statement carefully. After an additional half an hour of fluid conversation, punctuated by witty anecdotes and sparkling observations about their mutual interest, the two men parted with a warm handshake and promises to keep in touch. Simon watched this personable stranger saunter away, while his thoughts roamed over a landscape of employment possibilities.

Come to think of it, he concluded at length, *My company could use another salesman . . .*

PART ONE: THE FIX

Chapter One

May, 1967

Stewart Lawrence bolted up from his seat at Lakewood Downs Raceway and walked briskly on a long walkway that paralleled the restaurant, situated high above the track to offer patrons the best view of the action. He clambered down a few steps, strode through a cavernous room filled with television monitors hovering over attentive watchers, and stepped in line to the nearest betting window. Just as he reached into his pocket for his wallet, something bulky thumped him in the back, and he nearly lost his balance. His wallet tumbled to the floor. Cursing silently, he bent down to pick it up.

"Sorry about that, man," rumbled a deep voice above him.

Stewart looked up to a towering figure built like a wrestler. "Wasn't watching where I was going," the man said.

Stewart's irritation transformed to unease as his eyes traced the man's formidable outline. Blue jeans and a knit shirt stretched over a physique ready to burst rippling muscles from every seam. As if his body were not fearsome enough, the man's facial features resembled a moonscape plastered on a head that emerged from massive shoulders. Undisciplined eyebrows crowded intense, dark eyes. For a fleeting moment, Lawrence felt like an unarmed observer facing a gorilla in the animal's native habitat. He could only hope that the creature facing him was friendly.

Not that it mattered, of course. Stewart just wanted to place his bets and dash back to his booth. He nodded politely, and the man placed his massive arm on his shoulder. "Hope you win," he said, with a reptilian grin, while Stewart gaped at his sculpted triceps.

"Yes, well, I hope you do, too," he replied, wishing he could sneak to another line without seeming too obvious about it.

Fortunately, business was light at Lakewood Downs today, and

Stewart quickly stepped up to the window, laid cash on the counter, and grabbed a stack of tickets. He scampered back to his booth just as the trumpet sounded. The drivers were turning their horses to line up behind a specially designed Ford pickup with a raised platform on its bed and a mobile gate attached to its rear bumper. As the vehicle turned around the track, the gate unfolded from the truck's body like giant bat wings, nearly filling the distance from rail to rail. Horses trotted up to their post positions behind the mobile gate. The race was about to begin.

Stewart had reserved the entire four-person booth to himself, paying for the three empty seats so he could be alone. Nothing irritated him more than irrelevant drivel from noisy strangers who knew less about the sport than he did and took it less seriously. Most of all, he relished the crackling tension of the race, which electrified every nerve in his body. Such moments of private exultation or grief demanded absolute solitude; he would brook no invasions of his privacy.

The truck was equipped with microphones that picked up sounds off the track. The horses' pounding hooves produced a throaty, rolling rumble, reminding him of films he had seen of World War Two. The drone of four-engine bombers shown in Walter Cronkite's *Air Power* eerily resembled the sounds on the track and radiated the same throbbing power. He loved it.

Stewart gripped his binoculars and peered at the track. He caught sight of the burly intruder who had bumped him in line, leaning over the outside rail. The man's back muscles easily showed through his thin shirt and reminded Stewart of a mare's buttocks. Inexplicably, he turned his head in Stewart's direction, as though he were able to isolate him from his distant position. Stewart shook off his troubling presence and concentrated on the horses.

The loudspeaker's tinny squawk sliced through the clamor of thundering hooves to announce the race. *"PA-ce-r-r-rs* are OUT and behind the GATE! The gate swings around the turn, A-A-AND *the-e-e-e-e-re they GO!*

"The-e-e-re OFF! A-A-AND pacing for the lead, *RO-O-O-O-RING ANDY,* on the OUTSIDE, racing second, *FANCY DAN!* In the third, *SIMON SAYS.* ON the rail, A-A-AND fourth, *FLYING LOW! Pride-o-Jersey* racing fifth, *Junior Tee,* sixth, the trailer is *Da-a-a-ring Debbie.* ROUND the turn they GO! A-A-AND racing for the first quarter mark, GAINING on the front end, it's *FANCY DAN! SIMON SAYS* racing third. OPENING QUARTER in *TWENTY EIGHT AND ONE!*

"IN THE LANE for the first time, racing third, *FLYING LOW!* FOUR is *Simon Says! Pride-o-Jersey,* pacing fifth, A-A-A-ND, *Junior*

Tee. Down on the rail, seventh, TRA-A-A-ILING the field is *Daring Debbie*. The END of the turn and going for the HALF WAY POINT!"

Stewart's fingertips whitened as he squeezed his binoculars, his eyes gripped by the spectacle on the track. Every muscle tightened; sweat creeping from his forehead stung his eyes and traced warm paths down his cheeks, dampening his collar. Every feature on his face snapped to attention and bored on *Fancy Dan's* frenetic surge to first place. *Don't peak too soon!* he pleaded, as though his yearnings could leap across the track to instruct the lumbering beast's driver: *Save it for the stretch!*

"ROARING ANDY leads the way by a length and a half. Racing second, *FANCY DAN!* The END of the turn, third, *FLYING LOW,* by the half, fifty-nine and three. On to the back side they go! Racing fourth, *SIMON SAYS,* fifth, *Pride-o-Jersey,* sixth on the rail, *Junior Tee,* and the TRAILER, *Daring Debbie. Straight alignment at the five-eighth's mark!*

"FIRST to move on the outside, *FLYING LOW!* From fourth, *SIMON SAYS,* moving on the leader! Racing third, now, *FANCY DAN,* boxed in!"

Stewart silently screamed in anguish. *No! No! No!*

"OUT IN FRONT on the outside *FLYING LOW!* Drifting back, number four, is *FANCY DAN!* Three Quarters, one-twenty-nine and two! Toward the leader on the outside, *SIMON SAYS!* Three wide, *ROARING ANDY,* followed by *Pride-o-Jersey, Junior Tee,* A-A-AND *Daring Debbie! SIMON SAYS* on the OUTSIDE! Into the lightning lane, *FLYING LOW!* COMING TO THE WIRE! It's *FLYING LOW, SIMON SAYS, ROARING ANDY!* Streaking toward the finish, on the OUTSIDE, it's *SI-I-IMON SAYS!* TWO OH TWO and THREE! What a finish!"

Stewart threw his tickets down in disgust and glared at the tote board, hoping for the "inquiry" sign to flash, which indicated that the judges spotted some irregularity in the race. Nothing showed. Instead, the screen lit up with the horses' numbers after win, place, and show. *Simon Says* won at six-to-one, paying $11.60, which meant that a ten dollar investment returned fifty-eight dollars. Stewart glanced at the track one last time and observed satisfied bettors chortling over their winnings. He was convinced there had to be an explanation for the day's results, and he knew exactly where to go for it.

Stewart lifted his binoculars and studied the paddock area. Horses from race six were returning, some subdued and bathed in sweat, others bobbing their heads while they walked, like giant four-legged pigeons. Racing enthusiasts often gathered by a large gate, which separated the spectator area from the path linking the track to the paddock. They talked with drivers, patted horses that walked close enough, tried to inveigle "inside information" that might give them an advantage, and compared notes on the next race. Stewart scanned the area for one person in particular, a walking encyclopedia of harness racing who had spent most of his life around horses.

There he is.

Stewart scampered from his booth and walked briskly through Lakewood Downs' enormous spectator arena toward the paddock. Fortunately, the person he wanted to see was still standing there, his foot resting on a lower slat of the gate, explaining some finer point of horsemanship to a novice who obviously hung on his every word. When he saw Stewart approaching, he ended his conversation quickly. Obviously miffed, his attentive student tossed a look of irritation toward Stewart and sauntered away.

"How's your day?" he greeted with an inquisitive smile, which quickly vanished when he saw the expression on Stewart's face.

"I've had better," Stewart scowled, accepting Johnny Marlboro's leathery hand. Marlboro was a local trainer-driver who operated a public stable with a dozen horses. Acquaintances dubbed him the Marlboro Man for reasons that had little to do with his name, although that certainly helped. His ruddy complexion and coarse but handsome face suggested a rugged, outdoor type. He wore yellow racing trousers, a red striped shirt, and a white hat, which blossomed from his head like a fluffy ripe mushroom. His uniform made him look like a cross between a cowboy and a Lilliputian relative of the Mad Hatter from Alice in Wonderland. Even among the drivers, who competed with one another for the most colorful uniforms, he stood out.

Stewart had known him for only a few months, but the two quickly became fast friends. Marlboro had even used his influence to secure an owner's badge for Stewart, giving him the right to pass through the heavily guarded paddock gate, where he met some of the drivers and learned about the inner workings of the track. The knowledgeable trainer explained everything there was to know about horses, from forelock to hoof and muzzle to croup. He showed how the judges checked the horses, how sulkies were attached, and the function of every strap and hobble that kept the pacer's gait consistent.

"Bad day at the races?" Marlboro asked, retrieving from his assemblage of racing phrases the most annoying cliché that came to mind.

"The worst."

"How much did you lose?"

"Three hundred bucks."

Marlboro whistled. "That's a lot of magic markers," he commented, referring to Stewart's position as a sales representative for Office Products Unlimited, his "day" job. That is, when Stewart wasn't at Lakewood Downs, which was every afternoon after he finished his sales runs in the mornings.

Stewart eyed his friend carefully. "It doesn't have to be this way, Johnny."

"What do you mean?"

Stewart paused, calculating whether he dared pursue a subject that had been on his mind since the first time Marlboro had instructed him on the intricacies of harness racing. *Why not?* he mused, putting an end to his internal debate. *Given my record the last few weeks, I've got nothing to lose.*

"I think you know what I mean, Johnny. I just watched two races where the winners looked like they'd received 'help' from the other drivers. Yesterday, some bloke won with a horse at fifty to one odds and walked away with a thousand bucks. Last week, same thing. In fact, I remember the horses: *Dutch Treat, Peter's Principle, Albert's Way, Almahurst Run, Kentucky Bay*—need I continue? All long shots, every one of them."

Marlboro gave him a long, probing look. At length, the horseman broke into a wide smile. "You *are* observant, aren't you," he said.

"Yeah, and I've got good hearing, too. Several times when you've led me through the paddock, I overheard some drivers speculate on upcoming races. Frankly, everything they've talked about has confirmed what I've suspected for the past few weeks handicapping these races. Believe me, it's pretty hard to handicap a fixed race. Unless, of course, you're in on the fix."

"Naturally," Marlboro agreed.

"Not exactly kosher, don't you agree?"

Marlboro showed no offense. "You think the house percentage is kosher?"

Stewart scoffed. "The 'house percentage' is the biggest fix on the track! They sit back on their collective asses, do no work, and skim sixteen percent off the top. Scandalous, if you ask me." Stewart leaned forward and lowered his voice. "You handle their bets, don't you." It was a statement, not a question.

Marlboro darted his eyes about them to see if anyone was within hearing distance. Stewart was fully aware that Marlboro knew exactly the point he was making. Drivers could bet on their own horses but were forbidden to place wagers on others, for the obvious reason that such collusion was illegal. Betting on one another's horses provided incentive to give exactly the sort of "help" that Stewart had spotted on the track, so the favored horse would win.

"Of course," Marlboro answered quietly, a trace of pride twinkling in his eyes.

"How much do you wager for them?" Stewart asked eagerly.

Marlboro shrugged. "Small amounts, really. The drivers bet ten dollars to win and sometimes another ten or so on the exacta or daily double, but rarely more than that. They figured they earned it, and I agree with them. At least they work for a living."

Betting on the "exacta" meant selecting the number one and two horses in a race in the correct order. The daily double meant correctly picking the winners of the first two races. Picking any winner, of course, presented enough of a challenge to most handicappers, especially if the horse faced high odds, but correctly selecting two horses in the right order offered opportunities for excellent payoffs. Stewart immediately grasped the implications.

"You mean to tell me that you're in the position to win exactas and daily doubles, and all you've been betting is ten or twenty bucks a pop? I can't believe it!"

"I guess I'm not in your league," Marlboro admitted. "Keep in mind that coordinating the efforts of several drivers is risky business. Profitable, but risky."

"Not *that* risky," Stewart countered. "Maybe if I help, I can increase your profits. And mine, too."

Marlboro's gaze drifted to the track, deep in thought, then back to Stewart. "Maybe," he replied, regarding him carefully. "In that case, I suggest you get in contact with a special key player."

"Who might that be?"

"I'll let you know tomorrow," he said with a cautious grin.

"Why wait until tomorrow?"

"Because I know *you* want to meet *him*. But he'll need some convincing on my part before he'll agree to meet you."

Marlboro's answer only served to whet Stewart's appetite. "Okay, tomorrow, then," he agreed. The two shook hands, and as Stewart turned to leave, he spotted the man who had bumped into him by the betting window quickly avert his eyes toward the track, as though he were watching the horses warm up. Stewart sensed he had jerked his head away just in time, to disguise the fact that he was actually observing their conversation.

"Say, Johnny." Stewart called, stopping the driver before he entered the paddock. Stewart gestured furtively, and his friend joined him, a curious look on his face.

"See that guy over there, leaning on the rail?" Stewart said.

Marlboro glanced in the direction indicated by Stewart. "You mean, King Kong? Looks like he could pull a sulky."

"That's the one. Ever see him here before?"

Marlboro shook his head. "What's the problem?"

"Nothing, no problem, just curious," Stewart said, letting his eyes linger a moment too long. "I'll see you tomorrow then."

Stewart walked away, entered the main structure, and strode through the lobby where bettors were lining up for the next race. As he left the building, he glanced behind him one last time. King Kong was still there. *Is he following me?*

Stewart pushed the matter out of his mind, a task made easier by two exciting thoughts. Tomorrow he would meet Johnny Marlboro's "special key player." And tonight he would be with the love of his life, Lori.

Chapter Two

Ted Simon stared out the window of his third floor office, which was ensconced in a twenty thousand square foot warehouse filled with office products, with a single thought blaring in his mind. *I've got to get out of here. NOW!* The sales director of Office Products Unlimited tolerated confinement in his mahogany-lined roost no longer than six hours a day. Private demons propelled him to spend the remaining four or five hours on the floor chatting amiably with employees; or visiting the labs, checking on the latest developments; or, best of all, on the road, discovering new businesses, meeting new people, selling new products. That was the life! The thrill of creation, the excitement of sharing ideas with others, the warm pleasure of approbation. However, his boss, the company president, had insisted on ratcheting him upward, to higher levels of administrative misery, a process officially known as climbing the corporate ladder. Couldn't disappoint the old man, Simon thought. Got to take that new job he just offered me.

He hadn't started out that way. When Theodore A. Simon first approached Office Products Unlimited for a sales position, he was rudely rejected by the personnel director, a man who reminded him of Donald Duck with a speech impediment. In fact, Simon casually mentioned during his interview that the Disney character was actually *easier* to understand; a point he later admitted was better left unsaid. But trying to decipher a voice that resembled sounds of fingernails scraping across a blackboard, sputtered from jowls that looked stuffed with marbles, was not an easy task. When Simon honed his ears and clawed through piles of syllables tumbling from the man's cement mixer mouth, he discovered that the company frowned upon applications submitted in crayon. This policy admitted no exceptions; even those coming from ambitious applicants eager to display their originality.

But I want to be in *sales,* Simon had insisted. Originality should be considered a virtue. How else to gain the attention of busybodies scurrying about purchasing departments, quaffing sips of coffee between donut bites, while contriving novel ways to eject you from their lives? Try a job in the circus, growled the company's cartoonish official as he slammed the door behind him.

Undeterred, Simon returned the next day with a product he had developed himself, one he was sure would attract the attention of the company's executives, the more imaginative ones, at least. It was an innovative word highlighter that painted letters in florescent yellow. "Script nearly glows in the dark," he boasted, imparting new meaning to the expression, "striking prose." Super Animated Sun Honey— *SASH*, he called it. Sure to sweep through the Office Products industry with the same flourish it leaves on your documents. He carted his invention to the factory in his car, a dilapidated two-seater convertible liberated from an auto wrecker, which Simon filled with large glass containers of the stuff. "Room for your ass and a gallon of SASH," he quipped before stunned company officials.

Skeptical frowns greeted this new petition for employment. One executive, costumed in Brooks Brothers finest, summoned a fork lift operator to relieve them all of Simon's presence. This request was cut short by an arm slicing the air, ordering Simon's audience to respectful silence. It belonged to the company president, an elderly man who recognized this new twist on an old saying. He stepped forward, aimed his grizzled visage on the young upstart, and, in a commanding voice, asked to see more. Simon remembered that episode as though it had happened yesterday. He stood immobilized before the man's penetrating gaze, which pierced him to his foundation. More than words, it conveyed a single, unmistakable message: *none of these dolts understand you, son, but I do. We share the same spirit.*

That was seven years and ten promotions ago. Since then, Ted Simon had garnered a dozen patents in his name, sold millions of dollars of products he had developed, and now qualified as a genuine, potbellied Republican working on his first ulcer and his second or third wife. Except he was very trim, would never get an ulcer, and remained unmarried. Simon had learned how to pace himself, to vent his stress. *First, go to your roots.* He pulled out a huge binder and thumbed through product displays he had designed for his inventions over the years. The first one he loved the best. It showed an attractive lady wearing sunglasses, with a writing instrument in her hand, leaning over a manuscript that sprayed light into her face. Above her head glowed a sun in the shape of a honey pot, pouring a brilliant rainbow of colors on her paper as she highlighted sentences. *Animate your Words with Honey from the Sun,* it proclaimed above the bold, multicolored letters—*SASH.* It had won several awards, acquired him a fortune, and, as he had predicted, stormed through the industry.

Simon closed the heavy tome, leaned back in his chair, and let his eyes roam across the opposite wall. Wooden panels hosting pictures of restful ocean scenes soothed his vision. A regiment of plaques commemorating his awards were displayed across the wall to his right. On the wall behind him, portraits of company luminaries: the founder, a gaggle of vice presidents, and current salespeople, of which there were three for his division. Their territories included a one-hundred mile radius around company headquarters in East Meadow, Long Island.

They were all good men, but Stewart Lawrence he liked the best, perhaps because he reminded Simon of himself, at least in some respects. Simon mentally ticked off an inventory of characteristics. Brashness moderated by a polite demeanor; ambition that didn't overwhelm or threaten; not dashing good looks, but a pleasant appearance, agreeable. *I'm more handsome than he is,* Simon told himself, with an honest nod to his vanity. *But I can't match his most striking characteristic.* Truly, Stewart's winsome smile melted the resistance of even his most determined competitors, including Simon himself, as he recalled the first time he met his top salesman. *No question about it,* Simon mused. *Stewart is on the rise.*

Simon's second rule of personal rejuvenation skipped through his thoughts: *break up your day, do something different, sweep away stuffy ideas clogging your mind.* Simon checked his watch: twelve-thirty. Lunch time. Visit the floor, go to the lab, get out on the road—*do* something! he ordered himself. While musing about a variety of possibilities, the intercom buzzed.

"Yes," Simon acknowledged.

"Mr. Simon," crackled a voice, "there's a man here to see you. Says it won't take long. Do you have a minute?"

Simon inwardly groaned. "Send him in," he said, lamenting the intrusion. He put his plans on hold and fussed with a few documents before him, engaging in a well-rehearsed pretense of appearing interested in whatever cluttered his desk in case his boss ever popped in.

A knock on the door.

"Come in."

Simon's office door swung open and revealed a man whose size filled the doorway's width, jamb to jamb. Looked like a football player, Simon instantly concluded. No, make that *two* football players welded together.

"Can I help you?"

"Yeah. You're Ted Simon?"

Simon nodded.

"I'm looking for a guy. I think he works for you. Name's Stewart Lawrence."

Simon eased back in his chair and assessed the questioner. It hardly seemed possible that a man like this could ask innocuous questions about anyone. "Yes, Stewart works for me. He's one of my salesman. But he's not here at the moment. May I take a message?" Simon uttered his response in a tone suggesting he would have preferred to deal with this visitor over the phone. Preferably long distance. *Very* long distance.

His visitor glanced at the row of pictures on the wall behind Simon's desk. A feral look glinted from the intruder's dark eyes, as though discovery had animated some predatory instinct. "No, no message. Just wanted to see him, that's all."

"May I ask who you are?"

A sneer tugged the right corner of his mouth. "Let's just say that Lawrence and I are old friends. He's not expecting me, and I'd rather surprise him. So I'd appreciate it if you didn't tell him anyone was looking for him. Okay? Thanks a lot." Then he turned and left.

Simon sat for a long moment, replaying this brief encounter through his thoughts, pondering its significance. Stewart didn't strike him as the type who had such "friends," and this incongruity troubled him. He had gotten to know Stewart reasonably well over the previous six months, especially since Simon had allowed him to share his apartment until Stewart could find one of his own. Stewart had always been agreeable, conscientious, paying all his bills on time and never taking advantage. He remained silent about his past, however; Simon respected his privacy, assuming sooner or later his friend would confide in him. Based upon his experience with other salesmen, he suspected a bad marriage propelled Stewart's departure from his previous job, but this intruder threw a new element into the equation.

Simon considered the wisdom of acceding to the stranger's parting request and concluded to say nothing to Stewart. He glanced at a stack of papers on his desk, many with Lawrence's name written on them. *I'd rather be the bearer of good news,* he thought with satisfaction, fingering the top sheet.

Stewart fidgeted with anticipation as he drove his company car, a white Ford station wagon, across State Highway 85 along the southeastern coast of Long Island. He had a date this evening with Lori Armstrong, a demure secretary who had been quickening his heartbeat since the time they met during one of his sales runs. Lori worked for the president of a candy and nut factory called *Sweets Ahoy*, which was located a few miles inland near Millville. The manufacturing plant occupied several huge buildings that dominated an industrial park named after the business's founder. Its current owner was obsessed with security and had enclosed the sprawling complex with chain-link fence.

Both owner and factory had acquired legendary status among local inhabitants. Grandson of a famous sea captain, Jeremy Madison boasted that his forebears smuggled molasses and tea in flatboats under the noses of His Majesty's ships of the line during the American Revolution. No one knew if that were true or not, and no one much cared. The success of his business was unmistakable, and area residents often found it useful to identify where they lived by reference to *Sweets Ahoy's* location. Certainly Madison's factory contributed much to local lore, spicing up its smell as much as its stories. In fact, the phrase, "*Sweets Ahoy* is roasting its nuts again," was flavored with sufficiently risqué humor to make both Lori and Stewart chuckle every time they heard it.

Lori lived in an upstairs apartment of a Cape Cod home in Patchogue, about fifteen miles from where she worked. Her apartment was accessed by a rear entrance and protected by a security system that included a buzzer next to her door. Lawrence drove into the driveway, walked to the rear door, and pressed a button. A machine-like voice crackled through the intercom.

"Who is it?"

"It's me, Stewart."

"Okay, I'll be right down."

After a few minutes, the door opened, and Stewart put on his best smile. A slightly built woman emerged and greeted him by squeezing his hand and kissing him on the cheek. Her dark brown hair curled neatly below her ears, framing a face highlighted by flawless skin and an aristocratic nose. A whisper of Lauren Bacall crept from her sultry voice, a bit too low, perhaps, for a petite figure weighing no more than a hundred and ten pounds perfectly proportioned on a five-foot-four frame. Her smile radiated warmth and childlike innocence, but was compromised by worry lines that outlined penetrating blue eyes. She seemed to Lawrence like a goddess who had suffered hurt; purity afflicted by pain. He wanted desperately to help her, to expunge the hurt. Maybe tonight she would open up to him, Lawrence thought. But that's what he'd said all those other nights, after aching through days of longing for her.

"Where are we going?" Lori asked.

"Someplace special," Stewart said, beaming. He took her hand and they walked to the car. Soon, the white station wagon owned by Office Products Unlimited drove away and glided into the traffic on Highway 85. Their twenty-five mile trip took them close to the ocean and past several majestic homes that dotted the beach side on Long Island's southern shore. Finally, he pulled into a cobblestone parking lot next to a three-story home that looked like it had been built in the eighteenth century.

"Actually, early nineteenth century," Stewart explained, in answer to her question as she stood by the car taking in the structure's dimensions. "Around 1810, I think. The brochure says that a stray cannonball from a British man-of-war crashed through the kitchen during the War of 1812, and that room wasn't fixed until after the Civil War. It housed a single family until the 1930s, then sat idle for two decades until its current owners restored it."

Fenimore Cooper Inn cut a striking figure against the receding evening sun. The house was wrapped by red clapboards etched with white eaves and punctuated by orderly rows of windows, also cased in white. Three massive chimneys rose from the building's high-pitched roof, and flowers graced its foundation. They entered a generous foyer and were immediately greeted by seafood aromas and a figure dressed like Benjamin Franklin. He led them to a sawbuck table that hosted four bow-back Windsor chairs and "Flying Cloud" dinnerware, suggesting nautical themes from the early nineteenth century.

The Benjamin Franklin character seated Lori while chattering away in colonial English. When he asked their names, Stewart decided to play along.

"Horatio Octavius Hornblower," he announced.

Ben Franklin adjusted his spectacles, curled his lips downward, and raised his eyebrows, as though every feature on his face were collaborating to produce the proper response. He cleared his throat. "The veracity of your answer, sir, is attested by the extreme unlikelihood of your concocting such an extraordinary name on such extremely short notice." The two chuckled, and Ben Franklin sauntered away to dazzle other patrons with his ensemble of late eighteenth century wit.

Their evening at Fenimore Cooper Inn went splendidly, although spotted with painful revelations. Lori and Stewart savored every morsel of broiled rock lobster tail with melted butter, served with rice pilaf, and finished with the most delectable *chocolate sacher torte*, flavored precisely to salute their palates. As they raised their wine glasses to finish the last sip of *Cabernet Sauvignon Beaulieu*, Stewart was convinced he had opened significant chapters of Lori Armstrong's life.

She had grown up in New Mexico and moved to Long Island with her mother after her parents divorced. It had been a messy, brutal affair. Stewart could visualize a terrified child cowering in her bedroom listening to her mother's screams and her father's raging threats amidst sounds of crashing furniture in the background. Long pauses interrupted Lori's review. Tears seemed backed up behind her words, pushing them out in spurts. Frequently, she stopped to wipe her face, then smiled apologetically and tried to change the subject. Stewart offered no objection, and after a few more dips of lobster tail into her butter bowl, she returned to the same topic. He could tell it had been a long time—perhaps the *only* time—Lori had opened up this much to anyone. Their evening acted as a cathartic, exactly what he had wanted.

However, Lori's garrulousness ended in the car, and they drove home in silence. Stewart did not know how to interpret her rebuff of his gentle attempts to continue their conversation, and he wondered what additional horrors seethed beneath the surface, or if he had unintentionally made some stifling remark. Lori had poured out a litany of painful experiences, but Stewart wasn't sure which one, if any, explained her refusal to become physically intimate. *There had to be something else.* But what? Maybe he would find out when he dropped her off.

He pulled his car into the driveway to Lori's apartment. Stewart let Lori out and slowly walked her to the outside door, his heart thumping with anticipation. He had never been inside her apartment. Given the last half hour, he wondered how she would conclude their evening. Hot or cold? Passionate or aloof? They stopped by the door. Lori swiveled to meet his eyes, wrapped her arms around him and gave him a long, ardent kiss. Stewart met her lips hungrily. Desire surged throughout every part of his body.

"Thank you for a wonderful evening," she whispered.

Stewart said nothing. His craving for her pulsated through every breath; he felt flushed. Impossible to camouflage his arousal.

"Lori, may I . . . come in? Please?"

She stepped back slightly and stared at him, as though her searching gaze put his question on hold while a multitude of calculations played out behind her radiant blue eyes. He ached to be granted entry; her silent sentinel said, no.

His hands tightened around her waist, and he drew her closer. She stiffened. "Not tonight," she said, a slight tremor in her voice.

Anger flashed involuntarily, and Stewart saw his reaction immediately register on her face. *Alarm.* No, more than that. *Fear.* With one minor, but impetuous move, he had washed away the efforts, the progress, of an entire evening. Perhaps many evenings, or many months. He didn't know. *I'm a fool,* he scolded himself.

"Are you afraid of me?" he asked.

Lori's expression softened, and she gently put his hand in hers. "No, of course not."

"What, then? Tell me!"

Words tumbled from her lips. "I . . . can't. Not now. Not yet. It's late. I have to go."

She turned to open the door while Stewart stood there. Reading his expression, she again reached for his hand. "We'll see each other again? Soon?" she offered, as though words could provide compensation for what he had in mind.

"Of course, darling. You know that. I'll always be there for you."

Her smile washed away the tension. "Call me tomorrow," she said. She inserted her key into the lock, winked at him with smiling eyes, entered the house and closed the door behind her.

Stewart sighed and threw his head back toward the dark sky, as though petitioning the stars for some heavenly intervention on his behalf. They remained mute, reminding him only of his own insignificance. He walked toward his car and drove away.

Every minute of his ride home was consumed by thoughts of Lori and how to pierce the last barrier to her personal space, where she guarded the secret that kept the distance between them. Slowly the miles peeled away his thoughts about her as his station wagon neared the small town where he lived. Stewart ruminated about Marlboro's intriguing prospect, meeting his "special key player." He hadn't a clue what the trainer-driver had in mind, but Stewart was convinced that he was inching toward the breakthrough he had been striving for his entire life. Whatever he would encounter, Stewart mentally primed himself to make an audacious move. The prospect of winning a great fortune tantalized his imagination, lured him with hopes of achieving security, respect, everything he had ever wanted. Most of all, *power.* With power, a man could get anything. In fact, he might even . . .

In a flash, his thoughts coalesced with catalytic force, and he nearly demolished a corner post of the white picket fence bordering the driveway to his apartment. He stopped his car with a jerk and turned off its engine, his mind leaping to conclusions while the Ford's headlights glared at the garage.

Lori! To win her, I have to BE a winner. I CAN be a winner. But only if there were more to Marlboro's teasing than empty posturing.

Stewart walked behind the brick house and climbed the outside steps to his apartment, which overlooked a well-tended backyard studded with fir trees leading to a trickling stream. As he stood by the door fumbling for keys, he heard his phone ringing inside. Finally, he isolated the correct one, unlocked the door, and rushed inside. He grabbed the phone.

"Hello? Yeah! Johnny, how are you?" He shifted the receiver to his other hand, listened intently. "Right. Okay, fine! Yeah, I'll meet you then. Thanks Johnny!" He hung up the phone.

Beaming with delight, he tossed his keys on the table where they skidded across its top and clattered to the floor. Stewart twirled around, heaved his body on a sofa and let his mind roam over possibilities while he stared at the ceiling. He was too excited to sleep, but it didn't matter. Tomorrow he would meet Marlboro's special key player.

Stewart Lawrence was not the only one to have an important phone call that night.

Rexford Engels had a phobia about making calls from his motel room. You never knew when the local cops might be listening in; or worse, the Feds. So he didn't mind hiking one mile to the nearest phone booth, which stood next to a huge post supporting a Texaco sign. The "x" flickered on and off, obviously the victim of some kid with a BB gun. Which made him smile. That's what he did when he was a kid, before moving on to bigger targets. Live, moving targets.

Engels crammed his six-foot-four frame into the puny glass and metallic rectangle, stuffed his hand into his pocket and retrieved a fistful of quarters. He plopped a few into the slot and dialed an upstate number. The phone rang five times and then clicked. A familiar voice sounded on the other end.

"Mr. Arnoldi? It's me, Rex. Yeah, I found him." Engels maneuvered his bulky torso outside the phone booth, giving him more room for his wide shoulders. "I bumped into him so I could get a real good look and later stopped by where he works, talked to his boss. Right. He's the guy, no doubt about it." Engels paused, listened. "Right. I'll keep you informed. Good-bye."

Engels placed the receiver back on its hook and inhaled the damp, evening air as though he were taking a long, satisfying draught of cold beer. Pleased, confident, the man referred to as King Kong by Johnny Marlboro trotted back to his motel room, which was located a few miles from Lakewood Downs.

He knew exactly what he had to do.

Chapter Three

Morris Courtney bit off half of a Polish dill pickle with a loud snap and eagerly attacked his roast beef sandwich on rye, stuffing the small cavity that passed for his mouth with far more than it could handle. When he chewed, every facial muscle came alive for the task; even his ears moved. Since he obviously would be occupied for the next sixty to ninety seconds, Stewart scrutinized the gnome-like creature Johnny Marlboro had introduced to him.

He was a small man with eyes too large for his face, which possessed a prominent nose that overwhelmed an inadequate mouth, pencil-thin lips, and a virtually nonexistent chin. When he became excited, his nostrils flared, inspiring some of his friends to suggest that equine blood flowed in his veins, which explained his skills on the track. Stewart had a different metaphor in mind. Courtney's focused expression brought to his mind a state of repressed exasperation, as though the driver's facial features had conspired to produce the visage of an agitated rabbit.

But this rabbit had power. Marlboro had confided in him that Morris Courtney was not just respected among his peers; he was *feared*. Nearly a fourth of the drivers regarded him as their leader. Courtney handled their bets and coordinated efforts to block, harass, or somehow impede other drivers during a race so that favored horses would win and their earnings would increase. Even uncooperative drivers treated him warily, knowing that any one of Courtney's fixers was in a position to inflict serious harm. Unprotected bodies perched on diminutive seats pulled by eight or nine hundred pound beasts lumbering at thirty miles per hour presented ample opportunities for bone-crushing collisions, or even death. Marlboro related to him a chilling tale about a breaking horse that had caused a multiple crash in which one driver had his skull bludgeoned by a flailing hoof, and another who was nearly decapitated by a sulky's wheel. Drivers' battle scars often included shattered bones, ruptured spleens, and an assortment of facial lacerations. It was not a sport for the faint of heart.

Courtney's animated jaw muscles came to rest, and he trained his eyes on the man sitting across the table from him, as though wondering if this interruption of his lunch at his favorite restaurant were really worth his time. Lakewood Downs Diner radiated a 1950s ambiance, complete with juke boxes, Elvis posters, and chrome-stripped tables and counters, in a semicircular Quonset hut, a lingering structural refugee from some World War Two air base. The overall effect was odd. The uninitiated didn't know if the next patron would be Buddy Holly swiveling his hips or John Wayne toting a Thompson submachine gun; both luminaries had visited the diner some time in its history. Their posters, hanging high on the walls, stared at crowded rows of tables and booths, filled mostly by racetrack enthusiasts, meandering trails of cigarette smoke, and sounds of clattering dishes. Marlboro informed Stewart that it was one of Morris Courtney's favorite spots.

"Johnny tells me that you're a regular at the Downs," he stated in a clipped tone.

"That's right," Stewart said, offering him his most ingratiating smile.

Again, the scrutinizing look, as though Courtney were examining the hind legs of a trotter for cow hocks. "How much do you bet? I mean, typically?"

"Small amounts, really," Stewart said, with Johnny Marlboro's instructions in mind. "Well, more than small amounts," he corrected himself, quickly concluding that anything less than complete honesty would be detrimental. "In fact, I handicap as many races as I can, as thoroughly as I can, and wager twenty or thirty dollars. More, if I have great confidence in a particular horse. I study past races very carefully, the horse, the driver, and quarterly times. Only the record matters."

This answer seemed to please Courtney. "You're interested in working with me, in handling a few bets?"

"Yes, I am," Stewart said eagerly.

"Have you handicapped any of tomorrow's races?"

"Yes."

"Which one?"

"Race three."

Courtney's lips twitched while his tongue probed the inside of his taut cheeks for a wayward piece of roast beef. "What do you think of *Dollee May?*" he asked, taking a sip of coffee.

This is a job interview, Stewart thought. He reached inside his pocket for a sheet of paper, opened it up, and scanned its contents. "In his last race on a fast track starting from the five post, *Dollee May* looked impressive in the stretch, but I think that effort was deceptive. *Dollee May* immediately tucked in on the rail, gaining the two position. She stayed there all the way and picked up about three quarters of a length in the stretch. But, in the race before that, *Dollee May* started from the one post position but stayed in the fourth position most of the way. She made a move at the halfway mark, but didn't pick up any horses. She pulled back to the rail, saved ground, and tried again in the stretch, picking up one and three quarters to squeak in at third by a length. Good stretch drive. Didn't win the race, but showed great promise if she were handled properly. By you, for instance."

This time, Courtney smiled broadly, revealing dental work that undoubtedly had been rearranged by some refractory horse. "You've seen me drive?"

Stewart nodded. "You're one of the best. The *very* best."

"You think I'm swayed by flattery?" Courtney asked, but with little challenge in his voice.

"I think you're swayed by a straightforward answer," Stewart stated bluntly. "And if I didn't think you were the best, I'd have the good sense to keep my mouth shut."

Courtney smiled, giving Stewart an even better display of the few front teeth that somehow had escaped the ravages of his profession. He reached into his shirt pocket and pulled out a roll of bills. He carefully laid them on the table next to his plate, five twenties.

"Bet on *Whispering Pine* in race three," he instructed.

"Win, place, or show?" Stewart asked.

"Win," Courtney answered, wiping his mouth with a napkin. He slid off the shiny seat by their booth and stood up. "Meet me here again tomorrow for lunch. We'll discuss how the race went. Bring your program with you and other notes you've gathered."

Stewart nodded obligingly, and the two shook hands. He wanted to know why Courtney had selected *Whispering Pine*, but decided not to probe the driver's reasons for this tip. Not yet, anyway.

"It was a pleasure to meet you, Morris," Stewart said. "I'm looking forward to tomorrow."

"So am I," Courtney said. He turned, elbowed his way through several customers lining up to be seated, and left Lakewood Downs Diner. Stewart collected the twenties and stuffed them into his pocket, satisfied that their meeting had gone well. Finally, he paid their check, left a generous tip, and got up.

As he was leaving, Stewart noticed the sparkling grill work of a 1957 Edsel, which jutted out from a wall as though it had crashed into the building from the outside, and the owners decided simply to leave it there. A miniature horse and sulky, in gleaming chrome, was perched on top of the grill's yawning centerpiece as a hood ornament. Stewart once owned an Edsel, and this display made him smile. He stood there for a moment, admiring it. Then he turned for the door and caught sight of something else.

King Kong sat in the booth beneath the Edsel.

Stewart felt the same unease he experienced when that man had bumped into him at the racetrack. He averted his gaze, but not before glimpsing the man's intense, dark eyes and predatory grin. Stewart shuddered. *This guy shows up too much,* he thought. He quickly trotted out of the restaurant, tapping the shirt pocket filled with rolled twenties, just to nudge his mood back into the comfort zone. The prospect of winning a few bets for Morris Courtney and inching his way into the driver's confidence reclaimed his thoughts.

It's going to be a good afternoon, Stewart assured himself.

Three more quarters tumbled into the pay phone before the operator allowed Rex Engels to make another long distance call. He stood outside the same phone booth as the night before, fixing his gaze on the blinking "x" on the Texaco sign. Five rings, a click on the receiver, and the same familiar voice.

"Yeah, Mr. Arnoldi? Rex here. I did just what you said, and you were right. Yeah, sure, I can do that, but I'll need a little more money. You know, business expenses, and all that."

He shifted positions and listened patiently to instructions. A brown Chevy sedan pulled into the station, and a slightly built man wearing glasses got out. He walked toward the phone booth. Engels eyed his every step.

"Just a minute, Mr. Arnoldi," he said in a low voice into the telephone. "What do you want, buddy?" he called out.

"Um . . . the phone, please. How long will you be?"

"A while."

"I'll wait."

"Not here, you won't. Get lost."

His questioner, who stood a foot shorter and appeared a hundred pounds lighter than Engels, opened his mouth to protest. Engels dropped the receiver. It swung in a wide arc, clanked against the glass, and bobbed up and down on its cord.

"I said, get out of here!" Engels shouted, raising a beefy fist.

The intruder quickly turned around and trotted back to his car. Engels picked up the receiver.

"Yeah, sorry about that, Mr. Arnoldi. What? At a phone booth, why? All right, all right. Now what was you saying?" Again, he listened intently. Then a huge smile cracked the corners of his mouth. "That's a great idea! Sure. Yep. What? Of course he won't get away! I'm a professional. Right, I'll keep you informed. Good-bye." He hung up the phone and dipped his forefinger into the change return slot. Nothing.

Engels stared at the Chevy sedan, where the man who had interrupted him sat waiting, and toyed with the idea of walking toward his car and making life interesting for its occupants. Maybe crack a window, buckle a door; or, better, smash the little creep's glasses. He loved doing that: gently removing a guy's glasses, dropping them, and grinding them into the pavement, pulverizing them with his heel while the owner watched, quivering, helpless. Great fun. But not tonight. He had some planning to do.

This job was going to be more enjoyable that he had anticipated. More profitable, too.

Chapter Four

Johnny Marlboro stroked the nose of his prized horse, *Whispering Pine,* adjusted her breast collar, and tested the fit of her blinders to ensure that their strap, which looped around the horse's ears and below the neck, did not provide an uncomfortable squeeze. Everything had to be perfect. In last week's race, *Whispering Pine* had lost "by a nose," according to the familiar expression, in a photo finish that left spectators and bettors gasping. The difference between win and place was actually about an inch, according to the photographic negative he examined after the race. Since a fifth of a second represented approximately the length of a horse, Marlboro figured that an inch must slice that segment of time into hundredths, perhaps thousandths of a second. He wasn't sure. But he did know this: an infinitesimal shift of *Whispering Pine's* head at a crucial time had cost him, several drivers, and who knows how many bettors, several hundred dollars. Hence, the blinders, which prevented the horse from seeing to the side, thereby preventing distractions that would cost him any future races.

The paddock judge strolled by, clipboard in hand. He checked horses' identification numbers and any changes in equipment, which had to be registered with the racetrack at least one week prior to post time. The trainer obliged by lifting his horse's upper lip and folding it back, which exposed the soft interior that showed its identification number. Sometimes numbers embossed underneath the thick fold of skin were easy to read, if the background were light enough. Other times, the trainer had to stretch the slab of flesh for a longer time, an effort made more difficult by the horse trying to twist its head free from this annoying intrusion. Fortunately, *Whispering Pine's* number was easy to read, and the paddock judge glanced at it quickly. Then he checked his equipment card. Everything seemed in order. He walked to the next stall, where he repeated this procedure.

Morris Courtney ambled behind the paddock judge and uttered a few words to Marlboro. "Have you seen Stewart recently?"

"If by, 'recently,' you mean almost every day, then the answer is yes. How has he been working out for you?"

Courtney patted *Whispering Pine's* neck. "Good, real good. We've made a lot of money in the last five or six weeks. He wants to meet me tonight at the diner to discuss some proposal he's come up with. Do you know anything about that?"

Marlboro continued to check the multiplicity of leather implements that encased his prized pacer. "Not really, no," he said finally.

"What does that mean?" Courtney asked.

"It means I don't know *specifically* what he has in mind, but I've known for a while that he's wanted to work out a deal with you. That's all."

"What sort of deal?"

"Ask him."

"Come on, Johnny!"

Marlboro stopped fussing with his horse's apparatus and faced his friend. "Look, Morris. He's a straight-up guy, and he works in the big leagues. You know that by now."

Morris's gaze drifted to the other end of the paddock, considering his friend's remarks. "You still vouch for him?"

"Absolutely."

Courtney nodded. "Well, I do, too, frankly. I just wanted your insights."

Marlboro returned his attentions to *Whispering Pine*. "Ain't got much of them," he quipped. "Lots of horses, though."

Courtney slapped him on the shoulder and turned to leave. He looked down the paddock, hesitated, then walked back and tapped Marlboro on the arm. Courtney gestured toward a person three stalls away on the opposite side.

"You think Sergeant Sledge over there will give us any more trouble?"

Marlboro turned his head toward a driver standing by the paddock judge, who was nearly finished with his prerace checks. Courtney called the driver "Sergeant Sledge," and always with a sneer on his lips; others simply referred to him as "The Marine."

He looked the part. His erect, five-foot-seven frame carried a solid one-hundred-sixty pounds that seemed perpetually at attention. Thick neck muscles supported a square-shaped head, truncated at the top by a butch haircut. The Marine's sharp gaze shredded well-meaning attempts to engage him in friendly conversation, as though he instantly took the measure of person facing him and finding him lacking. A determined, pit-bull expression was permanently etched on his face. As far as Marlboro and Courtney were aware, the Marine had no friends. Even casual acquaintances carrying out official duties at the racetrack seemed to avoid him. He was all business, and his record showed it.

"You know, Johnny, I'd love to stick it to that son of a bitch," Courtney said. "Even when he wins, *especially* when he wins, which is too often, he's impossible to deal with."

"Stewart might have some ideas on that subject, too," Marlboro ventured, with a roguish wink.

Courtney brightened at this suggestion. "You know, I'll bet he does! Maybe between the two of us, we can get that strutting bastard's attention." He clapped Marlboro on the shoulder again and walked out of the paddock.

Morris Courtney had no idea how deadly accurate his statement would become.

"Okay, Morris, here's the deal," Stewart announced, immediately getting down to business. Courtney shoved aside his plate filled with the evening's meat loaf special, leaned forward, and listened intently. Lakewood Downs Diner was always crowded, which actually made it easier to engage in private conversation. One had difficulty hearing the person across the booth, much less someone across the aisle.

"You and your drivers let me handle your bets, which I'll increase to a standard fifty dollars per race, instead of the ten or twenty you've been betting," Stewart explained. "I'll assume all risks for any losses. We'll handicap the races first, and you let me know which drivers are cooperating with us. Then I'll make the wagers on the basis of the favored horses. What do you say?"

Courtney reached for his fork and carved off a slice of meat loaf. He dipped it into a puddle of gravy, stuffed it into his mouth, and chewed slowly, his eyes drifting to a glittering set of hubcaps on the wall behind his friend. Stewart had met with him enough times to recognize that this was Courtney's way of thinking: feeding his face while examining paraphernalia that cluttered the walls of Lakewood Downs Diner.

"Okay," he said, wiping his mouth. "Though I don't know about the figure you have in mind."

"That can be changed," Stewart stated quickly. "We just wouldn't make as much money."

"No, let's stick with the fifty. It's a nice round number," he said.

"Tomorrow, race two, pacers, five years old and up, class C. Fast track, good weather. Let me tell you who's in on the fix."

"No!" Stewart declared. "I don't want to know who's working with us until after we've doped out the race. Bad policy. Might affect my calculations, even if I try to keep it out of mind. Plus, it's bad luck, you know, like taking pictures of your horse before the race. And based on some of the horses I've bet on over the years, their pictures must have been plastered across every magazine in print. Let's handicap first."

Courtney chuckled and took another bite of food. "Okay. Care to know how *many* drivers we've got in our camp?"

Stewart couldn't resist this question. "How many?"

"Three."

Stewart whistled, but Courtney shook his head. "That doesn't make it as easy as you think. From my experience, the hardest race to set up is one involving a front-runner who's not one of our boys. The easiest, of course, is when there are few or no stretch runners working against us."

"Makes sense to me."

"Good. You told me you did race two?"

"Got my notes right here," Stewart said, patting his pocket.

Courtney leaned back in his booth. "Go ahead, professor."

Stewart pulled out a racing program, unfolded a few sheets of paper, and launched into a detailed breakdown of the horses' strengths, weaknesses, past histories, and likely outcomes of race two. Courtney imbibed every word with reverential attention, leaning forward as Stewart wound up his analysis with a flourish.

"As you can see, only *Margrave Hal* and *Scotch Plus* are strong enough to be potential winners," Stewart concluded. "Of those two, I pick *Margrave Hal.*"

"Why?" Courtney asked.

Stewart shrugged. "Simple. They're both strong on the stretch, but *Margrave Hal* has the post position advantage, which is worth eight lengths. That's too much to overcome, even for *Scotch Plus*. Now, tell me. Who's in on the fix?"

Courtney grinned. "In your wildest dreams, who would you *want* to be in on the fix?"

Stewart gritted his teeth. "What are you, a game show host?" he grumbled.

"Margrave Hal," Courtney announced.

"You're kidding!"

Courtney shook his head, obviously taking pleasure in observing his friend's reaction. "Plus the five and the two horse."

"That's perfect!" Stewart gushed. He quickly darted his eyes about the restaurant to make sure no one took notice. A ridiculous precaution.

"Exactly," Courtney agreed. "*Claire's Girl* can fade back and block out three and four. Number five will fake a stretch drive but go wide, and take out anyone trying to get around him. If the word doesn't get out, I think we'll get two-to-one odds."

Stewart gripped the chrome-stripped table, a panorama of glittering scenarios parading through his thoughts, all sparkling from what he believed eventually would burst into his life: that lightning strike of opportunity that would make him a fortune. Courtney continued to talk, but his tailored sentences about strategies, track conditions, the weather, instructions to drivers, and so forth, faded below audible tones to Stewart, who had retreated into his private world, relishing every second of this golden moment. Finally, the little driver finished, and Stewart's mind returned to the present.

"This is what I'll do," Stewart said. "I'll put fifty dollars on the nose for you, plus fifty each for the three drivers."

"Deal!" Courtney exclaimed, and the two shook hands. "Okay if we meet here after the races?" he asked. "I've got a long-term lease on the corner booth beneath the car with the big boobs." He pointed to a wall that hosted the front end of a '57 Cadillac, which apparently had mimicked the driving habits of its Edsel companion that faced it across the room.

Stewart agreed with his metaphor. If Jayne Mansfield were a car, she'd be a '57 Cadillac. "Let's make it a tradition," he affirmed, beaming.

Stewart trotted to his Ford wagon and drove home. Ideas for future deals danced in his mind. He mentally scanned his coming week's schedule, focusing on his impending luncheon date with Lori. He ached to confide in her, to share his excitement, but he wasn't sure how she would react. *Some day soon,* Stewart mused. *At exactly the right moment, we'll share each other completely. Our lives, our dreams, our bodies.* With that delicious prospect salivating in his thoughts, he turned on the radio. Instantly, he heard the twittering organ prelude to The Doors' hit single, *Light My Fire.* Perfect song. It was followed by The Monkees' *I'm a Believer.* Even more perfect.

Stewart arrived home in time to catch an episode of *Mannix,* but he decided to call Lori first to confirm their date. Three rings later, her breathy voice resonated through the receiver.

"Lori? I just wanted to touch base with you about tomorrow. Listen, if you can wriggle out an extra fifteen minutes to a half hour from the nut house for lunch, we can make it to *Le Petite Marmite* near Deerfield. Wickedly good food, and . . ."

Lori's words sliced off his sentence like a meat cleaver. A long pause. He listened intently. "Sure, I understand," he stammered. "Anything wrong? Okay, sure. I'll call you tomorrow, then. Good-bye."

He placed the receiver down and slumped into a chair. The thrill that had pumped him up during his conversation with Courtney slowly drained from his body. Lori never changed her plans like that. He had been making so much progress with her over the previous months, and now it seemed she had heaved him back to square one. And for what? Something about her job, her boss, she said. Sounded vague, evasive. *There has to be more to it than that.*

Stewart turned on the television and tried to push the matter from his mind. Tomorrow's race loomed ever larger in the grand design that had been forming in his thoughts, but a sliver of doubt nagged his earlier confidence. Now, more than ever, he *had* to win race two. And then find out what was troubling Lori.

Chapter Five

Lori glanced anxiously at her watch for the fourth or fifth time and resumed her cross stare at the man behind the counter. He looked like a desiccated, medieval burgomaster whose movements reflected his age. With tormenting deliberation, he adjusted the magnifying spectacles that jutted out from his glasses and inserted the key Lori had given him into his duplicating machine. He cocked his head back so his bifocals gave him a better perspective and picked out another blank from the multitude that jingled on a huge turnstile propped on the glass counter.

"Maybe zis one vill vork," he said with a thick accent and a smile that animated every crack lining his wizened features.

"I *hope* so," Lori pleaded. "Can you please hurry. I'm on my lunch break, and I absolutely must have this key made before I return."

He lifted his hand and waved her off. *"Ja, Ja.* Always in a hurry. *Old Hans* vill take care of *yoo. Ja."*

Another check of her watch. Twelve thirty-five.

The man called Old Hans inserted another blank, tightened a knob, moved a lever, and then started the machine again. A low hum filled the ancient Patchogue hardware store that had attracted Lori because of its sign in front: "Keys Made in a Jiffy!"

They don't make jiffies like they used to, she groused, observing his painfully slow routine. The cutter scored the blank key, spitting minute particles of metal on the floor. Lori hated its grinding, scratching sound, which reminded her of fingernails being scraped across a blackboard. So far, she had winced her way through two failing attempts by Old Hans to get the thing right. She now lamented her decision to travel to Patchogue for this task, but she didn't want to risk anyone seeing her at a hardware store in Millville. Chance meetings in a small town occurred too frequently, and the key she wanted to duplicate was too distinctive for a nosy acquaintance to forget.

Old Hans moved like a figure in a movie stuck in slow motion. After a minute, he shut off his machine and scrutinized the key. Finally satisfied, he turned on another machine with metallic bristles and held the key against it. More whirring sounds flowed through the empty store. *At least this time he's cleaning the thing up,* she consoled herself.

Lori continued to fidget. She checked her watch: twelve forty-one. Her employer was a fanatic for punctuality. Unexcused tardiness sparked accusations of sloth, or, worse, looking for another job, which was completely unforgivable. He once fired someone for showing up late after attending a funeral. Complaints about working conditions provoked threats of dismissal. Even failure to wear the company shirt at Little League baseball games incited his chiding comments. Thus, Lori's desperation mounted. She knew she had only a short time to dash back to Millville during lunch hour traffic and return this precious master key to its owner.

Without him knowing about it.

Old Hans manipulated the key in his fat fingers under the gaze of the quadrupled lenses protruding from his face. He looked up at his anxious customer through rectangular spectacles, which transformed his eyes into jittery gelatinous blobs, and allowed a wan smile to disturb his lips.

"Ja, I tink dis vill do it," he pronounced.

"Great!" Lori exclaimed. "How much do I owe you?" She thrust her hand into her purse, pulled out a dollar bill, and flashed it before his multiple glasses.

"Of course, I don't charge for *my* mistakes," he said proudly. "I only charge for one key, just ONE key, *Ja?"*

Lori waved the bill before his spectacles. "Fine! Will this cover it? Please! I must go!"

Old Hans lifted the money from her hand and examined it, as though he were surprised it wasn't a deutsche mark. "I get *yoo* change," he said, and shuffled toward a cash register that appeared even older than he was. He pulled down the handle on a machine covered with elaborate engravings, and its drawer opened with a sharp ping.

Lori checked the time again: twelve forty-five. It would take her twenty minutes to drive back to work and devise a way to slip the master key back where she had found it without arousing suspicion. She realized she wouldn't make it in time, and her empty stomach punished her neglect, especially for adding the insult of stress to the injury of a missing meal. Lori knew she had to eat something to prevent herself from becoming sick. She didn't know why she reacted this way, and whenever it happened, she resolved to ask a doctor about her condition. For some reason, she never got around to it.

"I don't seem to *haf* change," Old Hans said after an eternity of examining his cash register. "I *haf* to go in the back . . ."

"Oh, never mind!" Lori retorted, stuffing the keys into her pocket. She swiftly turned and strode toward the door. "Keep the blasted change!" she hollered over her shoulder as she left the store.

Lori climbed into her 1960 Volkswagen, turned the ignition, and its air-cooled engine zoomed to life. She revved it a few times and felt the engine's chirping rumble vibrate throughout the cab. Lori darted onto the street, sped through several traffic lights, and entered Highway 85 toward Millville. It was twelve fifty-three.

She lamented every wasted second in Patchogue's ridiculous hardware store waiting for Old Hans to duplicate her contraband key. *I should have stayed in Millville. How can I explain why I'm late?* Lori reached for her purse and pulled out some saltine crackers encased in cellophane. After an exasperating struggle keeping one hand on the wheel while the other manipulated the stubborn wrapper, she finally tore the package open with her teeth. Crushed crackers burst over her lap and on the front seat. She retrieved a fistful of crumbs and stuffed them into her mouth. A few minutes later, she felt better. More noisy duels with cellophane and fourteen crackers later, she pulled her Volkswagen up to the sliding gate by the parking lot of *Sweets Ahoy*. It was twenty minutes past one o'clock.

A middle-aged man dressed in a sharp blue uniform stepped from the booth adjacent to the gate and greeted her with a pleasant smile. Lori scoffed at Jeremy Madison's charade to provide security. Anyone able to climb a fence could break into this place. A fact she counted on.

"Howdy doody, Miss Armstrong," he said, conspicuously checking his watch. "Beautiful day," he added.

"Wonderful," Lori replied brusquely. "By the way, Oliver, has Mr. Madison returned yet?"

"Yep. Drove in ten minutes ago."

Lori bit her lip. "Thank you," she said. She engaged the clutch and scooted into a parking place. Lori brushed saltine crumbs off her skirt, ran a comb through her hair, and walked quickly toward the building's side entrance. She clutched her purse tightly in her right hand.

Her office was located on the second floor, sandwiched between the boardroom and an expansive suite with an excellent view of a picturesque stream leading to Great South Bay. She breezed by several offices down the long corridor that ended in stairs leading to Jeremy Madison's inner domain. A few staff persons flitted questioning glances in her direction, which she acknowledged with curt smiles. She opened the stairway door, slowly ascended the steps, turned a corner, and looked down the second floor hallway toward her employer's office. The door was opened a few inches, but no sounds escaped. Silence entombed the empty hallway.

Lori stepped carefully toward her office, eased her door open to see if anyone were inside waiting for her, wondering where she had been. Empty. A file folder on her desk caught her attention. *Maybe, just in case*, she thought. She reached over, grabbed it, and tucked it under her arm. She closed her door, quietly glided toward the boardroom, and stood before its huge double doors, which she knew were open. She slowly twisted the doorknob on the right. It squeaked in protest and opened with a sharp click that made her heart jump. Lori pushed it open a crack and peered inside. Not a soul. That left only her employer's office, the room with its door slightly ajar. She lifted her feet softly toward Jeremy Madison's executive suite, as though attempting to traverse the distance without her toes touching the floor.

As she approached his office, a blade of sunlight knifed through a window and stung her eyes, temporarily blinding her. Lori blinked, adjusted her vision, and scanned the room's interior. It was vacant. Soothing sounds of classical music intermittently stroked the room's emptiness. Cautiously, she stepped inside.

Lori examined the layout. Elegant pieces from Jamestown Lounge, including hand-carved tables, bookcases, and Victorian chairs lined the walls, all paying homage, it seemed, to a huge mahogany desk that dominated the room's center. A Tiffany lamp sat near the window, filtering sunlight and splashing soft colors on the wood's glossy surface. To her left, filing cabinets jutted out from a wall in a curious arrangement that created an aisle near the desk. Thus it was possible for a person to work on files and be totally concealed from someone else on the other side of the room. Lori counted on that peculiarity to carry out the next part of her plan.

To her right, a rolltop desk sat proudly beneath a large painting of George Madison, founder of the company. That was her boss's working desk; the big one in the room's center he used solely to impress visitors. Disheveled stacks of papers were perched on each side, and wooden compartments bulging with envelopes and documents gave the desk a cluttered, busy appearance. More papers were strewn across its top. A pencil holder, an ink blotter, a few tins filled with nuts, a telephone, and other implements completed the ensemble. Lori was glad the desk was messy; that suited her purposes just fine.

She walked toward it, passing by a sofa that sat beneath a majestic window. A stained glass design surrounded its beveled glass interior, which graced the room with a hint of religious ambience. Vivid memories prowled through Lori's thoughts as she glanced at that scene. *Nothing holy ever happened here,* she mused, bitterly.

She reached into her purse for the master key, found it, and was ready to sneak it beneath a stack of documents, when a horrible realization scooped her breath away. Jeremy Madison kept his office key on a chain connected to a pewter medallion, which she had removed in order to get it duplicated.

What did I do with that key chain?

Lori frantically searched her purse, spilling some of its contents on the floor. She shoved, poked, and fingered the small container, surprising herself at how much she was able to stuff inside.

There it is!

Lori grasped the key chain and pried open its tight ring, breaking a fingernail in the process. She shoved the master key on it and slipped it beneath a pile of papers under the compartments filled with documents. A portion of the medallion poked through the tousled stack. As she turned to leave for her own office, faint sounds crept from the hallway into his office and snagged her attention.

Someone was approaching.

Lori couldn't escape without being noticed by whomever was walking toward Madison's office. Probably one of her co-workers, she speculated, someone else wanting to see the boss; a salesman, maybe. Or, Jeremy Madison himself.

I've got to get away from his desk.

Lori took several long strides across the thick carpet, but her left foot skidded on some round, metallic object, and she fell forward, nearly crumpling to the floor. Heart pounding, she spied a tube of her lipstick near the center of the room in front of the sofa. Sunlight streaming through the window ricocheted from its burnished surface.

Footsteps became louder; the person was only a few yards from the door. Lori scooted behind the filing cabinets, cutting a glance toward the suspicious lipstick. She hunched down and tried to calm her breathing.

The door opened and someone entered. Sounds of a chair creaking under the burden of a heavy man poked through ripples of music floating across the room. It was Jeremy Madison, no doubt about it. Papers shuffled; a briefcase thumped to the floor; fasteners snapped open and shut. More crackling paper. Her boss had settled down for an afternoon's work.

Lori's guts churned. A wave of nausea welled from her stomach and pressed against her throat. She fought it back, but was still no closer to a solution. Finally dragging herself toward the obvious conclusion that she couldn't remain trapped behind the filing cabinets all afternoon, Lori decided to take action. She glanced at the file she had grabbed from her office. *This might work,* she counseled herself. *Be bold.*

Lori stood up, opened a drawer from the cabinet in front of her, and slammed it shut. She popped around the corner and gasped, nearly dropping the file she had been carrying. Jeremy Madison twisted in the chair and looked at her, mildly surprised.

"I'm *so* sorry, Mr. Madison," Lori stammered. "I had to get some records, and your door was open, so I, um . . ."

"That's all right," Madison said, waving her silent. He lifted his bulk from the chair, revealing a paunch that hung over the waistline of Brooks Brothers slacks supported by burgundy braces stretched to their limits. He was a handsome man, probably dashing in his youth, before fifty pounds of excess baggage accumulated on a body that had never recovered from college football injuries. He arranged his hair in that ridiculous fashion used by men who refuse to accept male pattern baldness; long greasy strands combed from the side over the top in a futile attempt to conceal the slick skin underneath. Still, his eyes sparkled with energy; or, as Lori knew too well, lust.

Before Madison advanced toward her, she closed the distance between them in several long steps and planted her feet by her wayward tube of lipstick. Madison stood before her, expression radiating desire. At the moment, this worked in her favor. Lascivious impulses smothered his naturally suspicious nature.

"I'm sorry I didn't wait for your permission," she repeated.

"You know you may work in these files whenever you need to," he replied, stating what they both knew to be true.

Lori positioned herself between him and her lipstick, which lay near her left foot. The only way she could kick it away was to do something that sickened her, and that was to accept his advance. "Yes," she said, "but normally you're in your office when I file something. I just was in a hurry, and . . ."

"No need to apologize," he interrupted. "Actually, I left the door open because I misplaced my keys. I feel a bit foolish, because they were on my desk the whole time." He stepped closer. "I still think we should talk, Lori. You know, it's been a while, now. Plenty of time for you to recover, settle down, think things over." Madison cupped her chin with his hand, drew Lori toward him. His hot breath fell on her face.

As he was about to kiss her, Lori coughed and at the same time kicked her left foot against the lipstick. It scooted across the carpet. She stepped back, eyes down, as though demurely retreating from his overture, but actually checking the accuracy of her slap shot to the sofa. The lipstick had vanished.

"I have to get back to my office now, Mr. Madison," she uttered softly. Lori knew he hated being addressed by her in such a formal way. She clutched her file, turned, and walked toward the door.

Madison shrugged, disappointment written on his face. "I'll see you later, then," he said, as she swiftly walked away.

Lori dashed across the hallway and into her office, shutting her door for more privacy. She sat down and released a long breath of relief. A close call, she admitted to herself. But satisfaction at what she had accomplished flowed through her body, electrified her thoughts. She had completed the first phase of her plan. She immediately set her mind on the next, crucial step.

Ted Simon leaned back in his chair, placed his hands behind his back, and aimed an expectant gaze at his prized salesman seated across his desk. Stewart rubbed his chin thoughtfully, then caught sight of something that triggered mild alarm.

"Do you have to put my picture up there?" he asked, staring at the company photographs lined up neatly across the wall behind his boss's desk. "I really don't like having my picture on display. Call it a superstition."

Simon swiveled around, then turned back to Stewart. "I always display our salesmen. In fact, our company president insists on it. Whenever he saunters in to make sure I'm keeping out of mischief, the first thing he looks for are these portraits above my desk." Simon cracked a smile. "Call it a superstition on *his* part. I hope you understand that my catering to his quirks takes more than slight precedence over appealing to your tastes. He happens to be higher on the food chain. Why don't you like to have your picture taken, by the way? Superstition aside, that is."

Stewart shrugged. "Many years influence of going to the races, I guess. Take pictures of your horses, and they end up dead last. Snap a photo of me and watch my sales come crashing to the ground."

Simon chuckled. "At least that point brings us back to our original subject," he said. "And you know as well as I do that your sales are breaking records in the other direction. Last month's figures soared above the charts, stabbed the ceiling. You have a very bright future with us, Stewart, if you continue producing as well as you have the past several months. Why, in five, ten years, who knows where you could be? I remember when I started out . . ."

As Simon launched into a rendition of his well-known success story, Stewart switched on an attentive expression and put it on autopilot, while his thoughts wandered to more exciting possibilities than those offered by Office Products Unlimited. Johnny Marlboro's words flickered through Ted Simon's sales pitch: *that's a lot of magic markers,* the trainer had said. Which was, of course, exactly the point. How many magic markers, or pieces of furniture, or tons of office supplies would Stewart have to sell, over how many years, in order to achieve financial goals that appeared attainable at Lakewood Downs in a few months? Or even in a few weeks, Stewart thought, depending on how well his plans with Morris Courtney panned out.

Stewart's ruminations came to an end about the time Simon put the finishing touches on his career-track sermonette. ". . . which means you have a very bright future with our company, especially with the additional training I have in mind for you," he concluded. "So, what do you say?"

Stewart cleared his throat. "I really appreciate the time you've spent with me, Ted. The special help you've given me to get started, letting me stay with you in your apartment, everything. But I would like to think about your proposals more, if you don't mind."

Simon's expression showed disappointment, but he smiled agreeably. "Whenever you're ready," he said, getting up, extending his hand.

Stewart acknowledged with a smile and firm handshake. He turned and walked toward the door, impatience adding quickness to his step. *I'm ready,* he thought, *to win a bundle at the racetrack and see Lori.* He left Ted Simon's articulate pleadings in the office as he closed the door behind him.

Chapter Six

Stewart's thoughts ran down columns of figures he had been tabulating while dashing through traffic on the way to Lakewood Downs. Eager anticipation for the second race had plagued his concentration all morning. At one of his stops, a minor slip of the tongue generated five minutes worth of verbal gymnastics to convince a potential customer that *Margrave Hal* did not refer to the name of a new desk offered by Office Products Unlimited. Actually, that was his uncle's name, who had bought many of his products, Stewart explained. "Then why call him by his last name first?" came the sensible question. Force of habit, Stewart had replied; that's how customers are listed in his rolodex, and his uncle's name just tumbled out of his mouth. Finally, to change the subject and cover his tracks, Stewart signed a deal cutting a larger break than his price lists allowed, leaving the satisfied owner of a department store no reason to ask further questions. He hoped he would make up the difference at the track.

Which he did. *Margrave Hal's* sterling performance vindicated the planning he and Courtney had painstakingly engaged in the previous evening. After the announcer breathlessly proclaimed race two's results, Stewart relaxed in his seat, exhausted and exhilarated at the same time. His shirt stuck to his chest; he pulled it out and let his damp skin suck it back again. Relief now flowed through his body like a sedative, checked only by a pesky reminder about a rival horse's impertinent challenge. *Famous Pixie*'s astonishing surge had sparked sufficient anxiety for anyone interested in handicapping the race, honestly or otherwise. Of course, that horse had an excellent driver who coaxed the best out of mediocre material. Courtney had warned Stewart about *Famous Pixie's* driver, a person everyone called "The Marine." And he was right; something had to be done about that guy.

But not at this moment. Stewart clenched a pencil in his teeth and excitedly fumbled through his pockets, probing for the soggy notebook overflowing with scribbled entries on race two. He jotted down figures, erased illegible scrawling, re-entered correct data, then rested the notebook on his lap. Finally, he extended the paper in front of him with his left hand, as though admiring intricate brush strokes flowing across a piece of Renaissance art. With no one to observe his actions or hear his voice, he giggled like a schoolboy, as he visually fondled the numbers etched on the paper.

Ten tickets on the daily double, one of which coupled number four horse in the first race with *Margrave Hal* in the second paid forty-six dollars for each two dollar bet. Winnings amounted to four hundred sixty dollars. *Margrave Hal* paid seven dollars forty cents for a two dollar bet, which, when multiplied by his five hundred dollar bet, produced one thousand, eight hundred fifty dollars. Minus his original outlay of eight hundred sixty dollars, his profits for that day were fourteen hundred fifty dollars. Morris and their drivers got off handsomely as well; for no investment at all, each cleared one hundred eighty-five dollars. Not bad for two minutes work. *And,* he assured himself, *this is only the beginning.*

Stewart emerged from his booth grasping his tickets tightly in his fist, convinced he had entered the front end of a gold mine. He strode through the lobby and stepped into a line to present his tickets when he felt a finger poke into his shoulder. Stewart's whole body stiffened. He had already bumped into King Kong at the track more often than chance encounters seemed to warrant and was in no mood to manufacture meaningless banter at his moment of triumph.

God, if it's that behemoth again . . . Stewart inwardly groaned.

He turned his head reluctantly. Then his jaw dropped.

"Axel!" Stewart exclaimed. "Axel Thomas! What are you doing here?"

"The same thing you are," beamed a tall slender man, who possessed a physiognomy apparently patched together by some deity with a cruel sense of humor. If a camel could be considered an animal put together by a committee, then Axel Thomas's face could be said to have been constructed by a committee of camels. His broad pate swooped down to an enormous nose which looped up like a ski slope. Bulging eyes hovered above oversized cheeks, which squeezed his mouth in a fashion suggesting some aquatic monstrosity. He hadn't earned his nickname, "Fish-face" for nothing.

All of these laughable features succumbed to an expansive, warm smile, then a look of concern. "I see you're still throwing around big bucks."

Stewart glanced at his stack of tickets, blushed, then stuffed them out of sight. "Now and then, yes," he admitted. "Nothing more than what you're used to."

"A *lot* more than I'm used to, Stewart," Thomas countered. "Or, at least a lot more than what I'm doing now."

"Come on, Axel," Stewart jibed. "We've both been bitten by the same bug. Lighten up."

Thomas presented a pair of tickets representing twenty dollar bets. "This is my limit, now. I will admit that I won big about a month ago on a real sweet horse, but promised myself to quit if that happened. Which is exactly what I did," he emphasized. "Used the money for a nice neat investment. I'm in business for myself, now." Pride glowed from his last words. "Maybe something you should do, too."

"I've got a job, thank you. And don't sound so righteous. You left for the same reason I did, from what I hear."

Axel Thomas's face clouded. "Good God, they *burned* me out, man. It was horrible! I had to leave, to get away."

Stewart didn't know what to say. Thomas hoisted his long arm over Stewart's shoulder and guided him away from the line, near a post. He spoke to his old friend in a low voice. "Look, I know I owe you money, man . . ."

Stewart gave a dismissing gesture. "Ancient history. Forget it."

"I promise to pay you back when my investment shows returns. But the best I can offer you now is good advice. Don't get caught up in this again, Stewart. Do it for fun, like me. A few twenty-dollar bets now and then, just for kicks. I saw what you stashed in your pocket. Get out of this high-stakes game before it eats you alive, before it's too late, before you have no choice. Get out before . . ."

Thomas's bulging eyes flickered alarm, looked over his friend's shoulder. He stepped back, behind a post, as though trying to hide. He peeked around it again, then back to Stewart. "I've got to go now, Stew." He reached into his pocket. "Here's my business card. Look me up sometime. Promise?"

"Yeah, sure, I promise," Stewart said, perplexed. Then he watched as his friend's long legs propelled him through the lobby and down a set of stairs. Stewart turned in the direction of Thomas's last look. He spied Double K's hulking figure walking away, a shorter, bald companion at his side. They vanished down a flight of stairs.

Stewart stepped back into line and tried to put these strange encounters behind him. He collected his winnings and walked toward the exit. He was eager to see Morris, but mostly couldn't wait to see Lori. Stewart's exuberance inspired imaginative leaps into their future. He might even retire from his job, do this full time long enough to retire, if today's winnings could be generated on a regular basis. Maybe he could persuade Lori to quit her job and release herself from that bloated, bovine fool who embellished his Napoleon complex with a bay window belly. *Maybe she'll even agree to marry me,* he ventured. An exciting prospect, but premature, he concluded. Still, he could at least invite her to the racetrack some time.

Now there's a thought.

And why not? She didn't have to be privy to his machinations; all she had to do was to enjoy the fruits of their triumphs. *Great idea!* As soon as he could, Stewart would ask Lori to join him at the races.

Alistair Dalton peeled off his racing uniform and whipped it across the concrete floor of the drivers' locker room, which jutted off from the show paddock at Lakewood Downs. He pried the helmet off his square-shaped head and heaved it toward a wall, where it crashed against a locker door with a clanging report that echoed throughout the nearly empty room. Two other drivers, who were watching television in quarters reserved only for them and their trainers, quietly got up and left. No one messed with the Marine when he was in one of those moods. Not unless you wanted your head ripped off.

Actually, the Marine's nickname was well-earned. He had served in the Marine Corps with distinction in Korea, receiving two purple hearts and a bevy of other medals, including the Bronze Star, awarded for conspicuous valor. After his military service, Dalton worked as a trainer for his father, who instructed him in the fine art of harness racing. He compiled an impressive record of victories over the previous fifteen years at racetracks in the New England States, including Bay State Raceway, Liberty Bell Park, Pocono Downs, Freehold Raceway, and Lakewood Downs. Awards studded his résumé like pearls glittering on a string. He took pride in his accomplishments and tolerated no excuses for his failures. The mere hint of chicanery sent him into a rage. It also inflamed the scar that cut an angry path from his left temple across his cheek down to his throat, compliments of a round from a North Korean assault rifle. After race two, this barometer of his disposition flashed red; other drivers had noticed and swung huge arcs around his stall to avoid him. They knew he was furious about something.

Scotch Plus, Dalton repeated to himself, while he examined his face in the mirror. *That bastard blocked me on purpose. Claire's Girl* might have as well. He was less sure about that, even though he finished just behind *Claire's Girl,* placing third. Dalton's thoughts ran through a replay of race two, scrutinizing each turn, each dart to the outside, every attempt to break free of the clump and dash for the lead. He shook his head, then looked at his dull reflection that glared at him from the ceramic tiles above the sink. Finally, he twisted a spigot, cupped his hands beneath it, and splashed cold water on his face. He grabbed a towel and wiped himself dry. Then he sat upright on the bench and surveyed the wreckage of his clothes and equipment strewn around the room. Although his temper had subsided, he still smoldered in anger.

Something's going on here, Dalton whispered to a room engulfed in silence. *And I am going to find out what.*

Lori screeched her Volkswagen around a corner and zoomed down Millville's main avenue, narrowly missing a pedestrian who threw her a curse and skipped out of harm's way. *It shouldn't take a rocket scientist to figure out what I want,* she murmured as she aimed her car through the town's quaint downtown streets. She had roamed through specialty stores, sports equipment sections of large department stores, and even a few jewelry establishments without getting what she needed. Salespeople continued to hand her instruments that looked powerful enough to identify craters on the moon, when all she wanted was something convenient enough to fit inside her purse.

She passed a store with gold letters embossed on a blazing red sign. Kresge's Five and Dime, a holdover from a previous generation, run by an old Millville family. *Kresge's,* she repeated. *Maybe I've been looking in the wrong places.* She abruptly swung her car around and squealed her tires into a parking spot in front of the store. She walked inside, quickly located the toy department, and roamed up and down the aisles, finally stopping by a glass counter filled with dolls.

That's what I need!

An elderly lady with white hair and pleasant smile approached her. "Can I help you, ma'am?" she asked, in perfect English, Lori thought with gratitude.

"Yes, you can. That pair of binoculars, may I see it?"

"Certainly." She opened the case and handed Lori the toy binoculars. Lori eagerly grabbed the small instrument and planted them in front of her eyes.

"Actually, they're quite powerful for a toy," the lady explained. "Very light, too. Very good for children. You can see . . ."

"I can see *excellently,*" Lori said, more to herself than to the lady. She spread the two cylinders to match the distance between her eyes, fixed on an object about fifteen feet away, and adjusted the dial in the center. Inch-high letters expanded to fill her vision. Blurred images clouded the lenses. More adjustments. Finally, the letters came into sharp focus. *Perfect.*

"I'll take these," she declared.

"We also have them in powder blue."

"Pink is fine, thank you."

"A dollar ninety-eight, please."

Lori paid for the binoculars and walked toward the doors, when she noticed a rack filled with novelty items by a checkout counter. A penlight encased in plastic hung from a hook.

How could I forget that? she reminded herself, and quickly purchased it as well. Then she left the store, entered her car, and slipped the small objects into the pocket of her dress. Plastic, lightweight, they fit perfectly.

Fifteen minutes of scooting down a dozen side streets brought her to the outskirts of Patchogue to her apartment. Lori had barely relaxed in her favorite chair when the phone rang.

"Hello, Stew," she answered sweetly upon hearing Stewart's voice. She immediately sensed relief on the other end of the line. "Yes, it has been a while. Tomorrow? What *time* tomorrow?" Lori paused, listening to him while a multitude of tactical computations sped through her mind. A tone of pleading and excitement radiated from his voice, which reminded Lori of how abruptly she had treated him the last time she saw him. He deserved better than that, she thought.

She would make up for it tomorrow. "Seven o'clockish at Lakewood Downs? Sure, sounds like fun! No, let's have dinner *before* the races, if you don't mind. I don't know if I'll be able to stay that whole time, but I'd like to see at least a few of your races. Okay, wonderful. See you then."

Lori placed the receiver down and contemplated the following day's activities. She enjoyed being with Stewart. He was kind, understanding, and gentle, not like the other brutes who had rampaged through her life. She kept her true feelings about him buried deeply, away from his prying questions. And away from herself, as well. Lori could only face one challenge at a time.

At the moment, Stewart's offer fit perfectly into the task she had set for herself. She had just completed another phase of her plan, and, although he didn't know it, Stewart was about to help her with the next, final step.

Chapter Seven

After scouring through his impressive repertoire of pleading expressions, Stewart selected one that had never failed to get him results in the past and aimed it directly at Ted Simon.

His boss grinned. "I don't know whether to stroke your head for the best imitation of a cocker spaniel I've ever seen or ask you to fetch my slippers," he quipped, peering over a stack of documents on his desk.

"I guess it's because you never explained your duck entrails theory of handicapping at that party last year," Stewart said. "I've read all your books several times and still can't find it. The continental drift idea didn't make the index, either."

"I'm saving both for my next book. Still need to do some testing at the track."

"When?" Stewart asked, this time putting on a pouty look.

"That would be your basset hound face, right?" Simon said.

Stewart nodded. "It's sold a ton of office supplies and furniture for our illustrious company last month. Store buyers place orders or I threaten them with *'The look.'* Works every time."

"Speaking of our illustrious company," Simon pointed out, "Have you given any more thought to my proposals?"

"Yes, I have, but I'd like to get more experience on the road. Then maybe we can talk more about the training you have in mind."

Simon gave him a probing look, as if appealing for a more complete reply. Getting none, he shrugged the matter off. "Fair enough. Back to our original subject, I'm sorry I couldn't make it at the races with you last week."

Stewart brushed off the apology. "That's all right, Ted. I do enjoy observing your expertise in action, but tonight I managed to persuade Lori to join me instead," he said brightly.

Simon looked impressed. "I won't ask you what look you used to finagle her into doing that, but I do have a favor to ask. Since I can't make it, would you mind placing a few bets for me and Phil Louis?"

"No problem at all," Stewart said, although inwardly he cringed at the prospect of doing anything that might benefit a man he considered a competitor. A person of enormous girth, he appeared to Stewart like a huge mound of cookie dough perched on a pair of wobbly pier pilings that jiggled when he walked. His head rested on his shoulders as though scooped from a tub of lard and plopped there by a careless chef possessing a cruel sense of humor. Ordinarily, Stewart didn't conjure spiteful metaphors for those with striking appearances, except he didn't much care for the man and didn't know anyone who did. Louis's sniveling demeanor had somehow won him numerous sales awards, a fact he brandished like a weapon. Listening to his boasting about his sales prowess was like being slapped in the face with a cold, dead fish.

Stewart put the image out of his mind. "Any instructions?"

"Oh, yes!" Simon stated. He opened his desk drawer, pulled out several sheets of paper, and spread them on his desk. Stewart leaned forward and examined them with interest. Names of horses, their drivers, past records, strengths and weaknesses filled the sheets in orderly rows, highlighted by carefully drawn charts summarizing information contained in Simon's efficient script. His explanations marched systematically from premises through evidence to logical conclusions, all of which converged with overpowering cogency on a horse named *A. P. Raven,* driven by a certain Alistair Dalton. *The Marine.*

Stewart stood up, mentally fondling a possibility that slowly blossomed in his thoughts. "Do you mind if I take these with me, Ted?" he asked.

Simon appeared reticent, then shrugged. "If you keep them to yourself," he said, handing Stewart a few twenties.

"I promise," Stewart said earnestly, collecting the money, then turning to leave. "I'll let you know how it comes out," he said as he left Simon's office.

Stewart's thoughts crackled with excitement. *Ted,* he mused, *you have just given me a brilliant idea.*

―――

Morris Courtney shoveled a scoop of chocolate chip ice cream into his mouth, his lean face betraying little excitement over the day's winnings. Stewart nibbled a blueberry tart, alternately switching his view between the gleaming grill work of the Edsel across the diner and his friend's contemplative expression.

"You don't seem very happy about our joint foray at the Downs," Stewart observed.

"I'm going to screw that Marine!" Courtney exploded.

"Don't think he's your type," Stewart countered. "I hear he's got bad breath and rough manners."

Courtney scowled. "Did you see what he *almost* did to us with *Margrave Hal?*"

Stewart nodded. "Hard to miss. We still won, though. And he's not in every race, Morris. We can work around him, when we have to."

"He's in enough races that are important to us," Courtney snapped. "And in a position to screw us up in future races if we're not careful." His agitated eyes darted about the restaurant while his jaw muscles pummeled great lumps of ice cream, reminding Stewart of a large, carnivorous bird masticating a struggling rodent.

"You know what would save us a lot of trouble?" Courtney mused. "If the horses could read the morning line and *know* the odds against them."

Stewart couldn't suppress a grin. "Oh, but they can! I forgot to mention that *Margrave Hal* joined me in my booth to celebrate after the race yesterday. We sat together, shared a few horselaughs and had a jolly good time. You just have to know how to communicate. If he pounds his hoof once, that means he agrees with you. Twice, he disagrees. And if he drops a road apple on your lap, that means he *really* disagrees with you. Fortunately, *Margrave*—he lets me call him that—displayed his contrary views only once, which was still terribly rude, not to mention, messy. But, after all, he *is* a horse. And he does have a way of making his point in a horselike way, if you get my drift."

Courtney refused to be mollified. "Stewart, does your wit get any better when you *lose?*"

Stewart mulled over his friend's consternation. "I think I've found a solution to our problem," he announced.

"And what might that be?"

"Who's the crowd favorite for race four?"

"That's easy. *Great Forwarder.* Probably won't win, though. Always fades at the stretch."

"Right. And who do you think will win the race?"

"*A. P. Raven,* most likely." Courtney scowled. "And Dalton's his driver. What's your point?"

"Simple," Stewart said. *"Let him win!"*

A grin spread across Courtney's lips, as Stewart's suggestion registered in his thoughts. "Of course! That's perfect," he exclaimed.

"I thought so. The best kind of fix, really. The winner's unaware of what's going on, and the race looks more natural. There are still judges watching, you know, and Dalton's reputation as a scrapper actually helps us. All we have to do is bet on his horse, guarantee his win, and while he's wallowing in self-satisfaction, we're laughing all the way to the bank. What do you think?"

Courtney twittered with glee. "I only wish we could tell him, so he could share in our joy over his victory."

"Darn right. A pity, don't you think?"

"A crying shame," Courtney chuckled.

"The question is, can we do that?"

Courtney pulled out a program and his eyes ran down the list of names. "We have the driver on two, *Red Riding Hood,* and six, *Seawall.* I'll have *Red Riding Hood* move at the three-quarter mark and ride shotgun on the outside. That'll make sense to any observer, because with a good starting position *Red Riding Hood* usually offers a fair stretch. *Seawall* will do the same and go three wide at the three quarter mark, and that will force late contenders to go four wide to catch up. With those two as blockers, this race's in the bag. *A. P. Raven* is four to one on the morning line. If those odds hold, we can make serious money."

"In other words, we can do it," Stewart persisted.

"Absolutely!" Courtney confirmed. "What inspired you to come up with this idea, anyway?"

Stewart hesitated. "Let's just say I've been working on it since you warned me about Dalton. Seems a sensible thing to do whenever he gets in our way."

"We'll see how it works out tonight, but I really don't have any doubts." Courtney splayed his hands out. "That's it, then, right?"

"We'll meet after race four," Stewart said, getting up and smiling. A date this evening with Lori, a sure fix on race four, and a brilliant trick played on everyone's favorite enemy added up to what he knew would be a perfect evening.

Although it was only eight minutes to post time for race four, Stewart couldn't pry his eyes away from Lori Armstrong's exquisite figure. She leaned casually against the back wall of his private booth clutching a ridiculous looking pair of binoculars. A soft summer breeze caressed the translucent scarf that fluttered from her neck. A white and pink striped halter top flowed across her ample bosom, deliciously accenting every movement. White pants hugged her provocative hips and legs, and flared slightly by her feet. *Ravishing*. Lori's fluid motions swam before Stewart's appreciative eyes, obliterating any other thought that strayed too close to his present object of concentration. *Innocent beauty unaware of itself,* he thought. Lori once complained that she didn't think she looked good in pink and white. She looked good in *anything*, Lawrence mused. Better, *without* anything.

"Darling, what is that over there? A scoreboard or something?" she asked, momentarily breaking the grip her presence had on his mind.

"That's the tote board," Lawrence said.

Lori lifted her binoculars and studied the wide rectangle animated by flashing lights. Her arm brushed against her left breast, which jiggled slightly as she leaned forward. Stewart nearly swooned.

"What do all those numbers mean?" she asked. "They're always changing."

Her second question yanked Stewart back to his real purpose, which now seemed like a distraction. "They reflect the changing odds on each horse as bets are placed."

Lori's quizzical expression indicated she didn't understand. Stewart continued. "The morning line establishes the odds against each horse winning the race. For example, you see the number twenty lit up next to number seven, which is printed on the board. The seven refers to the horse in the seventh post position; the number seven horse, in other words. It means that the odds against him winning are twenty to one. He has one chance in twenty-one, actually, to win the race. The favored horse in this race is number one, *Great Forwarder,* who is listed at nine to five. That is shown on the board as nine point five, so it is not confused with the number ninety-five. He has five chances in fourteen to win the race. More bets placed on each horse indicate greater confidence of bettors on that horse. That's why the odds are always changing to reflect bettors' actions."

That explanation seemed to satisfy her. "Win, place, and show," she stated. "That means coming in first, second, and third, right?"

Stewart nodded. "If you bet for show, you collect if your horse comes in first, second, or third. If you bet for place, you win if your horse comes in first or second. If you bet to win, you collect only if your horse comes in first. Obviously, the highest payoffs are attached to horses coming in first."

Although Lori nodded her acknowledgment, her attention seemed to drift. She checked her watch again and turned to survey their surroundings, finally fixing on some object about twenty feet away. She focused and re-focused her binoculars.

"What are you looking at?" Stewart asked.

"Nothing, really."

"The track's over there," he said, pointing toward the tote board.

"I know that, silly," she giggled. "I'm just . . . experimenting."

"I'll let you use my binoculars when the race begins."

"No, I prefer these, really."

"That's a toy, dear."

"They work perfectly. Do you want to see?"

Stewart shook his head. "Pink binoculars? Not my type." He checked his watch. Four minutes to post time. "I'll be back in a minute."

"I'll be waiting," she said, tweaking her nose and giving him a wink. Then she continued her curious sweeps with her pink toy binoculars, fixing on one point after another, each fifteen to twenty feet away.

Stewart remained mystified, but he was more interested in studying her than what she was doing. His eyes clung to her voluptuous figure, savoring every curve, every alluring motion. Just as Lori's liquid hips revolved in his direction, he broke off his gaze and turned away. He trotted toward the main lobby, his thoughts overheated with passion. Stewart concluded that blueberry tarts definitely placed a remote second in his hierarchy of irresistible delicacies. Lori Armstrong overwhelmed them all.

When he stepped up to the betting booth, two minutes remained before race four. Stewart placed fifty dollar bets for Courtney and his two drivers. Then he pulled out a billfold from the inside pocket of his sport coat and opened it, revealing a fat wad of one hundred dollar bills. He counted out each one and placed the stack on the counter. Twelve hundred dollars on the nose, *A. P. Raven*. With about a minute remaining before post time for race four, he walked toward his booth, checking monitors along the way. *Great Forwarder's* odds dominated the board at seven to five, while *A. P. Raven's* eased slightly to four to one, undoubtedly the result of his large wager. No matter; he would still win a bundle. If, that is, their unsuspecting dupe, the Marine, played his role in their scheme.

Stewart entered his booth and settled into his chair. Lori greeted him with a sweet smile, her binoculars resting on her lap, a detached look on her face as she stared into the distance. Sounds of rumbling hooves poked through patches of staccato chattering that crackled from the loudspeaker. Race four was ready to begin.

"PA-A-A-ACERS are *OUT* and behind the GATE! The GATE swings *AROUND*, and *the-e-e-e-ere they go!"*

Stewart's thoughts still floated above the charging reality of race four. The most important event of his wagering career was taking place before his eyes, while his mind had taken leave of the present to speculate about his future. Finally, as the horses turned the bend toward the back stretch, the urgency of the action seized his attention. He jerked his head around, snapped his binoculars into place, and focused on the track. By this point, the mobile gate had folded to the sides of the truck, and the truck moved to the outside rail. Eight frantic beasts pulling sulkies roared past the starting post. The race was on.

"SO-O-O-OARING to the lead, it's *Great Forwarder*. TWO is *Red Riding HOOD*. Three, and FLARING to the outside, it's *Macwyn*. FOUR, fading from his start position, is *A. P. Raven*. Five, hugging the rail, *Seawall*. Six, CHARGING to the *OUTside*, *Armored Knight*. Followed by *Hansel Direct*, SIX, and TRA-A-A-AILING the lot, it's *Golden Knight! Round the turn* they GO! RACING to the front end, *Red Riding Hood. POWERING* to the outside, *MACWYN! ONE QUARTER MARK* AT THREE ZERO AND TWO!

"INTO the LANE for the *FIRST TIME*, it's *Armored Knight*, racing third! TWO is *Red RI-I-I-I-DING Hood*, CLAWING for the lead! FIRST, *Great Forwarder*, BUT BEING CHALLENGED! *Macwyn* FA-A-A-ADES to four. Followed by *A. P. Raven*, FADING TO FIFTH! Slumbering *SE-E-E-EWALL*, SIX! *Golden Light*, SEVEN! *Hansel Direct*, TRA-A-A-AILING AT eight! *Straight alignment* charging toward the *HALFWAY POINT!* ONE-O-TWO AND ONE!

Stewart's fingertips ached in protest to the merciless grip he held on his binoculars. An avalanche of calculations from the previous evening tumbled through his mind, while he gawked, openmouthed, at twelve hundred dollars worth of horse fading to fifth at the halfway point. *Remember, he's a strong stretch runner. A. P. Raven will make it up.* Doubt still flickered in his thoughts. *Goddamnit, Marine, you had BETTER make it up!*

"Is your horse winning, dear?" floated a soft, low voice behind him. "Who are we rooting for, by the way?"

"A. P. RAVEN!" he retorted. He ripped his gaze from the racetrack and hurled an impatient glance in her direction. Lori wasn't even looking at the track. She was staring through that ludicrous pair of binoculars at some object behind them. Same thing as before, as nearly as he could tell. What was so fascinating about the third seat in the fifth row above their booth?

"INTO THE LIGHTNING LANE THEY GO!"

My God, I missed one fourth of the race! Stewart snapped his head back toward the track and thrust his binoculars to his face so hard, he bruised his cheekbone.

"*CHA-A-A-ARGING* from the OUTSIDE, it's *A. P. Raven!* He wants more! TWO Lengths! FOUR Lengths! AND MORE! *HE POWERS TO A HUGE LEAD!* Nobody will catch him! TWO and ONE are moving WIDE, it's *Red Riding Hood!* Followed by THREE, *Great Forwarder!* FOUR, it's *Golden Light!* A-A-A-AND, bunching THE LOT BEHIND HIM, three wide, *SEAWALL!* RACING TO THE WIRE! It's A-A-A-A-A. P. RA-A-A-A-AVEN! TWO-O-TWO AND THREE!"

Stewart released his grip on his pair of binoculars and let it tumble down his chest where it hung on a strap near his stomach. His face was slick with sweat. He slumped into his chair, exhausted and exhilarated at the same time. A sense of triumph welled within him, pushing a wide smile across his lips. Lori promptly leaned over and kissed him on the cheek.

"Congratulations, Stew. You won," she stated, as though casually offering a comment on the weather.

He reached out his arms and gripped Lori's shoulders. "*We* won, Lori. We won! You have no idea what this means, for me, for us, for our future!" he exclaimed. "This is just one race. There will be others, dozens more! And they'll all be like this, only *better!*"

Responding to the moment's fever pitch of victory, Stewart decided instantly to tell her everything, when Lori sat down in the front seat next to him and placed her hand on top of his.

"Listen, Stew, I enjoyed watching this race with you, but I really have to leave now. I'm wondering if you could do something for me."

Lori's blue eyes narrowed, accenting worry lines that transformed her expression to one of serious purpose. Stewart had seen that look before. Her reaction in the present circumstances puzzled him.

"*Honey,* we just WON!" he repeated, trying to coax her mood into line with his own. "What's the matter?"

"Nothing. I just want to know if you could do something for me."

"Of course, I will. What?"

"Actually, I need you to give me an alibi. If anyone asks, just say I was with you all night. Okay?"

Stewart tried to gauge her meaning. "Why *can't* you be with me all night?"

"I just can't. Now will you cover for me, *please?*"

Stewart's resistance melted as he lost himself in her pleading eyes. He cupped her hands in his. "Only if you promise to tell me why."

"Sometime I will. I promise," Lori said quickly.

"Fine, then. You were with me all night. The races last until about eleven o'clock. Is that enough time?"

"That's *plenty* of time," she said, beaming. She gave him a passionate kiss.

"Anything else you want me to cover?" he asked.

"Maybe later," she said, with a wink. "I have to go now." Lori got up and stepped out of their booth. Stewart watched her petite figure sashay down the walkway, collecting wolfish stares along the way.

He turned his attention to the track, where Alistair Dalton was standing in the winner's circle next to his horse. Several pictures flashed, and the Marine led *A. P. Raven*, still strutting and bobbing his head, back to the show paddock. Stewart lifted his binoculars and caught a glimpse of Dalton's face when he waved to someone behind the outer rail. The Marine grinned as though smiling were a distasteful but occasionally necessary duty, then he vanished beneath the stands by the show paddock. Stewart lowered his binoculars, savoring the moment. The victory was one thing; its magnitude, another. But the irony of it all just made everything sweeter.

He pulled out a crumpled stack of cards and rearranged them. His pencil scampered across the top note card, punctured it in two spots, and circled his own winnings with a wide, heavy stroke. Stewart's twelve hundred dollar wager had generated six thousand two hundred and forty dollars, of which nearly five thousand represented pure profit for him. *Five thousand dollars!* At the rate of one fix per day, depending on the odds, he could easily clear ten to twenty thousand dollars a week. Deductive leaps about future earnings spun off his thoughts like sparks flying from a grindstone. *Just a few months of this and I can retire!*

Giddy with excitement, Stewart left his booth to meet Morris Courtney, whom he knew was by the show paddock. He spied his collaborator leaning on the gate that separated the spectator area from the lane that led to the racetrack, chatting quietly with Johnny Marlboro. Both were nodding their heads, as though agreeing on some point. As soon as they noticed his approach, Marlboro broke off their conversation and walked toward the show paddock. Courtney met Stewart and motioned him back toward the grandstands. They walked briskly away from the track, into the lower level, ascended steps to the main lobby, and entered the men's room. A quick check indicated the room was vacant.

Finally alone, Courtney faced his friend squarely and clamped his hands on Stewart's shoulders, his face ablaze with exuberance. "We did it, Stewart! We did it! The biggest fix I've ever arranged in my life, and it went off without a hitch. *Absolutely perfect!*"

Stewart joined in the merriment and responded with a hearty slap on Courtney's shoulder. "Ready for payday at the Diner?"

"Absolutely! That Cadillac never looked better."

"Great! By the way, what were you and Johnny talking about when I came down to see you? And why did he walk away?"

"He doesn't think the three of us should be seen together at the track," Courtney said. "Don't want to draw too much attention."

Stewart regarded this point and nodded in agreement. "Sounds right to me. Is that what you guys were talking about?"

"No, there's something else Johnny came up with. About our fixes. You know, coming up with a system. Johnny's always looking ahead."

"I've been thinking the same thing!" Stewart exclaimed. "What does he have in mind?"

Two, then three men walked into the rest room and stepped up to the urinals. A fourth sauntered in and entered one of the stalls. Stewart and Courtney walked toward the sinks and busied themselves with soap and water.

Courtney lowered his voice. "Did you happen to check the stalls when we came in?" he asked in a worried voice.

"Yes! They were clear," Stewart whispered. "Now tell me about Marlboro's system."

"Here? Now? Ridiculous!"

Stewart had to agree. "Let's go up to the stands."

"No, wait till tomorrow. Lunch at the Diner. Johnny has to work out more details, anyway," he murmured.

Stewart pulled a length of paper towel from the dispenser and wiped his hands. "Okay," he said. "Meat loaf and blueberry tarts at the Diner, tomorrow. My treat."

Courtney grinned. Stewart left him standing there. He dashed into the lobby, stepped in line, and collected his earnings. He took great strides through the lobby and into the parking lot, springing along each step of the way. He climbed into his Ford station wagon and planted his hands on the steering wheel. As he gazed at its arrangement of gauges, lights, and instruments, the dashboard struck him as depressingly ordinary.

In a month or two, I'll have a BMW, he thought. *No! A Cadillac, a completely restored, mint condition, '57 Cadillac!* The symbolism of it glowed in his thoughts. *Yeah! That's what I'll do!*

Stewart started his company car and headed toward the Long Island Expressway for the half an hour drive to his apartment in Millville. A dazzling array of scenarios cascaded through his mind, reducing his travel time to blurred images of passing a few cars and making a dozen or so turns. He drove on mental cruise control, when suddenly his thoughts stopped short.

Lori!

I forgot she wanted me to cover for her at least until eleven o'clock. She needed an alibi for some reason.

Stewart pulled into the driveway to his apartment and checked his watch. He left immediately after the fourth race, and now it was only nine o'clock. He had told Lori he would be at Lakewood Downs the *entire* evening, until eleven or so. Did it make any difference? Stewart didn't know. Probably not, he convinced himself; he could fake it. When he, Morris, and Johnny Marlboro pooled their talents, created a system for future fixes, this minor slip wouldn't matter. The six-figure income he had in mind would demolish her need for an alibi.

Stewart clambered up the outside stairway, fumbled for his keys, and entered his apartment. He closed the door behind him and flipped a switch that turned on a lamp next to his sofa. As he was taking his sport coat off, he glanced across his living room.

Stewart froze.

Sitting on the sofa, glaring at him was the hulking figure of the man he only knew as King Kong.

Chapter Eight

Lori checked her watch and recalculated the time she needed to carry out an operation she had rehearsed in her mind a dozen times. With one hand guiding the wheel of her Volkswagen while the other fumbled through a knapsack, she swerved off the main thoroughfare onto a dirt road that snaked into a clump of trees. The road's stony, irregular surface pummeled her helpless vehicle, nearly heaving it against trees that loomed on each side and arched above her like the ceiling of a cave. Beams from the car's bouncing headlights stabbed into the foreboding darkness ahead. Finally, she angled into a clearing where the wheels slid to a stop on slick, grassy turf. Her Volkswagen snuggled easily into a copse of protective pines, and it was impossible to detect her presence from the road.

Lori turned off the car engine and pulled out a black sweat suit from her knapsack. She got out of the car, peeled off her clothes, and climbed into her sweat suit. She tied a scarf around her neck; always, Lori wore a scarf, regardless of the weather. Her clothing offered room for agile movement, but the forest's thick, damp air enveloped her, and she began to sweat. Lori knew that excess body moisture in this clammy environment constituted more than just an annoyance, but she was prepared for it. She pulled out a cotton diaper borrowed from a friend, wiped her face, and stuffed it into her right pocket, which already contained black gloves.

Her fingers probed the other pocket and were greeted by her binoculars' comforting outline. She stuffed her flashlight inside her bra, where it wedged between her breasts, uncomfortable, but secure. It joined another small object that had taken her considerable trouble to obtain: Jeremy Madison's master key. But since her car keys would be in the way, she opened the driver's side door and slipped them under the seat. Lori bent over, stood up, and was reminded of one more thing. The acid taste of guts in turmoil crept up her throat and stung her mouth, making her gag. She swallowed hard and reached inside the Volkswagen to the passenger seat for a box of saltines. After consuming eight or ten of the dry but functional crackers, Lori was ready to begin her task.

Ten minutes of disciplined walking separated her from the fence that enclosed Sweets Ahoy. A minute or two over the top, a dash to the side door, and several quick strides through the building's administrative area would take her to her boss's office. She figured she had to be there no later than nine-thirty. Then things would get interesting.

Lori started walking, then ran to Sweets Ahoy's outside fence, which she reached with five minutes to spare. She confronted the fence, grasped its metal with her wiry fingers to test its strength, then squeezed the pointed toes on her sneakers between the damp mesh. Lori took a deep breath, and with the agility of a monkey, scaled the fence. Its sturdy construction relinquished only a few squeaks as she made it to the top, where the links had been cut off, presenting a serrated edge she had to overcome before she could jump inside the parking area that surrounded the building.

Lori heaved her right leg over the barbed surface and angled her foot to catch a hold. She probed and stabbed the mesh for a secure notch with her toe.

Come on . . . Come on . . . Got it!

She shifted her weight and powered herself over the top of the fence, straddling its ominous teeth.

Almost there.

Lori grasped each side while gingerly hoisting her left leg past the sharp spikes. The fence's wire mesh squeezed her slender fingers to the bone. Pain shot up her wrists. Blood seemed ready to explode from her fingertips. Just as she was about to clear her left leg over the top, her right foot slipped from the mesh, and her thigh plummeted with all her weight on the fence's merciless prongs.

Searing pain.

Lori yelped. Her arms, legs, flailed helplessly. Toes probed, *clawing* for a foothold . . . *There!* She pulled her slashed leg free from the pitchfork grip that had knifed into her thigh. The fence's cruel hooks ripped her flesh and snagged her cotton sweat suit as she whipped her leg across the top. Lori threw herself free with such force that she lost her balance and tumbled to the ground.

Her body whacked the concrete surface in segments— elbows, left ankle, shoulder, wrist, back of the head.

Darkness.

Returning consciousness pried her eyelids open. Dazed, bleeding, she checked her watch. Nine twenty-three. A quick inventory of bruises and cuts. Multiple punctures lined the inside of her left thigh, like teeth marks inflicted by a ferocious animal. Blood blossomed from each stab. She tested her leg. Weight, movement, punished her effort. Still, it seemed fit. *I can go on.* Worried her fall might have been heard, she scanned the area with quick, nervous glances. No one was in sight.

She stood up. *Thank God, at least nothing's broken.* Her binoculars remained intact. Her flashlight and master key pressed against the soft flesh inside her bra, but she could put up with that for a short time. Lori brushed herself off and dashed to the side entrance of Sweets Ahoy. She reached it in ten seconds. Another time check. Nine twenty-four.

Six minutes left.

Lori reached inside her brassiere and retrieved the master key. She knew that for convenience sake, Madison had installed identical locks on the side entrance and on his office door. All Lori had to do was to open the door and waltz up to the second floor where she would conduct the next phase of her plan.

She inserted the key into the lock. It refused to turn. More pressure, twisting, jerking. Still nothing. Desperately, she jiggled it in and out, trying to coax the key into doing its job. No luck. Nine twenty-six.

That wretch changed the outside lock! Exasperation screamed through her mind, and in a fit of rage she pounded the door with a bloody fist. Again, she jammed the key into its slot. Completely stiff. *Insolent little piece of metal!* Once more, with all her might. It nudged a trifle, then groaned as it bent a quarter turn to the left. Something inside clicked. The door sprang open. The minute hand passed nine twenty-eight on her watch.

Lori swept into the hallway and ran toward the door opening to the second floor, where she came to an abrupt stop, the rubber on her sneakers emitting a tiny chirp. She froze into place. Beams from a flashlight glided across the pebbled glass of an office window to her left and traced a path across her forehead. Someone was approaching from the building's cavernous interior. She knew who it was: Oliver, the security man at the gate, who also served as Madison's night watchman and lived in a small apartment tucked away on the opposite side of the complex. He was making his evening rounds. For some inexplicable reason, tonight he was early.

Lori had no idea if he had seen or heard her. She gently pushed open the door to the stairway, eased it shut with painful care, and leaped up the stairs in several quick, silent bounds. Darkness shrouded the hallway, broken only by hazy light that spilled into the executive suite from streetlights outside. A door closed downstairs. Muffled sounds of footsteps seeped through cracks in the doorway and floated up the stairwell. The night watchman was approaching.

Lori pulled out her master key and frantically inserted it into the lock that secured Madison's office door. It turned without resistance. She pushed open the door with a whoosh that blew her hair back and eased it shut behind her, just as the stairwell door creaked its announcement of Oliver's entry. Weighty footsteps plodded up the stairs. Lori rushed behind the file cabinet, crouched in the murkiness, and waited.

The night watchman's heavy feet advanced in stops and starts. Through the office suite's pebbled glass partition, Lori spied beams from his flashlight sweeping across the hallway and stabbing into corners of rooms. Oliver walked a few steps, opened a door, sliced through darkness with his blade of light, closed the door, and then advanced to the next room. In a few seconds, he would check Madison's office.

Blood roared in Lori's ears. Every bruise, every scrape on her body protested against her enforced immobility. *Settle down,* she counseled herself. *He'll just peek inside, wave his flashlight around a bit, and then leave.* Lori felt warm moisture spreading from the inside of her left leg and trickling down her ankle. She dappled it with her fingers. They came back wet. Her punctured thigh oozed blood. Her sweat pants were sopped, squishy.

God! I can't bleed on the carpet! Sweat beaded on her forehead, as she feverishly tried to figure out what to do.

My scarf!

Lori clawed at the flimsy cloth circling her neck, poking into its loose knot with her fingers. Prying, probing into the tight, slippery silk . . . *Got it. Pull!* She gave it a yank and whisked it off her neck. She gently tried to extend her left leg, so she could fasten her scarf around it as a tourniquet. Like an animal trapped inside a cage too small for its body, Lori struggled to change positions without accidentally propelling an elbow or knee against the filing cabinet or the wall.

Carefully . . . Carefully . . .

Her left foot inched forward. *Keep leaning to my right, to my right!* Suddenly, her body twitched, uncontrollably. Her weight shifted to her left side.

Her wounded thigh revolted. Outraged nerve ends seized both legs, her arms, froze them into place. She eased her leg back and tucked it beneath her. Wooziness rushed through her head. The room swirled. *Nausea.* She winced, gritted her teeth to fight it off, keep a grip. Tears squeezed from both eyes. Another long, jittery intake of air. *That's a little better.*

Her fingers crawled to her wounds. Still wet with blood, worse than before. *Good God!*

I have to sit down first. Another try, this time to the rear, on her rump. She squiggled her hands backward, fingers extended, to ease her body on the floor. Her balance tipped; fingers on her left hand collapsed, skidded two inches toward the filing cabinet. *Can't do it. Might fall and thump on the floor. He would hear that.*

Tinkling sounds of metal, like tiny bells, pierced the air. Oliver was sorting through his crowded key chain for the master key to Madison's office. Metal clicked inside metal, locked into place, turned a complete revolution, then pulled away. The door opened slowly. Beams from Oliver's flashlight whisked back and forth across the room and probed the corners of Madison's office.

Lori cowered, her mind skipping across a dozen horrible thoughts, like bare feet hopping across hot coals.

The diaper, I'll use that.

Lori plunged her hand into her pocket and yanked out the diaper she had carried to keep her forehead dry. She stuffed it inside her pants. Pain streaked through her leg as additional pressure squeezed against her swollen thigh.

She crouched into as tight a ball as she could. *Any minute now, he'll be done with his routine check,* Lori thought, trying to calm herself. *Then he'll leave and not return until long after I've gone.*

Oliver's presence filled the room. An eternity passed with each second. Lori gaped at the sweeping yellow rays that poked into every crevice, chasing every shadow. She pressed her face against the filing cabinet to anchor her quivering body. Her breathing pummeled its cold metal skin. *Surely, he must hear me,* she agonized.

The heavy door brushed the carpet as it closed with a soft click. More footsteps. But they were louder, closer.

Inside the office.

Her heart thumped in her throat. Lori battled against acid invading her mouth, as she stared at fingers of light groping toward her hiding place.

Chapter Nine

Stewart stood transfixed by the sight of King Kong's mammoth outline sprawled across his sofa. He wore blue jeans and a light knit shirt that wrapped around his thick torso like a thin coat of paint. He straightened himself to an upright position, keeping his eyes trained on Stewart, like the deadly glare of a cobra fixed on its prey. Even casual movements animated his muscles, which twitched as though responding to sporadic electrical shocks.

For a fleeting second, the thought of escape streaked through Stewart's mind: dashing outside and running for his life. *Impossible*, he instantly concluded. He could no more flee from this man in his apartment than could a rabbit trapped in a wolf's den. King Kong would grab him in a flash.

"What are you doing here?" Stewart asked in a trembling voice.

King Kong lifted his heavy body off the sofa and approached him. He raised his hand to Stewart's throat and toyed with the lapel on his shirt, flicking it back and forth. Stewart felt like a mouse being pawed by a cat. Any second now, the playing would end, and he would be ripped apart.

"Never did make our acquaintance, you know, formal-like," Double K said. Stewart remained immobile, preparing for what he was sure would be a savage assault.

"My name's Rex Engels," he continued. "And I know you're Stewart Lawrence."

"What . . . what do you want, Mr. Engels," Stewart asked.

"What do I *want?*" Engels bellowed. Cruel laughter erupted from his throat. He clutched Stewart under his chin and backed him against the wall. Blood-lust flared from Engels's eyes, as words spat through clenched teeth. "I want what Mr. Arnoldi wants, and that's a hundred and ten thousand reasons not to break both your legs right now!"

Stewart felt as though his bowels had turned to liquid. "I don't owe him that amount," he stammered.

"I know you don't," Engels said. "Ten grand of that is my fee for finding you. Actually, I'm only charging him seven, but the extra three is your personal tip to me. You know, now that we're friends, and all." More sniggering, as though immensely pleased with his own joke.

Engels relaxed his grasp and let his victim touch his heels to the floor. Relief softened the tension gripping Stewart's body and allowed him to regain some control over his physical reactions. "How did you find me?" he asked.

"Actually, that wasn't too hard. You can run away from your bookie, desert your wife and kid, change your name, your job, where you live. But you know one thing you can't change?"

Stewart remained silent. Engels answered his own question. "The location of racetracks," he chortled, stepping back and folding his arms. "You also can't change the fact that you've got to come up with one hundred ten grand real fast. Or, I carry out my end of the deal with Mr. Arnoldi."

"I don't have that amount right now," Stewart said.

Engels's expression hardened. "Oh, but I think you *do*. I've been watching you, real close, man. You got something cookin' at that track with your friends. Normal bettors don't peel off twenties and hundreds like you do, and no salesman I ever met had that much dough." He took another step toward Stewart, who backed up against the wall. "So, I *repeat*. I leave here with what you owe, or you leave here in a box. Your choice."

"Wait a minute, *wait a minute!*" Stewart croaked in desperation, holding up his hands as if to ward off a blow. "You're right, I have arrangements with some drivers, and I do some wagering for them. But we just got started. I don't have that amount *now*, not yet. I can get it. I *guarantee* it!"

Engels's dark eyes narrowed as he regarded Stewart's answer. "Guarantee it?"

Stewart nodded quickly.

"How much did you make today?"

"About five thousand dollars," Stewart said. He figured there was no point in lying. He had the cash in his wallet, and Engels could rip it off of him if he wanted.

"I'll take that, then, as a down payment."

Stewart nervously shook his head. "That won't help either one of us."

"Why not?"

"Because I need that money to make bets. The more you bet, the more you win. And with the system we have in place, we're sure to make a bundle. Then I can pay you off."

Engels's slow reactions indicated mental processes that moved at tortoise-like speed. "How long will that take? Mr. Arnoldi ain't a patient man, and he figures he don't owe you no slack."

"It takes a long time to set up individual races," Stewart explained. "We have to study the horses, drivers, track conditions, weather, calculate odds, notify drivers . . ."

"How much time?" Engels repeated, impatient with details.

"Six weeks, I think. Maybe a little longer."

Another studied glare. "I'll give you a month, then," Engels agreed. He raised a thick forefinger and shook it in Stewart's face. "Keep in mind that I've got my eye on you, man. I know where you work. I'm at Lakewood Downs every day, and if you try to skip town again, I'll find you!"

Stewart responded with a quick jerk of his head. Engels held out his hand. "I'll take two grand right now, for expenses."

Stewart didn't argue. He thrust his hand into his back pocket and pulled out his wallet. Bulging with twenties and one hundred dollar bills, the fat leather container yawned open like a long, vertical mouth. He quickly flipped through two thousand dollars and handed the cash to Engels, who stuffed it into his front pocket.

The big man took a few steps toward the door. "There's one more thing you should remember," he said.

"What might that be?" Stewart said, aching to be rid of him.

"THIS!" Engels shouted, as he swung around and whipped a beefy fist into Stewart's stomach. Stewart doubled over and crumpled to the floor, gasping for breath. Engels loomed above him like a malevolent giant.

"And this!" he boomed, jackknifing his right foot into Stewart's back. Stewart writhed on the floor, vomit surged from his mouth. He choked for air.

"I guess that's *two* things," Engels said, cackling. "That's just a taste of things to come if you get any ideas." He opened the door. "A pleasure doing business with you. And *remember.* I've got my eye on you, man. You won't get away from *ME!"* Engels slammed the door behind him and left. Though blood howled in his ears, Stewart picked up tremors of Engels's footsteps bounding down the outside stairs.

He remained sprawled on the floor, sputtering and groaning, the side of his face smeared with vomit. Streams of air shrieked through burning nostrils, until his acid-coated mouth and throat were able to claw for larger gulps, without triggering his reflex to wretch. Grateful lungs pleaded for more air, and got it. Time and oxygen worked their sedative effects. He squirmed away from the wet stench near his face and coaxed his limbs to move. Pain knifed through his torso, as though a sword had impaled him in the back and protruded through his stomach. More deep breaths. His arms reached for the sofa. Fingers scraped for a hold. Bottom cushion . . . Arm rest . . . *Pull!*

Stewart dragged himself onto the sofa and lay there, wheezing. Heartbeats landed like hammer blows against helpless temples. He struggled to an upright position, inhaled deeply, felt a jabbing pain in his rib cage, and quickly tucked his right arm across his bruised midsection. He planted his left elbow on his knee and rested his hand on his palm. Although his side and back ached, Stewart slowly recovered, physically. Mentally, he was a wreck.

Guilt, bitterness vied for allegiance of his jumbled thoughts. Engels had confronted him with his debts, from which he had run away. *What else could I do? I couldn't pay them off.* If he had stayed where he was, Arnoldi would have had him killed, as Engels's actions this evening so vividly demonstrated. At least now he had a chance, although Stewart had to admit to himself that he had no intention of paying back his surly bookie from upstate New York. Anyway, why should he? It was Arnoldi's risk as much as it was his own. After all, his bookie would have reaped the benefits too, and he didn't have the guts or the energy to work on those bets as much as Stewart did. *It was OUR loss, not just mine! He should pay, too, not just me!*

The image of his wife, his child, glared at him, accusingly. Guilt flooded his mind. *Yes, I left them. I had no choice! I would have returned. Eventually.* All Stewart wanted was a fresh start. How was he to know that he would meet another woman, Lori, and fall in love? Did he still love his family, his real family? *Yes, but now everything's changed.*

Morris's parting words at Lakewood Downs seeped into his thoughts. Something about a system Johnny Marlboro had been working on, a way to make a lot more money in a shorter period of time. *Get a grip here, Stewart, and figure this out.* He did some quick calculating. Four to five thousand dollars a fix, one fix a day; four—no, make it five—fixes per week. That came to twenty thousand dollars a week, at least. For a month, eighty, maybe one hundred thousand dollars. Stewart knew the odds well enough to realize that he could not keep this up indefinitely. The longer he pushed his luck, the more likely something would go wrong. He would run up huge debts to recoup, and then be unable to pay them off. That's what happened to him before he moved to Long Island.

Axel Thomas's comments flickered through his mind, pointed a warning finger. *Get out of this high-stakes game before it eats you alive, Stewart. Before it's too late, before you have no choice.* Stewart shook his head, filled with remorse. *It's too late for me now, Axel,* he agonized. He was in over his head and had no choice. He had to make a lot of money fast, pay off his debts, get that huge monkey off his back, literally, and run. With Lori at his side.

Then the world would be right again. Stewart coaxed his thoughts into a positive direction. Arnoldi, Engels—they just delayed things a little bit, that's all. After three weeks or so, he could build his own nest egg and then leave, for good. It all depended on Marlboro's system, on Courtney's inside information, his instructions to his drivers. Morris Courtney. *I've got to see him. Immediately.* Stewart refused to be cornered by Arnoldi and his hired goon, to be a slave to their demands. He refused to be *trapped*.

Which, at this moment, is precisely how Lori felt.

Lori's eyes followed shafts of light bouncing toward the filing cabinet, where she crouched, trembling. Every ounce of her weight bored on the wound that throbbed inside her left thigh. Shrieks of pain seemed to pile up behind the knot in her throat, squelched only by a jaw locked firmly into place, but ready to burst forth at an instant. Sweat trickled down her forehead and stung her eyes, making her blink. Her whole body coiled in anguish; the slightest movement would set it off.

Any minute now, he'll sweep around the corner and discover me, she thought. Oliver's examination with his fearsome flashlight showed a pattern: first, he swept across the room's corners by the ceiling; then, he scanned the floor; next, he poked under tables, desks, and over burnished surfaces; and, most deadly, he probed *behind* objects. Like the overstuffed chair to the right of Madison's working desk. Or the sofa under the window. Or, the filing cabinet at the end of the room. Where Lori was hiding.

Closer the stabbing light approached. Sweeping . . . darting . . . probing corners.

Closer . . . Closer . . .

Lori bit her lip. Quivering fear peppered her breath. She shut her eyes tightly. A voice from her childhood leaped across the years and whispered in her thoughts that soothing, deceptive assurance that lurked in the breast of every terrified soul: *if I can't see it, it can't see me.*

Footsteps whisked near the cabinet. *Here he comes.* Oliver stopped. Lori riveted her eyes shut and clamped her body into place, motionless. Her breathing ceased. *Any second now* . . .

Nothing happened.

The carpet squeaked in protest to an abruptly turned rubber heel, and Oliver moved away from her. He strode across the room. Lori heard Madison's chair groan under a weight; Oliver was sitting on it. Tinny rattles from a metallic container filled with hard objects crackled through the air. Fingers rumbled through cashews and walnuts. Crunching sounds tumbled across the room: teeth grinding nuts. More rattling . . . Fingers groping . . . Oliver had his hand in the nut can again.

What happened? Didn't he see me? No way to know; Lori had her eyes shut. *But how could he miss me?* Impossible to tell, but this much was certain: Oliver simply did not know she was there. Apparently, some carping speck of desire in Oliver's head had snagged him away from Lori's refuge and cut his mission short. In this case, his impulse to munch on the boss's forbidden stash of goodies saved Lori from discovery. *Thank God!*

Lori shifted her weight ever so carefully, to ease the burden on her aching leg. She rearranged her limbs from a squatting position to one where she rested on her knees and hands. *That's better.* Soft crunching of teeth demolishing nuts continued to disturb the room's silence. Lori figured that Oliver's chewing was generating enough noise in his skull to obscure the slight sounds created by her minor body movements. She shifted into a more comfortable position. *I can wait him out,* she thought.

The muffled report of a door closing elsewhere in the building brought Oliver to his feet in an instant. Clattering of a metal top frantically screwed on a cylinder carried across the room. It was placed on a shelf. Brisk movements . . . Hasty footsteps . . . The door whooshed open, then eased to a quiet close. It clicked shut with authority. *He's gone.* Lori was alone again.

But not for long.

Morris Courtney sat at Lakewood Downs Diner across the table from Stewart and cocked his head at him, like a curious rooster scrutinizing an unfamiliar figure intruding into his private domain.

"You look terrible," he observed.

"So do you," Stewart countered. "But neither one of us are in this business for our looks, are we?" He coaxed a smile and took another bite of his blueberry tart. *Remain calm,* he ordered himself. *Like nothing has happened at all.*

It wasn't easy. Pains in his back and his gut conspired to produce the sensation of a baseball bat thrust through his chest, protruding from each side. Even minor movements felt like one of its ends got stuck on some vital organ and refused to budge. He had showered, changed clothes, and driven to the diner with the windows open on his station wagon, in hopes that briskly circulating air would blow away the pain that squeezed from his face every time he moved a muscle. Courtney's quizzical expression told him that this tactic hadn't worked.

"What *happened* to you, Stewart?" the little trainer asked earnestly. "You fall down the steps or something?"

Stewart cleared his throat and immediately winced. "I wish it were that simple," he said. Long pause. *Now what?* Stewart had spent that last half an hour straining his addled brains to produce a convincing reason to see Courtney this evening instead of the following day, as they had originally planned at Lakewood Downs. Courtney had pressed him for an explanation on the phone, but Stewart staved off his inquiries with the promise that he would explain later. Later had turned into the present, and nothing had gelled in his thoughts in the meantime.

Courtney filled in the silence. "Does your condition have anything to do with your insisting we meet tonight instead of tomorrow?"

Stewart nodded slowly, still without a clue how to respond in a way that would satisfy his friend's curiosity. "Let's just say I had a bad experience after leaving Lakewood Downs and wanted to end the evening on a positive note," he explained. "Plus, I'm eager to continue the conversation we had after today's race."

Courtney gave him a blank look. Then an expression of comprehension flooded his face. "Say no more." He raised his hand. "It's that woman of yours, right?"

Stewart leaped at this opening. "I could never lie to you, Morris," he admitted, which was true enough.

Courtney chuckled. "Let me guess. You went out with her to celebrate, some gorilla got the hots for her, made a wisecrack, and you took it on yourself to defend her honor. I knew it!" He slapped his hands together, relishing his insight. "Sure hope it wasn't that King Kong character Johnny told me about," he added. "That guy could have you for breakfast."

Stewart colored. *Tell me about it,* he groaned inside. "No doubt, you're right," he agreed, with more conviction in his words than he wanted to convey. He rubbed his aching stomach, testing a rib. "Morris, can we get *on* with things?" he asked in a pleading voice. "You said something about a system Johnny Marlboro has in mind . . ."

"Still in production," Courtney said. "Johnny indicated the three of us will do some brainstorming when everything's ready. Our immediate concern is our next race in a couple of days. Have you studied it yet?"

"Not as thoroughly as I intend to. It troubles me, though. Off the top, I'd say there's two, maybe three, horses that have a shot at first place, and I have a hard time imagining that we've got three of our guys driving each one, or who are in a position to block all three. The combinations here look complicated to me."

Courtney leaned over and spoke in a low voice. "Complicated, yes. But the payoff possibilities are *huge*, if we target our picks correctly."

"Target? What do you mean?"

"Stewart, what else did you note about race six?" Courtney asked intently.

Stewart shook his head and tightened his lips in a gesture of impatience. "That it consists of eight horses who have bad breath, bad owners, and bad attitudes. I *really* don't have the patience for this. Not tonight."

"It's an *exacta* race," Morris said quickly. "If we help the frontrunner and move a long shot into second place, we can win big! That's what I mean by targeting."

The prospect of winning big animated Stewart's interest. "You mean . . ."

"Here's what I think," Courtney began, launching into his analysis. However, ten minutes of the trainer's expert opinion succeeded only in heaping additional worries on Stewart's mind, a point he conveyed by shaking his head in doubt.

"Essentially, we're talking about taking out four to five horses in this race and forcing one of the long shots into second," Stewart muttered. "That's daring, to say the least." *Foolhardy is more like it,* he thought.

Courtney sat back and drummed his fingertips on the table. "Come on, Stewart! Our guys are *professionals*, and you know it. This is not a terribly new technique, and I'm confident they can pull it off. The notion of helping a noncooperating driver win a race was originally *your* idea. Remember?" he said, a whiff of indignation in his words. He leaned forward again. "Pardon me for saying this, but I think that broad's got your brains screwed up. You never used to be so skittish."

Anger flared, then subsided. Stewart collected his thoughts to produce the right response. "It's not her, believe me."

"Oh yes, it is!" Courtney countered. He picked up the check, irritated. "It's late. Why don't we both get a good night's sleep, you especially." Courtney patted him on the shoulder and got up.

"You got that right," Stewart said. He forced one last bite of his blueberry tart and slid away from their table. Courtney was already by the cash register, reaching for his wallet. Stewart nodded to him in departure and walked toward the door. He opened it, turned to let someone into the diner, and spotted the Edsel's familiar yawn hovering over two men seated in a booth.

One of them was King Kong.

Fear sliced through Stewart's guts like a knife. Engels threw him a crooked grin and raised his water glass, as in a toast. Silently, the words that Engels had spit in his face an hour earlier floated across the restaurant, shaking him to the core: *I've got my eye on you, man. You won't get away from me.*

The person sitting with him had his back to Stewart. He looked shorter than Engels and possessed a barrel-shaped, muscular back. Tight ripples of flesh piled up the back of his neck, like tufts of creased upholstery. Responding to King Kong's gesture, he turned to look at Stewart. He had smooth skin, a prominent jaw, pointed nose. His large brown eyes, no eyelashes or eyelids, studied Stewart carefully. Stewart had witnessed that gaze before. The look of a predator. He also thought he had seen the man before, but couldn't remember where or when.

"I see King Kong has a friend," Courtney muttered. "It *was* him that roughed you up, wasn't it?" the trainer asked.

"Yes," Stewart admitted.

They walked out of the diner and separated to their own cars. "Just stay away from him and keep your mind on the race," Courtney reminded. "And everything will be all right. Don't worry." He climbed into his car and left.

Stewart drove away as well, eager to get as far from Engels and his companion as possible. He put that part of his brain necessary to operate his vehicle on automatic pilot for the twenty mile journey back to Millville. From the moment he had returned to his apartment after their victory in today's race, everything had gone monstrously wrong. Worse, he had promised Lori to supply her with an alibi, now an impossible task, because too many people had seen him with Morris at the diner. Stewart struggled to get a grip, to console himself, rationalize his actions. *Lori always exaggerates,* he thought. She *really* didn't need anyone to say she was at the races all night, did she? Couldn't be *that* important, whatever it was . . . could it?

Self-reproach flooded his thoughts, as Stewart pulled into his driveway. He slumped his head on the steering wheel and for a long moment remained completely still. At length, he turned his blurred vision toward a star-filled sky. *I promise to make this up to you, Lori,* he pined. *But tonight, you're on your own.*

No one was more aware of this than Lori.

Chapter Ten

More footsteps, a determined gait, approached Madison's office. *That has to be Jeremy,* Lori concluded quickly. He stepped up to his office door, inserted his key into the lock, clicked the door free, and swung it open. Madison strode toward his desk, turned on a lamp, plopped his briefcase on the floor, and entered the cone of light beaming on his work area. Lori heard all the familiar sounds: chair squeaking to a comfortable position, documents shuffling, pencil lead scraping across paper. She knew her boss would work for a half an hour, rarely more. *Frighteningly regular habits,* Lori thought. Tonight, this worked in her favor. Judging from what she heard, he was performing all the tasks she expected so far, except one. He hadn't yet opened the wall safe behind the picture above his desk. Considering how her night had gone to this point, she wondered if he would.

God, at least let this part work!

Divine intervention must have responded to her entreaty, at least by making her less uncomfortable. Madison turned on the radio, adjusted its dial, and listened to soft music. *Excellent*! It was less likely for him to pick up whatever random scuffling might accompany her movements behind the filing cabinet. Which included muffled groans; her leg throbbed in protest even to minor demands she placed on her body to get a better view.

Although still trembling, Lori felt less threatened by Madison's presence than she did by Oliver's unnerving explorations. At least, Madison wasn't *looking* for anyone. With that in mind, she garnered her courage and peered around the filing cabinet. There he was; poring over his precious documents with the same obsession that inspired Ebenezer Scrooge to deny himself a lifetime of Christmas seasons in favor of his beloved accounts receivable. Lori wanted to believe that identical spirits of Christmases past lurked in this den of commercial computations, and that one of them, some day, would materialize and strike her boss dead. No warning, no additional visits, no possibility of redemption. Nothing. Just one deadly stroke of a ghostly hand. Except she was convinced Madison was a much tougher old bastard than Ebenezer; no chance of those spirits pushing *him* around. He would have fired them all for not wearing the company T-shirt, then blithely gone on with his business.

One of the robber baron spirits of eras past took the form of George Madison, the company founder, whose grizzled visage hovered over the room, its stern gaze admonishing descendants to follow in his avaricious steps. Which his great-great-great grandson did, with fanatic devotion.

Now if he would only open that safe . . .

Some benign ghost again came to her aid. Under Lori's dutiful watch, Jeremy Madison finally got up, stretched, and reached for the portrait above his desk. It hung on hinges and swung open to the left. A wall safe with a large combination dial was mounted behind it. Madison prepared to operate it.

Lori's thoughts quickened with electric force. *My binoculars!*

She plunged her hand inside her pocket, pulled out the small instrument, and snapped it to her face. Madison was already turning the dial. *Come on . . . FOCUS!* The numbers clicked away. *Got it. Crystal clear!* Madison spun the dial rapidly. Lori screamed inside. *Not so fast!* He stopped on the last number of the combination. He turned the handle, and the door to the safe opened.

Lori jerked her binoculars from her face in exasperation. *Missed it!*

She slumped in disappointment, feeling like a giant scoop had hollowed out her chest. She lowered her binoculars and observed the rest of his actions without its optical assistance. It hardly mattered to her what Madison did now; her main concern was to wait until he left, elude Oliver on her way out, somehow escape from *Sweets Ahoy's* miserable fence enclosure, and dash out of the area as fast as possible. Pain from her punctured thigh charged up her leg like jolts of electricity. At the moment, she didn't care. Remorse punished her thoughts. *I'll never get another opportunity like this again. Never!*

Out of curiosity, Lori continued to observe Madison. He held up a thick stack of sheets, raised each one to eye level, examined it, placed it down, then picked up another. Must be a couple dozen of them, Lori figured. She had no idea what they were; Madison guarded his personal documents with the ferocity of a wolf clamping its teeth on a succulent morsel of flesh, torn from an animal it had just killed. Bitter laments about her botched attempt this evening reminded her that she would never know.

Lori found a comfortable position leaning against the cabinet, confident that she could easily observe him, but that Madison probably could not see her, even if he tried. Like an actor on stage, Madison would have found it difficult to isolate objects shrouded beyond the pool of light surrounding his desk. Anyway, as long as she was careful not to punctuate his music with any discordant noises, Lori felt she had nothing to worry about.

Madison finished jotting down items in a ledger, stacked the documents in a neat pile, and inserted them into a manila folder. Then he stuffed the folder back into the safe, shut its door, and spun the handle. He swung the portrait into place, covering the wall safe. One last look at something on his desk. His eyes lingered, apparently caught by some incongruity that caused him to mumble a few profanities. He grasped a sheet of paper and stood up, scrutinizing it. Lori leaned forward, watching with increased interest. Another curse. Finally, Madison snorted in disgust, reached for George Madison's forbidding scowl, and brusquely swung his portrait to the side.

He was going to open the safe again.

Lori's heart leaped. She frantically groped for her binoculars, found them, and lifted them into place. They automatically focused on the action across the room. *Perfect vision.* The lighting was excellent, and her boss's head, conveniently cocked to the side, gave her an unobstructed view. Madison placed his hand on the dial, spun it to the right a few revolutions, and fixed on a number. The numbers were large, oversized; Madison had poor eyesight and had insisted on a specially designed safe with combination numbers he wouldn't have to squint to see. Lori picked up the first number without difficulty: *twenty-four right.* A spin in the other direction: *fifteen left.* Madison carefully approached the last number of the sequence, moving the dial back to the right: *eleven.* He turned the handle, and the door clicked open. A quick retrieval of a document; an impatient entry jotted in his ledger; a correction made, and a repeat of his actions of a few seconds earlier. The door shut, the picture knocked into position against the wall. Finally, Madison was done with his work. And Lori had the combination to his safe.

Madison swiftly gathered his things, checked his watch, and muttered another curse. Late for something, apparently. He flicked off the lamp and made it to the door in a few long strides. He departed quickly. Lori could hear his footsteps echo from the hallway, then down the stairs. In a minute, silence. A shroud of darkness reclaimed the room, broken only by hazy light filtering from outside street lamps. Lori was completely alone.

She stretched her limbs out and shook the tension from her arms. Signals of pain from her leg cautioned her to keep her physical exertions reasonable, but the movement actually felt good. The cloth inside her sweat pants gripped her thigh. It would be miserable peeling it off, she knew; at the moment, it functioned as she wanted, which was to soak up blood, stop the bleeding. Lori took a few tentative steps toward Madison's work desk, plagued by the irrational fear that someone lurking in the murkiness would vault forward and grab her. She brushed off this childhood terror and stepped up to Papa Madison's portrait.

Up yours, George, she mocked, raising a fist toward his homely face. She swung the frame away, reached inside her bra for the miniature flashlight, and aimed its sharp beam against the safe's protruding dial. Another look around the office, the door, the glass partition. No sound, no night watchman. Nothing. Lori studied the safe. The dull glare from its stainless steel front beckoned her eager fingers. Lori studied its large, inviting dial. She slipped on her gloves, spun the dial around to the right several times, and stopped it carefully. *Twenty-four.* Now to the left: *fifteen*. Lori took a deep breath. *Please, let this open!* she pleaded silently. Notch by notch, she turned the dial to the right. *Fourteen . . . Thirteen . . . Twelve . . .* Another quick breath. *Eleven*. With the care of a demolitions expert lifting the detonator from an unexploded bomb, she turned the handle.

The door opened with a soft click. *The combination worked.*

Exhilarated, Lori thrust her hand into the safe and grabbed the manila folder Madison had been working on. She slapped it on his desk and pulled out its contents, a bundle of thick sheets with smaller slips stapled on each one. Looked like official documents to her; she had never seen anything like them. Lori shined her flashlight on the top sheet and glided its yellow finger across a glittering array of symbols, figures, and ponderous legal sentences. Her eyes fixed on the numbers trailing dollar signs, which she quickly added up and committed to memory. The resulting sum from this regiment of figures made her purse her lips and exude a soundless whistle, her dazzled mind reaching to comprehend the magnitude.

Are these documents worth anything to me? Probably not, Lori concluded instantly, a sliver of regret for dropping out of high school whisking through her thoughts. *Another year or two I probably would have learned about this stuff,* she lamented. One thing, however, was certain: their absence would stun Jeremy Madison, if only temporarily. *Probably these papers are registered someplace, like mail or wedding dishes, and he can get them duplicated or replaced or something.* She thought she had heard of such practices. *But I can still shake him up,* she concluded. Lori gathered the papers and stuffed them inside the folder.

Now to look for something that had *real* value. She poked her flashlight inside the safe and searched for anything else that might be worth taking. A wad of currency bound by tape rewarded her probing eyes. She reached inside, snatched the small stack, and aimed her flashlight beam on it. Twenty dollar bills, clean, crisp. She thumbed through the currency with the satisfaction of a professional card player breaking in a new deck, fresh from the box. Lori lifted it to her nose. *The smell of money. I like that*. She stuffed it into her pocket and closed the door to the safe.

Lori swung Papa George's portrait next to the wall and shot a sneer at his wizened face. As her eyes focused on the manila folder lying on Madison's desk, questions about how best to proceed claimed her thoughts. She had been stabbed by Madison's fence and nearly apprehended by a nut-munching old fool, who fortunately allowed his infantile obsession with forbidden goodies to distract him from his job. She gained access to Madison's safe by sheer accident; only his carelessness over some computational error gave her a second chance. She still hadn't escaped from the factory complex, which was certain to be more difficult than her entry, given her reduced physical dexterity. Considering her miserable luck thus far, who knows what might happen if she tried to leave the building with those documents in her possession? Fear laced its icy fingers through her calculations, warning her not to burden herself by carrying an object when she again tried to scale that cursed fence. *Further, where's Oliver lurking at this moment?*

Rationally or not, Lori felt that somehow if she stumbled across the dimwitted night watchman in her attempts to escape, she would be able to explain herself. She kept a key to her office in a secret place, she could say; the front door was unexpectedly open; Oliver had neglected to lock it, and she simply walked in to do some leftover work. If she saw she couldn't elude his discovering her, Lori concluded she should then be *obvious* about her presence. Turn on a light; rustle some papers. Pretend to be busy. Drop something on the floor. Stuff like that. *Anything like that, I'll improvise*. But she could not cover herself if she carried a folder containing Jeremy Madison's property. And she doubted he would check her pockets for the cash.

Thus, Lori settled on what seemed to be the safest course: *take the cash, leave the folder here*. But not in Madison's office. Where, then? *My own office, back of my filing cabinet, bottom drawer*. Only two people had a key, Madison and herself, but no one ever looked there for anything special. That's where she stored her lunch. *That's where I'll put this folder; it's my meal ticket!* The irony of this choice made her smile. When Madison discovered his loss, probably the last place he would look would be inside his own building. *I won't be surprised if the arrogant old lecher even refuses to admit they were stolen!* Lori mused. Too big a blow to his pride.

Without further thought, Lori stuffed her binoculars into her pocket, buried her flashlight and Madison's key inside her bra, and grasped the folder. She strode across the room toward the door and stopped cold.

What did I do with my scarf?

Behind the filing cabinet. Lori pulled out her flashlight and walked quickly toward the bulky rectangle that had concealed her from Oliver's searching and Madison's working. She shot the narrow beam of light on the floor and darted it back and forth, across the carpet. *Where is that blasted thing?* Should be right there, where she had crouched for forty-five minutes. Where else?

Footsteps.

Oh, Lord, not again! She buried her light, scampered behind her familiar refuge, squatted down, and waited. Muffled sounds of plodding feet crept into Madison's office from the hallway, but from a more distant location. *Clump . . . Clump . . . Clump . . . Clump . . .* They trailed farther away, deeper into the building. Their fading echoes brushed against her taut eardrums.

Silence.

Lori resolved to escape *Sweets Ahoy* before she suffered a mental, as well as a physical, breakdown. *How could I lose that scarf?* Flashlight pulled out, switched on. She scanned the floor. In front of her . . . Behind her . . . Into corners . . . *Did the carpet swallow it up? Where is it?* Not in any of the likely places. *Good Lord!* How about the unlikely places?

More footsteps, drifting from some distant part of the building. Lori stopped, listened intently, breathless. Nothing. Back to the search.

There it is! By a corner next to the sofa. Must have kicked it there somehow, without knowing. She scooped it up, whipped it around her neck, one loop, no knot. *Now, get out of here.*

She straightened herself, stifled shooting pains from her left leg with gritted-teeth determination, and swept toward the door, manila folder gripped firmly in her right hand. She opened the door a crack and peeked out. Somber darkness greeted her scrutiny. Several quick strides brought her to an office door that said "Lori Armstrong" on it. She applied her skilled fingers to a removable panel at the bottom of the door casing to her right and retrieved duplicates of keys for her office. *No one else knows about these!* she prided herself, lifting the key to her lock.

The door key slipped into its lock easily. She took several long steps toward her own filing cabinet, opened it with the other key from her hidden ring, and gently eased open the bottom drawer. Scraping sounds, metal on metal, sliced through the quiet. *I've got to oil this thing,* she thought. A regiment of old files, marked by faded color-coded tabs, were stacked almost to the back of the cabinet, leaving a eight-inch-long cavity where Lori plopped her lunch. She pulled out an unused file folder different in color from the one she carried, stuffed her purloined folder inside, and jammed it flat into the rectangular pit. She lifted a few other scattered documents and threw them on top, just to be safe.

Done! Now, outta here.

Lori left her office, closed the door, and returned her key ring to its secret place. She stopped, listened again. Quiet. Down the stairs, now, *carefully.* Her soft shoes barely disturbed the steps; a few creaks, that's all—sounds easily swallowed by the carpet, she hoped. But too distant from wherever Oliver was lurking.

Into the downstairs hallway, toward the outside door. Still complete silence. Would the door open?

She tested its crash bar. Protesting metal emitted a tiny chirp. *Everything in this ancient place needs oil!* she lamented. Its hinges were worse. A low, metallic groan traveled through the hallway, as Lori opened the heavy door a few inches and peered outside.

As before, the parking lot was empty. Light flowing from lamps near the roof painted the building's brick walls with hazy yellow cones. Darkness loomed beyond. A soft, wet breeze caressed her face. Felt good.

Lori studied the fence, focusing on those fiendish claws that had ripped her leg open. Her thigh still ached, but mobility invigorated it, which encouraged her immensely.

A quick dash, a huge leap, and I'm gone! she told herself. She checked her pockets and her bra to make sure everything was securely stuffed into place and wouldn't fall out when she scaled the fence. Key, flashlight, binoculars, cash—all there. A thought struck her, which made her feel like an idiot: *why didn't I leave those items in my office, with that folder?* She chided her stupidity. *Should I go back? It's just up the stairs, after all.*

Sounds erupted from somewhere inside the building. That night watchman again, lumbering around. *Gotta get outta here, NOW!*

Lori glared at the obstacle that stood between herself and freedom, like a mountain climber staring at a cragged wall of rock. *That fence!* Lori was infuriated by its mocking indifference to the pain it had inflicted on her. *I'll conquer that monster! Come on, legs. You can do it!* She took a deep breath and dashed off.

The exhilaration of escape surged through her body like a jolt of electricity, as Lori galloped toward the fence. Larger it loomed as she raced for its wiry netting. Ten seconds of furious running . . . *There it is!* A huge jump . . . Fingers and toes, *grapple* that mesh . . . *Got it!* Firm grip, everywhere. CLIMB! *Now* . . . Right leg . . . Left leg . . . *Over the top* . . . *HEAVE!* The other side! *Okay, now* . . . LEAP to the ground . . . *Free!*

Lori landed squarely on her feet, using her legs coiled as shock absorbers. She bolted up. *I did it!* She looked at the building. The door she had just left was opening. As she readied to bound away, her eyes caught a sight that made her heart thump to a halt.

My scarf! She had hastily looped it around her neck in Madison's office; no knot. Lori was so intent on escaping, she didn't notice that it had been snagged by a wire spike as she vaulted over the fence. *I have to get it!*

The door across the parking lot opened wide. Oliver emerged with his flashlight and nosed around with its skittering beam. His light poked in her direction. He took a few more steps. *Is he coming toward me?*

Lori turned and ran. As she dashed into the woods, she threw one last glance toward the fence and saw her scarf at the top, fluttering in the soft breeze.

PART TWO: THE TRAP

Chapter Eleven

Alistair Dalton rubbed his eyes, leaned back, and let his weary body melt into the soothing enclosure of an overstuffed chair. He eased his throbbing head against the backrest and massaged his temples. His limbs felt like gelatin; fatigue hung from every muscle. He extended a heavy arm to open a curtain, and sunlight bolted into the room like cannon fire, slicing across furniture and carving a shaft of brilliance on his coffee-stained carpet. A thousand slivers of pain, like tiny arrows, assaulted his unprepared eyes and raced to the back of his skull. Dalton winced and hurriedly shut the curtain. He pried open a suspicious eyelid, tested the light, and checked his watch. A long sigh, venting twelve hours of relentless work, flowed past his lips and pushed the stuffy air. *Good Lord, I can't believe I was up all night.*

It had been worth it. At least if one measured productivity by the amount of work accomplished in the shortest period of time. In twelve hours he had gone through two, maybe three weeks of grueling scrutiny that would have sent the most conscientious judges into another line of work. Or, to the lunatic asylum. But Alistair Dalton specialized in such marathon sessions. Singleness of purpose, *intensity*, burned in his mind. He never quit until he accomplished his mission, and in this case that meant until he had found what he was looking for. Which he did. And what he found made him sick.

Dalton let his eyes rest on canisters of films stacked on a table next to the projector loaned to him by one of the racetrack officials. Each canister represented a day's filming of thirteen or fourteen races from the camera room, a small enclosure perched on top of the judge's stand, located over the stands high above the track. Each race usually ran eight horses; therefore, eight drivers, which, when multiplied by fourteen, came to one hundred twelve. That figure, multiplied by six days of racing per week, amounted to six hundred seventy-two. Times two weeks, representing the total quantity of races over thirteen hundred. *Thirteen hundred races.*

Fortunately, the real figure was lower. He wanted to study drivers, not horses, and many raced twice or three times within a two week period. Also, about a quarter of the races involved fewer than eight horses, so the actual number he needed to view was closer to a thousand. Each race lasted about two minutes, but Dalton figured that he needed only to look at the second half of each race, several times, if necessary. His efficiency in handling the machinery increased as the evening progressed, and by the time he switched off the projector, giving its hot metal time to cool, he had witnessed a week's worth of races. Another week awaited his examination, but he concluded that his single week provided him a representative sample, and he had seen enough.

Dalton let his hand flop on the end table, where he grasped a pack of Lucky Strikes. He pulled out his last cigarette, crumpled the pack, and tossed it next to an ashtray heaped with cigarette butts. A snap of his Zippo lighter, and the leather-lunged former Marine exuded a puff of smoke into the hazy blue that enveloped the room. His eyes stung; his chest rebelled against his chain-smoking determination by kicking wheezing protests up his throat. Weariness encased his body; every movement labored against the weight of fatigue, which beseeched him to call it quits. The harsh discipline of purpose pushed this entreaty aside; he had more work to do. *Gotta get up, gotta get some air.*

Dalton dragged his body out of the chair and trudged toward the window. Shutting his eyes tightly, he whisked the curtains to the side and cranked open a casement window in the den of his Hamptons Bays home. A rush of air splashed against his face, and he immediately felt refreshed. He coaxed his reticent eyes to accept the streaming light, and finally they opened to a panorama of lush greenery draped on the rolling mounds of Shinnecock Hills, eastern Long Island. He stood there for a long moment, letting the breeze and fresh air do its job, while his thoughts still groped to comprehend the magnitude of his discovery.

One fourth of the drivers, Dalton repeated to himself. *I can't believe it.* He had long suspected a handful of drivers conspiring to augment their earnings by wagering on favored horses and using their skills on the track to impede challengers. But twenty-five percent or so of the drivers? *Incredible.*

Dalton had been racing horses for the past decade and was aware of every trick ever devised by experienced drivers to win a race or prevent others from doing so. Blocking was, of course, the main technique, but it came in a variety of forms. Often sulkies and horses simply got tangled in clumps from which no driver, regardless of his skill, could escape. Galloping horses, who broke from their gait, posed the most serious danger, of course; but this, too, was understandable and hardly a reliable method of fixing races. However, when obviously inferior horses hugging the rail midway through the race floated to the outside and faded into strong three-quarter or stretch competitors, forcing them to go wide to pass and lose two to four lengths in the process, *something's going on.* Particularly if this occurred regularly, which is what Dalton concluded after reviewing some five hundred races. Further, the surprising number of drivers involved required careful, disciplined coordination. *There has to be a mastermind behind all this,* he was convinced. *Maybe several.* Dalton didn't know who. He intended to find out.

He stepped back from the window, feeling somewhat better, but still sluggish from exhaustion. He collapsed in his chair and let his eyes succumb to a restful gaze on the opposite wall, completely covered by a built-in bookcase. Military history dominated his library, along with a sprinkling of tomes on harness racing and horses. Dalton sat for a long moment, smoking his cigarette, staring at that wall for no particular reason. His gaze drifted to a thick, ochre-colored volume identified by a splash of acronyms and numbers along the binder. It was a military manual he had kept with him for years. *Classified.* He should not have possessed it, but there the book sat, next to a companion edition on chemical-biological-warfare components (CBW) in modern militarystrategy.

Dalton stared at that irrelevant manual, trying to sort through an avalanche of facts that swirled in his thoughts. For all the knowledge he had gained from watching those races, he still had no solid evidence of deliberate chicanery, something a judge would accept. *How can I prove what I know to be true?* Dalton grunted his way free from the chair, walked to the projector, and picked up a chart he had constructed while viewing the films. It listed every driver he suspected had been involved in fixed races, indexed by pencil strokes next to each name to denote frequency. He studied his scribbling. Only the most often cited perpetrators should be . . . *what?* Confronted? Accused? Threatened? *What can I do?* Dalton had a mountain of suspicions, but no real hard evidence. The films were suggestive, but not *definitive.* His charges could be countered by drivers who simply insisted they were jockeying for position or trying to win.

I've got to smoke them out, he concluded. Still . . . *how?* Dalton rested his arm against the bookcase and leaned his head on his wrist. He closed his stinging eyes to award them temporary reprieve, and opened them again, where they fell on that volume on CBW, just below his nose.

CBW. For no particular reason, he pulled the book out and aimlessly flipped through pages, as though this activity would stimulate his mental processes. No such luck. He replaced it on the shelf and sauntered back to his chair.

Smoke them out, he repeated to himself. *Trip them up. Force a mista—* Dalton halted his cognitive slide into somnolence. A mistake . . . *Of course!* A wrong move. An impulsive, disastrous decision launched by panic. *Yes!* He climbed out of his chair and returned to the bookcase. He pulled out his classified book on CBW and excitedly crackled through its pages, to the appendices near the back. He found what he wanted.

Poisons.

At least a dozen classification schemes were presented: by methods of administration, degree of toxicity, type of poison, length of reaction time, type of reactions, and so forth. Dalton ran his forefinger down the first list, methods of administration, and studied the categories listed: *breathed, injected, swallowed, skin absorption.* Which one did he need?

Swallowed.

He examined the entries, retrieved a pencil from his pocket, and marked several possibilities. His finger stabbed one in particular, which struck a memory from his time in the military: *Haloperidol.* He eagerly checked the index, located the page number, and thumbed through the book until he isolated it under the heading, *Soviet Psychiatric Hospitals, Medications Used.* A longer list marched down the paper . . . Finally, *Haloperidol.*

Description: a central nervous system depressant, used as a tranquilizer to address symptoms displayed by subjects experiencing severe psychotic states.

Dalton mulled over these words. *Sounds promising,* he thought. *How does it affect people?* He continued reading.

Reactions: Subjects given an overdose typically experience loss of breath, general disorientation, including speech impairment and hearing lapse, loss of balance, coma, convulsions, and collapse. Other indications include headache, confusion, hypotension, deep breathing, chest pain.

The plan coalescing in Dalton's mind had charged through his thoughts like a freight train, but some of the drug's more severe reactions gave him pause, siphoned off his enthusiasm. He scoured the inventory of reactions and plucked from the list the ones that interested him the most. *Loss of balance, speech impairment, headache, chest pain. Hmmm . . . Possibly useful.*

Still, the extreme indications jutted out like swords in a wheat field.

Coma . . . Convulsions . . . Collapse . . . That's a bit much.

Check the toxicity level. *Down the page again . . . In bold . . . Bottom of the page . . . There!* Wait a minute. *Nope. It's something else.*

Legend: on a scale of one to six, one indicates mildly toxic; six indicates lethal.

Fine. *What about Haloperidol? Can't be too lethal if it's used in a hospital,* he reasoned, trying to recall what he remembered about it from some distant military briefing during his time in the reserves. Something about use of drugs, Russian dissidents, prisoners of war, and Soviet psychiatric hospitals. Even Soviet hospitals, although not known for their bedside manners, were still hospitals, he thought.

Dalton's eyes cut through a forest of technical terms, probing for the heading he figured should be easy to find. *Gotta mention toxicity level for this drug somewhere!* Finally, near the bottom, buried in the middle of the page. Toxicity Level for Haloperidol . . .

Five and a half.

Dalton rolled his eyes back. *Lord, I can't use that!* he concluded. *What else is there?* Hundreds of drugs, he discovered, had identical reactions but differed in their method of administration and lethality. And he had to investigate each one. Even if he found the perfect drug for his plan, could he obtain it?

Dalton clapped the book shut and carried it with him to his chair. He massaged the bridge of his nose, trying to counteract pressure driving from the inside. *Somewhere* in that book was exactly what he needed, but his depleted mental state didn't permit him to investigate further. He reached for his coffee, sniffed the brackish liquid, and with a scowl on his face, put the cold cup back on the table.

Time to sleep for a few hours. Then he would figure it out.

Dalton laid his head back, closed his eyes. Although drained, he still couldn't sleep. He felt jittery and exhausted at the same time. Miserable. *It's that damn coffee,* he concluded. *Twelve cups of it. Too much. Even got a few chest pains because of it.* That's what his doctor had told him when Dalton feared much worse, like heart problems, an ulcer, or something. He just drank too much coffee, which gave him all sorts of annoying symptoms. Bad stomach. Jitters. Severe anxiety, even. *If you drive a sulky, don't drink too much coffee, doctor said. Damn cof—*

Once again, Dalton's musing stopped cold. Coffee? *Of course!*

He scrambled through the book on his lap and quickly isolated the word he sought: caffeine. *Description: although commonly regarded as harmless, caffeine, taken in larger doses, induces hyperexcitability, gastric irritation, rapid mood swings, palpitations, manic-depression, convulsions, and sometimes death. Reaction time: one to two minutes. Toxicity level: three.*

Dalton marked the page with a scrap of paper and placed the book on an adjacent table. *Caffeine does all that stuff?* he muttered under his breath. *Of course it does, known that for years. Great!*

Now for the set up. He reached for the phone, dialed a number. "Mable? Yeah, it's me. No, not today. In six days, I drive *A. P. Raven* again. Listen, how'd you like to help me out with, um, a special assignment. Actually, it's for the racetrack. You would? I *knew* I could count on you! What? Simple. Just listen carefully and do *exactly* as I say . . ."

After a few clipped instructions, Dalton placed the receiver back on its cradle and smiled. *None of those scheming fools thinks I've got any friends around here,* he mused. *They have no idea . . .*

He picked up the phone again and dialed another number. "Hello, *security?* Dalton here. Yeah, I'm fine, thanks. Look, I've been working on something that's important to the racetrack, and I'm wondering if you could help me out. Yeah, that's right . . . *Very* important . . . What? I'll explain it more when I see you. In the meantime, this is what I'd like you to do . . ."

Chapter Twelve

Ted Simon lifted his one-hundred-seventy-pound frame from his chair and walked to a window overlooking Office Products Unlimited's expansive parking lot. As though his thoughts had wheeled Stewart in, a white station wagon with a minor dent in its right fender squealed into the lot beneath his view. Stewart got out and stepped toward the back end of his vehicle.

Simon opened his window a bit farther. "Stewart!" he called. Stewart looked up. "Come on up here before you leave, would you please?" Stewart hesitated. Finally, he waved his acknowledgment, shut the back door of his station wagon, and vanished into the building.

A few minutes later, a knock on the door. "Come in," Simon said, still standing by the window.

The door swung open, and Stewart emerged, head first, then the rest of him, slowly, as though entering a courtroom and expecting to be greeted by a hostile jury. He closed the door behind him and stood without uttering a word.

Simon strode to meet his valuable employee, extending his hand. It wilted before his friend had a chance to reciprocate, and Simon gracefully withdrew his arm and let it hang to his side as he gaped at his friend's drooping countenance. Worry clung to his features, flowed from his expressive brown eyes. He reminded Simon of a chastened animal, struggling to marshal his strength, to lift his eyes and face a victorious adversary who had just physically mauled him.

"Stewart, are you all right?" Simon asked.

"Yes . . . I'm fine," Stewart said. "A lot of things on my mind, that's all. Behind in my calls."

Simon regarded this statement. "Not according to *my* records, you're not," he countered.

Stewart shrugged, wiped his brow with his sleeve.

"Listen," Simon continued, "I need a break, you sure look like *you* could use a break, so I have an idea."

Stewart cocked his head.

"Let's go to the races tonight!" Simon proposed in a bright voice.

Stewart reacted as though Simon had just recommended a trip to the Everglades for a relaxing afternoon of alligator wrestling.

"The races?" he repeated.

Simon nodded. "We haven't done that together for a long time. It'll be a good change of pace. Plus give us a chance to talk."

"A change of pace . . ."

"Of course! I thought we could ask Phillip Louis to come with us. He enjoys the races, too." Simon approached Stewart and clapped his hands on his shoulders. "It will take your mind off whatever's bothering you, I'm sure."

Stewart responded with a look suggesting he had just witnessed an execution. Perplexed, Simon considered asking a few questions about his friend's mental state, dropped the idea, and returned to his desk. "Shall I pick you up around, say, six-thirty?"

"Um . . . why don't we just meet each other there," Stewart muttered.

"Sure, that's fine, too," Simon answered agreeably. "I'll rent a booth so we can have a little more privacy."

Stewart paused, blinked. "Sounds fine to me," he finally managed to say. "I really have to go."

"Fine. Tonight, then? Say, seven o'clock? The first race is at seven-thirty."

Stewart nodded, fumbled for the doorknob, and backed out of the room.

The door closed. Simon sat at his desk for a long moment, staring at the phalanx of company officials mounted on his back wall. He shook his head, pondering Stewart's behavior.

I wonder what's wrong with him today? he uttered softly to himself.

When Lori's alarm clock went off at six-thirty in the morning, its clanging report assaulted her ears with the force of a brick crashing through a picture window. The sludge of exhaustion clung to every fiber in her body, and she could hardly move. Drugged by the torpor of sleep, the best her mind could produce was a fleeting dream *about* waking up, without actually prodding herself to do so. Five minutes passed. Again, the alarm clock's ringing clattered through the room, forcing Lori to succumb to its harsh reminder and drag herself out of bed. After spending an hour showering, doing her hair, and disciplining her face to exude that "natural" look by applying a menagerie of skin treatments, she trudged to work in her faithful Volkswagen. Her muscles responded well to her recuperative regimen, which consisted mostly of stretching and limbering up exercises, but her leg reminded her, with stabbing protests, about the previous evening's indignities. Antiseptic ointment, gauze, firm wrapping, and several aspirin quieted it down to the level of a few spikes of pain now and then.

Lori's mental condition was in worse shape than her body. Anxiety stalked her thoughts, forcing anguished review of every scenario she feared awaited her at the office today.

Did Oliver figure out there had been an intruder? Was he approaching the fence as I ran, or did he just happen to poke his flashlight in my direction? Did he retrieve my scarf? Did he tell Jeremy Madison? Did Madison discover the theft?

Lori approached the gate to *Sweets Ahoy's* parking lot with her heart thumping in her throat. She couldn't bear to face the man who had nearly stumbled on her last night and wrecked what otherwise had been a successfully, though painfully, executed plan. Still, she knew Oliver never actually *saw* her. She clung to that notion. Like a record needle stuck into place, Lori's thoughts feverishly repeated her sole defense: *he never saw me, he never saw me, he never saw me.*

She pulled up to the gate, pulled down her window. She turned her head, which at first resisted, then yielded to sheer force of will. *Act normally, as though nothing has happened.* She peered into Oliver's booth.

Oliver wasn't there. No one was there. What did that mean?

More tormenting possibilities. He was talking to Madison, she imagined, telling him there was an intruder last night, and that it was probably Lori, because he grasped her scarf from the fence where she had escaped, and Madison checked his safe, discovered the theft, called the authorities, the police are waiting . . . Lori's ruminations choked on this tortuous progression. Her mind stopped functioning. She sat there.

"Something wrong, lady?"

Lori's body jerked. The car behind her. Some guy called out.

Without turning her head, she engaged the clutch, and her Volkswagen lurched forward. She drove it around the lot, trolling for a parking place, when a simple idea struck her, offering a whisper of relief. *Maybe my scarf's still there!*

Now, to get to the fence without seeming obvious about it. Parking lot's loaded, she could drive around. *Do it slowly, don't attract attention.*

Her Volkswagen crawled down an aisle leading to that part of the fence where she had climbed and ripped her leg open.

Lori approached it gingerly. Her Volkswagen's engine putted at idling speed, patiently waiting her anxious conclusion, as she leaned over the steering wheel to get a better view. Couldn't see the top at that angle. She turned right, cranked down her window, and looked up.

The scarf was gone.

Lori slumped over the steering wheel, rested her head on her forearms, and fought back tears. The same wretched avalanche of thoughts that had immobilized her by the gate again tumbled through her mind. *They know, they have to know it's me!* What to do, now? Every part of her screamed to escape, to run as far away as possible. *Can't do that, too obvious.* Then they'd *surely* know it was her. Against raging emotions that beseeched her to flee, Lori decided to park her car, enter the building, and go to work. As though nothing had happened at all.

Lori angled her body out of her Volkswagen and walked toward the side entrance. She swept past rows of parked cars, shielding her eyes from stinging arrows of sunlight exploding from windshields, when a clicking sound caught her ear. She stopped, turned, scanned to her right, then to her left. Again, she heard it. *Click! Whir-r-r-r . . . Click!* She jerked her head to its source, a dark sedan, two vehicles to her left, no more than twenty feet away. Its driver-side window cranked up, hurriedly. Stillness. Lori peered at it, curious. Couldn't see a thing, too much blinding sunlight. She sensed a presence in that car. *Someone just took a picture of me,* she concluded. This new danger, inexplicable, cut an additional slice of fear into her heart. Suddenly, she felt terribly exposed. Flinging her gaze forward, she trotted toward the side entrance, swung open the door, stopped and leaned against an inside wall. *Settle down, Lori. You're imagining things.* But why would anyone want to take her picture?

Forget it, get on with the day. It was a few minutes past eight o'clock when Lori strolled through the first floor hallway to the stairs leading to her second floor room. She exchanged banal pleasantries with a few friends, which calmed her nerves a bit, and settled down to work. Madison was nowhere in sight; out of town on a business trip, maybe? Talking to police? She didn't know. *Did he hire a private detective to follow me, the person in that car?* Dismiss that idea, get to work. Lori settled down to her tasks, working mostly alone. Aside from the familiar tromp of footsteps announcing the arrival of co-workers or a few salesmen, she carried out her duties in her second floor compartment undisturbed. Time inched along at a turtle's pace, but Lori worked. She placed phone calls, answered phone calls, typed reports, chatted with co-workers, drank coffee, *lots* of coffee, filed papers, checked lists . . .

Lunch time.

Lori had forgotten her lunch. She stared at the bottom drawer of her filing cabinet where she had stuffed Madison's folder. There it sat. Lori gazed at that steel enclosure as though it were a time bomb ready to explode at any second. *I've got to get that package out of here!* An idea materialized: maybe it was a good thing she hadn't taken her lunch today; now she could jam the documents into a valise and casually cart them away. Although she usually carried a lunch bag, Lori frequently left the building with work under her arm. No one would suspect a thing. Then a quick trip home, to safety. *Good idea!*

The door opened. A blonde head popped in. "Say, Miss Frugality, I didn't see you carry your lunch in today. Care to go out for a sandwich?"

Lori's heart sank. "I'd love to, Valerie," she replied evenly. "I'll be with you in a minute."

"I'll be downstairs."

"I'll stop by your office."

The door closed, leaving Lori wondering why she had even bothered to take documents whose meaning she couldn't grasp. She should have just absconded with the cash, something she *did* understand. *No, if Madison had those papers locked up, they must be important,* she reminded herself. Off to lunch. She joined her friend, walked through the parking lot, and threw a glance in the direction of that dark sedan. It was gone.

An hour of mindless banter, a barely digested tuna sandwich on rye, dill pickle, cole slaw, and it was one o'clock. Still no Oliver at the gate. *Where is he?* Lori didn't dare ask. She didn't want to know.

Her afternoon replayed the morning, a routine she would have found comforting, other than her strange encounter with that car in the parking lot and Oliver's inexplicable absence. The first she dismissed as an unwarranted flight of fear, exaggerated by other anxieties. Oliver posed the more immediate puzzle. *Maybe he's just sick,* she told herself. What about Jeremy Madison? He's always gone, of course; comes and goes as he pleases, for days at a time. Only his habits in his office are predictable. *But why is he gone today?*

The approach of quitting time put an end to her queries. She made it through the day with no problems; simmering worries, but nothing she couldn't handle. Oliver never materialized. Of course, for all she knew, he had returned to his spot near the gate or was strolling about the factory floor someplace; rarely did she see him during her daily routine. *I'm sure that's it.* All she had to do was to grab Madison's folder, stuff it into a valise, and leave the premises. After she was in her apartment, she could think more clearly about what to do next.

Lori got up, retrieved the key to her filing cabinet, and unlocked the ponderous metallic box. She pulled out the bottom drawer and squatted to reach inside for its contents in the back. She rifled through stacks of documents she had jammed on top as camouflage and grasped the stolen folder. Lori stopped. Sounds of footsteps trickled through the cracks of her office door. Someone was coming up the stairs. *Not another salesman, I hope.* Lori checked her watch: four forty-five. *I'll give him ten minutes, max.* Footsteps came closer, passed her office, stopped. Keys jingling . . . Metal scraping into a lock . . . Door opening . . . That was no salesman.

Jeremy Madison.

Lori felt her stomach tighten. *He could breeze in here any minute.* She hurriedly stuffed her package into its pit, covered it with assorted files, and eased the drawer shut. She locked the cabinet, slipped the key inside her blouse, and walked toward her desk. She sat down. *A few minutes more and I'll leave.* More footsteps. Heavy, plodding gait, up the stairs. She recognized those sounds.

Oliver.

His big feet pounded down the hallway, passed her office, stopped. Knuckles thumped on heavy wood. Pause . . . Door opening . . . Muffled conversation . . . *What are they talking about?*

Lori bit her lip, gripped the armrests on her chair to steady her nerves. She had to admit that she did not think through her plan of action *after* investigating Madison's safe, what she would do next. She had intended simply to unnerve him, that's all. *Get a hold of yourself,* she admonished. *Sooner or later, Madison will discover the theft, and I'm going to have to act cool during the investigation.* Still, Lori sat there, immobilized. Her window opened to the parking lot, but Lori couldn't summon enough courage to steal a look at who or what might be lurking beneath her office outside. Could be police. Or someone with a camera, who, for God knows what reason, wanted to take another picture.

This is ridiculous, she thought, scolding her own trepidation. Lori got up, tiptoed toward her door, and eased it open a crack. She peered out. Madison stood in his office doorway, nodding, talking, cracking an occasional grin; Oliver had his back to her. The night watchman's resonant voice punctuated the drone of his employer's soft replies. Lori's eyes roamed over the two figures and caught on a sight that froze her soul. A flash of color sprouted from Oliver's back pocket, like a flower petal. It was her scarf.

Lori eased her door shut. Bile crept up her throat, seeped into her mouth. She swallowed hard. *Crackers.* Lori scurried back to her chair, rummaged through the top drawer of her desk. No crackers. More sounds, this time footsteps leaving. *Thump . . . Thump . . . Thump . . . Down the stairs . . . Door opening . . . Shutting . . . Thud! Gone.*

The phone rang. Lori punched a button. Madison's voice crackled from the tiny phone speaker. "Miss Armstrong, would you come into my office, please?" *Click.*

Oh God!

Lori buried her head into her hands. There had to be police out there now, she was convinced. *Trapped!* Madison wanted to see her. *Got to face him, no choice.*

Lori stood up, brushed her clothes down, collected herself. She walked out of her office, down the hall, and stopped in front of Jeremy Madison's office door. She raised her arm, in halting, jerky movements. She tightened her fist and tapped the heavy oak door.

"Come in," muttered a voice inside.

Lori took a deep breath, opened the door, and stepped inside.

Chapter Thirteen

Lori peered around the half opened door like a child stealing a forbidden glance into her parents' bedroom chamber. Her eyes met Jeremy Madison's steely gaze, which hovered over his massive mahogany desk like the cannon barrel on a tank turret sighting its target. Lori scolded her idiocy for being caught in such a predicament. It was not clear what she lamented the most: forgetting to maintain an ample supply of crackers in her desk to dampen the tide of acid surging up her throat, or committing the act that made this tasteless balm necessary. She would soon find out.

"Can I help you, Mr. Madison?" she asked putting a tight clamp on her quavering voice.

"Sit down, please," Madison said in an even tone, motioning toward the sofa next to his desk.

Lori did as she was instructed. Madison followed her movements and studied her carefully. "How long have we known each other?" he asked.

"About two years, I think," Lori said.

"Two years, yes. We've had our ups and downs, wouldn't you say?" he stated. A grin lifted one side of his mouth.

Speculations about the meaning of this cryptic remark sped through her mind at light speed. She had seen this expression before; lust pouring from narrowed eyes, every facial feature at attention, probing for flickers of a positive response, ready to leap at the slightest gesture of acquiescence.

"I told you that we would have to get some matters between us resolved," Madison said. His eyes continued their searching gaze.

Fear returned. *He knows it all,* she thought. *And now he wants to blackmail me.*

Madison leaned back in his chair. "I think we're in a position now to get a better understanding of our relationship," he continued with icy composure.

The yearning to confess, to obtain absolution, beckoned for a place in Lori's thoughts. Still . . . A better *understanding,* was that all he was asking? What did Madison mean by that? Did he *really* know about his missing papers and cash, or hadn't he checked his safe yet? Was this just another ploy, another sexual advance? Her previous ruminations struggled to insert a degree of rationality into her thoughts. *Even after Madison discovers the theft, would he have any reason to suspect me?* Oliver, after all, had kept her scarf in his back pocket. Maybe he drew no conclusions from finding it. Or, maybe he did.

Madison stared at her, an expectant look on his face. Lori furiously assessed her alternatives. Should she confess? Or should she act as though nothing had happened and politely dismiss him, as she had the other day? *What should I do?*

She cleared her throat. Madison took this as a sign that she was about to say something, and leaned forward, and looked at her intently. With taut nerves and labored breath, Lori opened her mouth and began to speak . . .

A mocking twist of fate plunked Stewart's sweating body next to Ted Simon and in front of their corpulent colleague in a private booth at Lakewood Downs. Phil Louis needed the back seat—actually, the back *two* seats—to himself, forcing Stewart to the front and making him feel like he was caught inside a losing exacta box; he wasn't placed in the right *order.* Simon and Louis chatted amiably, while Stewart clawed through his stress-fogged mind for appropriate responses to their innocent comments. Fortunately, as a salesman, he had garnered an impressive collection of affectations for uncomfortable situations. By the time race six approached, he had used them all up.

"I think I'll bet on this one," he said. *Please don't go with me,* he silently pleaded.

"Okay," Phil Louis said. "I'm going to get another hot dog, so I'll meet you back here." Simon nodded agreeably and buried his nose in the program.

Stewart trotted across the long walkway in front of the restaurant and scampered down a flight of stairs to a different part of the lobby, departing from his usual route to the betting windows. He resolved not to use the same window every time, not to become a familiar fixture to racetrack officials, if he could avoid it. A conspiracy of apprehensions stalked his thoughts: King Kong's threats, Courtney's daring departure from their usual methods, his own shameful betrayal of Lori's trust, even Axel Thomas's prudent warnings—on top of which Ted Simon had heaped his virtuous attempt for a recreational outing, to *relieve* his anxieties, of all things. Talk about miserable timing . . .

Got to concentrate! Stewart considered his wagering options and decided to wheel the exactas, to put all the other horses in second place behind *Thergus*. This would cost more—fourteen dollars for every two dollar wager—but would ensure a winner, provided Thergus came in first. His thoughts danced about numbers and decimal points. For each driver, twenty dollars to win and an exacta wheel, totaling sixty-two dollars. For himself, three hundred dollars on the nose and fifty exacta wheels, coming to seven hundred dollars. Total race outlay: one thousand dollars. Engels's warnings hovered over these calculations, like a vulture circling its prey, sending a shiver up Stewart's spine. *I've got to win!* Stewart repeated to himself.

The shortest line still had a dozen people. Stewart stepped to the back of it and stared at the person in front of him. He hated this part of the cavernous building. The track's security office, a long room that jutted into the lobby a half-story above the floor, loomed over the bustle of activities below like a censorious schoolmarm. Worse, the room's facade was lined with a regiment of one-way windows covered by a chromium glaze. This ominous, multi-eyed monster defied efforts to penetrate its interior, to spy who was inside, looking out. Efforts to do so were met by tiny explosions of light that ricocheted from a multiplicity of lamps glowing from the ceiling or bunched in corners like hornets' nests. Somehow, one got the feeling that the beast was watching you, piercing your innermost thoughts. Stewart instinctively kept his back to that room. It gave him the creeps.

The line shrunk as bettors peeled away from the window. In just a minute or two, Stewart would place his bets, dash back to their booth, observe the race, and then concoct an excuse to leave so he could contact Morris Courtney and assess their situation.

"Boy, you look determined!" It was Phil Louis.

Oh no!

"What are you doing here?" Stewart asked testily.

"This is an exacta, so I thought I'd be daring and bet a few bucks," he mumbled through cheeks that protruded from his face like golf balls filled with food. He took another huge bite of his hot dog and groped for his wallet. Stewart kept his eyes forward.

"Hope you win," cracked another voice. Stewart felt his chest tighten. He recognized its owner immediately. He didn't want to acknowledge the man's presence or face the glowering monster with its dozen shimmering eyes. Evil lurked behind him.

"Yeah, well, I sure hope you do, too," Louis responded pleasantly. Mindless banter followed between two complete strangers—Phil Louis from Office Products Unlimited and the man Stewart still referred to as King Kong. Engels's deadly admonition again cut through his thoughts: *I got my eye on you, man.*

Stewart was about to step up to the window when a hand suddenly thrust in front of him, grasping an envelope. Startled, he met the earnest face of a person he recognized from the show paddock, a friend of Morris Courtney.

"This is for you," the young man whispered, then quickly strode away.

Stewart eyed the envelope as though it contained an arrest warrant. He began to open it, then stopped. Quick glances revealed eager eyes focused on his every move. But Morris wouldn't have interrupted him in this fashion unless the driver wanted him to open this envelope now, *immediately.*

"You got people waiting behind you, mister," stated the person behind the booth in a flat voice.

Stewart looked up and noticed those in front of him had departed and he stood three feet away from the booth. He stuffed the envelope into his pocket and stepped up to the window. He retrieved his wallet, and hunched over the counter, trying to conceal his activities. He splayed down a fan of cash, the clerk thumbed through it, and handed him a stack of tickets. Stewart stepped away, flitting a glance behind him. He caught Phil Louis's look of astonishment below King Kong's confident sneer, against glimmering rectangles of chrome in the background. Everyone was watching him, it seemed. *Hunting* him.

Stewart headed back to his booth. He sensed Phil Louis's ponderous form huffing behind him, but he didn't wait for his friend to catch up. He had to watch race six, get it done with, get away from Simon and Louis, get away from King Kong, *get away!* Focus, he commanded himself again. *I must win. I WILL win!*

Stewart scampered up the steps toward his booth and walked quickly along the restaurant hallway. As he was about to enter his booth, he heard the track's public address system crackle a terse announcement:

Stewart Lawrence. Calling Mr. Stewart Lawrence. Phone call for Mr. Stewart Lawrence from a Miss Lori Armstrong. Report to the Security Office at once!

Alistair Dalton stood behind his protective barrier of windows in the security office, sipping coffee, studying the crowd below. A half-dozen uniformed figures lined up in chairs on either side of him, each engrossed in some matter relating to the security of Lakewood Downs Raceway. A few concentrated on rows of bettors outside; another, on the phone; a fifth studied a clipboard; one stood next to Dalton.

"That's the only one today," stated a slender man adorned in a gray uniform etched with black shoulder boards, charcoal buttons, and badges on his sleeves.

"Who was it, Jack?" Dalton asked.

"One of the groomers from the show paddock. He works for the track. I'm sure you know him. Doubt if he's on your list."

"Just a messenger, then."

"That's about it, probably. Or, he's simply betting for himself."

"Did you catch who he was talking to?"

The gaunt official with a serious look on his face shook his head. "Impossible to tell. Somebody behind a couple of huge guys. Didn't see who it was."

"Didn't you see him leave?" Dalton pressed.

"He melted into the crowd, Alistair," his companion responded, irritated. "Look, drivers and their trainers float around here all the time. It's not illegal. They're allowed to bet on their *own* horses, you know. *You* do it."

Dalton continued sipping his coffee, staring at the lobby pensively. This part of his plan wasn't working out terribly well, but he admitted to himself that his sleep-fogged mind hadn't sorted out the practical implications, either. *Just what the devil am I looking for that would constitute suspicious behavior?* he pondered. Dalton concluded that it was impossible to stumble upon the hard evidence he needed. He had to *force* the issue. He was confident he knew exactly how to do that.

A hard knock on the door. All eyes turned left. One of the officials opened the door, displaying a man with brown eyes, a high forehead, and pleasant features, though slick with sweat and contorted with worry. He saw Dalton and flinched. Dalton regarded him coolly.

"I'm Stewart Lawrence. There's a call for me?"

A security official closest to the door handed him a phone. "Line three," he instructed.

The man identifying himself as Stewart grabbed the receiver, turned his back to the men in the room, cupped the mouthpiece with his hand, and cowered next to the door. A few words punctuated his anxious voice and floated across the room. "What? Where . . . Are you sure . . .? Fine!

You mean, *now?* Okay . . . Right!" He fumbled the phone on its cradle and backed out the room.

Dalton's companion shrugged and smiled. "Another guy in trouble with his wife," he remarked, as though accustomed to such situations.

The Marine considered this statement. "Ever see *him* before?"

"Nope," came the reply.

Dalton returned his gaze to the lobby, then shook his head, and pulled out a piece of paper listing names studded with hash marks. He scrutinized it carefully. He groped in his other pocket and whipped out a schedule saturated in tiny script with a forest of names, dates, and horses for the coming month. He compared the two lists, slowly running his forefinger down the schedule. The racetrack announcer peppered the air with his excited broadcast of a race in progress. Dalton's finger continued running down the paper, ignoring the announcer's screeching report of race six's final seconds:

"Powering to the lead, into the LIGHTNING LANE, it's *Ther-r-r-r-GUS!* Five lengths BEHIND, *First Lass,* followed by *Irish Bird!* Win, place, and show!"

Dalton's searching ceased, isolated a date. He compared it to his other list. *Got to be absolutely sure.* His eyes drifted up, rested on one of the monitors in the lobby. He noticed the "inquiry" sign flashing on the tote board. Dalton snorted, disgusted. *Probably caused by one of those bastards fixing races,* he thought. *Can't prove it, though.* Back to his lists. Found a date, unquestionably the most certain one, best combination of drivers and horses. *But I can prove this!* he concluded, circling numbers and letters in heavy pencil. *Time to give Mable her instructions, so she can prepare in time.*

Dalton stuffed the papers into his pocket, satisfied. He casually observed the crowd in the lobby, picking out disgruntled looks as well as excited faces belonging to pleased bettors, who lined up to collect their winnings. One in particular caught his attention, somebody in a hurry. He darted through a thicket of bodies to the nearest window, fidgeted while his cash was being doled out, stuffed a wad into his pocket, and raced away. The same guy who had come in for that phone call.

Stewart Lawrence.

Chapter Fourteen

Flickering candlelight danced in Lori's glistening blue eyes, which signaled distress with every wayward glance. Stewart sat across from her in a booth at Fenimore Cooper Inn, which had become their favorite place, and where she had insisted they meet in her frenzied summons to him at Lakewood Downs. Stewart pushed his station wagon to the limit of its performance envelope and made the distance in record time, in spite of a delay caused by a skeptical policeman, who, fortunately, accepted his labored explanation about a family crisis. He arrived breathless and agitated, spied Lori immediately, and strode toward her booth, draped in sweat. She looked distraught. Worry lines creased her eyes, cracked her porcelain beauty. Stewart sensed a torrent of emotions seething within her, ready to burst forth at any moment.

"I'm *so* glad you came," she gushed, extending her hand, which Stewart quickly grasped.

"What is it? What's wrong?"

Lori withdrew her hand and reached to her seat. She darted a few glances about them, then thrust a manila envelope across the table.

"Take this from me, *please!*" she instructed. "Hide it. Don't tell me what you've done with it; just put it in a secret place where no one can find it. Not even me."

Stewart eyed the sealed package suspiciously. "What is it?"

Lori pursed her lips. "Something . . . I took from the office, that's all."

Stewart gave her a sideways glance. "Something you took from the office?" he repeated. "Care to explain that?"

Lori buried her head in her hands. Her long, white fingers slid down her cheeks and folded together, resting under and supporting her chin. Her eyes melted to tremulous pools of liquid. A single droplet traced a path down her right cheek and fell on her hands.

"Let me begin at the beginning," she said, collecting herself. "You know most of it, my dropping out of school, running away from home, leaving New Mexico, coming to New York City—" she sighed, collected a tear from her cheek—"settling in Long Island, getting a job at Sweets Ahoy."

Stewart nodded.

"Madison gave me a job because"—her low voice wavered—"he *wanted* me. He wanted me *bad!*" Lori lowered her head, then wrenched herself up to meet Stewart's intense stare. A deep breath, a stuttering exhale. "We had an affair, and I got pregnant."

Rage surged through Stewart's breast. *So he's the one who defiled her.* "Go on, dear," he whispered.

"He promised me everything, *everything!* He said he loved me more than anyone. He would divorce his wife; we would get married . . . I was young, naive . . . I *believed* him. I mean, the wretched men I've known before he came into my life . . . He was a dream come true! But after he got me pregnant, he brushed me aside. Threw me away, like . . . like . . . *garbage!*" Her tone sharpened. She took a moment to regain her composure. "I couldn't keep my baby, *his* baby . . ." Lori's voice crumbled to a hoarse whisper. *"I had to . . ."* Words sputtered on her lips, then collapsed.

Silence. A horrible premonition loomed in Stewart's mind, awaiting the trigger of her next utterance, her slightest gesture. Instead, Lori remained mute, an icy expression on her face. She riveted her gaze on something behind Stewart, over his shoulder. With the hesitation of a child jerking his head around to face some unknown terror, Stewart slowly turned to catch the object of her fixation.

His eyes roamed the nearly empty restaurant, scrutinizing sights possibly in Lori's line of vision. Tables . . . Chairs . . . Booths . . . Objects on the wall . . . A few people murmuring, soft conversation. Colonial bric-a-brac. *What is she looking at? All I see is . . .*

Stewart's looking stopped. He caught sight of a bar that extended between two posts. A tangle of metal coat hangers clumped to its side. A few dangled separately, at crazy angles. One hung alone.

A coat hanger.

He turned and looked at Lori again. She sat transfixed. Stewart jerked around again, then back. No question about it. Lori was staring at that coat hanger.

She had aborted herself with a coat hanger.

Searing images of ripped flesh, spurting blood, shredded human tissue, exploded in Stewart's mind. Wrath seized every particle of his body. *"I will kill him, Lori."*

"NO!" Lori blurted, the spell broken. An expression of relief flooded her face, as though she had descended to the depths and pulled herself free. Then, in a more controlled voice, "You can't do that. That's not you. If I thought you were even capable of violence, I never would have gone out with you."

Stewart accepted that point in silence.

"Anyway, I got even, Stewart. *I GOT EVEN!*"

"What do you mean?"

"After I healed—I was in the hospital for a spell, you know . . ." Stewart gave her a look that indicated he did not know that, which Lori acknowledged with a curt shrug. "That was before I met you," she added. "Anyway, I got better, went back to work, and he started coming on to me again, you know, like before. He said he was sorry, we needed a new understanding, matters would be resolved between us, stuff like that. I tried to fend him off, but couldn't. One day he forced himself on me again, and I happened to notice that he keeps a safe behind a portrait over his desk." She leaned forward, her face brightening, eyes gleaming. "So I thought up this plan, see, to sneak in there and take something that's important to him. And that's what I did!"

"What was the emergency, then?" Stewart asked. "I nearly killed myself getting over here."

"He came in late today and called me into his office. I was afraid he had discovered that it was me who had stolen some of his things. I was so terrified that I nearly confessed!" Lori shook her head. "But it wasn't that at all. He just wanted to proposition me again. He wanted me to agree to have sex with him, without him having to *rape* me whenever he wanted me. *Can you believe that?* And to think what I almost said!"

Stewart considered her explanation and decided not to explore the subject. Too painful for her to review, too painful for him to hear. "Lori," he ventured thoughtfully, "sooner or later he's going to discover whatever's missing from his safe. By the way, what *is* missing from his safe? What did you take?"

"Just some documents, that's all."

Stewart gave her a searching look. *I love you, but you're a poor liar.* "What makes you think he would suspect you?"

"Nothing, really. I had just done it, and I got scared, I guess. Leaped to conclusions."

Another lie.

"You're sure?"

"Yes," Lori replied, a bit testily. "You can still vouch for me for last night, right? I was with you, remember?"

Oh no! Stewart thought. *Now I've got to cover up.* "Of course. We were at the races."

"Good! Now will you hide this package for me? Keep it safe and secure?"

Stewart unbuttoned his shirt and stuffed it inside. "Hope it's moisture proof," he cracked.

Lori reacted with a warm, but weary smile. Her eyelids were red, her cheeks puffy, her brown hair streaked, disheveled. Still, she appeared angelic to Stewart. "You look awful," he observed with a smile.

"So do you," Lori said. "I feel drained, completely spent. But somehow, better. *Much* better. I'm sorry I sent you on this wild-goose chase, put you into a panic. It was a harrowing day, I just about blew it all, and I had to see you. *I need you!*"

"That's all right," Stewart responded in a soothing voice. "I need you, too, Lori. Always."

The two remained silent for a long moment. Stewart pondered her words. Lori's little lies tonight didn't matter to him; he had to lie to her also, he admitted. Nor did he much care about how she got into her boss's safe; that was her business, and some day she would probably tell him. What mattered to him more than anything else in the world was her stunning confession, which removed the last barrier between them, and, judging by her reactions, seemed to act as a cathartic for her as well. He would hide her package and not trouble her with questions about its contents. He admired Lori's cleverness, but believed she was not sophisticated enough to comprehend what she took, if they were company documents. But most likely she snatched some personal letters, mementos, perhaps; items that meant something to *her.* She just wanted to unnerve Jeremy Madison, and that was fine with him, too.

"It's been a long day for both of us," Lori finally said. She leaned forward, her eyes glowing with warmth, and, strangely, *desire.* Stewart had never seen her look at him like that. Lori stroked the palm of his hand with her forefinger. "You've really come through for me, Stewart. You've always been there for me, no matter what. I cannot tell you how much that means to me."

Stewart said nothing, mesmerized by her alluring gaze. "I'm too tired to drive home tonight," Lori continued, "and I'm sure you are, too."

"Absolutely," he agreed.

"There are rooms upstairs," she whispered.

It took Stewart a moment to comprehend her point. *"You mean . . ."*

Lori didn't have to reply. Her eyes, her smile, the tilt of her head, said it all. With no further words, they both got up and walked, hand in hand, toward a desk that sat near the foot of stairs leading to the upper floors. Stewart muttered some questions, an elderly man checked a register, nodded, and handed him a key. As they walked up the stairs, Stewart adjusted the folder inside his shirt and felt the envelope the young man at the track had thrust into his hand. He stopped at the landing, pulled it out, ripped it open, and read a note in Morris Courtney's hasty scrawl. A satisfied grin claimed his lips.

Tomorrow will be an exciting day, he thought. He turned to Lori, who was standing by the door to their room, smiling at him with beckoning eyes.

But tonight will be heaven!

Chapter Fifteen

Stewart burst into Lakewood Downs Diner bathed in sweat and wheezing for breath. A rush of refrigerated air coughed out by a half-dozen machines hanging precariously at strategic points in the Quonset hut smacked his face as he entered. Stewart's body odor announced his presence. He slithered through a dozen patrons standing in line, who accommodated him by stepping back to avoid his damp torso brushing against them as he passed. He glided into the booth under the Cadillac's toothy grill to face Morris Courtney, who glared at him with the visage of an agitated rooster. Even his sloping chin struggled to contribute to his scowling expression, by twitching in indignation as Courtney began to speak.

"Where have you been!" he erupted. "I send you a message at the track to see me *immediately* about a fantastic opportunity, and you dash off with no explanation. I don't count your breathy phone call at *two in the morning*, with that broad fingering your chest hairs, as a suitable excuse. You should have seen me right away!" He folded his arms and glowered at Stewart accusingly.

Stewart didn't know what to say. Of course, Courtney had every right to be indignant, but it was not just an evening of bliss with Lori that had detained him. After his morning sales runs, he had to drag his weary but wonderfully satisfied hulk up to Ted Simon's office to explain how a stack of tickets, which Phil Louis *thought* he saw sprouting from Stewart's fist, actually represented a little more than a hundred bucks or so.

"Fifty to win and fifty to place," Stewart had explained earnestly. "So I did okay."

Simon had arched a suspicious eyebrow, wondering how an inch-thick pile of tickets, according to their insistent friend, had somehow melted to scraps of paper indicating fifty to win and fifty to place.

"You're sure?" Simon ventured, as though it were possible to be mistaken about such matters.

"The only thing that thick was the hot dog he was chewing on," Stewart had retorted. "And that was *two* inches. Of course, I'm sure!" Ted Simon accepted this answer, with an admonition that he still had bet too much and a reminder about his professional responsibilities. To satisfy him further, Stewart agreed to meet him regularly after hours to learn more about the company's sales operations. This pleased Simon immensely. Stewart felt it best not to share with Courtney his encounter with his boss; the little trainer was already upset.

He assayed his friend's demeanor and groped for a reply. "Would it help if I told you Lori and I explored new depths of erotic ecstasy?" he offered with a broad smile.

"No, because I don't know what that means."

"I scored big, so to speak," Stewart clarified. He savored every delicious minute he spent with Lori and was repulsed by his own vulgar reference, but thought this answer might assuage Courtney's feelings as well as satisfy his curiosity. Might even appeal to his prurient interest, if the passion boiling in Courtney's breast had any other outlet besides the attention he lavished on winning horseflesh.

Courtney shrugged the matter off with a salacious grin. "All right, all right. So you got your horns clipped. Now, are you ready for some *real* scoring?" He leaned forward, eyes gleaming. Stewart shifted positions to hear him.

"There's another group that fixes races at the track," he murmured. "Johnny Marlboro's been in touch with them, and they've agreed to work with us. We've got to be careful, though. We can't screw these guys!"

"Why would we want to do that?" Stewart countered. "There's enough for everyone." So *that* was his momentous news!

"There's conditions," he continued. "We've got to give them our fixes so we don't accidentally screw each other up . . ."

"No problem," Stewart interrupted.

". . . and they won't give us their fixes until five minutes before post time."

"That *is* a problem," Stewart said.

"Not really. I can't make it up to the lobby in time to place bets, but, of course, you can! You're our secret resource."

Stewart liked the sound of that.

"I've worked out a series of hand signals," Courtney proceeded. "Focus your binoculars on me before the race. If I stretch with both hands above my head, that means one of their races is set up. No stretch, no fix.

Other gestures signal which of their horses to bet on. For example, if I lift my cap off my head, the fix is on number one. If I lift my cap off and scratch my head, the fix is on two. And so forth." Courtney handed him a three-by-five card filled with instructions. "You'll have to place bets for their guys, too."

"I can handle that."

"One more thing. This other group is more active than we've been, usually arranging one fix per day, compared to our three or four a week. I don't think we should try more than that without risking both our operations. Remember, we also have to let them into our races."

"Sounds fair to me!" Stewart gushed. In the fraction of a second it took for Courtney to take a breath before continuing his explanation, Stewart's imagination vaulted to that exalted region inhabited only by prancing dollar signs leading six and seven figure numbers. Thereafter, he allocated only part of his attention to the task of acknowledging Courtney's words, by nodding agreeably and smiling at appropriate times, while reserving the higher part of his mental faculties for rapid-fire mathematical calculations. Eight, nine races a week. Four thousand dollars a fix, and, say, eight fixes a week comes to thirty-two thousand dollars. Maybe thirty-five or forty grand . . . who knows? *Two, three weeks, I've paid off Arnoldi and his goons. After that, all gravy!*

Courtney's conclusion put an end to these reveries. "Any questions?"

"Just one. When's their first fix?"

"Tomorrow, race nine. But wait until I confirm it with an arm stretch."

Exuberance surged through Stewart's body. "Morris, this is *fantastic!*" He lurched forward, reached across the table, grasped his small collaborator by his shoulders, and shook him.

Courtney threw off his friend's embrace. "Save that stuff for your broad, for crap's sake." Then, with a grin, he cackled, "Yeah, it is exciting, ain't it." He gestured toward the plate by Stewart's hand. "I ordered you a blueberry tart, though it's probably dried out now."

"I'll munch on it in the car. Tomorrow, then? Here at noon?"

"Be on time!" Courtney warned, sliding off his seat. Stewart walked out with the trainer, paused at the door, and scanned the dining room before leaving. King Kong was nowhere in sight. *Maybe you don't ALWAYS have your eye on me, you big bastard,* Stewart thought. *Anyway, in a couple of weeks, you'll be history.*

Stewart climbed into his station wagon and caught sight of the large envelope Lori had given him, its yellow corner poking out from his front seat cover. He toyed with the prospect of ripping it open to examine its contents, but decided against it. *I've already lied to her,* he scolded himself; *I can't betray her trust again.* Still, what was he going to do with her envelope? His mind sauntered across a landscape of places he'd been, people he knew, exotic sites he'd visited, until a stunning possibility erupted in his thoughts. *Of course!* he beamed. *The perfect hiding place. She'd never figure this out; no one would!*

Stewart started his engine, feeling satisfied with the day's events. Two problems in his life would be eliminated: the one, after a few weeks or so of successful betting. The other, right now.

He knew exactly where, and how, to conceal Lori Armstrong's precious package.

If that insipid fool wanders in my direction one more time, I'll strangle him! Lori resolved, grinding her teeth. Never had she accidentally bumped into Oliver more frequently than she had today. At the gate to the building, by the water cooler downstairs, in the parking lot near her car, in the hallway by the copier, by the storage room next to a mountain of supplies . . . *Maddening!* And always, he shot that same sideways glance at her, a corner of his mouth lifting a flaccid jowl in an expression that implied more than just a casual greeting. An upward scoop in the tone of his voice hoisted his guttural words to a suspicious, unnatural level. *Good to see you again, Lori,* he repeated, with a knowing look. Then he turned, plodded away. Lori always cut her eyes toward his back pocket; no scarf. Still, the same sickening indictment trumpeted through her mind: *he knows, he knows, he knows!*

Closing time. Madison had ensconced himself in his office all day, no calls, no requests, nothing. Lori collected items scattered across her desk and prepared to leave. Another day consumed. Although Oliver's intermittent presence disturbed her, she no longer found the prospect of facing Madison quite so daunting, especially since Stewart relieved her of those documents. He had relieved her in other ways as well; their rapturous encounters last evening vented months of anxieties. And their consummations bequeathed her a contentment she hadn't relished in years. Then morning arrived. Another day waiting for the ax to fall.

Sooner or later . . . she kept reminding herself, as she grabbed her purse and prepared to leave. She fumbled for her keys, opened the door, took one step . . .

Oliver.

Lori jumped. There he stood outside her door. *How did he get here without my hearing him?*

"I'm sorry I disturbed you, Miss Armstrong," he muttered sheepishly. His countenance drooped. "Um . . . I've got something for you." He reached into his back pocket. Out whipped Lori's scarf.

Lori looked at it as though it were a gun pointed at her head. She looked up to Oliver's face. *Something's wrong with him.* Guilt flickered in his eyes. He looked like a smitten puppy. Not what she expected.

Oliver coughed nervously. "I found it in the parking lot, next to where you park your car. Actually, a few spaces away. Someone ran over it, I'm afraid," he added apologetically, raising it for her to examine. "I know I should have returned it to you right away, but . . ."—his voice crumbled to a hoarse whisper—"it smelled so good, and . . . I kind of thought about it, your wearing it around your pretty neck, your getting dressed in the morning . . ."

Oliver blushed, no longer able to face her. The expression on his face completed the explanation that now mushroomed in Lori's mind. This mettlesome fool, now instantly transformed into a pitiful old man, had apparently indulged in some adolescent fantasy by clinging to her scarf, smelling it, caressing it, letting it inspire some imaginary sexual exploit lingering from his lost youth. *To think how I let this harmless, nut-crunching character with a room-temperature IQ terrify me!* Lori mused.

She gently lifted her scarf from his mottled hand. "That's fine, Oliver," Lori said soothingly. She angled her head to meet his lowered eyes. "I appreciate your getting it for me, really."

Shame clouded Oliver's face; sympathy poured from Lori's words. *"Really,"* she repeated. "Thank you."

"You're a beautiful lady," he murmured. "Inside and out." He turned and shuffled away toward the steps going downstairs.

Lori watched him leave, shut her eyes and sighed. *At least that's off my mind. Now, to get home . . .*

The door to Jeremy Madison's office opened with a rush of air. His head emerged, then his body, propped against the wall. His paunch hung out, his shirt slopped over his trousers. Madison's face was ashen; strands of hair pasted against his glistening bald pate spilled down his forehead, his cheeks. His right hand grasped his chest.

"*Lori . . .*" he croaked.

"Mr. Madison! What . . . what's wrong?"

"*Come . . . in . . . here . . .*" Madison stumbled back into his office. Lori dashed after him, burst into his room just as he crumbled on the sofa next to his desk. A quick scan revealed the portrait of George Madison swung aside, safe open, contents strewn about the desk.

He had discovered the theft.

Lori rushed to his side, eased him to a prone position, and cradled his head. Anguish flowed from Madison's flickering eyes. "I've ... been ... *robbed!*" he wheezed. His left hand, drained of color, crawled up her arm, grasped her shoulder. "Can't replace them. Can't replace them. They're ... *Gone!*"

Lori struggled to make sense of this utterance, when he pulled her toward him. "You *didn't,* Lori. Tell me that you didn't ... *Please! Tell me ... you ... didn't ... take ...*" Madison heaved, coughed. Loathing flowed from his anguished expression. He looked not at Lori, but beyond her, over her shoulder. He was glaring at Oliver, standing behind her.

"You!" he croaked. Madison's arm crept up his chest, clutched his shirt.

Stillness.

"Call an ambulance!" Lori shrieked. Oliver scrambled to the phone, dialed a number, stuttered instructions. Lori sat by her boss, her thoughts swirling. The ghostly hand lurking in her imagination had materialized to strike down her nemesis, Jeremy Madison. She gazed at his limp, ashen hulk, wondering if he would live.

Another thought occurred to her as well. Madison wouldn't get a heart attack over a small stack of missing twenties, or over something he could easily replace. It had to be the documents Lori took from his safe. *They must be much more important than I realized,* she concluded. She had committed to memory every detail of those sheets before handing them over to Stewart: symbols, words, as much of the legalistic morass she could manage to stuff into her head, and numbers—*especially* numbers. At the time, she just couldn't comprehend their meaning, whether they had any value to *her.* Now, she thought differently.

As co-workers rushed into the office, offering help, exclaiming concern, a single idea burned in Lori's thoughts.

I've got to get those documents back.

Chapter Sixteen

Stewart examined sheets of glossy product reports strewn across Ted Simon's desk, picked up a company report, and let out a soft whistle. "There's one thing I don't understand," he mumbled, nose buried in a forest of numbers.

"What's that?" Simon said.

"Our operations in England. That's kind of a long commute for one humble salesman in a white Ford station wagon, isn't it?"

Simon chuckled. "Didn't I tell you? That territory comes with a company yacht painted in our latest Magic Marker colors. Some of them even glow in the dark."

Stewart clucked his tongue. "Bad policy, it seems to me. That's taking advertising of our product lines too seriously. Not to mention how it makes our ship an easy target for German U-boats."

"Only a former submariner would think of something like that," Simon laughed. "The last I heard, there weren't many U-boats left, but I'll still pass your observation on to the head of our overseas division. He'd really appreciate your input, because he served in the Merchant Marine during World War Two. Which probably explains why he acquired our ships under some kind of reverse Lend-Lease agreement with the Brits. They're all old destroyers, I think."

"Glad to know my suggestions are taken seriously around here," Stewart quipped. He picked up another advertisement. "What's this?" He handed a glossy paper across the desk to Simon who glanced at it.

"One of our latest products. A refillable highlighter. You just insert the nib into the aperture and it refills by capillary action. Quite clever, really. Did you see the one designed exclusively for military use? Writes over everything—grease, cordite, canvas, painted metal, you name it."

"With all due respect, I refuse to sell that. Too many bad memories."

"Rank insubordination," Simon commented.

"So, court-martial me," Stewart said, as he continued to thumb through a stack of documents on his lap. He looked up. "Didn't these companies we acquired have their own sales forces?"

"Some of them did, yes. But they weren't as dynamic as ours." Simon winked, and Stewart caught the compliment instantly. "As a regional sales manager in training, you will become familiar with all these product lines, which is why I want you to study the literature and also spend time in the lab testing products for demonstrations to customers. Obviously, you don't have to test anything in our stationery line, but everything you see in our graphic arts division you should know thoroughly."

Stewart nodded agreeably. "You mentioned something about quarterly reports, stock options, and whatnot. When do we delve into that?"

"We hold classes in the boardroom after hours. Something like a military sub-course, complete with homework assignments. I scheduled you for that as well. The next cycle begins quite soon, in fact."

Stewart looked concerned. "When?"

Simon raised his hand and grinned. "Don't worry. It will start after your vacation. Do you have any plans, by the way?"

A wide smile animated Stewart's comfortable features. "You might say that. Lori and I plan to spend some time together."

"That's great, Stewart. If your relationship with her develops half as well as the work you've accomplished with us, you two should have a bright future." Simon glanced at his watch. "I've kept you long enough. Your vacation officially begins right now."

Stewart gathered the items before him, arranged them in neat piles, and placed them inside his briefcase. He shook Simon's hand. "I'm sure I'll have a chance to review this while I'm away. Thanks for everything, Ted. I'll see you in two weeks."

Simon patted him on the shoulder. "Have a good vacation."

Stewart left the office swiftly, and Simon relaxed in his chair, musing about his early days with Office Products Unlimited, comparing his experiences with those of Stewart Lawrence. He found training a bright prospect and a thoroughly rewarding task, something he looked forward to as he advanced on his own career track. Stewart in particular had vindicated his early assessment of him, which fed Simon's self-satisfaction immensely. He hoped Stewart's promotions would parallel his own so they could continue working together. Simon smiled whenever he pondered his trainee's future.

A rising young star in the company, he concluded, as he turned his attention to the next stage of Stewart Lawrence's professional development.

A dozen towns bursting with historical memorabilia jutted off Long Island's Highway 27 like pearls on a string leading to the ocean, and Stewart and Lori visited them all. It had been a spectacular four-day vacation rummaging through the East End's mélange of quaint villages, bays, beaches, boutiques, trails, parks, landmarks, and other tourist attractions generously sprinkled within and around an assortment of small cities collectively referred to as The Hamptons. They imbibed as much whaling history as their stomachs could endure at Sag Harbor; gawked at a king's row of stately homes gracing East Hampton's tree-lined avenues; sauntered off the coast of East Quoque, staring at hosts of white sails pricking the blue horizon like a myriad of shark teeth clawing the innocent sky; took pictures, and more pictures, of Montauk Lighthouse while crisp sea breezes whipped across their faces and ruffled their clothes. Absolutely fabulous.

Their days ended the way they began: in bed, fulfilling mutual sexual fantasies. Their last morning together before driving back to work found Lori and Stewart snuggling beneath the sheets of a pencil-post bed festooned at its top by a tangle of rose hip vines. A stupendous view of Southampton Bay offered occasional diversion for eyes lost mostly in each other's gaze. At the moment, Stewart was sitting on the edge of their bed. He pried his attention away from a ravishing swatch of Lori's flesh, which had escaped their sheets' soft embrace, to examine a bruise sprawled across the side of his leg to his right buttock. He gently touched it, winced, and turned to gape again at Lori, who was smiling at him with a contented look on her face.

"How's your leg?" she asked.

"It hurts. But I give you credit for doing your best to take my mind off it."

Lori giggled. "I know what a pain in the leg feels like, believe me," she quipped. "I'm sorry I insisted you go horseback riding with me."

"So am I!" Stewart retorted, in mock irritation. "I told you, I only *bet* on those smelly beasts. I don't *ride* them."

Lori slid her nude body over to his side. She brushed her creamy skin against his arm and gave him a hug. "There's only one part of your body I'm interested in right now, and that's doing great." She tweaked her nose, offered her luscious lips to his, which Stewart accepted hungrily. He embraced her, they tumbled backward, and wriggled themselves into the luxurious silken folds that had caressed their bodies all night. The pain in his leg and buttock vanished.

After several minutes of playful wrestling, they relaxed, casting appreciative glances outside at sea gulls hovering in the brisk wind against a backdrop of white clouds splashed across an azure blue sky. Stewart could not remember a time when he felt so utterly content, happy.

"Stewart," Lori said, shifting over to her side. She toyed with his chest hairs, reminding Stewart of Courtney's exasperated comment at the diner one time after he had showed up late for their appointment. The little trainer's prescience made him smile.

"What did you do with that package I gave you a few weeks ago," Lori asked.

Stewart didn't answer immediately. He felt deliciously depleted and didn't want to exert the energy to answer a question.

"That package . . ." Lori repeated.

"Huh? Oh, that. I put it in a safe place, like I told you."

"Where?"

"You didn't want me to tell you, remember? In fact, you insisted on that. By the way, how's your boss?"

"Still in the hospital, convalescing," Lori said without expression. "Mild heart attack. He should be back in a week or two."

"Did the police ever investigate?"

"No . . . They didn't."

Stewart shrugged. "I'm not surprised. Especially if the package you took just contained personal stuff. You know, between you and him. He wouldn't want the police to snoop into that."

Lori didn't challenge his statement. "So, are you going to tell me where you put my package?"

A speck of concern perturbed Stewart's thoughts. She loathed Madison, he knew. Then why was Lori so interested in retrieving a paper trail recounting his depraved attentions for her? Assuming, of course, Stewart was right in his guess about her package's contents. *Puzzling.*

Still, he would permit nothing to mar their perfect vacation. "It's safe, don't worry."

"Where?" Lori persisted.

Stewart studied her intent expression, then let his eyes rest on the crown of vines looped across their bedposts. A thought blossomed in his mind, pushing a mischievous grin across his lips. *I wonder if I remember that correctly . . .* Finally, he got up, stepped into his boxer shorts, pulled on some trousers, walked toward a chest of drawers, and rummaged through a stack of glossy brochures and other paraphernalia they had collected over the previous week. *Here it is!* He picked up a large shiny pamphlet with the words Lakewood Downs sprawled across the front and thumbed through it. *First race, second race, third race . . . There!* His forefinger glided down the page. His eyes plowed through a thicket of numbers, probing to isolate exactly the right sequence . . . *Found it!* Stewart stabbed the paper with his finger. *What do you know?* he exclaimed to himself, congratulating his powers of recall. *I was right.*

He shut the program and faced Lori, who was looking at him with a curious expression. He tossed the pamphlet on the bed where it landed on her lap. "Number four's a winner at two-o-two and three," he announced.

"*What?*"

"That's where your package is hidden."

Lori looked at him sideways. "I ask you a question and you give me a puzzle?"

"Just following instructions, lady—*your* instructions. If and when Madison recovers and makes inquiries, you can honestly say you have no idea where his package is."

"What if he asks me if I took it?"

Stewart shrugged. "You'll have to lie about that. Any problem?"

"No," Lori said, with a hint of annoyance. She picked up the program, flipped through a few pages, and rolled her eyes back. "You say the answer's in *here?*"

"Number four's a winner at two-o-two and three," Stewart repeated. "Let's not talk about this any more, please? We have a few hours left before we have to head back."

Lori closed the program and nodded agreeably. "Let's make the most of it!"

They spent the remainder of their morning lingering over a breakfast that tasted as elegant as its French appellations suggested. Then, after a quick job throwing their things together and heaving them into the storage compartment of Stewart's station wagon, they took a picturesque journey westward with the sun intermittently peeking through clouds and shooting bolts of light into their eyes. Although they were both tired, their conversation remained animated until they approached points west, Millerville, Patchogue, Deerfield.

Quiet enveloped the car, broken only by brief comments and short answers about the traffic, the weather, passing scenery, their sight-seeing tours—anything but what had apparently claimed Lori's attention for the last hour of their trip. Stewart wheeled his station wagon into her driveway, hauled out her suitcases, and lugged them to her door. Lori offered him a radiant smile and gave him a passionate kiss.

Stewart let his lips linger on her soft flesh. "How about one last fling? You know, before we both trudge back to the salt mines," he ventured.

Lori grinned. "You're *insatiable!*"

"For you, yes."

"Store your energy for another time. Frankly, I'm exhausted."

Stewart had to admit to himself that he also needed time to recuperate. "I'll call you tomorrow."

Lori nodded, picked up her luggage. "One more thing, Stewart," she said, in a tentative voice. "That racing program . . . May I have it?"

Stewart hesitated, but Lori's supplicating expression melted his resistance. "Why not?" he said. He trotted off to his car, retrieved it from the glove compartment, and returned with program in hand. Lori clutched it as though the glossy pamphlet held the key to a treasure. One last embrace, an ardent kiss, a lingering squeeze of hands. Lori grasped her suitcases, flung Stewart a departing wink, and vanished into her apartment.

When Stewart's station wagon roared away from her driveway, his thoughts immediately switched to a different channel. *Immerse yourself in that racing form as much as you want, dear,* he mused, confident his clue would remain impenetrable to her most determined probing. *I've got more important numbers to ponder.*

He reached into his shirt pocket for the notebook he kept with him at all times. His eyes darted back and forth, from the road to his jottings on paper, and back again. Stewart's notes sent his imagination soaring. Date, race number, name of horse, amount wagered, profit gained—all meticulously catalogued. *Rows of figures marching to the heavens,* he thought with glee. Two months of betting with Courtney and Marlboro's other group had netted him a six figure sum, more than enough to pay off Arnoldi's goons and eliminate that avaricious reminder from his troubled past. *Pay him off and the rest is all mine,* he thought. *Mine and Lori's.*

He pulled into his driveway, turned off the car, and hauled out his suitcase from the back seat. Stewart clambered up his stairs, fingering through his key chain. He opened the door to his apartment and lifted his suitcase inside. He looked up and stopped breathing.

Two men sat at his kitchen table: Rexford Engels and that bald hulk Stewart had seen with him at the diner some weeks ago, the one possessing a wrestler's body, no hair or eyelashes, folds of skin piled up the back of his neck. T-shirt, jeans, cowboy boots comprised his clothing. Engels wore his trademark tight knit shirt. They were playing cards.

King Kong's companion ignored him, but Engels lifted an arm in greeting. "Howya doing, lover-boy?" he said. "Haven't seen you for a while."

That was true enough; it had been several weeks since Stewart had caught sight of Engels's bothersome presence at Lakewood Downs, and on only a few occasions during his sessions at the diner. Stewart had even toyed with the notion that Arnoldi might have written off his debt and called in his attack dogs. Their invasion shattered that fantasy.

Stewart kept the door propped open with his suitcase. "I've . . . been busy," he said. His chest tightened.

Engels flipped a card from his hand. His colleague picked it up, plugged it into the stack clutched in his fat fist, then triumphantly fanned his cards on the table. Engels glanced downward and muttered a curse. Back to Stewart. "Told you I've got my eye on you, man. You won't get away from me." He gathered the cards and began to shuffle. The clean-shaven gorilla facing Engels kept his head riveted forward, scrutinizing fingers snapping crisp cards into random order.

"Oh, forgot to make your acquaintance here," Engels blurted, dealing out two hands. "This is Bernie. Bernie, Stewart."

No acknowledgment; the man didn't even grunt. Cards sailing across the table, caught beneath his meaty hands consumed his attention.

Stewart stood rigid at the doorway; too afraid to flee, too stunned to speak. The notebook weighed in his pocket, stuck to his clammy skin, giving him a reminder that spiked his courage. "I've got your money," he said. "I can pay you off. That would settle things between us. Completely."

"Good, good," Engels murmured without expression, arranging cards in his hand.

Silence.

Cards slipped into sequence. Forearms darted back and forth. Cards slapped on the table.

"Call!" snapped the hairless one.

"Whatcha got?"

"Full house."

"Damn!" Engels hurled his three-of-a-kind down with such force that they collided with the deck, launching a spray of playing cards from the table. His partner grunted.

Stewart coughed, nervously. Engels looked up, his dark eyes bored on Stewart's stationary figure. He got up from the chair and walked toward him, the floor creaking in protest to his every step. Engels pulled out a toothpick from the pocket in his knit shirt and began chewing on it.

"So, you say you can pay us off," he said.

Stewart nodded. "I would like to settle things between us once and for all."

Engles snickered. "You *would,* now!" He took a step closer. Engels's nose, inches away from Stewart's face, filled his vision.

"There's been a change in the rules," Engels announced.

Stewart gave him a puzzled look. "What do you mean?"

"You're working for us, now," Engels declared.

Stewart didn't know what to say. Finally, "but, our agreement"—his voice crumpled to a squeak—"you can't . . ."

"Oh, but I CAN!" Engels shouted. "And just to make sure you don't skip town *this* time, we have insurance. BERNIE!"

Engels's companion turned toward Stewart. He plunged his hand into his right boot. With terrifying speed, he whipped out a knife, cocked his arm, and hurled it across the room. The weapon stabbed the wall with a sickening crack. It stuck into a photograph clinging to a thumbtack. Its blade slashed across the throat of the person in the picture. Stewart focused his eyes on that cruel metal, scrutinized the figure in the photograph. A female. Brown hair. Her head turned toward the viewer. Unmistakable features.

Horror surged through Stewart's chest. The woman in the picture was Lori.

Mable Osgood's facial features paraded the decades of her life the way lines on a road map display directions and distances. Every harrowing episode of her checkered past had carved a new wrinkle on her visage; but when she smiled, some ineradicable glow burning within animated her lithographic countenance in a fashion that melted away those years engraved with perils and pitfalls. Throughout it all, she had maintained her resilience and good humor. That's what Dalton loved about her the most: she was a *survivor*. Dalton, twice divorced, had once threatened a proposal of marriage to her; Mable, three times divorced, had threatened to accept. And there they had left the matter for the last five years.

Most important, Dalton trusted her more than anyone else he knew. Confiding in Mable meant entombing one's secret forever; she'd die before revealing it. And assigning her a special mission, especially one shrouded in conspiracy, fired her enthusiasm in a way Dalton never saw in any soldiers he commanded. He once told her she was the best marine he ever knew. Mable's eyes flashed anger; she cracked his face with a vicious slap, and then they made love. A perfect relationship between two very tough people.

Dalton knew Mable viewed her current task as a way to take advantage of an opportunity to get even with the world. Her position in charge of the snack bar in the show paddock afforded Dalton exactly what he needed as well: a means to carry out his plan against the fixers.

Dalton slipped through the back door of the show paddock's snack bar and observed Mable's efficient motions, as she took orders, poured coffee, and handed out burgers, desserts, and snacks to the throng of drivers and trainers who bustled into her shop between races. She spotted Dalton, snapped her fingers, and one of her employees quickly took over her tasks. She brushed her willowy body past him and trotted into a back room, where he joined her in a private corner.

"Okay, stripes, who's on the hit list?" Mable asked, unknotting her apron.

Dalton grimaced. He hated it when she used one of his military nicknames, this one earned when his commanding officer ripped off his sergeant's stripes for the minor infraction of accidentally driving a brand new Patton tank through the colonel's orderly room. He eventually regained his rank, but the name stuck.

"We're not going to *kill* them, for crap's sake. Just make them a little nervous."

"You mean, make them a *lot* nervous," Mable corrected. "By the time I'm done with these guys, they'll be charged up enough to supply the power needs of a small city."

"Mable, you've got to be careful," Dalton cautioned.

She shrugged him off. "Of course I will. Now tell me, who gets spiked?"

Dalton pulled out a sheet of paper, opened it, and handed it to Mable. Her eyes widened.

"Well, I'll be . . ." she grinned. "You're sure?"

"Positive. They're both in the fifth race."

Mable folded the paper and handed it back to him, a confident look on her face. Dalton gave her a gesture of doubt, which Mable immediately picked up.

"Don't worry!" she assured. "I know what I'm doing. In fact, these guys' habits help us out. You know, like when they come into the snack bar. Should work out perfectly."

Dalton stifled his inclination to inquire about details and stuffed the sheet back into his pocket.

"Gotta get back to work now," Mable said, putting on a fresh apron.

"You're a real trooper," Dalton commented appreciatively. He patted her on the rump as she walked past him toward the kitchen.

"Don't touch my ass unless you intend to pay my rent," she quipped, tossing him a coy grin over her shoulder. Dalton watched her vanish into the next room and resume her duties. He sauntered out of the kitchen area and stood by the door leading to the show paddock. He leaned against the wall, reached into his pocket, pulled out his Zippo lighter, and snapped its flame on a Lucky Strike. He took a deep drag, exhaled a stream of blue smoke, and observed drivers and trainers guide their animals on the track for the next race.

Tomorrow, he repeated to himself with quiet satisfaction, *we'll nail these bastards to the wall.*

Chapter Seventeen

Six minutes before the fifth race.

Stewart focused his binoculars on Morris Courtney's familiar perch and visually scoured the track area to isolate his diminutive figure among the kaleidoscope of colorful uniforms, wandering spectators, and clumping horses. No need to check Courtney's card filled with explanations of his hand signals: he had memorized these gestures the moment the little trainer had given them to him. They joined Stewart's formidable array of intellectual equipment that routinely sprang into action whenever he handicapped a race. However, at the moment, other anxieties clouded his thoughts.

That mental picture: knife yanked out, arm cocked, like the hammer of a pistol; flashing blade whipping through the air, stabbing the wall, slicing across the throat of Lori's innocent visage . . . *Harrowing!* Yet, what could Stewart do? *We can't run away. No money left, they've ripped it off. We're trapped.*

A changed digit flashed on the tote board and caught his attention. Four minutes left. Binoculars lifted to his face, bolted to the track. *There he is!* Stewart watched Courtney weave through clusters of bodies and horses, step up to the spectator gate, and hoist a leg onto its bottom slat. He stretched, threw a look upward, toward Stewart. Another stretch to confirm. Cap off, head scratched. Horse number two instantly registered in Stewart's thoughts. His right hand darted to his shirt pocket, grasped a sheet of paper, crackled it open. He probed his summary sheet and jabbed his finger on Courtney's choice. *Adam's Jet.* Classified as a strong stretch competitor, great post position. *Sensible choice,* Stewart concluded. Back to the tote board. *Five to one at three minutes to post time.* Didn't promise a great payoff, but Stewart at this point would eagerly scoop up whatever offering Marlboro's wagering system threw before him.

Stewart walked down to the betting booths, his calculations skittering across a jumble of figures. *Play it cautious today,* he concluded. *Make three, maybe four thousand bucks if everything goes without a hitch.* He glimpsed dancing reflections of those awful rectangular spies that shielded the security office, then scurried to the shortest line. Stewart didn't feel like waiting for the last minute to place his bets today. *Get this over with, then think about what to do next.*

In a few moments, he would have much more to think about besides Engels and Lori.

Three gulps of coffee . . .

That's all it took to reduce Tim Booker, driver of *Adam's Jet,* to a quivering assemblage of arms and legs. He shook all over; air tumbled past his lips in stuttering capsules of breath. Desperate, panicky, the driver folded his arms, grabbed his elbows with his fists in futile attempts to take control of his convulsing body. Impossible. Enflamed nerve ends exploded in revolt against every attempt. He staggered off his sulky, crumbled to the ground and clutched his chest with both hands, knuckles white, fingers rigid, their icy grasp clamped on his uniform. Seizures jerked his body across the track's gravel surface, as though he were assaulted by a barrage of electrical jolts. Onlookers witnessed his anguish with dropped jaws. It was like watching a human slice of bacon crackling on a hot griddle.

"Dalton, get over here!" someone cried.

The Marine ran toward the victim of Mable's special concoction, dismayed his assistance was demanded. He hadn't planned on that. Obviously, he couldn't observe how the fixers reacted if he was absorbed in helping a stricken driver.

"You've got first aid training. Do something!" It was the patrol judge.

Dalton clamped his powerful hands on the driver's body and poured soothing words over his terrified countenance. In a flash, decades of military training took control of the Marine's reactions, guided his motions. He was in Korea again, embracing a fallen comrade, rescuing him from the clutches of enemy fire. Nothing else mattered. Booker responded with a beseeching look and grateful eyes, which anointed Dalton as his rescuer. A pinch of guilt nudged the Marine's thoughts. He genuinely regretted causing such misery. *How much of that stuff did Mable sneak into his coffee?*

Other drivers and trainers hovered over him, eyes riveted on his every move. A question squeaked through the confusion and bustle: "Heart attack?"

"Don't think so," Dalton answered quickly. "Seizures like this can come from a number of sources." That's all he dared say; you don't explain medical alternatives under emergency conditions to others while the afflicted one lies helplessly before you, treating your every word like a potential gun pointed at his head. Especially if you happen to be the cause of his condition.

"There seems to be a delay by the show paddock . . ." The announcer's metallic voice scraped Dalton's taut nerves.

He withdrew his eyes from Booker's shaking body and quickly scanned his surroundings. A bevy of figures huddled nearby, the patrol judge, other track officials, a few drivers, trainers. Clipped questions and answers . . . Crisply nodding heads . . . A voice hurled over Dalton's spectators . . . "I got *Adam's Jet,* Tim. Don't worry!"

Was this substitute another fixer? Dalton didn't know.

A flash of uniform bolted away. Dalton looked up. Couldn't catch who it was. *Has to be one of the fixers, racing to the lobby to warn their chief.* And Dalton missed him.

A break in phalanx of bodies huddled about him offered a peek at the track. Dalton cut his eyes toward the tote board. *Two minutes.* He wondered about the other driver Mable was supposed to have poisoned. Or, had she just managed to juice up the coffee of one of them? *I hope she didn't do both!* Dalton suddenly thought. *I don't want to handle another tinderbox right now.*

Booker seemed to be settling down under Dalton's skillful ministrations. Someone patted him on the back, undeserved thanks. He helped the driver, still shaking, to his feet. Booker embraced him eagerly, treating Dalton like a savior, words of thanks tumbling from lips still stuttering to regain control.

"Fine, fine," Dalton repeated, his own thoughts coping with disappointment laced with regret. His perfect plan had collapsed in a jumble of unanticipated consequences and unmerited plaudits. For all his trouble, he had learned nothing.

"BACK on line! *PA-A-A-ACERS* are OUT! A-a-a-a-and, *the-e-e-e-re* they GO!" Race five was beginning. The track routine remained on schedule, the announcer hadn't missed a beat.

Dalton released Tim Booker to several official-looking men with competence written over their faces. They assisted the driver into a truck, which then roared through the parking lot and vanished on the street. Dalton trudged past the snack bar, caught a wistful glance from Mable Osgood, and continued toward the locker room, collecting expressions of gratitude along the way. He did not disappoint those who expected little in the way of an effusive response to their outstretched hands.

"All in a day's work, eh, Marine?" somebody offered, as though trying to excuse Dalton's boorish lack of acknowledgment coming from others who genuinely appreciated what he did.

"Yeah, something like that," Dalton mumbled. He reached for his Zippo lighter and a Lucky Strike. The excitement brought on by Tim Booker's unnerving breakdown now subsided to the normal bustle of activities associated with the show paddock's routine. *I'll never nail these bastards,* Dalton groused, blowing out a stream of smoke.

"Dalton!" someone shouted. He turned toward the show paddock office, a small enclave tucked into the corner of the building. "Telephone, for you," called a track official, holding the receiver.

Dalton walked toward him, grabbed the phone, ducked into the office. "Dalton here," he said.

"Alistair?" boomed a voice on the receiver. Only one person called him that. Jack, from the security office, upstairs.

"Yeah," Dalton said.

Triumph surged through Jack's words. *"We've got your man."*

Chapter Eighteen

The announcer's shrieking report of race seven assaulted Stewart's ears like a barrage of cymbals clanging inside a tunnel. He fixed his binoculars on the track. White knuckles punctuated his rigid fist like fluorescent road bumps on a highway. *This is insane!* Stewart screamed inside.

"*INTO* the lightning lane they *GO!* Number one, but *straggling* to the outside is *IMPORT!* TWO, it's *Quick Jo-ANN!* Three, *SURGING* to the outside is *Major Prim-m-m-ROSE!* FOUR, and *powering* to the inside, CHALLENGING *for the lead,* it's *FRIS-CO-O-O-O!"*

Stewart's heart thumped in his throat. He popped his binoculars from his eyes, rubbed moist lenses against his damp shirt, and whipped them up to his face again. Didn't help at all. His attention returned to the track. *Impossible!* he repeated. Frisco didn't belong in the same race as those other horses. Or, the same class. *Or the same planet!*

"*HERE* he comes . . . INSIDE! No one can stop him! It's *IMPORT,* number ONE, but fading . . . *FRISCO,* on the inside, CHARGING FOR THE LEAD! Quick Jo Ann moves toward the *rail! Frisco* . . . JAMMED! *FRISCO* . . . powers THROUGH! To the finish! It's *Frisco! Import! Major Primrose!* Win, place, and show!"

Stewart released the grasp on his binoculars and let them fall where they dangled from his leaning posture like dead weight attached to a hangman's noose. He shook his head, the announcer's terse observation echoing in his thoughts: *Frisco* . . . JAMMED! Stewart's jaw tightened. *Of course he was jammed,* he thought, grinding his teeth. That was *supposed* to happen, but at the halfway mark, *not* down the stretch. *Quick Jo Ann* was driven by one of Courtney's boys. *One of ours!* His last desperate attempt to ram the charging horse to the rail shrieked FOUL! to anyone possessing half a brain that was half-awake and watching the race. *Did the judges see it, too?* They *had* to see it, Stewart concluded. An idiot could see that.

The inquiry sign flashed. Stewart fumbled for his binoculars, locked them on the tote board. *Oh no, after the last few weeks, not this!* Agonized waiting. The tote board's yellow bulbs flickered at him accusingly, like a dozen hot coals poking him in the chest. Stewart let his binoculars collapse in front of him, slumped in his chair, and waited, pondering the implications of losing another fixed race.

It doesn't get any worse than this, he thought, ruminating over the last few races. *What's going wrong?* Among the short list of explanations, the most comforting possibility was also the most simple. *Quick Jo Ann's* failed maneuver represented nothing more than a fluke, one that happened to reduce their most painstaking calculations to a useless jumble of numbers, ratios, and names, but a fluke nonetheless. Stewart had suffered through similar mishaps, but his fortunes had always changed for the better in subsequent races, which confirmed the soundness of their system. But *too* many flukes constituted a pattern. The dismal performance of their drivers over the last several weeks suggested a more dire possibility, one that *blared* in his mind: a leak, a break in their security. A serious break, too. Slender victories brought in their wake disastrous defeats, the kind he had never experienced earlier, not at Lakewood Downs, at least. Guessing winning horses using a dart board at twenty paces would have been no less effective than their careful plotting; *more* accurate, probably. But who was responsible?

The inquiry sign continued flashing. Stewart fidgeted. *The judges had to see that jamming maneuver,* he repeated. *That's what they're reviewing right now, deciding how to handle the infraction.* Stewart pulled out a damp handkerchief, dappled his face, and matted his sopping hair behind his ears, above his shirt collar. *Come on . . . Come on . . .* he pleaded silently. *ANNOUNCE something!*

The inquiry sign still blinked.

Stewart's thoughts meandered to his last meeting with Johnny Marlboro. Scared the life out of him. He had been standing in line by the hundred dollar window, the trainer rushed up to him, under the watchful glare of those shimmering, devilish windows, peppered his ear with frantic words . . . Something about one of their drivers suddenly taking sick. *The fix is off,* he had croaked. *I'll explain later.* Then he scurried back to the show paddock. Stewart had nodded and decided instantly to slash his wager by four thousand dollars. Then he walked briskly through the lobby, careful to keep his face angled away from the security office. Had anyone seen him, or Marlboro, and suspect anything? Stewart didn't know. The track was busy that day; Marlboro mumbled to him while both had been buried in a clump of bodies, shielded by Engels's massive form and that of his shorter partner—the only time Stewart had actually been grateful for their presence. This much, however, was clear; their profits had plunged since that meeting. Something was very wrong.

Lights ceased blinking. Final winners, win, place, and show flashed on the tote board. No further announcement. Stewart sighed heavily. At least today would yield no additional traumas, he concluded. He grunted out of his chair, left his booth, started walking toward the show paddock, determination pounding through every step. *Got to see Morris, tell him to lay low for a while. Maybe talk to Marlboro, convince him to sever our connection with that other group. Maybe . . .*

The track's public address system crackled an announcement that cut through sounds of the bustling crowd. *Mr. Stewart Lawrence. Please report to the Security Office at once. Call for Mr. Stewart Lawrence . . .*

Stewart stopped suddenly, stood in place. Bodies bumped into him from behind; people flowed around him, flitting him looks of irritation as they passed. A multitude of fears cascaded through his thoughts. The security office was just down the stairs, around the corner. A few steps, he's there. Or, he could leave, run away. By the time they realized he wasn't going to show up, he could be ten, fifteen miles away. Unless they left guards at the entrance, ready to stop him. That possibility made him pause. *Might as well go to their office,* he concluded with resignation.

Stewart made the distance quickly, stepped up to the side entrance, and knocked on the door. He quickly whisked a handkerchief across his face. *Settle down, act normal, see what they want.* The door opened, a lanky man with a deeply lined face and a gray uniform motioned him inside. Stewart stepped up, a rush of cool air brushed against his face. A half-dozen pairs of eyes turned in his direction, then away, to other things. The man who had opened the door cocked his head, gave him a curious look. A shiver knifed up Stewart's spine. His eyes jerked toward the official's nameplate above his pocket. It read, JACK.

"Phone call for you, Mr. Lawrence," Jack said.

"Thank you," Stewart said, grasping it with a sweaty palm. "This is Stewart Lawrence."

A shaky voice on the other end. Distraught, struggling to maintain control.

Lori.

"I'll be right there!" Stewart blurted. "What? Okay, fine! I'll meet you there." He handed the phone back to Jack who placed it on its cradle, a smug look pasted on his face. Maybe something else lurked behind those sneering lips; Stewart couldn't decipher his countenance. As though he *knew* something. Or, was Stewart just imagining things?

"Hope everything's all right," Jack offered, with an expression that evaporated the veneer of concern in his words.

"Everything . . . is *fine!*" "Thank you." He swiveled, closed the door, and scampered through the lobby toward the entrance and to the parking lot.

Stewart made the distance to his apartment, where he agreed to meet Lori, in half the time it normally took him. As he screeched into his driveway, he saw Lori's Volkswagen parked on the street. He ran up the stairs, fumbled for his keys, reached the top landing, and saw the door was open. Stewart burst into his apartment, slammed the door behind him. Lori was sitting on the sofa, her body hunched forward, her hands clutched together on her lap. She tilted her worried expression to Stewart.

"What's wrong, what happened?" Stewart asked.

"I've been fired."

Stewart rushed to her side and put his arms around her. "What happened?"

Lori collected a tear from her cheek. "Madison got back from the hospital a couple of days ago. He called me into his office. He looked awful. He babbled something about company security and asked me accusing questions."

"What did you tell him?"

"Nothing! I acted innocent. He continued accusing me. I fended him off. The more he talked, the worse he looked. He took a few pills, for his heart, I guess. Then he told me I was fired, to get out. He called Oliver in, too, and fired him. That was *really* bad. I could hear them from my office. Lots of shouting, cursing. Then I left and called you." Lori nestled her body into Stewart's arms. He patted her back, consoled her. They heard footsteps outside.

Their eyes darted toward the door. The rumble of heavy feet pounding up the outside stairs shook the floor, rattled windows. Stewart and Lori stayed on his sofa, clutching each other's bodies. Footsteps stopped . . . On the landing now . . . Pause . . . A mammoth foot rammed against the wood, the door crashed open, shattered glass exploded across the room, rained on the floor. Engels stepped into the room. And that other guy, too, the one with the knife. Bernie.

Like a pair of massive grizzlies bursting into their lair and confronting intruders, Engels and Bernie glowered at the two seated before them. Bernie whipped out his knife, ran a forefinger across its shiny blade, and cut his fierce eyes toward Lori, as though pondering what part of her to slice up first. Engels gnawed on a toothpick, a look of contempt on his face. He glanced at Lori, then turned to Stewart.

"You've been late, man. Mr. Arnoldi ain't happy with you *at all.* Neither is my associate here." He nodded toward Bernie, who was still thoughtfully testing the edge of his knife's razor-sharp blade. Pale light glinted off its cruel metal surface. Bernie's flat lips widened in an expression that could not be called a smile. More like a snake stretching its mouth, preparing itself to devour a prey it had stunned with its poisonous fangs.

Stewart pushed words out. "A few setbacks, that's all," he stammered.

"Mr. Arnoldi don't see it that way," Engels countered. "He figures you got some explaining to do."

How can I explain what I don't understand myself, Stewart thought. "This is temporary. I've been on time in the past. *Almost always.*"

"That was then. Now is now. I ain't heard from you in a couple of weeks." He folded his massive arms across his chest. "Mr. Arnoldi expects you to be *punctual,* man. No more delays."

"Give me one more time," Stewart pleaded. "I promise to be on schedule. *Please.*"

More gnawing on his toothpick. An exchange of glances with Bernie. Engels shrugged. "We got your number, you know," he reminded, casting a wicked look at Lori.

Stewart felt her body shiver. "I promise," he repeated.

"All right. I'll talk to Mr. Arnoldi and see you again. *Real soon!*" He gestured toward Bernie, who somehow had buried that huge knife into his trousers where it vanished, then turned, and the two tromped away. Stewart and Lori waited until they heard their footsteps trail away into the driveway. Car doors opened, then slammed; they drove off.

Stewart collapsed against the sofa. Lori gaped at him, fright and astonishment written on her face.

"Who *were* those men? What is this all *about?*" she demanded.

Stewart closed his eyes, his stunned thoughts groping for answers to her questions. Worse, for a way to pay off Arnoldi. He had blurted that response just to get rid of his goons, not because he had a clue how he was going to do it.

Stewart met Lori's indignant expression. He didn't know what to say.

The phone rang. Stewart flopped his wet palm on the receiver, lifted it off its cradle, dragged it to his ear.

"Hello."

"Stewart?"

Stewart recognized Morris Courtney's voice. "Yeah," he said weakly, massaging the bridge of his nose.

"It's me, Morris." He paused. *"They've got us . . ."*

The image of Alistair Dalton approaching him in the show paddock locker room would be embossed on Johnny Marlboro's memory forever. One ominous step after another, like a stalking leopard, muscles twitching with every movement, coiled for a ferocious lunge to tear its victim's heart out . . .

It was late at night when Marlboro had dragged his exhausted body from the show paddock, grunted a few good-byes to departing friends, and ambled into an empty locker room, still pondering the mysterious affliction that had abruptly wrecked their day's fix of race five. He unzipped his uniform, peeled it off, and slumped on a bench, facing his locker. He was grateful that at least Tim Booker hadn't died. Then again, no one had a clue what happened to him, either. *Temporary setback,* Marlboro had told himself. *I'll find out in the morning.* He found out sooner than that.

The door had creaked open, then slammed shut. A sharp click. *Locked already?* Marlboro paid it no mind. Just as he bent over to pry off a shoe, a metal object whizzed over his head, missing him by inches, crashed against his locker, clattered by his feet. A horseshoe. Who in God's name would throw a horseshoe at him? *Why, you could get killed . . .* He jerked around, outraged by such a reckless act. And there stood the Marine.

The look in Dalton's eyes told it all. Marlboro knew he could kill a man with his bare hands. But why was he after him? Fear of discovery knifed through his thoughts. *Could be only one reason . . .*

Dalton then pulled out another horseshoe, slapped its metal against his palm, and stepped toward him. Arm cocked, whipped forward, another shot, this time buckling the locker door next to Marlboro. The next instant, the Marine was in his face. Powerful hands grasped his shirt, lifted him off his feet, slammed him against the wall, then heaved him across the room, where Marlboro collapsed on the cold concrete floor. Dalton towered over him, hoisted him up again, pinned him against a row of lockers. Eyes ablaze, every feature taut with rage, Dalton spit words in Marlboro's face. *"You and I need to TALK!"* he had said through clenched teeth.

That's when Johnny Marlboro's betrayal began.

Presently, he sat in a room filled with authorities who looked at him with accusing eyes and grave looks, hunched over a desk covered with official-looking documents. Three inspectors from the State Racing Commission, a few judges from Lakewood Downs, and Alistair Dalton. The Marine locked his chilling gaze on Marlboro with an expression that cut him to the core. Dalton thought he knew everything. *Almost* everything, that is. The question remained how much more Marlboro was willing to confess.

"Mr. Marlboro, the purpose of this inquiry is to determine the extent to which irregularities in the wagering procedures at Lakewood Downs Raceway reflect illegal activities," intoned a metallic voice issuing from an official who possessed the sort of cadaverous countenance that could only belong to a bureaucrat.

Reflect illegal activities. The accuser's words echoed in Marlboro's thoughts. *That's the last of my concerns.* Since Dalton's murderous threats in the locker room—*did these pompous asses know anything about that?* he wondered—Marlboro had leaked crucial information to racetrack functionaries and selected drivers on a regular basis. He parceled out tips sparingly so that his two betting groups would not suspect their activities were being monitored by watchful judges. Snare them tightly in a web of self-incrimination, Dalton had ordered; *let them hang themselves.* Marlboro knew that sooner or later Stewart and the others would catch on, but by that point it would be too late. In the meantime, Marlboro had to pretend he knew nothing. He parried anxious inquiries from men who trusted him with their livelihoods by shrugging and mumbling a disingenuous pledge to look into things.

"Our main concern," the official continued, "is to determine how many outside individuals are involved with trainers and drivers in efforts to fix races." A half-dozen pair of eyes bored on him.

"Outside individuals?" Marlboro repeated.

"Yes. Persons not officially connected with Lakewood Downs, but who monitored activities, shall we say, from a distance."

Marlboro remained mute, his reasoning caught in a moral vise grip between two alternatives. Confess everything, protect yourself, perhaps earn official lenience for your sins, but at the expense of incurring the hatred and contempt of your friends; or, protect the few they don't know about yet, and remain tainted, subject to additional punishment if the lying is discovered later. Or did they already know who else was involved, and they just wanted him to substantiate their facts? *Which is it?* His mind locked on that dilemma and froze.

"Mr. Marlboro?"

"I'm not sure I understand . . ." he murmured.

"The mastermind, you idiot!" Dalton shouted. "Who else is involved? Who's in charge?"

"Mr. Dalton, please," one of the commission members cautioned.

"Oh, for crap's sake, he knows what we're talking about!" Dalton sneered. "Come on, Johnny. No sense holding back now."

Group sentiments obviously clustered around Dalton's view: why hold back now?

A multitude of faces cascaded through his mind: drivers, trainers, owners, people he knew and trusted, and who had trusted him. Courtney, Lawrence, many others.

"Need I remind you that this commission will view with great favor any additional cooperation you provide on matters pertaining to this investigation," came a reminder.

Cooperation.

Marlboro evaluated the expressions arrayed before him. Expectant, eager, *hungry* for his words. He took a deep breath, which everyone understood as a signal that he had resolved some inner struggle. They were right. Johnny Marlboro had finally decided what he was going to say.

Now all he had to do was to open his mouth and say it.

———

A dark evening . . .

Gentle ocean breezes brushed across Stewart's face, soothing his weary countenance with their soft, moist caress. He fixed his gaze on the seamless black horizon where the Atlantic's murky waters gripped the sky so tightly that he had to lift his eyes to spy distant stars rising from the clinging darkness of the ocean's surface. *Those stars . . .* So far away, so constant, so indifferent to anyone's concerns. He wanted to leap up and join them, escape the turmoil of his life. A view from the heavens is what Stewart yearned for. Certainly his answers could not be found on this earth.

He had reached this conclusion after driving across Long Island, unconsciously retracing the route he and Lori had taken several weeks earlier, until finally he stopped by the coast near one of the Hamptons. He parked his car off the road as close to the water as he could get. Stewart recognized the site; he and Lori had made love on this very beach. Memories of ecstasy flickered through his thoughts—fires of passion coursing through their bodies beneath midnight stars against sounds of surging waves crashing on the shore. That time seemed an eternity ago. A flood of fears washed it away. He sauntered toward the beach, collapsed on the sand, and let the distant sepulchral darkness swallow his tired gaze.

Stewart mentally tiptoed through the minefield of disasters that had stricken him over the past several weeks: Engels's threats, Lori's dismissal, Morris Courtney's devastating revelations—all rising like cragged peaks from the wreckage of a perfect operation smashed to rubble. And he had not a clue what to do next.

Stewart's thoughts recoiled from each catastrophe, then returned, only to leap backward again, like fingers testing a hot oven and getting burned. Engels planned to kill him, this much was certain. Lori too, probably. Unless he could figure out a way to pay him off in the near future, which seemed impossible. It got worse. Courtney told him he had been called before an investigatory panel and that Johnny Marlboro was the source of the leak that had demolished their race-fixing business, their means to acquire a huge fortune in a short period of time. Now shot to pieces. *Can't believe it.*

Stewart fingered through the moist sand, groped for seashells, liberated several from a watery pool formed by his digging, and cradled them in his palm. He manipulated the shells in his hand, listened to their porcelain tinkling against the background music offered by gently lapping waves. Felt good. His eyes rested on a fluff of salty foam, chased by reaching waves, then sliding back toward the ocean across the slick sand. Wide tongues of water scurried after the elusive fluff, but it always got away. Finally, a more determined wave with an overbite consumed the stubborn conspiracy of salt bubbles, but another one immediately formed again, in mocking defiance to the persistent waters. The foam always won. The more furious the waves, the more numerous the splotches of fluff.

Stewart again jingled his seashells, thoughtfully regarding the minuet of salt foam and ocean waves that played before his eyes across the glassy sand. Elements of a plan coalesced in his thoughts, formed a pattern, offered a solution. *That's how I should be*, he concluded. *Like that elusive patch of foam, a phantom chased by adversaries, but always coming back and never getting caught.*

Stewart turned his back to the sea, allowing his eyes to linger for a parting glance across the shore. One last thought scurried through his mind, capping a welter of conclusions he had reached from his meditations on the lonely beach. *Only this time, I'll work alone.*

He stuffed his seashells into a pocket and walked back toward the parking lot. He tossed a final look at that tar-like expanse that welded ocean to midnight sky, then turned, climbed into his car, and drove off.

PART THREE: THE CHASE

Chapter Nineteen

September, 1967

Reflections from dazzling autumn colors glided across the windshield of Stewart Lawrence's company car, as he sped across Long Island Parkway toward New York City. Usually he relished such scenery, but the two tasks he had set for himself dominated his thoughts. The first involved delivering the package that sat in the passenger seat beside him. A necessary job, and relatively easy. The second task made his blood run cold. It was equally important—more so, in fact—and dangerous. Of course, anything remotely connected to King Kong, his morbid sidekick, and their sinister boss could be considered dangerous.

At least he didn't have to worry about being pursued by authorities poking into his former race-fixing business at Lakewood Downs. Fortunately, racetrack officials had kept news about illegal activities out of the press as well, undoubtedly to preserve public confidence in the sport. More important, Morris Courtney assured him that he hadn't implicated Stewart in any way, in spite of repeated questioning by officials from the New York State Racing Commission. Stewart poured out his thanks, which Courtney accepted with a shrug, explaining that he saw no sense in satisfying the Marine's appetite for revenge.

Johnny Marlboro was a different matter. Courtney heaped scorn on his former collaborator and commented bitterly how he wished that Dalton had killed him when he had the chance in the locker room. One good development did emerge from Marlboro's treachery, however. Apparently drenched in remorse, he also refused to do anything that would assist the Commission's investigation into their activities at Lakewood Downs. His guilt complex worked in Stewart's favor; Courtney emphasized that Marlboro needed no additional incentive to remain quiet. Neither did Courtney, but the trainer needed another kind of help, and that Stewart intended to provide when he completed his first task.

He turned his car into a tree-lined avenue that snaked through the campus where Morris Courtney's son attended college. Stewart pulled out a piece of paper, glanced at an address, and peered through the window searching for the right dormitory. Three- and four-story buildings rose from a lavish carpet of well-tended lawn outlined by wide walkways, which flowed around majestic maple trees bursting with a kaleidoscope of fall colors. A gorgeous campus, he mused, allowing himself perhaps the only pleasant thought he had experienced for the past several weeks. Another check on the address: Timberlane Hall, it read. Stewart found a parking place, grabbed his package, climbed out of his car, and headed toward the building. He looked at his watch. Most students were eating dinner, but he had made arrangements with Craig Courtney to meet him in the lobby of his dormitory around this time. Not as private an encounter as Stewart desired, but it would have to do. Stewart wondered how much of Morris's travails had been confided to his son. Perhaps he would find out.

Stewart entered the building and looked around. To his right, a lobby; to his left, a door leading to stairs; straight ahead of him, a counter attended by a student whose complexion matched the seasonal array outside. He looked up from a book and gave Stewart a grin.

"Can I help you, mister?"

"Yes, I'm looking for Craig Courtney." Stewart glanced at the empty lobby. "I believe he is expecting me."

"Oh, yeah. Craig said you'd be coming. You can go up to his room, 203B. The stairs are over there."

Stewart thanked him, headed up the stairs, and walked toward Craig Courtney's room. Grateful for an empty hallway, Stewart stopped before 203B and knocked. A few seconds later, the door opened, displaying a young man who looked like a replica of Morris Courtney, only younger. No need to confirm identification here, Stewart thought with amusement. Brown hair sprouted below a New York Giants baseball cap, which topped a figure resembling how Jiminy Cricket undoubtedly would appear if he had been a college student. A glance beyond the young man revealed a room that brought to Stewart's mind the sort of wreckage expected from a drunken brawl involving harness racing drivers in full regalia. The word "mess" failed to capture the extravagance of the disorder.

"You're Craig Courtney?" Stewart asked, just to be polite.

"Yeah. You're a friend of my Dad's, right?"

Stewart nodded and handed him the package. Courtney took it and gave him an inquisitive look.

"What's in the shoe box?"

"Something for your Dad. I'd greatly appreciate your giving it to him. Be sure to guard it carefully. Please don't open it. It's personal."

Craig nodded somberly, as if he understood the gravity of Stewart's purpose. "Dad's in some sort of trouble, I guess," he said. "Can you tell me anything about it?"

"I'm afraid I can't, Craig," Stewart said. "But you can help by giving him that package the next time you see him. Unfortunately, I'm not in a position to do that." *Mostly because I can't take the chance of being seen with him,* he thought.

Craig acknowledged with a nod, and Stewart patted him on the shoulder. "Thanks a lot. You, um, have a good semester, now," Stewart added, a bit awkwardly. Then he turned and left young Courtney standing there, wondering what this college sophomore would think if he knew he had just been handed twenty-five thousand dollars cash. Inside the package, Stewart had also placed a note, reading: *Morris: for your legal expenses. You're a real friend. Very best wishes.* Period. No signature: too risky. Stewart had no doubt that Craig would deliver the package to his father unopened. He would keep his word, not violate Stewart's confidence. Like father, Stewart reasoned, like son.

Now on to the second task. The tough one. But before he could accomplish that, Stewart had something else he had to do of vital importance.

Romulus Ignatius Arnoldi lifted his gaze from the stack of cash splayed on the table before him and aimed his hawk-like nose toward the two men seated on the sofa. Both fidgeted like errant schoolboys called into the boy's vice-principal's office for smoking in the rest room. Arnoldi let his eyes roam around their surroundings, then shook his head.

"I'll give you credit for one thing, Engels," he snorted.

"What's that, Mr. Arnoldi?"

"Your taste in motel rooms is wretched, but at least you're saving money."

Engels's expression indicated he wasn't sure if he had received a compliment or not. "Thank you," was all he could manage to say.

"Where's the rest of what Lawrence owes me?" Arnoldi asked sharply. "I gave him twenty grand seed money for his operations at the track, and all I see here is ten. He owes me double that amount in return. Is there some problem I should know about?"

"Actually, Mr. Arnoldi, Lawrence hasn't been at the track too much recently, and I haven't seen him with those guys he usually hangs around with. Not at the diner, either."

"Then how does he expect to pay me back?" he asked in a condescending tone. "With office furniture?"

"He told us he intended to borrow the money," Bernie cut in.

"Borrow it?" Arnoldi exclaimed. "Who's he going to borrow it from? Another bookie? That doesn't make sense."

"We're just telling you what he told us," Engels offered.

Arnoldi folded his arms, looked out the window, considering this information. "Lawrence belongs to me and *only* me. If he's working out some sort of deal with someone else, I want to know about it. Is that clear?" Both men nodded their assent. "And I want you to find out why he's not at that track working his system. Working *our* system."

"You want us to shake him down?" Bernie inquired.

Arnoldi stroked his chin, pensively. "No, not yet. Just keep an eye on him and keep me informed." Engels and Bernie looked disappointed, drawing a further comment from their boss. "Mostly I want to make sure he's not dealing from the bottom of the deck. Let me know what you find out about that first, then I'll decide what to do."

"Whatever you say," Engels replied, disgruntled.

"That's what I say!" Arnoldi fired back. "I've got to go back to upstate New York. I'll see you again in a couple of weeks." Then Arnoldi got up, left the motel room, climbed into his Cadillac, and drove away.

He lamented not keeping tighter control over Lawrence, whose skills he appreciated, in spite of his penchant for running up huge debts. In fact, Lawrence had paid Arnoldi the full amount he originally owed him, but when the bookie caught wind of a betting arrangement he had set up with a number of drivers at Lakewood Downs, Arnoldi decided to take advantage. Using Engels and Bernie to enforce his demands and having Lawrence's girlfriend available as a potential hostage, Arnoldi felt sure he could milk this system for huge profits before letting Lawrence go. Until recently, his captive bettor had obeyed orders, which is why news of his absence from the track bothered Arnoldi. He wondered if his race-fixing scheme had somehow collapsed, which would explain why Lawrence hadn't been at the track recently. If that were the case, Lakewood Downs was being very quiet about it.

Arnoldi pondered the meaning of Lawrence's cryptic answer about borrowing money to pay him back. Had Engels and Bernie gotten their facts right? Both had been reliable men, but neither possessed sufficient mental acuity to discern anything beyond the obvious. Lawrence's talents remained very important to Arnoldi; he wanted to make sure he remained their sole proprietor. The question about what Lawrence had in mind gnawed on the edges of his thoughts.

Arnoldi would soon find out.

Midnight. Crisp breezes howled through the parking lot and whipped across Stewart's face like a splash of cold water. Icy fingers from the damp fall evening penetrated his clothing, sending shivers through his body as he got out of his car. Stewart pulled up his collar, rubbed his hands together, and looked around the area. Evening darkness shrouded the mostly full parking lot, punctuated here and there by the hazy glow of street lamps and light spilling from windows in the apartment complex looming beyond. He stuffed his hands into his pockets and trotted toward the building.

He stood before a side entrance, pulled out his key, and applied it to the lock. It opened perfectly. Then up two flights of stairs, a short walk down a hallway, another door. The master key slipped effortlessly into its lock, the door opened. Total darkness. No matter, Stewart knew his way around. First, to the bedroom. Several quick strides brought him to a chest of drawers located inside a closet and covered with clothes. He slid the bottom drawer open. Stewart pulled out a flashlight, directed its beam to the drawer's contents. Papers, certificates of achievement, assorted memorabilia greeted his scrutiny. A mahogany box occupied a corner. *That's what I want.*

Stewart opened the container and aimed a beam of light on a chrome-covered pistol called the Colt Ace. Built on a forty-five caliber frame, the weapon fired twenty-two caliber long rifle ammunition and looked exactly like its military counterpart, except for its distinctive covering. He picked the weapon up, tested its weight. The Colt's agreeable contours melted into his hand, felt good. Into his pocket it went.

Now for the other items. Out of the bedroom, across the living room, toward the closet. Stewart opened the door, glided his flashlight beam across a row of coats, suits, and jackets. *There it is.* Stewart pulled out a brown London Fog raincoat and tucked the heavy garment under his arm. What else . . . Examine the top shelf . . . *Hats!* Two brown fedoras. No good, too bulky, hard to conceal or carry. A baseball cap. *Perfect!* Stewart grabbed the cap, stuffed it into his other pocket. Still need more though . . . *But what?* Glasses. Dark sunglasses, of course. He knew where to find those, as well; in fact, snatching a pair now would save him a trip to the store. Across the room, into the kitchen, open a drawer . . . Got them! Into the pocket with the hat they went. Stewart probed the rest of the kitchen drawer's contents with his flashlight. *What's this?* Looks like bandages. Big, wide bandages. A devilishly clever idea tweaked his imagination. *Why not?* he thought. He grabbed the whole package and jammed it into the pocket laden with the Colt Ace.

Now Stewart Lawrence had everything he needed for the next crucial mission he had set for himself.

Melissa Barkley smiled pleasantly at the elderly woman standing across the counter from her at the Main Street Branch of County First Federal Bank, Nassau County, in Deer Park. She had been a teller for eight years and enjoyed most aspects of her job, especially chatting amiably with folks she knew in the community. This relieved the tedium of paperwork, gave her fingers a rest from their ritualistic dances across the keypad, and provided her a way to offer smiles to occasionally grumpy customers. In fact, she viewed the adverse dispositions that marched up to her counter every day as a challenge. Crack the gruff veneer of an impatient businessman, soothe anxieties of delinquent bill payers, answer simple questions posed by innocent souls unable to balance their checkbooks—all these tasks inspired her to begin each day on a positive note. To her knowledge, she was the only teller who approached the job in this way. That, too, made her feel special.

"There you go, Mrs. Ewing," she said, after cashing a Social Security check. "Glad to hear your arthritis is getting better. Give my best to your grandchildren."

The elderly woman's smile animated a road map of facial wrinkles, as she extended her hand and gave Melissa's fingers a squeeze, thanking her profusely. Then the woman collected her money, turned around in carefully calibrated steps, and walked out of the building. No one behind her, Barkley observed; lobby looked empty. Slow day today, she was the only teller on duty. She directed her attention to the cash register on her right, dipped a forefinger into a small jar of *StickyFinger Deluxe* supplied by a company called Office Products Unlimited, and started sorting through cash.

Someone stepped up to the counter, seemed to materialize out of nowhere. Barkley arranged stacks of twenties and fifties into order. "Yes, sir, how are you today? May I help . . ." She looked up and faced the muzzle of a chrome-plated forty-five caliber pistol, pointed at her chest.

"Yes, I believe that you can," uttered the response in a measured tone. A man stood before her, dark sunglasses wrapped across his round face, a baseball cap squatted tightly over his head, squeezing the top half of his ears, large bandages covered his cheeks. A brown London Fog raincoat draped over the stocky figure, collar turned up, concealing most of the lower part of his head.

Terror streaked through Melissa Barkley as she viewed this apparition. She began to shake.

"Scoop up all the cash in your cash register and hand it over to me, please. I assure you no one will get hurt if you do this quickly," he ordered, again in a soft but firm voice.

Barkley applied her trembling hands to the stack of twenties and fifties she had just assembled and placed them on the counter. The man rapidly stuffed them into his pockets.

"To the other cash drawer, please. Do it fast!"

Barkley complied instantly, turning over several stacks of fifties, twenties, and a single bundle of one hundred dollar bills. They vanished into the robber's bulging pockets.

"You have been most cooperative. Thank you," he muttered, then swiveled around and swept out of the bank.

Melissa Barkley watched him leave, as she stood behind a teller's booth, trembling uncontrollably. Ten seconds passed; perhaps twenty. She swooned. Lingering strands of consciousness that had kept her functional long enough to obey the robber's commands finally snapped. She crumpled to the floor, an image of the gun pointed at her heart succumbing to the refuge of total darkness.

Chapter Twenty

November, 1967

Arnoldi wet his fingers, thumbed through a crisp stack of fifty dollar bills, and shook his head in disgust. "Still ain't enough," he groused. He glared at Engels and Bernie. "Four-figure amounts don't do it, gentlemen. He owes me more than that. A lot more."

Engels shrugged, by this point accustomed to his boss's dismissal of Lawrence's weekly offerings. "This is the fourth shoe box he's given us. Maybe he's keeping some of it for himself," he suggested.

"That's what I think, too," Bernie added. "He's holding back as long as he can, keeping most of what he gets for himself. I think he figures that if he makes regular low payments, he can keep you satisfied long enough for him to collect enough money for himself to get his girl and skip town again. He's just throwing us a bone now and then to keep us off his back."

Arnoldi's anger flared, he started to say something, then settled down, considering their words. The possibility that either of those two could come up with such a logical explanation astonished him. Worse, they might be right, in which case Stewart Lawrence was making him a fool. "What did you find out about his racetrack operations?" he asked.

"He still goes to the races now and then, sometimes with his boss. I still don't know what happened to those other guys," Bernie said.

"You want we should bring him in for questioning?" Engels ventured, as though pleased for uttering what sounded like a phrase borrowed from the police.

"No, I want you to invite him over for tea and crumpets," Arnoldi snarled. "Yes! By all means, order him to come here. I want to talk to him!"

Gleams of satisfaction greeted this command. "We'll get him here right away," Engels promised, sharing a feral look with his partner. "You can count on it."

Stewart Lawrence squealed his white Ford station wagon around a corner, cut off a lumbering Buick sedan bursting with a troop of second graders, nodded an apology toward its outraged driver, and sped toward a road leading to Deer Park. It was the third or fourth turn he had narrowly missed; his mental cruise control worked only on highways, but today he stretched his luck beyond tolerable limits. Arnoldi demanded to see him again; Lori told him she had something important to discuss this evening; and Ted Simon expected him to complete the last part of a training course he had set up for Stewart's professional development. Plus, Stewart had his own plans, which called for doing things he hoped would make his obligations with Arnoldi and Simon irrelevant.

Stewart turned another corner, grasped the map from the passenger seat, propped it next to the steering wheel, and flitted looks at it while keeping an eye on the traffic. He jerked his head around to catch a road sign. Railroad Avenue. *That's right.* Deer Park, County First Federal of Nassau County. Needs some rubber stamps for a mass mailing. Immediately. *I'll deliver those, dash back to the office to see Ted, meet Arnoldi, then Lori at our special place.* Stewart's guts twisted in protest. He wondered if he would even be *alive* to keep his date with Lori after confronting Arnoldi and his hired goons. *Get the priorities straight,* he instructed himself. *First see Lori, THEN Arnoldi, and tell Ted I can't make it.* The thought also occurred to him that he might never see Arnoldi, Simon, or anyone else again, depending on the momentous revelation Lori had in mind. Anguish radiated from every possibility Stewart considered. He might end up killing himself, save King Kong the pleasure.

Grim satisfaction hung on that thought. What did Lori have to tell him? A confession, she had noted cryptically, something affecting their lives, their future, forever. Stewart reached across his passenger seat and scooped up a blueberry tart he had been nibbling on all day. *KK, Arnoldi, Simon, Lori . . .* Premonitions of disaster hovered over his thoughts like vultures circling an animal in its death throes.

Stewart pulled his station wagon into a parking place across the street from County First Federal Bank. Another few nibbles of his blueberry tart, then he reached behind him and hoisted a package over the seat. He climbed out of his car and tromped toward the bank, eager to deliver his package and be on his way. He swung through the building's double doors and scanned the cavernous room. A partition divided the floor area in half, separating the vault and a half-dozen desks from the main lobby and the tellers. A few desultory figures littered the lobby; each desk behind the partition hosted a customer and a bank official with serious looks on their faces, looking at documents.

All the tellers were available, heads down, flipping through papers, slips, currency. Stewart stepped up to one of them and plopped his package on the counter. He fumbled through his pockets and pulled out a receipt ready to sign.

"Perhaps you could help me," he said, pushing a pasty smile across his lips. "I have a package here. Rubber stamps . . ."

The person behind the counter, an attractive woman Stewart guessed in her late twenties, looked up pleasantly, settled her brown eyes on his face, and stopped breathing. She looked at him in horror, raised a quivering finger, then shrieked. Her piercing scream cut through the room's comfortable murmur like a scythe. Silence. Stewart gaped at her, then looked around.

All eyes in the room focused on him and the teller. Her eyes rolled back into her head. The teller's body seemed to transform to liquid as she collapsed before him, sweeping a limp arm across the counter and spraying the floor with a confetti of checks, receipts, and deposit slips.

Stewart stared at her for a few seconds. Then he grasped his package, bolted toward the doors, plowed through a bevy of figures entering the bank, and raced down the street toward his station wagon. He scampered through crossing traffic like a running back hurtling through tacklers. A Ford Mustang screeched to a halt to avoid him, its driver flinging an epithet that he ignored. Stewart feverishly attacked an uncooperative clump of keys with his thick fingers, isolated the right one, plunged it into the keyhole, and unlocked the passenger side of his station wagon. He threw his package inside, accidentally brushed his hand across the seat and swept a half-eaten blueberry tart on the pavement. Then he scurried to the other side, opened the driver door, and leaped inside. Key into the ignition . . . Engine turned over . . . Into gear . . . Check the traffic . . . Turn the wheel . . . *GO!*

Stewart squealed his station wagon onto Railroad Avenue, nicking the left rear fender of a shiny new Dodge parked in front of him. He floored the accelerator, spiking his company car through traffic, down Main Street. He turned a corner . . . another corner . . . then rocketed toward the highway, east, as fast as he could drive.

He did not see the outraged owner of that shiny new Dodge focus his twenty-twenty vision on the back of the car that had marred his proud possession, carefully taking down each digit of the white station wagon's license number.

Knock! Knock! Knock!

Ted Simon looked up from a desk strewn with documents sprayed with a multitude of sales figures, company reports, accounts receivable, and regiments of other data to cast a sharp glance toward the door. He checked his watch and shook his head. *About time he got here,* he murmured under his breath. *A great salesman, conscientious, punctual, and all that, about everything except these sales meetings.*

"Come in, Stewart," Simon called, burying his nose into his figures. No response. He glanced at the door again, puzzled.

"I said, come in!"

Still no reaction. *Strange.*

"Mr. Simon?" murmured a voice from behind the door.

Definitely not Stewart. Simon got up from his desk, stepped toward the door, and opened it. Two men stood before him, dressed in gray suits. Grim expressions clamped on their faces.

One of them, a taller man possessing chiseled features and piercing blue eyes, nodded curtly, flashed him a police badge, and cleared his throat in that official manner that announced something important was about to be said.

"Mr. Simon, my name is Lieutenant Lyon Belcamp of the Suffolk County Police, and this is Sergeant Harold Minck. May we have a word with you, please?"

"Um . . . certainly!" Simon replied. "Please, have a seat." He gestured toward several chairs that had been intended for his sales staff, and the two police officers sat down. Simon returned to his desk.

"Well, gentlemen, I can't imagine your gracing my office to investigate a few renegade parking tickets, so it must have to do with my recent release from that Turkish prison. Remember, I was acquitted of all charges." He flung a sheepish grin in their direction, which shattered to pieces against the officers' stone demeanors.

An awkward cough, another try. "Don't tell me Office Products Unlimited is late in one of our deliveries. If that's the case, I'll fire the salesman who's responsible, immediately." Simon's company had many accounts with local police departments, including Suffolk County. He was half-serious in offering that comment.

Lieutenant Belcamp lifted a corner of his mouth, out of sympathy, it seemed, and shook his head. "No, Mr. Simon, this isn't about parking tickets or your release from a Turkish prison, although my partner here"—he nodded toward his companion—"may want to ask you about that later." A broad smile lit up the Sergeant's ruddy complexion, which had a calming effect on Simon's anxieties. "However, we do want to ask you about one of your salesmen."

"One of . . . *my* salesmen?"

"Please understand this is just a routine inquiry," Belcamp emphasized. "In fact, it may be a wild-goose chase. We've had a *number* of those but we have to follow every lead. Tell me, does your company own a white Ford station wagon?"

"Yes, we do, several, in fact. We lease them. What's this all about?"

"Would any of your salesmen have occasion to be in Deer Park this afternoon," Belcamp asked, ignoring the question.

Simon rubbed his chin thoughtfully. "As a matter of fact, yes. One of them had to deliver some rubber stamps to a bank. Again, I would appreciate your telling me what this is all about."

"My apologies," Belcamp offered. "We're investigating a bank robbery. Several, in fact. At least four, to be exact."

"Bank robberies!"

Belcamp nodded. "We have reason to believe that one of them was carried out by a person driving a white Ford station wagon." He reached into his suit pocket and retrieved a notebook. "Would you mind giving us a rundown on your employees?" he said, flipping through a few pages.

Simon parted his lips to respond, when Sergeant Minck's transformed expression caught his eye.

"Never mind that," the officer said, hoisting his barrel-chested figure from the chair. Recognition flooded his face, as he stepped around Belcamp, eyes riveted on something over Simon's head, behind his desk.

He walked behind Simon's chair, turned his back to the two men, stood motionless, and stared at the wall. "We've found our man," he announced.

"What?" Simon said.

The Sergeant pointed to a picture and turned to face Simon and Belcamp. Confidence surged through his gravelly voice. "There he is!" he boomed. *"The Blueberry Tart!"*

Arnoldi glowered at his two henchmen, then jerked his wrist over and checked his watch. "Well, where is he?" he demanded.

"He's *supposed* to be here, Mr. Arnoldi," Engels said, obviously smoldering in anger. "I told him it was *really* important. He's always showed up in the past. I figured he'd be here."

"Obviously you didn't stress that point sufficiently," Arnoldi snapped. "I wait for no one. Do you understand that?"

"He told me he would get here right after his sales meeting. Maybe it ran overtime or something."

Arnoldi snorted. *"Maybe,* he decided not to arrive at all because you failed to stress the importance of our meeting." He got up, headed toward the door. "I'll be back at exactly nine o'clock. I expect you to be here, with Stewart Lawrence. Do you understand?"

Engels nodded vigorously. "We'll go out and get him, I promise."

His companion pulled out a long blade, and ran his finger across its razor edge. "Or," Bernie said, a sinister grin flashing a row of shark-like teeth, "we'll make *him* come to *US.*"

———

Ted Simon drummed his fingers on a stack of documents and studied his two interrogators. "Let me get this straight," he said. "You say a guy who looks like my salesman and drives a white Ford Station wagon held up County First Federal Bank about three months ago, using a chrome-plated forty-five automatic pistol. Right?"

Both police officers nodded.

"And that he disguised himself by wearing sunglasses, bandages on his cheeks, a baseball cap pulled over his ears, and a London Fog raincoat over the rest of him. Is that so?"

More nods, each with a whiff of irritation.

"Furthermore," Simon continued, thrusting out his forefinger, "he delivered a package to a *different* branch of that bank to a person who positively identified him as the one who waved a pistol in her face during that earlier robbery. And in his haste to leave, he dropped a receipt and a half-eaten blueberry tart on the road."

Sergeant Minck pried his gaze from Stewart Lawrence's picture and leaned forward. "Something we should add here," he noted.

"About the incriminating tart?" Simon quipped.

"No, about that lady who identified him. She's been a mental case since the robbery, which is why the bank transferred her to its Railroad Avenue branch, to settle her nerves, get her away from that bad memory. She's called in a half-dozen sightings, all of which we investigated and which turned out negative. But when she saw your salesman, she really went ballistic. And the rest of the facts fit together pretty well. *Too* well, for this to be, say, circumstantial."

Simon picked up a pencil, tapped it on his desk, incredulous. "I still can't believe it, gentlemen. I mean, I *know* Stewart Lawrence. He once stayed with me for a couple months when he first worked for our company, and we've been friends ever since. He's one of our best salesmen, a rising star in our company. I've been training him for a regional sales manager post, for crying out loud! He's a businessman, definitely not a bank robber type."

"And what type would that be, Mr. Simon?" Belcamp inquired.

"Well, I don't know!" Simon retorted. He manipulated his pencil through his fingers like a miniature baton, in quick, nervous movements. A thought blossomed. His eyebrows arched, right hand sprang forward, pencil waved for emphasis. "That gun part," Simon ventured, shaking his head. "Stewart doesn't even *like* guns. In fact, he hates them."

"How do you know that?" Minck asked.

"Guns are my thing, not his. I once collected guns for target shooting. Sold off most of my collection years ago. All except a few pieces. In fact, I happen to own a gun like the one you described in that bank robbery."

Lieutenant Belcamp's stone demeanor quickened to full alert. Sergeant Minck's dark eyes burned with intensity. "You *do?*" he exclaimed.

Simon flinched, suddenly aware of what he said. "Yes," he said.

"And you said he stayed with you for a few months?" Belcamp pressed.

"About six weeks, actually," Simon clarified. "You see . . ."

The phone rang. Simon's hand jerked to the receiver, whipped it to his ear. "Barbara, I said hold my calls. I can't be interrupted. Just take messages, and . . . Say again?" He cupped his hand over the mouthpiece. *"It's Stewart,"* he whispered to the policemen. They both leaned forward.

"Stewart!" Simon exclaimed. "Listen, I got a call from the bank. They never got their rubber stamps, and I'm wondering . . . What's that?" Simon cut his eyes toward the policemen, whose eager expressions showed they were taking in his every word. "As a matter of fact, yes. Two officers are here with me right now. What's this all about, Stew? Yes . . . Traffic violations! Then why don't you come in and we'll get this straightened out right now . . . No! Wait . . . Your mother? Okay, but . . . Wait a minute . . . Stewart! Stewart!"

The line went dead. Simon placed the receiver down. "Traffic violations," he repeated softly. "Can't make it to the sales meeting. Also said his mother was sick, and he's going to Buffalo to help her. He'll call back later, tonight sometime. Or maybe tomorrow."

Skepticism claimed Sergeant Minck's features. "A sick *mother?* I don't buy it."

"Neither do I," Belcamp agreed. "The gun you own, the chrome-plated forty-five. Do you still possess this weapon?"

"Yes, I do," Simon answered. "At home, in my apartment."

"You have a permit, I assume,"

Simon nodded, expecting the question and relieved he was able to answer it without difficulty. "I was in the military police in the service, and after my discharge, I used it in state competitions. Stewart doesn't even know I have it."

"You're sure about that?"

Simon opened his mouth to answer, but Sergeant Minck cut him off with a wave of his hand. "There's only one way to find out," he asserted with authority.

Lori stood before a full-length mirror in her bedroom adjusting a blue, diaphanous scarf around her neck so that one of its loops spilled down her flawless skin and sneaked into her cleavage, a display sure to invite visual fondling of her ample bosom. Such fastidious arranging was hardly necessary, but Lori knew Stewart relished the attention she devoted to her attire, especially on clothes that flowed with the liquid movements of her exquisite figure. *If you've got it, flaunt it,* he always advised, a remark that made Lori feel special, desired.

Stewart's frantic phone call indicated that her evening dress was the last thing on his mind. He sounded panicky. *Meet me at Fenimore Cooper Inn!* he had sputtered. Lori's inquiries about the nature of the emergency only provoked Stewart's insistence to hurry, that he would explain when he saw her. Then the line went dead.

Lori still refused to dash out of her apartment without swishing, tugging, and stretching uncooperative articles of clothing into position, like an obsessive drill sergeant disciplining his parade dress uniform for a command inspection. Finally satisfied, she stood before a mirror and let her eyes roam over the results of physical preparations that had capstoned several hours of mental gymnastics over this long anticipated discussion with Stewart. *Perfect,* she concluded. *For what I have to tell him, I have to look perfect.* Lori knew Stewart would gape at her appearance, which would perhaps relieve his anxieties. Or, better, redirect them.

Lori had pondered the wisdom of confiding in Stewart and would have done so after she had gotten fired, if he hadn't been acting so strangely for the last few months. His puzzling behavior began after those two thugs burst into his apartment, threatened him over money he owed them, then left only after Stewart promised to pay them off. But why did he owe them money? Stewart never explained the reasons to her. Therefore, Lori decided not to confide in him either, in spite of the fact that he had been supporting her financially until she found another job. In the meantime, Lori had worked on his maddening clue and had come up with nothing, and clearly she needed his help. Maybe then he would explain himself. Maybe then the solution would sweep away problems for them both. She would find out tonight.

Lori picked up her purse, swept her arms down her skirt for a finishing touch, and stepped toward the door. She snapped her purse open, groped for her car keys, clutched them in her left hand, and opened the door.

Lori stopped cold. A barrel-chested man with wrestler's arms, a clean-shaven face, and a completely hairless head stood before her in the doorway, filling her vision. Stubby fingers on his right hand wrapped around an enormous knife. He tested its savage blade with his forefinger and glowered at her. A row of jagged teeth emerged from the dark crack formed by his colorless lips, slowly widening. Lori had seen him before. It was the man Stewart had once referred to as Bernie.

Chapter Twenty-One

Rexford Engels pounded his massive feet up the steps of Stewart Lawrence's apartment, his thoughts boiling in rage over Lawrence's defiant failure to show up as commanded. *I'd kill that little skunk if the boss didn't want him alive,* he groused. Engels wondered if he could somehow stage Lawrence's death, in self-defense, maybe. Not likely, he concluded, although after more thought than that possibility deserved. *Might as well grab him and haul him back to the boss.* Anxiety lurked beneath Engels's anger toward Lawrence. What if he and Bernie couldn't produce him by nine o'clock? Engels knew Arnoldi could hire other guys that made even him quiver.

Engels cocked his leg to ram against the door when he noticed it was open a crack. He stepped through the doorway and examined the apartment. Silence. No Stewart Lawrence, which didn't surprise him. *Probably skipped town again,* he concluded, a twinge of worry about Arnoldi's reaction holding his anger in check. He walked through the living room, peered into the kitchen, then stepped toward the bathroom and walked inside. He stood before the sink and spared a second to greet his enraged reflection in the mirror. He whipped the cabinet door open.

Engels took a minute to look at the cabinet's contents. *Something strange here . . .* Toothpaste, toothbrush, shaving cream, razor, a few combs, other overnight stuff—all still here. *If Lawrence left for good, why didn't he take these things?* Engels walked into the bedroom. Everything looked in place, no evidence of a hurried departure. Didn't make sense. To the closet, door opened. Full. What about the dresser? Engels whipped open every drawer, dumped contents on the bed, heaved items across the floor. Everything one would expect spilled out: underwear, socks, a stack of folded shirts, a few sweaters. *What's this?* A bunch of brochures fanned across the carpet, their shiny surfaces reflecting pale light glowing from the lamp next to the bed.

Engels sat on the bed and scooped up a handful of the glossy folded papers. He flipped through them, scrutinizing each one. All tourist stuff on Long Island attractions—parks, monuments, beaches, trails, restaurants, hotels . . . *Hold it.* Engels moved a brochure next to the light for a better look. Had some writing scrawled on it. A smile tugged at the corners of his mouth as he visually pawed the carefully scripted endearments, obviously written by a woman. *Lover-boy, you've shown me your hand,* he thought with satisfaction.

Engels stuffed the brochure inside his shirt, got up, kicked a few items across the floor for the pleasure of it, and stomped through Lawrence's apartment. Down the stairs, into the car, engine started, out the driveway. Engels checked his watch, made some quick calculations about driving distances, then set his eyes on the road, satisfied. *Bernie's got the bait, I've got the hook. All we have to do now is to snag him and reel him in.*

Which is not exactly how Bernie felt at this moment.

At least he didn't rape me, Lori thought, quivering in a straight-backed chair, hands clasped on her lap, body rigid. Her eyes locked on Bernie's fearsome outline as he hovered over her dining room table concentrating on a game of solitaire. He snorted in disgust over some adverse turn, muttered an obscenity, then reshuffled the deck and started over again. The snap of cards on the table's cold Formica top cracked the room's tense silence. Every minute or so, Bernie cut his eyes in her direction, flashing a glint of animal lust that froze her soul. *Not yet, at least,* Lori reminded herself.

Nausea welled up her chest, pushed against her throat, taunted her reflexes to gag, vomit. Lori straightened her neck, her back, clenched her teeth, garnered every ounce of strength in her body, and swallowed . . . *hard.* The flood of bile retreated, regrouped, then returned. Lori knew the next assault from her stomach would overwhelm her, and she'd throw up. *Crackers . . .* She glanced toward the kitchen.

In a nearly disastrous concession to the relentless nausea, Lori set her jaw and clamped down her turgid guts long enough to clear her throat. "I need to go to the kitchen," she said.

"What for?" Bernie snapped, not looking up.

"Saltine crackers . . . My stomach . . . *Please!*"

Bernie regarded her with cold eyes. "Don't think so," he said.

"I'll throw up," Lori threatened. "Just a few crackers to settle my stomach."

Mental calculations flickered in Bernie's dark eyes, as though he were pondering the risk of letting her out of his sight for a few seconds versus the prospect of enduring the stench of Lori's vomit. "Go ahead and make it snappy."

Lori got up, went into the kitchen under his watchful gaze, retrieved a box of saltine crackers from the cupboard, then returned and sat down. She attacked the wax paper enclosure with a ferocity that even startled her captor, who watched as she nibbled, then stuffed a half-dozen white crackers into her mouth.

Not in time. A wave of bile gushed up her throat, caught near the back of her tongue, jammed, squirted into her mouth. Lori's neck lurched forward, she bolted up and scampered to the bathroom.

"Wait a minute!" Bernie shouted.

Spasms pounding up her chest, Lori managed to lift the lid on the toilet just in time to release a torrent of undigested crackers and stomach acid that surged from her mouth and through her nose.

"Aw, *Ge-e-e-e-ez!*" she heard Bernie exclaim. Lori heard the door close behind him, as she sputtered and coughed into the toilet bowl.

Better, much better, Lori thought, still gasping but slowly regaining control over her trembling limbs. As she braced herself for a second round, an idea squeaked through layers of fear and whispered a tantalizing possibility to thoughts still reeling from the pounding inside her head. *Just might work, if he leaves me alone long enough.* Lori got up from the toilet, grabbed a towel, and wiped off her face. She went to the sink and turned the water on. A slow stream splattered into the bowl against the plug and gurgled down the drain, noisily. *Perfect.* She inched toward the door, opened it a crack, peeked out. Bernie's attention seemed consumed by his solitaire. *Just stay that way, don't move!* Lori silently pleaded. She closed the door, carefully eased the dead bolt into place, locked tight. In his haste to get away from her, Bernie hadn't noticed that, *thank God.* She stepped toward the bathroom window.

"What's going on in there!" bellowed his voice from the other room.

Lori raced back to the sink. She turned the water off, stuck her finger down her throat, and made loud retching sounds. She heard a muffled curse from the living room. Silence. Then, more cards slapping on the table . . . Back to the faucet. Water on again . . . Now, to the window . . . Open it, *slowly . . . carefully . . .* No noise. *God, not a sound, please!*

A minor peep escaped from the rising window, swallowed by sounds of water trickling down the drain. Lori rushed to the faucet. Water turned on, *louder* this time. Then off . . . On again . . . *Pretend I'm wash-*

ing up. Wait, see what he does . . . Any reaction? *Nothing.* Back to the window. Lift it up, carefully . . . All the way open . . . *There!*

Lori stepped onto the rim of the bathtub and hoisted her left leg through the opening. She crouched beneath the bottom pane, straddled the sill, wriggled herself through the tight aperture and on the roof, which sloped at a manageable angle from the dormer hosting the bathroom window. She thanked God that her negligent owner hadn't attached the storm windows yet, and that the punishing cold of previous weeks had abated, leaving a delightful Indian summer in its wake.

Now, how do I get down?

Lori sat on her haunches on the rough shingles and scrutinized possible escape routes from her perch on the Cape Cod house. Best way, toward the main entrance, on its roof, maneuver by the gutter, grasp the down spout, plunge into the bushes . . . *Without a sound.* Lori dragged her way toward the roof over the entrance hallway, moving her bottom supported by her arms, then both her feet alternately, like a crab. The shingles' sandpaper talons clawed at her skirt, bit into the heels of her hands.

Closer . . . Closer . . . Almost there . . .

Suddenly, her left foot twisted, and her ankle skidded across the grating surface. The roof's merciless exterior sheared off a layer of skin. Lori yelped in pain. She instinctively kicked out her leg like a switchblade, launching a shoe in a wide arc across the lawn, where it clattered on the sidewalk. Quickly tucking her bruised ankle beneath her buttocks, Lori darted a look toward the window. Still quiet. *At least my stomach isn't revolting,* she thought, gratefully.

She tested her ankle. Not bad, still worked, more like a minor cramp, nothing more serious. Make it to the entrance roof, it's lower, closer to the ground. She shuffled toward it again. A few more moves . . . *Right there, good!* Now, climb on the roof, no unnecessary thumping, scraping . . . *Made it!* The gutter . . . Turn around . . . Back down, grasp its lip . . . *Will it hold my weight?* It has to!

Sounds rumbled through the air, furious, threatening. Bathroom door shaking, savagely. No time to lose!

Lori positioned herself into the crotch where two roofs met, grappled the gutter near the down spout, eased her body where she could swing off the roof. A deep breath . . . *Now!* She let her weight collapse on the gutter, hung for a second or two. The agonized squeal of tearing metal pierced the air. The gutter ripped off, collapsed, swung down, crashed her against the house. Grip released . . . On the ground, behind a bush . . . *Thud!*

She landed squarely on her feet. Lori cowered behind the foliage, then looked up, toward the bathroom window. Raging curses erupted from the glowing aperture jutting out from the dormer, punctuated by ferocious clamor, shaking the bathroom door. *Any minute now, Bernie will crash through, spy the open window, chase after me . . .*

A single thought screamed through her mind: *escape!* Lori burst from her hiding place, scurried around the entrance, and dashed across her backyard. She darted between houses, raced into the street behind where she lived, and ran away as fast as her legs could propel her. Not once did she look back to see how close, or even whether, that loathsome man with the hideous blade was pursuing her.

A dark, depressing evening. Ted Simon shook his head in disbelief as he replayed the drama that had taken place in his apartment earlier that day. *Gone, all gone.* He couldn't believe it. His chrome-plated Colt Ace, a twenty-two caliber pistol made on a forty-five caliber frame, along with several boxes of ammunition and a spare clip—*missing*. Nor was that all.

"Do you own a blue baseball cap, a London Fog raincoat, and sunglasses," Minck had asked, a hard edge of suspicion cutting his words.

"As a matter of fact, I do," Simon had admitted.

"They're gone, too. Exactly the items used for disguise by the perpetrator."

"You said Lawrence had a key to your apartment for several weeks. Ever get it back?" Minck inquired.

Simon had to think. "No, I don't believe he ever returned it."

The two officers looked at Simon as though they both had quietly reclassified him in their mental rolodex of criminal types. "The FBI will be in contact with you," Belcamp had said. "Bank robbery is their primary jurisdiction." Then, as both readied to depart, Minck tossed one last comment over his shoulder. "Please be available for additional questioning," he had warned. They closed the door with authority, spiking an image in Simon's thoughts of metal bars on a door clanging shut against a chilling cubicle enclosed by unpainted concrete walls.

Far worse was the trauma that had shattered what remained of Simon's comfortable world filled with reassuring routines and confident expectations. *Everything the police have told you is true, Ted,* Stewart had confessed in a telephone call to him after the detectives left. *Except I robbed seven banks, not four.* Stewart then promised to call him back the following day at the phone booth in the parking lot around noon.

The line went dead. Simon then slumped in his chair and hadn't moved since. He could do nothing except wait for Stewart to call back, which at least gave him time to think of ways to persuade his friend to end this nightmare and turn himself in. Just wait for Stewart Lawrence, salesman, bank robber, fugitive.

And, of course, for the FBI.

"You mean, you let her get away!" Engels thundered, glaring at his shorter companion.

Bernie shrugged. "Come on, Rex. She was puking all over the place. Bathroom stunk. I didn't think she was in any condition to pull off a stunt like that."

Engels shook his head, stepped toward the front door of Lori's apartment, and examined the wreckage of her escape. A torn gutter hung by a metal strap and leaned against the down spout. A metallic scrape arced across the siding. Darkness shrouded the corner where Lori had fallen; a few broken branches signaled evidence of her dash to freedom.

Bernie stepped next to his partner. "My fault I lost her," he admitted. He jutted his chin upward, in a gesture of resolve. "I'll tell Arnoldi."

Engels merely smiled. "Don't matter."

"What?"

"I say, it don't make no difference. Although having her as insurance would have been nice."

Bernie looked puzzled. "Care to explain that?"

Engels reached into his pocket, pulled out a brochure, and unfolded it so they both could view its contents. "Know where this place is?"

Bernie scrutinized the pictures, the address. "Yeah, I do. About an hour from here. What about it?"

Engels turned the glossy paper over and pointed to some handwriting. "Read that," he instructed.

Bernie moved closer to the paper and let his eyes dart across the flowing words: *To my love, from your love, at our special place.* Bernie grinned. "She was leaving when I came here, you know. All fixed up."

"To go to *this place!*" Engels confirmed. "What do you say we join them, for tea, what?" he cackled, with an affectation rendered absurd by his thick voice and crude accent. They both walked toward the driveway. Engels stopped by his car door, unfolded the brochure, and looked at its glossy exterior. *We got you, lover-boy,* he mused with wicked delight. He stuffed the paper into his pocket, flitting one last glance at its title, graceful letters embellished in colonial script: *Fenimore Cooper Inn.*

It sputtered, coughed, and backfired with heart-stopping explosions, but at least it ran. Lori thanked God that her forties-era pickup truck managed the distance between her friend's apartment and Fenimore Cooper Inn, without expiring from internal hemorrhaging of bruised bearings, collapsed pistons, blown gaskets, and a multiplicity of engine belts finally surrendering in a shrieking protest of scorched rubber. She was even more grateful that her friend accepted her desperate request to borrow it without embarrassing questions or undue delay. But Lori was a half an hour late; Stewart had said to meet her at seven-thirty, or thereabouts. Had she missed him?

A multitude of anxieties besieged her thoughts. *If Bernie grabbed me, that other guy must be after Stewart. Did he find him? If so, Stewart won't show. Or, he's still free and waiting for me, inside.*

Lori pulled her truck by the side of the road, which was lined with other vehicles, the overflow from a crowded parking lot by the Inn. With hesitation, she turned off the engine, fearing she'd be unable to persuade this army surplus refugee to start up again. She visually scoured the murky panorama of parked cars along the side of the road. No white station wagon. *Might be in the parking lot.* Lori got out of the truck, swept off particles of roof clinging to her skirt, straightened her clothes, and tried to settle her nerves before entering the restaurant. Fortunately, she didn't smell as though she had been sick; her friend had seen to that—the *only* condition insisted on before the loan of the truck.

Lori walked toward the Inn, when she caught sight of something that made her stop. She peered into the parking lot, tried to focus. That car over there, buried in a flock of vehicles under the lights. Something familiar about it. She stepped closer, trying not to appear too conspicuous, and examined its outline. Dark-colored vehicle, utterly ordinary. *Why did it look familiar?* Uncertainty gnawed at her thoughts. *Now I'm imagining things*, she concluded, struggling to appease that part of her brain that flashed alarm. Back to the restaurant, hand to the door . . . *Stop!* An image popped into her mind, seized her attention. *Time . . . Place . . . Context . . .* Lori knew where she had seen that sedan. In the parking lot, outside Sweets Ahoy, a few months ago.

That was Bernie's car.

Lori backed away from the building, out of the light. Questions raced through her mind, demanding answers. How did he know she and Stewart were supposed to meet at the Inn? Bernie, maybe his friend as well, had to be inside, watching. Waiting to nab Stewart. Or her. *Maybe me first, as a way to get to Stewart.* That *had* to be part of their plan; that's why Bernie kept Lori captive in her apartment in the first place. *Run!*

Lori turned, galloped toward the truck, climbed inside, slammed the door shut, and sat there. She tried to make sense of the situation, until a few elements emerged from the tangle of facts. One of which astonished her: *they never even noticed me, even when I approached the entrance!* Lori felt like kissing the steering wheel of her jalopy, which Bernie obviously didn't expect, never looked for, and, therefore, didn't see. Another conclusion: they weren't looking for Stewart to *enter* the Inn; they intended to grab him *before* that point. They were looking for Stewart's white station wagon. Lori had to get to him first. *But how?*

She had one advantage: Stewart would be approaching from her side of the restaurant, so she would have a chance to spot him before they could. Apparently, they believed Stewart would drive through the parking lot first, where they intended to take him by surprise. She had to keep him from going that far.

Lori looked back and examined approaching traffic. No way could she stop Stewart before he drove past her, into the lot, into their hands. *He* had to see *her* first. *Get out of the car, show yourself.* Could Bernie see her from that angle as well? Lori opened the door, took two steps toward the road, and scrutinized his car's line of vision. *Just barely.* She had to back away, then make herself conspicuous to coming traffic, and pray Stewart would slow down and stop before going any farther.

A car passed. Then two more. Then a whole bunch. One slowed down . . . *Was that Stewart?* No. It swept by her, into the parking lot, trolling for a space. *Exactly what they want Stewart to do,* she thought with a chill. Another car, then several whizzed by. Two more slowed down. Part of a group, apparently. They filed into the lot. Eyes back on the road. *Come on, Stewart . . . Show up!*

Time passed slowly. Evening dampness crept into Lori's clothing, spiked by the whoosh of each passing car. Icy chills raced up her spine, as she wrapped her arms across her blouse. The traffic subsided, until a lone pair of headlights poked through the distant murkiness, slowed, and approached the Inn. Lori squinted, as though her determined gaze could pierce the impenetrable darkness and identify the oncoming vehicle. Was that him?

Yes!

Stewart pulled beside her, leaned across the seat, and lowered his passenger window.

"Lori, I'm sorry I'm late!" he cried. "Why are you standing . . ."

"Get out of here!" Lori rasped. "Turn around, drive away, they're waiting to grab you!"

Stewart looked stunned; then, recognition flooded his face. "How did you . . ."

"No time to explain! Get out of here!"

Rapid-fire calculations played across Stewart's features. "Okay. Meet me at our beach, tomorrow, nine o'clock in the morning," he instructed. "They'll never find us there!"

"Fine! Just leave! Go!"

Stewart reached for Lori's head, pulled her toward him, hungrily wrapped his lips around her mouth, released her, and cranked his window up. He darted his head back and forth to check traffic, then squealed his station wagon into a U-turn and vanished into the distance.

Lori climbed into her truck and switched the key in the ignition. Each groaning turn of the truck's engine felt like a fist grabbing her guts and twisting. Finally, the old mechanical war horse sputtered to life, and Lori spun it around in a U-turn, following Stewart's departure from Fenimore Cooper Inn. A single thought skipped through Lori's mind as she drove farther from the danger lurking at what used to be their special meeting place. *What beach is he talking about?*

Chapter Twenty-Two

If idiots were flowers, those two guys would be walking botanical gardens, Romulus Arnoldi grumbled as he guided his Cadillac down Montauk Highway on a morning tour of the Hamptons. Crisp air laced with ocean aromas streamed through an open window, swirled inside the car, and whipped across his face. Felt great, a bracing effect. He needed that, especially when he wanted to clear his mind, to sort out complicated situations. Bernie and Rex had waited practically all night for Lawrence to show up at that Inn; they gave up only after he instructed them to leave, return to their motel, and await his instructions. Engels had chortled with delight over his momentous "discovery" of Lawrence's special meeting place with his girl, convinced he had him completely figured out. Ditto with Bernie, who took pride in never failing an assignment. They both blew it, although Arnoldi had to admit their conjectures struck him as sound. But this lady of his, Lori, had more pluck than Bernie reckoned, and Lawrence's cleverness outclassed anything Engels could put on the table. *So, what to do now?* He decided to drive along Montauk Highway on the way to Fenimore Cooper Inn and ask a few questions himself.

Arnoldi drove slowly and impatient drivers soared past him, hurling petulant looks in his direction. That didn't bother him, but he hated to be squeezed between two vehicles, particularly when one of them was a freight train masquerading as a tractor-trailer combination charging toward him at the exact time he had to avoid another vehicle parked near the white line on his side of the road. He gripped the steering wheel, muttering curses at the idiot who planted himself on the shoulder close enough to be sideswiped by passing traffic. Sure, parking there put you near the beach, but still . . .

Who-o-o-o-sh!

Arnoldi slowed down and moved past the car just as the truck zoomed by him from the opposite direction, walloping his Cadillac with a gush of trailing wind. Arnoldi murmured another profanity and checked out the parked vehicle from his rearview mirror. Looked like a station wagon. White. A Ford, judging from the grill work. A white Ford station wagon . . . *Something significant about that.*

Arnoldi slowed down, pulled to the side of road, screeched into a U-turn, and raced back toward that car. He curled another U-turn, wheeled behind it, and climbed out of his car. He instantly spotted the cargo portion of the station wagon filled with boxes. He peered into its back window, scrutinized labels. *Office Products Unlimited* emblazoned several packages. Arnoldi stepped back, pondering his discovery. *This has to be Lawrence's car!* He circled the station wagon, searching for some evidence of malfunction. *Did he abandon it?*

He walked toward the front, placed his palm on the hood, sniffed near the grill. Warm metal. Fresh, hot fumes. No question about it, this thing had just been driven. Lawrence was in the area somewhere, probably near the beach. He examined the front seat. A lady's handbag lay on the passenger side. And his girlfriend, too. Seems they had more than one "special" meeting place.

Arnoldi walked back to his Cadillac, climbed in, turned the engine over, and backed up. Check traffic . . . Turn the wheel, hard . . . On the road . . . Now, drive, fast! Ahead of him, not more than a mile, stood a phone booth, next to a gas station. Call up Rex, Bernie, get them over here. *For what has to be done, I need THEM!* After that, return to Lawrence's station wagon, figure out how to disable it before he returns.

A satisfied smile crept across Arnoldi's lips. He knew how to do such things.

———

Agent Kenneth Benton of the New York City Federal Bureau of Investigation Office flipped through a few pages of a spiral notebook, glanced over his reading glasses, and aimed a slightly amused expression at the man seated across the desk. "Mr. Simon, you'll be happy to know that we have checked you out thoroughly and are pleased to inform you that you are not under suspicion for collusive behavior in this case."

"Thank you, Mr. Benton," Simon replied officiously. "I find that comforting."

"However, our preliminary findings do not preclude the possibility of further inquiries into suspected nonpayment of traffic tickets. Which is *not*, however, our jurisdiction." A mischievous grin lit up a face marked by pleasant features, easily animated smile lines, a broad forehead, and thick, dark hair. "I must say I find this Turkish prison affair intriguing, but again, out of our jurisdiction. Maybe the CIA will want to look into that, though."

Simon's laughter rippled through every part of his body and vented twenty-four hours of accumulated tension. "Word does get around, doesn't it," he exclaimed in mock relief, thankful he was dealing with at least one official who possessed a sense of humor. Obviously, the Suffolk County police had briefed these agents thoroughly.

"I wish we could convey better news about your salesman, though," added Agent Michael Green, on a more serious note. His deeply lined face managed a wan smile, then he looked at his yellow legal pad. "Everything we've learned about Stewart Lawrence indicates that he is the man we're seeking." Green's eyes darted across the paper before him, and he recited Lawrence's record with the crisp efficiency of an evening sportscaster. "We know that your man is a gambling fanatic, that he's been involved with horses. We know he won a seventy-two thousand dollar twin double at Roosevelt Raceway in Westbury, New York, last year. We know he hit several banks, between four and seven, based on the M.O.'s involved." He glanced up at Simon. "That expression means, of course . . ."

"Modus Operandi," Simon interjected, having become painfully more familiar with police jargon over the past day.

"Correct. The perpetrator in question wore a London Fog raincoat with the collar pulled up, green sunglasses, a baseball cap over his ears, and was armed with a chrome-plated forty-five automatic, probably a Colt. He also wore bandages on his cheeks as part of his disguise. At two locations he was identified as entering a white Ford station wagon. We believe he may have hit banks in New Jersey, New York, Long Island, and northeastern Pennsylvania. Hempstead, Deer Park, Stroudsburg, New Rochelle, and Rye, New York are also strong possibilities. He was courteous, swift, efficient, and netted ten to twenty thousand dollars per robbery."

Each accusation hit Simon with the force of a fist whammed to his belly. "It seems I had the honor of employing the politest bank robber in FBI history," he quipped in a humorless tone.

"That doesn't mean he's not dangerous," Benton cautioned. "We do not know his state of mind, and my experience has been that even nonviolent types can be murderous, if provoked. That is where we need your help."

"I'll do what I can," Simon offered. The tug of friendship yanked his thoughts in Stewart's direction at the same time that whispers of betrayal echoed through his mind. "He said he'd call me today around noon."

Both agents snapped to attention, eyes wide, alert. "Really?" Benton exclaimed. "Mind if we listen in. Could be helpful. *Very* helpful."

Did you really expect me to say no? Simon thought. "Let's hope that it is," he agreed.

"One other matter of information," Agent Green pointed out. "We've distributed his picture, hundreds of them, actually, to public avenues of departure from this area. Railroad terminals, bus stations, airports, ferries, and so forth. If he tries to leave by such routes, we should know very soon. Almost instantly, in fact."

"Do you want me to tell him that?" Simon inquired.

"No!" Benton stated firmly. "Say nothing. Just try to talk him in, if you can." He leaned back in his chair and folded his arms, looking confident. "If he tries to escape by public transportation, we'll nab him," he proclaimed. "No problem."

Simon acknowledged this statement with a polite nod. *Don't count on it,* he thought.

The ocean's surface cut a line across the horizon with the precision of a surgeon's scalpel, setting off a pale blue sky nipped by flickers of white from wings of distant sea gulls. Other gulls, nearby, hovered in place against swirling gusts, like kites thrashed by the wind, tugging against invisible strings attached to the ground. Cool breezes swept across Stewart Lawrence's face as he listened to their chirps pierce the rhythmic slapping of waves against the shore. He gazed at the sun's reflections dancing on the shimmering waters, then let his eyes drift across the shoreline. A few desultory figures walked along the beach, lonely souls who, like himself, preferred the ocean during autumn or spring instead of summer. He wondered how long he would be able to experience this glorious panorama of sun, wind, surf, and sound. Not long, he concluded grimly.

Lori stepped to his side and wrapped her arm around his waist. "I'm so sorry, Stewart," she lamented. "I had no idea."

"I'm just glad that you found me," Stewart replied in a consoling voice.

"Found you! I practically sideswiped your car on the way to this place." She trained her eyes on some distant point. "Good thing you made it obvious. Otherwise, I never would have figured out what beach you were talking about."

"We made love here once," Stewart commented wistfully. He turned and gestured toward a hollow sculpted out of a sand dune by wind and sea and surrounded by tall grass. "How could you forget that?"

"I didn't," Lori replied. "But you'll recall we anointed several beaches that way during our vacation."

Stewart silently conceded her point. *"Bearer bonds,"* he stated, as though in a trance. "With the delivery receipts still attached to them. No wonder Madison had a heart attack when he discovered they were missing. All the interest coupons were still affixed to each document as well, isn't that right?"

Lori nodded, as though accepting a rebuke from a parent. Stewart sighed deeply. "As good as cash!" he exclaimed. "The documents you took from his office are as good as cash. A half million dollars worth of cash. And you had no idea. *Incredible!*"

Lori inclined her head and looked at him sharply. "A sum that remains in *your* hands," she reminded.

Stewart avoided her gaze. "If you had only told me sooner . . ." he muttered. "I . . . no, *we* could have avoided more misery than you can imagine."

"The source of which," Lori persisted, "still remains a mystery to me. Do you have any idea what I've been through, Stewart? That monster with the knife trapping me in my own apartment, me tearing my guts out and nearly breaking a leg trying to get away . . . I was *terrified,* Stewart. And for what? You still haven't told me what this is all about!"

This time Stewart faced her indignation squarely. "No, I haven't," he admitted. "I will. Right now, in fact. But let's not fight." He gestured toward their private cove and picked up her hand. "Over there."

The two walked away from the water and nestled into the hollow that had served as one of their love-nests. Stewart held her hand while Lori looked at him intently. He groped for words. "It all started with horses . . ."

Lori's expression turned immobile. She stared at something past him, near the water. Fright seized her features. Stewart followed the direction of her gaze and immediately spied what had traumatized her. *Bernie.*

"Down, get down!" he whispered. "He can't see us if we duck down."

They both crouched behind the dune, peered through strands of grass, and studied his movements. Bernie shielded his eyes and scanned the area, jerking his head around like a nervous pigeon, obviously searching for them. Stewart cradled Lori's body, felt her quiver in his arms. *"How . . ."* she rasped. No other words came out.

Although stunned by Bernie's presence, Stewart felt a sense of rage overwhelm his fear. "Where did you park?" he asked.

"By the scenic lookout point, up the road," Lori said.

"In that old truck?"

Lori nodded.

Stewart studied the path behind them that snaked into the dune, shrouded by mounds of sand and tall grass, leading east, toward the scenic lookout point. "The others are probably waiting near the station wagon. They must have decided to go back to the Inn and spotted it on the highway along the way. We can get to that truck"—he gestured toward their avenue of escape—"without them seeing us. Let's go!"

The two crawled through the sand beneath a fold in the dune that concealed them from the beach, and dashed away. Fifteen minutes later found them collapsed behind a hill rising next to the parking lot overlooking the ocean, catching their breath. Recovered, Stewart peered around the hill and then yanked his head back, a spike of adrenaline surging through his chest.

A black Cadillac was parked next to Lori's truck, along with a few other vehicles. Window down, a man inside. Hooked nose, shadowy features, unmistakable profile. *Arnoldi.*

"What's wrong?" Lori asked.

Stewart didn't answer her. More hard thinking, plotting. Finally, he met her anxious gaze. "Tell me, Lori, have you ever met Arnoldi? Does he know what you look like?"

Lori shook her head. "No, I haven't, because I don't know who you're talking about."

"No, of course, you don't," Stewart confirmed. Images of Lori's picture on his wall with Bernie's knife slashed across her throat whipped through his thoughts. Did those two ever show that picture to Arnoldi? He didn't know. But there was only one way to find out. He peered over the rise again. A few people were sauntering along the walk toward the parking lot. Stewart turned to Lori. "Okay, this is what I want you to do . . ."

One minute later, Lori Armstrong emerged from their hiding place, wearing sunglasses that concealed most of her face. She stepped behind several people who were casually strolling on the walk in front of the parking lot. She sashayed past a row of cars, walking conspicuously in front of Romulus Arnoldi's Cadillac. Stewart watched her every movement, his heart thumping in his throat.

Arnoldi spotted her walk by—*who wouldn't?*—and followed her as she climbed into the truck. He continued to watch with interest, but didn't move. Lori started the truck, or tried to. Engine turned over . . . Slow, mournful cranking . . . *Come on,* you stupid thing . . . *start!* Stewart silently pleaded. Finally, the vehicle coughed to life, and Lori backed it out of the parking lot. Arnoldi returned his gaze toward the ocean, as Lori wheeled around and drove off.

It worked.

Stewart doubled back, raced along a meandering path in a gully beneath their protective sand dune, clambered over a rise that shielded the road from the ocean, and tumbled to the other side. He ran to the road, waited. Lori approached in her truck. The door yawned open, Stewart leaped inside, they raced away, free.

After a few minutes, Stewart's breathing returned to normal. He turned toward Lori. "I am going to settle this whole mess once and for all," he proclaimed, with steel in his words.

Lori's hands gripped the steering wheel, attention on the road. Her eyes flickered in his direction. "How?" she inquired.

Stewart pulled off a shoe and sprinkled sand on the floor of the truck. "I'll need your help."

"First tell me what it's all about, and I'll promise to help."

"I promise," Stewart resolved, "that we can make it get-even time for both of us."

Lori smiled. "I'm game."

A wave of affection, mixed with wicked delight, gushed through Stewart's thoughts. "Good! Then listen to me, darling. Here's my plan . . ."

The phone booth in the parking lot by Office Products Unlimited sprouted enough cables, earphones, and recording devices to make it appear as though it had dropped out of a science fiction movie set. Three men hovered over this apparatus, two with earphones attached, and the third glaring at the receiver like an expectant father. At one minute past noon, the phone rang. Simon eagerly grasped it, and a gaggle of machinery whirred to life.

"Yes, of course," Simon's words spurted out. "Two agents from the FBI, Stewart, and they're both listening in. What? Who? What are you talking about?"

Benton snapped his fingers, and Green quickly produced a pen and notebook. Scratchy sounds of Stewart's voice leaked from the receiver, as the three men listened intently, Green furiously jotting down information.

"Why didn't you tell me?" Simon muttered, but Benton waved him off. Green's hand skipped along his notepad. "Well . . . I don't know, Stewart . . ."—he glanced at Benton—". . . you'd have to ask them directly . . ." Benton vigorously nodded his assent. "I guess that's all right, then," Simon quickly added. "When? Okay . . . Where will *you* be?

Okay! Sorry I asked. Tonight, then. At my apartment . . ."

The line went dead and the machinery automatically tripped off. Simon placed the receiver on its cradle and looked to the FBI agents for their reactions. Benton appeared pensive, while Green studied his notes. Simon broke the silence. "Well, what do you think?"

"I think we can do that," Benton said. "We'd have to contact local law enforcement agencies, but it can be done."

"On what pretext?" Green inquired.

"I don't care," Benton said. "Make it anything. An article one, section eight offense."

"What the devil is that?" Green asked.

"That's the part of the Constitution where the powers of Congress are listed. Get them for interstate flatulation without a federal license, anything that works. We know what we have to do. Now find a legal excuse and do it!"

Agent Green gave him a puzzled look. He picked up the phone and dialed a number, wondering how to explain to the person on the other end that breaking wind in the privacy of one's car while crossing state lines constituted a federal offense.

"I told you he was one slippery bastard!" Engels stated earnestly. "His car was there, his broad was there, but somehow they got away. Mr. Arnoldi, he ain't an easy guy to catch."

Arnoldi shrugged. "None of this would have come about if you hadn't scared him off," he insisted. The phone rang. Arnoldi waved Engels off and picked it up.

"Yeah. *Who?*" A pause. "You're putting me on, lady . . ." He furiously motioned Bernie toward the receiver. Bernie tilted his head, listened for a few seconds, then mouthed the words, *that's her.* Arnoldi listened intently.

"Oh, you *do,* now. Right. Where? Yeah, that could be done, I suppose. Repeat that amount, please? Yeah, that would do it, all right. Which one? When?" He looked at his watch. "Sure, we can make that. Let me ask you this, lady. What's in it for you?" Engels and Bernie gaped at Arnoldi as he listened to an explanation. "Yeah, I can believe that. And you got my promise, too, don't worry. Yeah, bye."

He placed the phone on its cradle, a satisfied grin creeping across his lips. "Boys," he announced. "We just got an offer we can't refuse . . ."

Chapter Twenty-Three

"Let's review this one more time, please," Simon asked. "How did we leave it with him? He was supposed to call us . . ."

"And we were to convey, through you, that his instructions had been carried out to the letter," Agent Benton said.

"And will they?" Simon ventured.

"Yes!" Benton said, indignant. "He said you're the only one he trusts, so you must be the one to tell him. You do trust us, I assume."

"Of course!" Simon stated firmly. "I just hope all this can be pulled off without a hitch. Without anyone getting hurt."

"Once he receives the confirmation from you, Ted," Agent Green added, "he agreed to negotiate terms for his surrender. Which may take some time, but I'm confident we can pull it off. Believe me, this part we couldn't have arranged better if we had done it ourselves."

That's what bothers me, Simon mused, a vague uneasiness gnawing at the edges of his thoughts. Plus, Stewart was late. He showed up late for sales meetings on occasion, but always kept his other appointments to the minute. *Something's wrong, I can feel it in my guts.*

The phone rang and a gaggle of electronic surveillance machinery clicked into operation. "That's probably him now," Green said.

Simon picked up the receiver. "Hello. Who?" He handed the phone to Benton. "It's for you."

"Agent Benton, here . . . *What?*" His expression animated, Benton turned to Agent Green, who responded with an eager look. "Really? All right . . . *good!* We're on our way!" He placed the phone down, his voice filled with excitement. "An Eastern Airlines ticketing agent at La Guardia positively identified Lawrence purchasing a one-way ticket to St. Louis. First flight out, ten-thirty." He checked his watch. "That's just over two hours from now. If we push it, we can make it."

"You want me along?" Simon asked.

"Absolutely! We need you for another positive identification and to talk him into surrendering peacefully, if necessary." Triumph surged from Benton's voice. "With any luck, we won't need to go through any negotiations"—he uttered the word with a sneer—"to bring this guy in. And I don't think he's smart enough to buy an Eastern Airlines ticket and then travel via American or some other airline. Let's go!"

Simon, Benton, and Green stampeded down the stairs from Simon's apartment and sprinted toward a government-issued sedan. They climbed into the car and screeched away, heading for Southern State Parkway, west, toward New York City.

A nagging reservation wormed through Simon's thoughts about what to expect once they arrived at La Guardia Airport. *He's a lot smarter than you think,* he mused.

Sweet revenge. Stewart Lawrence savored every delicious detail of events that paraded before his eyes, as he observed the professional actions of Federal agents seizing, handcuffing, and hauling away his tormentors. He felt as though he were watching a Charlie Chaplin movie, filled with pantomime characters moving with exaggerated, jerky movements, like a flock of excited pigeons. Arnoldi's Cadillac pulled up, Engels and Bernie emerged, and Federal agents immediately surrounded the pair. Their faces radiated astonishment, then rage, mouthing curses as they were shoved into a black government sedan. Then came Arnoldi's turn. Agents stopped his car before he could get away, hauled him out, searched him, then yanked him away, his agitated lips spitting threats, undoubtedly about the government hearing from his attorney, unlawful arrests, and whatnot. It was beautiful!

They never even had the chance to enter the airport and pick up the storage box key Lori had promised to leave them at the Eastern Airlines ticket counter. A key opening a container supposedly filled with forty thousand dollars neatly stacked in twenties and hundreds, all in shoe boxes. Instead they would have found a note, written in Lori's flowing script: *Congratulations! You have just won an all-expenses-paid vacation to federal prison.* Lori's offer to Arnoldi over the phone sounded so convincing that even Lawrence felt flickers of doubt about her loyalty. *He's caused me nothing but trouble,* she had explained earnestly, in her low, alluring tone. *Promise to leave me alone and I'll tell you where he's stashed the money he owes you.* Arnoldi and his goons swallowed it all, and the Feds had kept their end of the bargain as well. *Grab these guys, and I'll turn myself in,* Lawrence had promised. They did, and now he was free.

Almost, that is. "They're on to me, Lori," he commented, as he cradled his partner and observed from their shadowy enclave at a bus station across from the airport entrance.

"How do you know?" Lori asked.

"After you dropped off the key, I stepped up to the ticket counter and asked about flights out of the city. The lady I questioned flitted her eyes between me and something under the counter, out of my sight. My picture, I assume. So I bought a one-way ticket to St. Louis to throw them off. This means we'll have to drive out of town, take back roads, no toll booths, no turnpikes, ferries, or stuff like that. They're looking for me."

"How can you be sure?" she asked.

Lawrence checked the time. "Just wait," he said. "Wait and watch."

Yellow traffic cones skipped off the car's hood, arced across its top, and whipped through the air like sparks flying from a spinning grindstone, as Agent Green plunged their black sedan through the wrong way of an empty toll booth guarding Southern State Parkway. Ted Simon turned around and spied several Long Island Parkway officers move toward their cars, climb inside, and screech after their racing vehicle. Some primeval instinct honed by years of military training took hold of Simon's body and pushed him down, below the level of the back window. Green quickly zoomed their cruiser above ninety miles per hour. Benton furiously cranked down his passenger window. Air shrieked through the opening, as he stabbed his arm outside, FBI badge clasped in his fingers. Simon lifted his head and tossed a cautious glance behind him; apparently Benton's message connected, because the police cars trailed off, then vanished into the distant gloom.

With one hand gripping the steering wheel, Agent Green reached for their radio receiver. His instructions produced brusque acknowledgments in voices crackling through radio static. *FBI vehicle in hot pursuit, do not interfere* zipped through the airwaves, clearing their path to La Guardia airport. A spark of whimsy flickered through Simon's thoughts; *Mr. Toad's wild ride has got nothing on this trip,* he mused, as he watched the speedometer needle tickle the number one hundred on the dial. Another, less pleasant thought occurred to him: *if they don't kill Stewart for putting me through this,* he resolved, *I will.*

At exactly eight minutes past ten o'clock, their sedan squealed in front of the Eastern Airlines terminal and stopped in the "No Parking, No Standing" zone. Benton leaped out of the car and scanned the area. Several men, obviously FBI agents, stood by identical vehicles ahead of them. One of the men gave Benton an "A-Okay" sign, which he acknowledged with a wave.

"They've got those guys who were tailing Lawrence," Benton announced with a smile. "Now all we have to do is nab Lawrence himself, and call it a wrap on a good night's work."

Green, Benton, and Simon trotted toward double glass doors leading to the terminal and were immediately stopped by a tall, pipe-smoking man, dressed in a sport coat, with a suit bag slung over his shoulder. Looked like any other businessman, or tourist. "We've got the place covered tight," he murmured to Benton, as though imparting a casual traveling tip. "A mouse couldn't get out of here without us knowing about it. We'll get him."

Maybe a mouse couldn't escape, but that doesn't mean Stewart can't, Simon thought. Benton gestured toward him and addressed the other agent. "Keep in mind that Lawrence is armed, possibly dangerous, and that we have a civilian with us."

Simon felt a pinch of indignation. "I was in the service, you know," he reminded. "Military Police, no less."

Benton shrugged. *"Now,* you're a civilian," he snapped. Back to the pipe-smoker. "What gate are we looking for?"

"E-Nine."

"Let's go."

The three strode through the airport, Green and Benton flashing their badges at appropriate times. They checked passengers at four boarding areas and encountered only looks of curiosity or irritation. Ten-thirty passed, no Stewart Lawrence. Green scanned the area one last time before signaling permission to airline officials to board their flight. The three studied the monitors, searching for other departure times for flights to St. Louis.

"We'll wait for the next flight," Benton instructed.

Eleven-thirty passed, the three men studying every passenger in the area before permitting the flight to board. Still no luck. More intense scrutiny as the twelve-thirty flight approached. The same sea of expressions, now etched with fatigue, greeted their impatient stares. Benton radioed several agents and angrily stuffed his communicator inside his suit pocket. He slumped into a chair, exasperation written on his face, along with the conclusion that hung in the air about them like a bad odor. Stewart Lawrence simply was not in La Guardia Airport.

Simon took a seat opposite the two agents and rested his arms on the chairs beside him. Mixed emotions tumbled through his weary thoughts: a sense of relief besieged by guilt. He wanted Stewart somehow to elude their grasp, at least temporarily, to vindicate his faith in Stewart's cleverness. Yet his friend had to be apprehended, for his own good. Rationality succumbed to pride: *Let Stewart play with these guys first,* Simon reasoned, *then* they can haul him in. At all events, that is how events seemed to be unfolding.

Agent Benton turned to Simon, as though some sixth sense picked up his musings. "You suspected something like this might happen, didn't you?" he said, but with no animosity.

"Honestly, Ken, I had my doubts about how easy it would be picking him up. I know Stewart is smart, and you seemed so sure of yourselves . . ." His voice trailed off.

Benton's jaw muscles twitched. *"Too* sure," he repeated, more to himself than to others. "Okay, look. Let's get back to your apartment and wait. Do you have two extra beds?"

Uncle Sam wants YOU! Simon thought, as a military recruiting poster flashed before his mind's eye. He nodded, yes.

"Then we'll stay with you until Lawrence calls back and tells us what's on his mind," he said in resignation.

The three men shuffled back to the entrance near the Eastern Airlines booths, passed through the double doors, and stepped toward their sedan, which was still parked in the restricted area. Simon paused before entering the car and scanned the surroundings one last time.

You're out there somewhere, Stewart, he murmured. *I can feel it.* Then he climbed into the back seat, let his head collapse against the cushion, and quickly dozed off, as Agent Green drove their vehicle back to his apartment.

Triumph surged through every passionate embrace of the most intense lovemaking Lori and Stewart had experienced since their storybook trek across eastern Long Island months earlier. Their bodies spent, they collapsed on their backs and let their gaze drift to a spacious motel window, which offered a soothing view of sunlight sparkling on calm ocean waters. Sounds of chirping sea gulls and gently lapping waves seeped through the partially opened window, along with slivers of crisp morning air and the aroma of fresh coffee from a nearby restaurant. At this moment, everything seemed right with the world.

Lori wriggled closer to him and slung her right leg over the sheets and across his legs. She threw off her covers and brandished a generous portion of pearly flesh before Stewart's drooping eyelids, with predictable results. "darling," she murmured, training her radiant blue eyes on his. "Can't we pick up those bonds now?"

Stewart's eyes flowed over every delicious curve of her nude body. He gave her a squeeze and kissed her cheek. "Let me think about that," he replied lazily.

"What's to think about?" she said, a cutting edge to her voice. "We've accomplished what we set out to do. Those thugs will be in prison long enough for us to get out of here. The FBI has no idea where we are. And with that amount of money, we could even leave the country!"

Stewart hoisted himself on his elbows. "It may not be that simple. The Feds are still after me. I want to cut a deal . . ."

Lori's expression hardened. "Cut a deal? What are you talking about?"

"So I don't have to serve any prison time," Stewart said.

Lori got off the bed and threw a sheet over her shoulders. She glared at him coldly. "That's *your* problem, not mine. If you hadn't gotten mixed up with those brutes in the first place, you wouldn't have to face the police now. I *trusted* you, Stewart. I gave you those bonds for safekeeping. They're not yours, they're *mine*. I took them, and I want them *back!*"

Stunned, Stewart met her look. There she stood, rigid before him, all beauty drained from her face, features contorted, eyes ablaze with . . . *what?* Impatience? Anger? No, he concluded. He saw in her expression something he had never witnessed before. And it took his breath away, chilled him to the core. It was *greed*. Unsheathed, undisguised, ugly.

"I . . . I would like more time," Stewart said. "You know, to work things out."

"You've had all the time you need!" Lori snapped, a guttural tone scraping her naturally low voice. "To repeat: whatever you work out with the FBI is your business, not mine. Those bonds belong to me, and I want them back, Stewart. *NOW!*"

Stewart gaped at her, uncomprehending, a sense of shock gripping every part of his body. *This can't be Lori,* he thought. *Not my Lori!* He averted her eyes and tried to rationalize her demands, to fit this uncharacteristic burst of rage into some familiar and less threatening category of behavior. Didn't work. Everywhere he turned he encountered the same bald display of the evil he knew all too well. What he saw in Lori was a mirror of his own depraved soul glaring back at him, locking him in its icy gaze. He recoiled from it, sickened.

"Of course, darling," Stewart said softly. "I know where they are. I'll get them right away. Then we can leave and put all this behind us for good."

Lori's expression transformed instantly and assumed its natural appearance. "Wonderful!" she exclaimed. "We can figure out how we want to spend it on our way out of town." She climbed into bed and nuzzled herself in Stewart's embrace, chattering about things she wanted to buy, the house she wanted to build, furniture she wanted to purchase, clothes she needed immediately . . .

Stewart cradled her with limp arms. Lori's girlish drivel shattered against the wall that had arisen between them, and her words tumbled away in heaps of unconnected syllables. Stewart paid her no mind. Instead, he stared out their motel window, deep in thought.

Chapter Twenty-Four

Agent Kenneth Benton shut his eyes and massaged his forehead in a futile attempt to assuage the pounding inflicted by a miniature jackhammer that had been playing across his skull for the past two days. In mocking defiance of these efforts, his invader simply changed venue, then returned after Benton's fingers succeeded in pushing an internal assault of drumbeats away from his temples. Back to his forehead to propitiate his relentless adversary; more rubbing, with the same results. *Hopeless.* He reached for another sip of black coffee, tossed two more aspirin into his mouth, felt every inch of their gritty crawl down his throat, and chased them into his stomach with a more convincing swallow of the tepid, black liquid. He put his cup down and stared out a window from his office in the Federal Building, located in the downtown section of Manhattan. It was going to be a long day, he knew it.

I have to admit, that guy's got style, he thought, as he picked up a picture of Stewart Lawrence. No sooner had he, Green, and Simon dragged themselves to Simon's apartment about four in the morning one week ago, when Lawrence called up to inform them that he had been across the street from the airport all along. To prove it, he provided a blow-by-blow description of their actions, at least as far as he could observe them, which was accurate enough. He even took a bus ride around the airport; worse, *he waved to them as they were departing!* Now, that's style.

Nor was that all. After laboriously explaining to Lawrence that the FBI could not arrange for him to work off prison time with an additional stint in the Navy, Benton thought he had convinced him to surrender the following day on the steps of the Federal Building. Time was set at eleven in the evening. He readily accepted Lawrence's conditions: no gunplay, no physical abuse, and Simon had to accompany him through the arrest, booking, and subsequent legal procedures. Sounded reasonable, although Green remained skeptical and thought it was another ploy to gain time. Simon, though eager to help put an end to this charade, clearly had been smoldering in rage against his former employee. Benton understood that; he was tired. They were all tired. As before, a dozen agents had been strategically placed around the entrance to the Federal Building, across the street in a restaurant, in parked cars, standing by adjacent buildings. They waited for four hours. Lawrence never showed.

For all Benton knew, Lawrence had witnessed the whole thing from a bus, as he had at the airport. *Wouldn't surprise me a bit,* Benton groused, thinking of the buses that had rumbled by while they waited in the wee hours of the morning on the steps of the federal building. *Boy, is that style!* And smarts, too. Simon had been right all along: Stewart Lawrence was one clever operator. *He's probably halfway across the country by now,* Benton mused painfully, as he tried again to counteract the pummeling from what felt like a tiny herd of buffalo stampeding inside his cranium.

The phone rang and Benton picked it up. "Benton here . . . What? Why me? I'm busy. Won't another agent do? Yeah . . . Yeah . . . Okay, why not. I'll be right down." He cradled the phone, put on his suit coat, and departed his office. The physical activity of trotting down the steps seemed a better antidote to his headache than any other nostrums he had tried, and when Benton arrived at the front desk at the reception area, he actually felt better. Two people stood there. One, a lady receptionist, propped behind a long counter, fussing with some papers. Another, a man about five-foot-eight, dark hair, had his back to him, staring at the entrance. An open suitcase sat on a table next to the counter. Benton glanced at it. A chrome-plated pistol lay on top. Looked like a forty-five.

The man turned around, flashed a smile. "Agent Benton?" he asked. Benton slowly dropped his jaw, as recognition flooded his senses.

"I'm Stewart Lawrence. I've come to turn myself in," he said, offering his wrists before him to be handcuffed.

Agent Benton nodded to the guards flanking the door, one of them opened it, and he motioned Ted Simon to enter. Simon glanced into the room and saw Stewart Lawrence hunched over a table, head resting on his hands, a haggard, defeated expression written on his face. Stewart looked up, brightened when he saw Simon, who then turned to the FBI agent.

"How much time do I have with him?" Simon asked.

Benton shrugged. "How much time do you need?"

"Hard to tell. Probably not much. I have some questions for him, things I want to know."

"Me, too," Benton said with a grin. "Chat with him as long as you like and stop by my office when you're done." He patted Simon on the shoulder, then closed the door behind him. Simon walked over to the table and took a seat.

For a long moment, neither said anything, until Simon at last broke the silence. "How are you doing?"

"About as well as can be expected," Stewart replied with a wan smile. "At least this time they kept their word. Thanks for walking through the booking process with me, Ted."

"I'm glad I was able to help." The exasperation piled up over the previous week melted as Simon gazed at his former employee's downcast countenance. "What do you mean, this time they kept their word?"

"There were no agents planted all over the place when I turned myself in," Stewart explained. A grin of satisfaction crept across his lips. "No one stopped me when I came in, and the lady at the counter didn't even know who I was. I wanted to turn myself in on my own terms, and that's what I finally did."

"How did you know there were agents planted around the area when you first agreed to come in?"

"Easy. I passed the building in a bus—twice, in fact—and saw the same couple of guys seated at the restaurant across from the building. I figured they weren't there to drink coffee all night, and that Benton broke our agreement."

Simon shook his head and smiled, marveling at his friend's ingenuity. "Actually, Benton told me that he suspected you might have done something like that. Then you disappeared. The FBI figured you skipped town, maybe out of the country. What happened then?"

Stewart rubbed the back of his neck. "I almost did that," he admitted. "I traveled. Flew from one city to another. Chicago, St. Louis, finally back to New York City. Went to a hotel room a dozen blocks away, spent my last cent on breakfast this morning, then walked over here. Benton came down the stairs, greeted me, called you. Thanks for showing up so fast, by the way."

"You're welcome," Simon said. "You owe him some thanks, too, for waiting until I got here." A long pause. Stewart averted Simon's probing gaze. Finally, Simon asked the question that had been burning in his thoughts. "Why, Stewart? Tell me why."

"I told you, I ran out of money. I figured I couldn't keep running away the rest of my life. Eventually they'd catch up to me. I'm surprised that didn't happen when I was at all those airports."

"That's not what I mean, and you know it."

Stewart finally met his friend's stern expression. He sighed. "I had no choice, Ted, I had to rob those banks. Arnoldi and his goons would have killed me if I didn't pay them back. They would have killed Lori, too. I had to get the money *somehow*, make regular payments until he would leave me alone. Anyway, I just intended to borrow it for a spell. Plus, my gun—your gun, actually—wasn't loaded. I never would have hurt anyone. I just needed to pay off those gambling debts."

Simon inwardly gasped at this colossal rationalization. "The FBI doesn't see it that way. And that lady who identified you is still in a state of shock."

"I never meant to hurt anyone," Stewart repeated, again lowering his eyes to the table. "I explained that to Benton, who's actually a pretty good guy, by the way."

"I agree."

"While we were waiting for you, I asked him what would happen to me next, what to expect from the judge, and so forth. I've got to talk to my lawyer yet, but Benton said that based on his experience, my being a first offender and all, I might not have to serve that much time. Maybe one-third or less of a seven-to-ten-year sentence, depending on the plea bargain my lawyer works out. I served four years in a submarine when I was in the Navy, the toughest kind of duty. I ought to be able to do two or three years in a prison. Then I'll start all over again. Clean slate." Stewart's expression took on a distant look, as though he were pondering something else while speaking.

"Probably, you're right," Simon said agreeably. "What's the next step? Did Benton tell you anything about that?"

"Apparently, I go to a place called Jackson County Jail, where they send federal holdover prisoners until the trial date comes up. Benton refused to tell me anything more. Seemed kind of stiff about it, in fact, as though he wanted to avoid the subject."

"When's your trial date?"

"I don't know. They'll tell me before too long, I'm sure. Meanwhile, I'll just have to do some jail time."

"You'll make out all right," Simon said reassuringly. "Provided you serve your time and put this thing behind you forever."

"Don't worry, I will." Stewart responded to Simon's uplifting tone. "I'll end up in a federal prison someplace. Of course, I'll have to do some time in that county jail, but it can't be all that bad."

Simon nodded. "I'm sure it won't be," he said, trying to end their meeting on a positive note.

Neither could have been more wrong.

PART FOUR: THE DUNGEON

Chapter Twenty-Five

A sense of foreboding darkened Ted Simon's thoughts as he climbed the steps leading to the white granite edifice with the words "Jackson County Jail" etched on its cold facade. After the eleventh step, he paused on a concrete slab leading to the doors and took a quick scan of the lower-middle class neighborhood that surrounded this baleful structure. Rows of ramshackle buildings hovered over the street like a slatternly platoon of combat-weary troops, their windows glowing with watchful malevolence at the somber night and spilling pale light on the charcoal pavement. Simon felt a chill race up his spine. He pulled his collar up and faced a heavy glass and metal filigreed door, accessed by a flat glass lever. *Looks like a door leading to a library,* he thought, in a pathetic attempt to fit this scene into some less threatening category of experience.

Simon entered a gray room with a white plaster ceiling, etched with a design that fell pitifully short of imparting any elegance to the chamber below. He followed directions and walked toward a second door, which opened to an office area, where he was greeted by a black Bakelite sign embossed with white letters announcing the visiting hours. *Prepare to identify yourself,* warned the message at the bottom. An arrow pointed to the left, where two guards were seated behind a counter-high partition separated from visitors by a high glass window. Simon stepped up to it and turned over his pre-approved letter authorizing him to visit a federal holdover prisoner. A middle-aged guard shot him an impatient glance.

"Collateral I.D.," he growled.

Simon handed him a driver's license and a firearms permit, which he accepted, then returned. The guard gestured toward a row of wooden chairs lining the wall opposite his desk. "Next!" he snapped, and the person behind Simon took his place.

Simon watched others repeat this procedure. Several brought packages, which they placed on a long oak table that had long ago relinquished whatever natural beauty it once possessed to age and rough use. As the clock hands crawled toward seven o'clock, the table became heaped in disarray; numerous food containers, grocery bags, and miscellaneous parcels spilled over the top and cluttered near the table's straight, unadorned legs. The jail's visitors comprised an assortment as varied as the packages they toted. More women than men, by a factor of at least three to one; a few children scurried about as well. All wore haggard looks, coarse features, tired eyes, and submissive expressions, battered by life. Their dress was simple, particularly on the women, who observed another sign's strict prohibition against provocative attire.

A bell clanged. Visitors picked up their packages and formed a rough line in front of a heavy door guarded by two prison officials, one male, one female. They filed past the guards and had packages inspected, announcing their own names and those of inmates they wished to see, including inmate numbers. Using a magic marker, the guards brushed bold, colored swaths on each package and placed some on wooden shelves nearby, below a sign indicating the goods in question were not permitted. Visitors who passed with cleared packages appeared to give the guards something before advancing to the next set of doors. In tandem, the doors appeared like a pair of Cyclops sentries staring at onlookers with evil, rectangular eyes, hovering over grimy brass locks that seemed to blow a foul breath against those who approached too closely.

Scruffy wooden chairs flanked the doors. One of them was occupied by an enormous man, easily three hundred pounds, whose corpulence spilled over the chair's flimsy armrests like bread dough overflowing a baking pan. His flaccid countenance hung from bulbous features streaked with tiny red veins, bringing to Simon's mind images of melting wax drooping over the sides of a multicolored candle. His slick pate reflected pale light through strands of wispy gray hair. The man's jowls jiggled as he spoke to a priest, a pencil-stick figure dressed in black, whose spidery outline next to his bulk presented an absurd, though amusing, contrast.

A guard standing nearby caught Simon's attention with a brusque question. "Who are you here for?"

"Stewart G. Lawrence," Simon replied.

He took Simon's pass and slid the door window open by its brass knob. A face materialized, filling the small rectangle.

"Lawrence, one."

"Right," said the face.

The guard applied a key, twisted its metal shank, and the heavy door creaked open with a sepulchral groan that chilled Simon's soul. He motioned Simon to pass through. The door clumped behind him with ominous finality, flinging a macabre echo into the gloom.

What Simon next witnessed nearly made his heart stop. A hallway shrouded in dim light stretched before him, flanked by cages double-barred from floor to ceiling. The two sets of bars, which were about eighteen inches apart, sandwiched a heavy metallic mesh studded with sharp prongs throwing off a pale reflection. Simon advanced slowly, as though descending into Dante's *Inferno,* each step immersing him deeper into an oppressive atmosphere reeking with odors of urine and sweat. He spied eight army-type cots lining each side of the cells, which also contained two coverless toilet bowls, and a wash basin. Simon stopped by Stewart's cell. Shadowy figures loomed in the obscurity. One of them stirred, climbed off a cot, and approached the bars.

"Ted! Ted!" rasped a voice.

"Stewart?"

Stewart's face emerged from the shadows, like a corpse's head thrusting through the murky surface of a stagnant pool of water.

Simon could not help but gasp. "You don't look so good," he remarked, before he could stop himself.

"I don't feel so good, either," Stewart uttered in a low voice. "Welcome to the dungeon, Ted."

"What . . . have they done to you?" Simon asked.

"Physically? Nothing. Not yet, anyway. Listen to me. You got a twenty dollar bill?"

Puzzled, Simon nodded, yes.

"Then do exactly as I say," Stewart said. He reached for a broom, tossed a glance toward the guard, a motion that Simon followed, then flattened the broom on the floor and eased its straw part beneath the bars and the mesh. "Stick the twenty in the broom," he instructed.

"I don't understand."

"Do it!"

Simon bent down and shoved the twenty into the straw bristles. He nervously inclined his head toward the closest guard, who looked in the other direction, as though he were purposely ignoring them.

Stewart retrieved the broom and snatched the twenty. "That will keep me in food for a week," he said in a relieved voice. "Can you spare a twenty every week?"

"Twenty bucks every week!" Simon exclaimed, and Stewart immediately gestured him to lower his voice. "Stewart, what is going on here?"

Stewart's head hung with fatigue. "They don't feed you here," he whispered. "What you just did is standard operating procedure. That's why there are a couple of brooms in each cell. The guards put them there for this purpose."

"What?"

"Simple as that. They don't feed you. The only way I've been able to eat is by other guys sharing their food with me. This jail charges you to eat. Fifteen dollars a week. The poorer guys get fed by others' sharing. That's how we survive."

"What about prison-supplied food?"

"They sell it, pocket the proceeds, then charge us to eat. Everything here has a price. If you've got the money, you get a fourth floor suite with TV, and even a call girl, if you can afford it. They come and go in county cars, paid for by the government. It costs fifty to one hundred bucks a week to live up there. More for extras. Mostly the organized crime types inhabit that floor, because they've got the most money." Stewart leaned forward, eyes burning with intensity. "Only money matters here, Ted. Not race, color, or creed. Cash is king."

Simon remained incredulous. "Can't you notify the authorities?"

Stewart sneered. "Are you kidding me? First of all, they'd kill you, or at the least beat you up. Second, the *authorities* are the ones *in charge* of this hell. They run the dungeon for fun and profit."

"Who, exactly?" Simon inquired.

"The warden, of course. And his entourage of guards."

"Who's the warden?"

"A big, fat guy. Often hangs around outside the cells to check new visitors, like you. You may have seen him on your way in."

An image of the man Simon encountered on his way in flashed before him. "Rumpled suit, red tie, white shirt, sixtyish, about three hundred pounds?" he ventured.

"You *have* seen him," Stewart confirmed.

"And he . . ."

"Runs the place," Stewart said. "The Dungeon Master. He's got a price list for everything. TV's, radios, food packages. You name it. Costs you five bucks to bring in a food package, for instance . . ."

That explains what the other visitors gave to the guards, Simon thought.

". . . and the warden has to okay it. *Personally.* These guys are so organized, it makes administering the Normandy Invasion look like running a family picnic. I've never seen anything like it. We call the warden 'Boss Hogg,' but never to his face. By the way, could you bring in packages of food?"

"How . . . do I set that up?" Simon asked hesitantly, as though conspiring with another fourth grader to pilfer an extra carton of chocolate milk after recess. "I mean, how do I let him know that I want to be in the Boss Hogg feeding program?"

Stewart's features radiated disdain. "You're already in it," he said.

Simon still had not exhausted his capacity for astonishment. "What?"

"When the money hits the broom, the whole place knows. I wouldn't be surprised if the guards turned in broom tally sheets," Stewart commented bitterly.

Simon shook his head. "I'll see the bastard, then," he said harshly.

"Don't call him a bastard," Stewart cautioned. "To him and the guards, it's just business. And don't expect him to be surprised, either."

He wasn't. After a guard signaled the end to visiting hours, Simon was led out of the cell block into the room where Warden Gerald Kennedy remained seated, nodding at visitors as they left. Simon approached him and quickly discovered that introductions were not necessary. The warden knew who Simon was and even addressed him by his first name, as though they were old friends. Unctuousness flowed from a voice that sounded like heavy machinery being scraped across a concrete floor, as he explained prison rules, including delivery charges for food and other expenses for "nice little nourishing extras" that helped new prisoners adjust. In an effort that unquestionably taxed his physical dexterity to its limits, Warden Kennedy hoisted one of his flabby, pier-piling legs over the other and inquired about Simon's ethnicity. He concluded with a comment about the excess of Jewish lawyers over Jewish inmates and gave Simon his "special permission" to return after official visiting hours with a supply of food for prisoner Stewart Lawrence. After, of course, paying the small service charge for delivery.

Simon retraced his steps through the bleak entrails of Jackson County Jail with the sense of a man who had been consigned to hell and was somehow miraculously granted a reprieve. He took a deep breath to rid his lungs of jailhouse stench, and brushed his clothes off, as if symbolically to sweep away any lingering elements of his descent into that depraved abyss. He again surveyed his surroundings and quickly concluded that it would be faster to pick up a few items from a local grocery store two blocks away than it would be to leave the area for a larger store and come back.

Simon collared his neck, trotted down the steps, and walked toward the store, still struggling to comprehend the evils of what they called The Dungeon. No wonder Benton didn't explain any more about Jackson

County Jail, he thought. The FBI agent didn't want to terrify Stewart.

Simon's determination gathered strength with each step. By the time Ted Simon returned to the jail with an armful of groceries, a conclusion hardened in his mind with the firmness of forged steel.

Somehow, this wicked place has to be exposed, destroyed, he resolved. *And Stewart's got to get out of there.*

Warden Gerald Kennedy splayed his pudgy fingers across an oversized mahogany desk and swept his eyes from one end of his office to the other, catching the gaze of each collaborator seated before him. He lifted the lid on a box with *Dutch Masters* printed on its top and removed a large brownish-black cigar, the shape of a miniature torpedo. He passed it beneath his nose and sniffed loudly. Then he clamped his tobacco-stained teeth on the fat projectile, which extended from his mouth like the jib boom of a British man-of-war. He reached inside his suit pocket and picked out a lighter that operated by depressing its trigger, which struck a flint and ignited its wick. His fat digits fumbled with the ridiculously dainty object, clicking it several times, until he finally succeeded in striking a flame. Several loud sucking puffs smacked the room's silence, and soon rolling balls of blue smoke floated up from his face toward the ceiling, where the office's clanking air circulation system whisked them away. The meeting of the executive board of Jackson County Jail was ready to begin.

"I'm wondering about that new guy in E-7," he said.

"He's caught my attention, too," agreed Albert Conner, who witnessed the warden's rituals with barely suppressed amusement. Conner lifted his lean but muscular right arm, and thoughtfully fingered the ends of his handlebar mustache, meeting his boss's stare directly. "One of our guys overheard him threatening to sneak information out using his brother, who's a regular visitor. Sounds to me like he hasn't figured out our rules yet."

"Is he a state prisoner or a federal holdover," asked another guard.

"He's federal," replied a third, lighting a cigarette. He wore a troubled expression on his face as he blew smoke out of the side of his mouth. "That doesn't make him any less of a problem."

"Sure it does, Ed," Conner snapped irritably. "He doesn't have the guts to contact federal officials, nor the knowledge to deal with state people. In any case, who would he report to? The judges unfamiliar with our jail won't believe him, and the ones on our side won't care. Plus, I'm sure we can devise ways to make his brother think sensibly about what he says outside these walls." A sly grin tugged at his lips, but the guard he addressed as Ed didn't look convinced.

Kennedy removed his cigar and stabbed the air for emphasis. "Still, I think he should be taught a lesson, one that is not lost on the others, if you get my drift. It wouldn't hurt the federal holdovers or the state prisoners. Or anyone on the pecking order."

The five men facing Warden Kennedy nodded their agreement. Everyone knew their prison social register ranked organized crime figures at the top, followed by counterfeiters, bank robbers, gamblers, hijackers, and white collar criminals. Child molesters, rapists, and other perverts lurked near the dregs of prison society.

"What'd he do, anyway?" inquired a fourth guard. "It's best we not fool with mobsters, or someone with enough connections or money to be promoted to the fourth floor."

The last person in the room to offer his view answered the question quickly. "He's a counterfeiter. Mousy little guy, thick glasses. Thinks he's smarter than the others, and he's probably right. Not that it matters here. Definitely nonviolent, though, and easily scared. I say we give him a few close encounters with our professional persuaders," he cracked, eyes gleaming, hand on his billy club. "That should cure him of any desire to take any chances. The word will get around fast enough."

Ed shook his head vigorously. "Too dangerous," he objected. Looks of disdain floated across the room. "Well, it is!" he insisted. "Look what happened after the last beating, or the one before that. The one thing we don't want is an inquiry, a *real* inquiry, one that looks into our operations carefully."

Conner snorted and gave Ed a look of contempt. He continued to stroke his mustache thoughtfully. "I've got a suggestion. We can teach our counterfeiter a lesson *without* implicating ourselves. And, we can make our point to the whole population at the same time."

The warden puffed his cigar energetically and trained his eyes on Conner. The others also listened intently. When Conner finished, he whisked his fingers across his captain's bars, folded his tightly muscled arms across his compact torso, and smiled in satisfaction.

Warden Kennedy's lips widened, pushing into his ponderous cheeks. "Great idea!" he proclaimed. "But don't you think our guests on the fourth floor might wonder about our choice?"

Conner shrugged. "I doubt they'd want to get involved," he said. "They keep pretty much to themselves anyway. Plus, it might be useful for them to learn what we're capable of doing *without* their help."

"Then do it!" Kennedy ordered jubilantly. "I put you personally in charge, Albert." He surveyed the room, checking reactions. "Any other business?" Curt nods traveled from head to head, answering his question in the negative. Kennedy took another huge drag from his cigar and shot two streams of smoke out his nostrils, reminding Conner of fire-breathing dragons depicted in children's fairy-tale books. "Well, I've got just one item to bring up. That new prisoner in E-4 . . ."

"Stewart Lawrence," Conner interjected. The others generally deferred to his knowledge of prison operations, as well as to his adroit management of the warden's domain.

"Right," Kennedy confirmed. "He had a visitor today, a guy called Ted Simon. A Jewish fellow, earnest, concerned—you know the type. And my guess is, *loaded.* Get this. He asked if he could return with food for Lawrence *after* prison hours. Naturally, with my expansive generosity . . ."—Kennedy chortled, his huge chest pumping out hearty guffaws—"I said, yes. I think we've got a real pigeon here."

"Probably you're right, but one thing at a time," Conner reminded. "My philosophy is to solve problems first, then slurp up the gravy."

"And I agree!" Kennedy blurted, not looking comfortable about being lectured by his chief henchman. "I just thought you would like to know. You'll get on that counterfeiter, then?"

"Yeah, but I want to wait a while," Conner said, getting up. "See how things develop. Maybe he's a slow learner and just needs a few weeks to pick up on things." He glanced at Ed, who acknowledged with an appreciative nod. Conner turned toward the warden. "In the meantime, I've got some further thoughts about that new prisoner in E-4 . . ."

Wispy strands of cirrus clouds burst into streaks of fiery orange and yellow, as sunlight cracked over the horizon of the Chiricahua Mountains in southeastern Arizona. Each morning splattered the foothills with patches of burnt red, reflecting the land's rich mineral deposits, checkered with splotches of dark green and brown. Lori Armstrong shielded her eyes from this explosion of morning light, as she watched Aurelio Rodriguez tromp toward his decrepit 1954 Chevy pickup truck plunked about twenty feet from their trailer home, a rusted out hulk squatting on four flat tires. She had known him since her high school years in New Mexico, and when she traveled from Long Island to more familiar haunts, he promptly sheltered her like an abandoned puppy. Together they moved to Arizona where he began a new job in Bisbee, the copper capital of the state. Holdings of the Phelps Dodge Corporation enveloped the territory like a protective quilt and included most of the copper bearing regions, along with several buildings downtown, a hotel, and three large stores. Town inhabitants simply referred to it as "The Company," realizing that the ebb and flow of corporate fortunes connected to each resident like intravenous tubes hovering over patients in hospital beds. To remove them meant slow death.

Lori worked in one of the company stores, located in a town consisting of a cluster of buildings jammed inside a deep gorge, only a few blocks wide but stretching about two miles in length. From one of the adjacent hills, Bisbee appeared like an elongated heap of rectangles festering inside an angry scar that had been ripped open by a gigantic scalpel slicing across the earth's surface. Numerous houses clung to the slopes of surrounding hills, and from a distance appeared like rectangular beetles crawling up huge mounds of earth. Lori dearly wanted to move into one of the those, and Aurelio gave her every reason to believe that was his intention. Except he had no money; at least not yet, he explained, between draughts of Jack Daniels or tequila, chased by hearty swallows of some Mexican beer. First, he earns money, he promised, then they get a house, then he might get her pregnant and even marry her—in that order. When Lori had renewed their friendship in New Mexico, he greeted her like a lost love reclaimed, and she looked on him as her lifesaver. After months filled with physical beatings, which included daily verbal attacks in alcohol-soaked profanity, Lori Armstrong yearned to escape—again.

But where to? *I'll figure that out on the road,* she decided, watching her tormentor's truck rumble into the distance and vanish into a cloud of reddish-brown dust. *California, maybe. He'd never find me there.* She scurried to their bedroom, pulled out two battered suitcases, and opened several drawers. She hurriedly scooped out her clothes, stuffed them inside her suitcases, and sat on the tops to snap them shut. She trotted into the tight little cubicle that had passed for her bathroom for the last several months. Lori paused by the mirror, studied her face. Her eyes remained puffy, and her left cheek still stung from the slap he had inflicted last night. Forehead looked better, though; the gash ripped open by an empty liquor bottle skipping across her skull the previous week was healing . . . slowly. She reached inside her purse, pulled out a pair of large dark sunglasses. *That's better,* she concluded. *Hardly noticeable, now. Even covers my cheeks.* She tossed them back into her purse, along with scattered toiletries collected from the bathroom cabinet. Back into the bedroom, one last check to see if she had missed anything.

Where's that map?

Lori scanned the small room, walked to the chest and whipped open a drawer. Nothing there, just wrinkled contact paper, a little dust and sand. Everything was lined with dust and sand. She cursed under her breath, opened another drawer. Empty. *Maybe it's with Aurelio's stuff,* Lori surmised. She threw open a drawer containing some of his shirts and underwear. The mere sight of his grubby clothing ignited fires of rage. Lori whipped out every article in sight and hurled them about the room, screeching, laughing insanely. Finally, she pulled out the whole drawer and with all her strength heaved it across the room, where it crashed against the wall and crumpled to the ground, a twisted mess of plastic and cheap thin plywood. Lori stood there gaping at it, breathing heavily. Felt good. Felt great! *Do it again.*

Another drawer fell victim to her onslaught and met the same fate, tumbling next to the first one. This time she hadn't bothered to empty its contents completely, and several magazines spilled on the floor. She spied one of them sticking out from a jagged edge of splintered wood. Looked like a map. Lori walked over and extracted the folder-like packet from the debris. She held it up to the light for a better look. She saw instantlly it was not a map. The words *Lakewood Downs* sprawled across the pamphlet's glossy exterior. Lori's heart skipped a beat.

It's that racing program Stewart gave me.

No, she quickly remembered. This was *more* than a simple racing program. *This holds the key to my treasure!* Lori sat on the bed and scrutinized the program she had misplaced, then forgotten, quickly flipping through pages, searching for . . . *what?* She wasn't sure, couldn't recall. Stewart told her the clue to where he had stashed those bonds was buried somewhere in these pages. *Now if I can only remember his precise words* . . . Lori combed her memory for the proper sequence of syllables that Stewart had smugly rolled off his lips. A bunch of numbers, she remembered that; *mostly* numbers. She flipped through the pages again and felt her heart sink into her stomach. A veritable sea of figures flowed before her eyes, saturating each page. She didn't understand them the first time Stewart introduced her to harness track racing, and she surely had no clue what they meant now.

Lori checked her watch. Eight o'clock. *I can't sit around here thinking about this. I've got to put distance between me and this hellhole.* Lori figured that twelve hours of driving in her trusty Volkswagen would put her far enough away from Bisbee to discourage Aurelio from trying to follow her, once he discovered she had left. She doubted he would make the effort. Lori believed that deciding between chasing after her and keeping a steady job, the first he'd had in years, would not be a difficult choice for him. But just in case, she planned to throw him off her trail. Aurelio expected her to return to Arizona, back to her roots. Lori planned to travel *through* that state without stopping until she had arrived on the east coast. He would never follow her that far.

Lori stuffed the racing program inside her blouse, looped her purse strap over her shoulder, and grabbed her two suitcases. She trotted outside to her car and heaved her baggage into the back seat. A half an hour later found her cruising along Highway 80 toward Lordsberg, New Mexico. As the efficient, air-cooled engine in her indestructible Volkswagen powered her down the highway, her thoughts probed through details of her last week in Long Island before Stewart surrendered to the authorities. *Double-crossing skunk!* Lori suspected what he had in mind. He planned to serve part of an eight-to-ten-year sentence, get released on parole after serving only a few years, then retrieve those bonds, *her bonds,* and live off them for the rest of his life. *All men are pigs,* Lori thought bitterly. She grudgingly conceded that at least Stewart had never abused her, but still, he had absconded with her money, abandoned her. That made him as rotten as all the other brutes who had ravaged her life.

If I could only remember that clue! Of course, recalling it was not enough, she knew. She also had to decipher the *meaning* of an obscure code buried somewhere in a forest of numbers about as intelligible to her as hieroglyphic symbols splattered across an ancient Egyptian tomb. Lori also had to determine whether the bonds' location was as easily accessible to her as it was to Stewart. She possessed great respect for his cleverness. Had he concocted some devilishly ingenious obstacle to prevent others from tracking them down? New traps designed to mislead those unsophisticated in the intricacies of harness racing jargon, such as herself? Lori didn't know, but based upon hearsay information about prison sentencing and parole, in addition to what Stewart had told her, she could confidently assume he would be confined for the next two to three years, perhaps longer. That gave her plenty of time to figure these things out.

That comforting conclusion inspired a train of words to wriggle through her memories and parade before her mind's eye with the brash clarity of a neon sign flashing in bold letters, the clue Stewart had dropped in her lap six months ago.

Number four's a winner at two-o-two and three.

Chapter Twenty-Six

Albert Conner relaxed in a leather chair opposite the warden's desk and opened a folder that looked like a United States Army 201 file with the name *Stanton, Timothy A.* printed on its tab. He examined mug shots, thumbed through several papers, and isolated a canary-colored document from the local Federal District Court office. Rows of criminal charges marched down the sheet with military precision, but he focused on explanatory notes attached to each item. One in particular caught his attention and pushed a grin across his lips. From scores of elements that enabled investigators to distinguish the authenticity of paper currency from counterfeit substitutes, it seemed that *Stanton, Timothy A.* got tripped up on the most elementary: number spacing. Everything else he matched to near perfection. The color, Treasury seal, portrait, check letter, series letters—all he reproduced with sufficient skill to escape the notice of casual observers and the first scrutiny of professional craftsmen. Even the lathe work, minute striations that flowed across the picture, he captured with a remarkable degree of finesse.

But he didn't get the numbers right. An odd angle here, a slightly tilted figure there, and other microscopic variations triggered alarm bells under the probing gaze of Treasury specialists and launched an investigation that ultimately sent a platoon of federal agents bursting into his basement catacomb, where he was caught in the act. Conner glanced at Stanton's previous job and chuckled at the irony of it all. *Occupation,* it read: *Accountant.* A number cruncher who couldn't get his numbers right.

Warden Gerald Kennedy drummed his fingers on the desk and shifted his sagging eyelids toward his chief lieutenant. "You got things set up on Stanton's brother, too?"

"Yep," Conner replied without looking up.

"Too bad it's got to come to this," Kennedy remarked without emotion, reaching for his cigar box.

"Some people have to learn the hard way."

"How did your choice react to our proposal?" Kennedy asked, commencing his cigar-lighting ritual.

"Like a kid who can hardly wait for his birthday present." Conner placed another file on his lap, opened it, and scanned its contents. *Lopez, Roberto, E.,* read its tab, trailed by a succession of other names, all aliases, all in Spanish. Conviction: *First-Degree Murder.* It seemed Roberto had concluded at the tender age of nineteen that his previous criminal forays, which consisted of car thefts, petty burglary, and simple assault could not support him in the lifestyle to which he aspired. Doctors make the big money, he reasoned. He cased a physician's office, broke into it when he thought only the doctor remained, and stabbed him thirteen times when his victim refused to relinquish his wallet. Unfortunately for him, Roberto did not detect the presence of a patient in an adjacent room, a formidable man who overheard the commotion, apprehended him, and chased the young Puerto Rican out of the building and into the street, where he was picked up by a passing patrol.

Conner examined Lopez's picture. As a captain with twenty years' service, he had seen thousands of such photographs, most of which returned pallid expressions, dead eyes. Not Lopez. His dark eyes gleamed with malevolence, defiance etched his sharp features. Other prisoners avoided him, concluding that only a lunatic would kill a doctor in his office for a few tens and a twenty. You just knew this devil's spirit would rip your heart out for the sheer thrill of it. But give him some *real* incentive, and there's no limit to what he would do. Conner counted on that.

"Any danger your man would convey information that would best be kept within these walls?" Kennedy asked.

Conner looked up. "Who'd believe him?"

Kennedy accepted that answer. The door knocked, two quick thumps, a pause, another thump.

"Come in," Kennedy called.

A slightly built man entered the warden's office, followed by a prison official. The guard closed the door and stood behind the prisoner, arms angled behind his back, parade rest. His diminutive charge, who once worked in a bank, looked like he dropped out of the pages of a Charles Dickens novel. Black hair looped over his large ears and hooked around his bald head like a dust ruffle surrounding the foot of a bed. His eyes appeared like gelatinous pools of liquid, shimmering behind thick lenses perched on his fleshy, turned-up nose. A neatly trimmed Charlie Chaplin mustache hovered over puffy lips. Pale and gaunt, his stooping frame twitched in response to every slight movement of others in the room, as if to ward off anticipated blows.

Warden Kennedy cleared his throat. "I understand that you've voiced some criticisms about the administration of this facility."

Timothy Stanton's features sprang to life. *"Criticisms?"* he repeated in a tone surprisingly deep and resonant. Conner mused that some barrel-chested hulk must somehow be lurking inside that frail physique in order to supply such a heavy voice.

"More like extortion, don't you think?" Stanton boomed.

Kennedy's pudgy hands balled into fists. He champed on his cigar and glared at the little man. Conner observed in silence.

"Five dollar delivery charge for food packages. Twenty-five percent of all goods and packages taken by the guards, in addition to the service charge . . ."—he spat the words out contemptuously—"before they reach us. Twenty, now twenty-five dollars a week simply to live, to eat in this hellhole. Mice, rats, cockroaches in the cells, and we can't set traps to catch them. No showers, no facilities . . ."

"You have toilets," Kennedy interrupted.

"Some of us have . . ." Stanton hesitated, ". . . special problems." The blurred images behind his glasses seemed to flutter with embarrassment.

Like a prostate problem, Conner thought, remembering Stanton's file. *He's so nervous much of the time, he can't urinate.* Based upon what Conner knew about the man, he found Stanton's present outburst frankly surprising. And alarming. If a wilting flower like him could flare up, how about other, bolder types? He dismissed the possibility for the moment. One thing at a time.

Kennedy relaxed his fists, removed his cigar, and forced an expression of sympathy. "This facility is run for the good of everyone, Mr. Stanton," he said earnestly. "To prove this, I'm ordering you transferred to another location inside the building."

Stanton looked at the warden suspiciously. Kennedy gestured toward Conner. "Captain, if you don't mind?"

Conner got up and wrapped his hand around Stanton's weak, fleshy arm. "You'll come with me," he ordered.

"Where are you taking me?" Stanton asked.

"You'll see."

The guard behind Stanton stepped back, flickered a look of puzzlement. Conner shrugged him off. "This way," he instructed, leading Stanton out of the warden's office.

Conner led his prisoner by the arm along a narrow hallway, up three flights of stairs, until they reached another hallway lined with doors.

They stopped. Stanton obviously recognized the area and turned to Conner.

"This is the fourth floor," he said. "I can't afford to stay up here."

"I assure you, that won't be a problem," Conner said.

Stanton looked relieved. "I can't believe it," he murmured. "Listen, I really have to use the bathroom . . ."

Of course, you do, Conner thought. *I counted on that.* "Second door on the right," he said.

Timothy Stanton's face glowed with gratitude. "Do you have to accompany me?"

"You can go in by yourself," Conner said generously, motioning toward the door. "I'll stand outside and wait."

The two men walked toward the fourth floor lavatory, and Conner positioned himself by the door so he could easily peer inside after it opened. Stanton turned the knob and walked in. Conner braced the door open a sliver by his foot, so he could observe. Stanton walked up to a urinal and unzipped his trousers. Behind him, one of the doors to a stall swung aside. Stanton turned to look. Color drained from his face, fright gripped every feature. Standing before him in a T-shirt, muscled like an assemblage of coiled springs, fingering the edge of a knife, was a person known to every guard and nearly every inmate in Jackson County Jail.

Roberto Lopez.

Stricken with terror, Stanton jerked his head toward Conner, who tossed him a fiendish grin, then moved his foot back from the door. Like vertical jaws of a strange beast clamping tight around its victim's body, the door slowly eased toward the hallway, erasing Conner's window of vision and clicking shut behind him as he walked away.

Andrew Stanton clamped his small hands on the counter's edge, glaring at a prison official whose eyes returned his stare with equal intensity. "What do you mean I can't see my brother!" Stanton demanded.

"Just that!" the guard snapped. "He's indisposed."

"Indisposed? What does that mean?" Stanton snarled. "Is he sick? What's going on here?"

The seated guard rose to his full height, revealing a thick torso perched on spindly legs and covered by a crumpled gray uniform. His looming hulk combined the appearance of a wrinkled sea lion and an unmade bed on which some careless child had scattered various metallic objects. Pale light reflected from a brass badge attached to his left pocket; his revolver, covered by a jet-black swath of leather snapped over the holster, jutted out from his waist. "I *said* . . ."—he leaned forward for emphasis, spreading his large hands speckled with liver spots on the counter—"that Mr. Stanton is *indisposed.* You'll have to come back later."

"When?" Stanton asked.

"Later," the guard repeated, then sat down. "Next!" he shouted.

Andrew Stanton remained standing at the counter, fuming at the prison official, who now looked past him to the person next in line. Stanton swept his eyes across the room. Their altercation had clamped a lid on the normal bustle in the reception area; even the children were quiet. A dozen pairs of eyes trained on him, including those belonging to three other guards, who fixed their chilling gaze on his every move. One of them smacked his billy club against the palm of his left hand, a sound that cracked the room's tense silence. Stanton concluded he would learn no more about the status of his brother at this time.

He threw one last hostile glance at the man behind the counter. "You haven't heard the last from me!" he uttered in a hoarse voice. Then he scooped up his package and stomped out of the room. Stanton left the building and trotted toward his car, a blue Cadillac parked two blocks away from the jail. His ponderous chrome chariot stuck out from its surroundings like a prom queen at a biker's convention. Stanton was eager to dash away as quickly as possible. *Next time I come back,* he resolved, *I'll bring help.*

Traffic besieged him at every turn, and it took a half an hour for Stanton to extricate himself from the jumble of slum-like, inner city structures surrounding Jackson County Jail. Finally, he found himself cruising along a major highway toward his posh residence in Morris County, New Jersey. His thoughts grinding against one another in suppressed rage, Stanton mumbled quietly to himself about his next course of action. *I'll notify the authorities,* he murmured. *State, no, FEDERAL authorities. I'll blow that place apart! I'll . . .*

"Don't move," uttered a voice.

Stanton jumped. His Cadillac skidded to the shoulder, then lurched back on the road. He peered at the rearview mirror. A dark shape loomed behind him in the back seat, emerging from the gloom like a ghoulish apparition rising from the grave. Headlights from passing cars cut slivers of light across the murky figure. A ski mask shrouded his head; only his eyes showed, icy blue dots sparkling against intermittent invasions of light.

"Who are you?" Stanton muttered.

"Keep driving," the voice commanded.

Stanton clutched the steering wheel with both hands, riveted his gaze on the road. Several minutes passed . . . Five, ten, thirty . . . He didn't know. Finally, "What do you want?"

The head leaned forward. Hand raised . . . Metal against flesh . . . Stanton flinched, eyes jerked toward the mirror. The black outline of a Smith & Wesson .38 caliber revolver pressed against his ear. Like a giant fist, the cold grip of terror wrapped around Stanton's chest, squeezing his life away. Sweat beaded on his forehead. Every breath, a gasp.

"Oh my God!" he whimpered. "Money! You want money! I got money! Plenty of it. Just don't kill me . . ."

"I don't want money."

"What then? What! Just name it!"

The head inched closer. Stanton jerked away. Pistol barrel pressed against his temple, steel against bone . . .

"Don't ask any more questions about your brother," came the command. "If you value your life and his, no more questions."

Stanton kept his head inclined, watched the road. "My brother. Is he . . ."

"You'll find out. No more questions. Clear?"

Stanton nodded yes in abrupt movements.

"Say it!"

"No more questions! I promise. No more questions."

The pistol lowered, the head leaned back. Stanton took a huge breath.

"Take the next turn," the man ordered.

Stanton drove as he was instructed. The next half hour he followed directions that took them into a densely populated thicket of apartment houses. Several onlookers viewed his garish car with an interest that only made Stanton more jittery. The man in the back seat instructed him to stop near an alley. He leaned forward. Stanton instinctively veered his head away.

"I'm getting out of the car now," the man said. "You will drive away and tell no one about what happened. You will not look back. Clear?"

Stanton nodded vigorously.

"Say it!"

"I'll do exactly as you said," he stated quickly.

In a fluid motion that took only a few seconds, his intruder opened the back door, slipped away with the quickness of a cat, and vanished into the alley. Stanton checked traffic, slammed his foot on the accelerator, screeched into the road, and rocketed his luxury car through the brick forest of tenements as fast as he could.

He did not see his intruder whip off his ski mask and follow his escape. Nor did he witness a satisfied grin pushing up the handlebar mustache of Captain Albert Conner, Head Guard, Jackson County Jail.

The hallway extending from Stewart Lawrence's gaze in E-4 stretched across his cell block like a dark catacomb leading to the gates of hell. Its lone attendant stood between the double doors' rectangular eyes, which must have drawn their baleful reflection from some reservoir of evil emanating from The Dungeon's murky depths. Certainly the chamber's pitiful illumination offered no such sustenance. The guard's gray outline blended into the shadowy background, his presence a reminder that any moment could launch a skull-bashing invasion of inmates' quarters, for reasons of "prison security." Against this contingency, Stewart and his fellow conspirators devised a plan to pry the lid off their personal version of Devil's Island.

"What's he doing?" came a furtive question behind him.

"Nothing. Just standing there like he always does," Stewart answered in a low voice.

"That gives us an hour," whispered another voice.

"That's all I'll need," Stewart said.

He stepped to the back of his cell and sat on a cot. After flitting one last glance toward the bars, Stewart pulled out a sheet of white, blue-lined paper and flattened it on a file folder pilfered from an inattentive guard. He hunched over the paper with the concentration of a medieval monk inscribing holy writ on a delicate parchment for presentation to His Holiness. His collaborators placed themselves at strategic locations around him, shrouding his work as much as possible. Cones of light from hanging bulbs painted the hallway's charcoal grimness with a hazy glow, which sifted through steel bar and wire mesh filters into their cell. Yellow shafts probed inside their cramped quarters, and Stewart positioned himself to catch their fuzzy pale light as he applied his number two pencil with strong, thick strokes on E-4's precious document. With Jeffersonian flourish, he began his carefully printed script using the words, *"We, the prisoners of Jackson County Jail . . ."* Stewart proceeded with an itemized list of abuses and usurpations, each with a price tag attached.

"How much apiece for those private rooms?" he asked quietly without looking up.

An inmate took two steps toward him but kept his eyes on the hallway. "Forty to fifty bucks a week," came the whispered response.

"Times fifteen private rooms for the prisoner elite," Stewart muttered. "I'll round it off to six hundred bucks a week. Commissions on whores . . ."

Everyone had an opinion on that price. "About a hundred a week," ventured another voice. "We could be off by a hundred percent, but what does it matter?" snarled his companion, who leaned over to examine Stewart's entries. Eight men exchanged nods of agreement.

A sudden noise pierced the low murmur that enveloped their cell block like the drone of heavy machinery. Eight pairs of eyes trained on the cell bars; scores of anxious glances from their block knifed down the hallway. A spike of adrenaline surged through Stewart's chest, as he grabbed the paper and shoved it inside his shirt. "What was that?" he rasped, getting up.

Silence.

A hand waved him back. "Nothing. Nothing. He's still standing there. Go on!"

Stewart pulled out his paper and carefully flattened it on the cot. "Okay," he continued, "four hundred fifty regular inmates at an average price of twenty-five bucks a week, or twenty bucks a week. We don't know if the higher price applies to all."

"Still don't matter," murmured an inmate over his shoulder.

"Right," Stewart agreed, quickly calculating an average. *That doesn't count the price increase to thirty bucks a week to support me,* he thought bitterly. *All because Boss Hogg thinks he's spotted a pigeon with Ted Simon.* Stewart pushed this reflection aside and worked with what he knew. "Comes to nine thousand bucks a week," he announced.

A low, breathy whistle. "Bastards!" croaked a cell mate seated on the opposite cot. "Miserable, stinking, rotten bastards," another chimed in, which inspired a chorus of vivid profanities that rumbled in low voices through the cell.

"They're the criminals, not us," stated another, a sentiment seconded by all.

Each stroke of Stewart's pencil scored the paper in fury, as he plunged deeper into the muck of Boss Hogg's corruption. Nearing the end of his calculations, he gaped at the mounting profits of The Dungeon's enterprises. A thousand a week profit from package surcharges; three hundred a week charges for "miscellaneous favors," such as television sets, radios, phone calls, drugs, alcoholic beverages. Untold hundreds of dollars per week for the twenty-five percent of food packages pilfered by guards before they reached the prisoners, in addition to their normal "service charge." Plus all the other stuff he had just tabulated. *Incredible.*

Stewart chewed on the nub of his pencil, then jotted down a figure. "Comes to over eleven thousand dollars a week," he concluded.

"What about the food they sell to the outside," came a question. "That's got to be worth a lot."

Stewart nodded in agreement. "Impossible to know for sure. But even without that amount . . ."—he scrutinized a column of numbers and added their total—"their yearly profit comes to five hundred seventy-five thousand dollars." He shook his head in disbelief. "Add estimates of their other profits and you probably get about six hundred grand. No wonder some of those guards brag about how much they're making." He paused, striving to comprehend the enormity of it all. *"When this stuff is exposed . . ."*

The agonized groan of heavy doors grinding open on tortured metal hinges cut through the undertone of their cell block like a scythe. Deathly silence claimed the chamber, punctuated by sounds of footsteps plodding down the hallway. Their eerie, irregular cadence echoed through the ghostly, tomb-like atmosphere. One set pounded the concrete with authority, while another shuffled intermittently between heavy thuds of military boots.

Scrape . . . THUD! Scrape . . . THUD! Scrape . . . THUD!

Inmates stumbled over each other, rushed to the bars, strained their necks to peer at the approaching procession. What they saw pushed gasps of shock into the stuffy air.

Two men passed by, as if on display. The first, a guard, dragged a prisoner across the hallway, like a Devil's henchman leading another condemned soul down the road to eternal damnation. Limp arms dangled from the stooped shoulders of the prisoner's battered frame. His pitiful assemblage of shuffling limbs appeared to have been stitched together by some mad surgeon feverishly spearing through helpless flesh in a frenzied attempt to cover up his mistakes. Angry red welts laced his ashen features, as though an earth tiller had raked across his face. A wicked gash tore a path up his cheek, skipped past a eye bludgeoned to a sickening pulp of black and blue, slashed an arc across the tight skin on his forehead and scalp, and clipped a half inch off the top of his ear. A regiment of stitches marched down his throat, vanished into his shirt. Whatever this man went through, Stewart wondered how he came out of it alive.

"That's Stanton," whispered an inmate beside him. "The counterfeiter."

A few shaking heads. "He's been shooting off his mouth, saying he was going to tell people on the outside about this place."

"How was he going to do that?" inquired another.

"Through his brother, I think. He's a lawyer, or something."

"Wonder what they did to him?" whispered a worried voice.

Stewart's heart plummeted to his stomach, as these words, with their frightening implications, echoed in his thoughts. *Ted said he was going to help us,* he thought. *After I gave him this letter.* But Simon had become so furious after his last visit, he indicated he might even approach federal authorities on his own initiative, with or without the prisoners' list of indictments. Stewart stepped back into his cell, picked up the incriminating sheet of paper, and folded it carefully into a tight, two-inch square. He stuffed it into his pocket. He couldn't phone, he couldn't write. Boss Hogg had taken those privileges away. Stewart couldn't devise any way to get in touch with his lifeline to sanity, to warn him, perhaps even to save his life. Stewart was helpless until Ted Simon returned for his next visit.

If he returned.

Chapter Twenty-Seven

Theodore A. Simon hoisted a weary arm up to his desk and grasped the cold handle of a coffee cup with the Office Products Unlimited logo emblazoned across its side. He lifted the tepid liquid to his lips, took a sip, winced at its metallic flavor, and placed it down again. He preferred not to work this late, but his last visit to Jackson County Jail had showered his agenda with a flood of concerns, and he couldn't leave the office until he had sorted matters out. An avalanche of worries tumbled through his mind, all launched by the same agonizing quandary: what course of action should he take to deal with the hellhole Stewart had fallen into? *Why should it be my problem at all?* he queried.

Simon's thoughts drifted to a previous visit. When the inmates in cell E-4 overheard his pledge to return the next time with a armful of corned beef sandwiches and blueberry tarts, they showered him with gratitude. Simon simply nodded his head and prayed that the tear tracing a warm path down his cheek would not betray his emotion by throwing off a twinkle in the pale light. Such gratification assuaged the misery of his periodic visits and buoyed his hopes for a less painful return. He assumed that their thanks during his follow-up visit would wash away the discomfort he felt every time he entered Boss Hogg's imperial domain. He assumed wrong.

At his next visit, Simon detected something amiss as prison officials guided him into the bowels of The Dungeon. Playful smirks tugged at the lips of every guard he encountered. *Loved those sandwiches,* several quipped. *Great tarts,* added another. He expected as much; they snatched twenty-five percent from all food packages, which is why he bought a dozen of each item, with several to spare. That left plenty for the prisoners in E-4.

The guards had taken them all. When Simon approached Stewart's cell, a half-dozen inmates flocked to the bars and glowered at him. *Where were the sandwiches?* they demanded. *The tarts?* Simon's explanation failed to mollify their fury. Nor was that all. Another price hike, this time to thirty dollars a week, had been put into effect especially because of him, Stewart had complained after the other inmates stepped away. Actually, Stewart went on to explain, the warden had several empty wards upstairs, wanted to fill them, and raised prices on everything to goad prisoners out of their cells and into the higher rent area. He even promised Stewart a place. Provided, of course, Simon paid up.

Rage overwhelmed Simon during that visit. Stewart asked for his help to convey information he was gathering, a written indictment of sorts. Simon agreed to help. Stewart then asked more questions, always the same ones, with identical answers.

What about Lori?

Nothing to tell you, Stew. She's disappeared.

The bail bondsman? Can't he get me out of here?

Not unless you can come up with twenty-five thousand dollars in collateral, Stew. Do you have that amount stashed away?

Flickers of deception had played across Stewart's partially shrouded visage.

No, I don't have that amount. Then he turned away.

Simon wanted to believe his friend, but didn't. The bail bondsman had emphasized to him that bank robbers were bad risks and often failed to show up for their hearings. Furthermore, they always kept a stash hidden, somewhere. *Always*, he repeated.

Stewart was holding back on him. Still, Simon resolved to help. By himself, if necessary. Stewart had indicated there might be risk in doing that and asked him to wait until his cell mates had collaborated with others and prepared a statement. But the degree of risk to Simon personally was never made clear, and he didn't feel like waiting any longer. His moral sense hovered over every calculation, and, like an Old Testament prophet, stood in judgment. *To be confronted with evil and hesitate? Or worse, do nothing?* Unthinkable!

Simon's thoughts returned to the present and he checked his watch. Eleven fifty-five. Time to wrap things up, return home, get a good night's sleep, and . . .

Muffled sounds of soft footsteps climbing the stairs leading to his office patted the lonely silence. Several people were always in the building, but everyone that came to Simon's mind broadcast their approach by thumping up the steps loudly, either in frustration or determination. *Maybe a very gentle thief,* Simon mused, his mental processes thick with fatigue. He returned to his desk and waited.

Footsteps stopped. A gentle tapping on his door.

And polite, too. But here, now, at midnight?

"Come in," Simon called.

The door opened a crack. A woman's face emerged, radiant blue eyes skittered about his office. Then she stepped inside, faced him.

Simon's mouth opened slowly as he let his eyes rest on the lithe, attractive figure of Lori Armstrong.

Warden Gerald Kennedy retrieved his delicate cigarette lighting instrument and applied its flame to the black projectile jutting from his lips. Loud puffs smacked the air, and rolling orbs of blue smoke drifted away, their pungent odor invading every corner of his office. He eased back in his chair, plopped his pudgy hands behind his neck, and stretched open the side of his mouth. A dark aperture the shape of a horizontal teardrop materialized, and a ball of smoke huffed out like exhaust shooting from the pipe on a steam engine. A smile shoved his cheeks up his face, reducing his baggy eyes to narrow, dark slits. He appeared to Conner like a pregnant Saint Bernard smoking a stogie.

"Do you have to light up one of those stinking things every morning?" Conner groused. "Smells like wrapped donkey dung."

The warden just laughed. "Celebration, m'boy. Celebration. We nearly got every room on the fourth floor filled. Helps the cash flow immensely."

"At least you could use a man's lighter," Conner persisted, "instead of that pinko lady thing."

Kennedy ignored his protests. "How's your boy doing with his new accommodations?"

"Lopez? Says it's better than what he ever got at home. He wants to take up permanent residence. Too bad we can't keep him for special assignments."

"Very useful lad," Kennedy observed. "And I must commend you for the job you did on Stanton's brother, the lawyer. He sends in his fifty bucks a week very faithfully." The warden cackled, his whole body jiggling with merriment. "To think every cent of it goes to support the guy who nearly sliced up his brother into filets of counterfeit baloney." That piece of self-inflicted wit overwhelmed him, and Kennedy spent the next minute chortling, coughing, hacking himself into a state of quivering helplessness.

He recovered just in time to hear an alarming suggestion from his head guard. "I'm thinking of a change of venue for Lopez," Conner stated.

Kennedy heaved an arm forward and lurched his bulk toward the desk. "You can't do that, Albert! Violates our rules. Help our friends, punish our enemies. He's our friend. Mighty useful one, too. Keeps the whole jail in line."

"It would just be temporary," Conner pointed out. "He can hear as well as he can fight. And after he's done, we can move him back to his hotel suite. Maybe with a reward, depending on services rendered."

"What services did you have in mind?"

"Snooping, mostly. Or at least at first. We've gotten drift of something brewing in a few of the cells, inmates passing information outside. Like the Stanton case. Maybe worse."

A map of concern formed on Kennedy's fleshy face. "What could be worse than what Stanton's brother was going to do?"

"Written stuff, obviously."

Kennedy puffed on his cigar thoughtfully, considering this. "Can you identify the ringleader?" he inquired.

"I believe so, but I want to send in Lopez to make sure. After we confirm, then it's a judgment call about what to do next."

"You're contemplating another excursion to the fourth floor with Lopez to, shall we say, *educate* the offender?" Kennedy's words constituted more of a statement than a question.

"Exactly," Conner replied.

Kennedy chucked his cigar against an ashtray. "Who are we talking about here, Albert?"

Conner pulled out a document and flattened it on the warden's desk, so they both could scan its contents. Lists of inmate cells studded the sheet, each room highlighted in bold script. Indented beneath cell numbers were rosters of prisoners. Kennedy examined the names carefully and snorted.

"I'd say your suspicions are well-founded," he observed, lifting his fountain pen. In deep, bold strokes, Warden Kennedy signed his name at the bottom of the document, authorizing the temporary transfer of Roberto Lopez to Cell E-4.

———

"Thank God, you're all right!" Stewart exclaimed.

"Why should that be so surprising?" Simon asked.

"Where have you been for the past few weeks? I've been worried sick about you. We all have." He gestured to his cell mates behind him.

"I've been away on business," Simon replied, throwing a glance over Stewart's shoulder, then scanning the hallway. The guards struck him as unusually attentive today. Simon lowered his voice and moved closer to the triple-partitioned barrier. "Do you have the item you told me about?"

Stewart gripped the bars tightly. "There's been a change of plans," he whispered. "No document. Too risky."

Simon gave Stewart a long hard look. Flickers of rage had always played across his features since his confinement in this diabolic pit, but this time Simon detected more than what he had become accustomed to facing. A deeper layer of fear radiated from Stewart's expression.

"What happened, Stewart? Something must have happened."

"Something *did* happen. Lots of things I can't tell you about. Just take my word for it. If we risk passing something to you through the broom and get caught, they'll kill us both, maybe others, too. You can talk to the Feds and tell them we'll testify. Then don't come back. *Ever!* Or they'll get to you, Ted. Like they got to . . ." His voice trailed off.

"Like they got to who?" Simon pressed.

"No one, nothing. Just don't come back. We'll make out somehow."

Simon pondered the implications of Stewart's warning. Finally, "I did talk to the FBI. Agents told me they've been building a case against this place for a long time. But they need *affidavits*, something in writing. They need assurances prisoners will testify. They need what you said you were going to provide me, and I told them I would sneak it out. Apparently they've been burned in the past and they need more than just verbal promises. Naturally, they guarantee everyone protection."

"That's easy for them to say. They're on the *outside!*" Stewart glanced at the guard, a motion Simon followed. The guard seemed to jerk his head away just as they looked at him, in a gesture of practiced indifference. "Talk to them again," Stewart repeated. "Tell them they'll have to move against this place without any written stuff from us." He retreated into his cell, raised his right forearm onto the wall, and rested his head against it.

Obviously, Stewart was holding back on him, but on a matter that clearly involved mutual survival, and not just his individual gain. Simon had been holding back on Stewart as well. More than that, he had lied, or at least withheld the truth, pending his decision on how best to present it. Business obligations had delayed Simon's return, true; but a more important reason had burst into his life. Lori.

Why had she returned? Simon hadn't a clue, and their encounter in his office several weeks earlier only confused him even more. Their conversation hobbled along in fragments, consisting of a disjointed series of queries on her part followed by hesitant responses on his, while he probed for the correct meanings that seemed to lurk behind her wayward glances, her awkward pauses. *This is what she said; is that what she meant?* Simon had wondered. *This is how I answered; is it what she was seeking?* And so their conversation stumbled along for two hours, like a Model T bouncing across uncertain terrain. *MY answers chasing HER questions,* he concluded later, after Simon showed her the door. One point, however, did stand out, a phrase that seemed to possess special meaning to her. Thus, like a desperate Marine besieged in his foxhole, and tossing a hand grenade into a murky jungle fraught with unknown dangers, Simon plunged forward with words that meant nothing special to him, but might evoke a reaction from Stewart.

"Number four's a winner at two-o-two-and three." he said in a loud, clear voice.

The scene before his eyes froze. Stewart lurched toward him and clutched the bars.

"Where did you hear that?" he hissed.

"From Lori."

"She's here? You saw her?"

"She stopped by my office several weeks ago."

"And you didn't tell me?" Stewart rasped accusingly.

"I told you, I was out of town. Besides, you've been so distraught, I wasn't sure how you would react."

"Did she ask about me?"

"Yes. And she wants to see you, but after I told her about The Dungeon, she became frightened, begged off. Said something about waiting until you were transferred or something." Simon knew he was a lousy liar; he hoped Stewart wouldn't detect the catch in his voice.

Stewart gaped at him for what seemed an eternity. "What did she say about those words you just said?"

"She asked me, with my knowledge of harness track racing, if the phrase had any special meaning. I told her that, beyond the obvious, no."

Another studied gaze. Suddenly, Stewart swiveled around, stepped to his cot, retrieved something from a spot Simon couldn't determine, and returned to the bars. "I'm going to stick a folded sheet of paper into the broom. Reach down and take it just like you always do, like you're shoving in a twenty," he instructed.

Stewart obviously wasn't going to offer reasons for his change of heart, and Simon didn't ask. "Right," he said.

Stewart grasped the broom, laid it on the floor. Eyes toward the guard. Same straight-ahead look, like a uniformed mannequin. Note into the bristles . . . Slow, careful shove beneath the bars . . . Simon leaned over, plunged his fingers into the straw. He looked up.

The guard was watching their every move.

Stewart whisked the broom away, set it against the wall. Simon jerked to an upright position and tried to appear normal. Too late. The guard walked toward them and stopped. Accusing eyes burned beneath a heavy, short forehead. He'd caught them in the act and knew it.

His hand rested on his pistol. "Will you come with me, please?" he commanded.

"Why?" Simon asked.

"You will come with me, Mr. Simon," the guard repeated. He gestured toward the two doors. Simon glanced at Stewart, whose face had turned ashen, then reluctantly got up and preceded the guard toward the double doors leading out the cell block.

"Where are we going?" Simon asked.

"To the warden's office," the guard said.

As the pair approached the end of the long hallway, the doors opened and two other guards entered the cell block, flanking a prisoner. Simon and his guard stepped aside to let them pass. Simon watched the trio walk down the gloomy hallway and stop before cell E-4. A heavy key chain jingled off a guard's belt. Key lifted . . . Cell door opened . . . Prisoner shoved inside.

Before the guard prodded him to continue, Simon caught a glance of E-4's new inhabitant. The chamber's dim light cut cruel shadows across his dark features, rendering his countenance even more striking. As he was being led away, Simon clawed through his memory, trying to isolate Stewart's comments about an inmate whose appearance seemed to match what he saw. Finally, it came to him.

It was that Puerto Rican kid. The one who had murdered a doctor, according to Stewart. Why were they moving him into Stewart's cell?

Chapter Twenty-Eight

Gerald Kennedy glared at the guard who sat upright with a stricken expression on his face, hands folded on his lap, like an errant schoolboy. Unspoken communication flowed from the warden's angry countenance, prompting the object of his attention to avert his scornful glare.

"I could have sworn Lawrence was passing something back to him inside that broom, warden. Honest," Delbert said.

Kennedy snorted. "You swore that *twice,*" he huffed. "Damned embarrassing bringing a man up here a couple of times to be searched on suspicion for carrying out contraband. Each time, *nothing!* You searched him yourself, Ed, *in my presence.* What did you expect to drop out of his pants? A typewriter!"

Ed colored, let his gaze drift toward the window, nursing the warden's verbal slap with a scowl. Conner chuckled, which drew a sharp look of rebuke from Kennedy.

"And the last time," the warden continued, stabbing the air with his cigar for emphasis, "that Simon guy, that arrogant son of a bitch, muttered something about talking to state officials and accusing us of harassment! And you know what, Ed? *He'd be right!*" Kennedy blew a ball of smoke out the side of his mouth, where it rolled through the air and swished against a window, dissipating. "Anyway, you're the one who's been fretting and sobbing about bringing an investigation down on our heads," he accused. He turned toward Conner. "Any news from your man?"

"Nothing, I'm afraid," Conner said.

"You told me he could hear as well as he could fight," Kennedy said derisively.

Conner shrugged. "Only if people talk loud enough for him to hear. But other inmates pretty much leave him alone, and he's not overheard anything. They all know he sliced up Stanton. I thought one of those weak ladies would confide in him, try to curry favor, and tell us what we want to know." Conner shook his head. "Guess it didn't work," he admitted.

"Well, something's going on!" Kennedy boomed, pounding the desk. "Ed, you said Simon blurted something before Lawrence used the broom. What was it?"

"Number four's a winner at two-o-two and three," he repeated, like a Sunday school child reciting a Bible verse.

"Aha! See?" Kennedy cried triumphantly. "Number four's got to mean E-4, their cell. *Right?* Two-o-two and three's got to mean a time, a date, or something. That's the part we've got to figure out! They're planning something. I know it. I feel it in my bones." A tinge of purple colored the warden's jowls.

Conner raised his hand in a gesture of dismissal. "Warden, it may mean nothing. Haven't you ever been to the races?"

"Car races, yes. Well, demolition derby."

"Try *horse* races," Conner corrected. "Actually, harness racing. That's what Lawrence did before he started robbing banks. In fact, that's the reason he robbed banks, to pay off his gambling debts. All those words mean is that the number four horse came in first with a winning time of two minutes, two and three-fifths seconds."

"But it still might be their secret way of communicating something," Ed ventured. His expression brightened. "I know what to do! Let's make this visitor search thing part of our standard operating procedure. Tell him it's a new policy. Search a few others while we're at it, so he doesn't feel singled out. Who knows what might turn up?" He appealed to Warden Kennedy, who responded with a thoughtful gaze as he puffed on his stogie.

The head guard of Jackson County Jail slapped his fist into the palm of his hand. "If those words mean anything we should be concerned about," he said, with steel in his voice, "I guarantee to you both, *I will find out.* In the meantime, I think we should look into this random search policy. Especially if we arrange to insert the wrong things into the pockets of selected guests . . ."

Like a network of tributaries feeding a river, a tangle of worry lines converged on the furrow carved on Stewart's forehead by five months of anxiety accumulated in The Dungeon. He glared at Jackson County Jail's lifeline to the world. "What did they say to you the last time?" he asked his most faithful visitor.

"They were embarrassed," Simon answered. "I mean, *really* embarrassed. I even threatened to notify their superiors about the facility's handling of prison visitors." Simon chuckled at a slice of humor that failed to make an impression on his companion. Noting this, he continued in a low voice. "The bottom line here is that I think the heat is off, so to speak, and I don't think they suspect anything beyond the normal. Or, what's normal for this place. In fact, that guard who hauled me up there stumbled all over himself just letting me in. Bumped into me, practically knocked me down. I just think he wanted to let off steam for not catching me with anything incriminating."

"Thank God you stuffed that note back into the broom when you saw him looking at us," Stewart said.

"Thank God *you* retrieved it after I left," Simon said. "Do you have that document?"

Stewart looked worried. "The last couple of times we thought about doing this, they hauled you in," he warned. "If they catch you with this sheet of paper . . ." He left his sentence unfinished and glanced down the hallway. Ed Delbert remained standing there, a Dick Tracy character trimmed in black straps wrapped around a gray outline, highlighted by a gaggle of weapons jutting out from his waist. No change in his demeanor; a yawn even gaped from his mouth. Finally Stewart met Simon's gaze with a look of determination. "Let's do it this time!" he whispered.

Stewart retreated into the murky confines of his cell, groped for something near the base of his cot, and returned to the bars. He reached for the broom, stuffed his note inside, and eased it beneath the barrier. Simon observed his motions, then looked over his shoulder at E-4's muddle of prisoners, their shadowy figures etched in charcoal lines against the dim yellow haze of light flowing into their enclave from the hallway.

"Where's that Puerto Rican kid?" Simon asked.

"They took him out of our cell this morning," Stewart said. "He's Conner's stooge, and he returned him to the fold, I guess," he commented acidly. "Which is why I think you may be right about the heat being off."

Simon checked the guard again, who now had his back turned to him. His posture struck Simon as a bit too casual. *He wouldn't dare trot me up there a third time,* Simon tried to reassure himself. *Would he?*

Finally, Simon leaned toward the floor, plunged his hand into the straw. Note grasped . . . Eyes cut toward the guard . . . No change. Just like the dozen or so other visits—before Guard Delbert took him to the warden's office, of course. Still . . .

Is he toying with me?

Simon palmed the two-inch square of paper and raised it to his waist. Where to put it? He poked for a hiding place on his clothing, anxious to get it out of sight before the guard's vision drifted in their direction. He lifted the flap of his suit pocket and stuffed it inside. *Something strange, here* . . . Simon probed his pocket, felt an object, fingered its contours. Long, slender, weighty—metal and plastic, he guessed. Unmistakable outline. Horror flooded his thoughts.

It was a knife. From his manipulation of it, he guessed a switchblade. Somehow, someone had sneaked a knife into his suit pocket after he entered the building. Simon closed his eyes, spun his thoughts back to the point where he entered the jail, checked in by the reception desk, took a seat, waited. Got up . . . Stepped toward guards . . . Quick, visual examination, check for contraband . . . Small door window sliding open . . . Shaft of light spilling out, face filling the rectangle . . . Into the cell block . . . Guard still standing there . . . Took one step toward E-4 . . .

He's on top of me.

That's when it happened. The guard's artful clumsiness planted a switchblade into his pocket. *A frame-up.* Fear knifed through his guts. Getting caught sneaking a weapon into a jail—Simon shuddered at what they could do. *But what was their purpose?* Certainly they didn't expect him to pass it along to Stewart, did they? Like fingers sorting through a jumble of puzzle pieces, Simon's thoughts rummaged through elements of what he imagined constituted a pattern, a coherent design lurking in Boss Hogg's mental architecture. A single fact pierced into his speculations like a sword thrusting through his heart: *he had Stewart's document in his possession . . . Could he put it back this time as well?*

Stewart followed Simon's motions with an expression of disapproval. "That's the first place they'd check," he protested. "Try to put it someplace else . . ."

"*Stewart!* That guard slipped a knife into my pocket!" Simon muttered.

"What!"

"Must have slipped it into my pocket. You know, when he stumbled on me."

"Bastards!" Stewart's eyes twittered back and forth, as though registering the calculations skipping through his mind. "Give it to me!" he ordered.

"Give it to *you?* But what are you . . ."

"Do it! Shove it into the broom!"

Stewart grasped the broom, slid it under the bars again. "Quickly!" he whispered.

Simon's fingers plunged into his pocket, five thick, quivering digits bumping into one another, frustrating their common purpose. Finally, he grabbed it, started to lift it out. A furtive peek toward Ed Delbert . . .

He was staring at them.

Simon released his grip on the knife, whisked his hand out of his pocket. Knife felt heavy in his clothing, like an anchor hanging from his side, broadcasting its presence. *Might as well have a brick strapped to my waist,* Simon fumed. Stewart's countenance had turned ashen. Ghostly light gouged murky depressions into his cheeks. "Talk!" he croaked. "Act perfectly normal."

Simon moved his lips, pushed out meaningless drivel that neither he nor Stewart paid any attention to. Delbert sauntered toward them, right hand resting on his pistol holster, left fondling his billy club. Premonition of disaster hovered over Simon's thoughts. *Can I drop this thing into my shoe?* The corner of his eye caught a flicker of blurred motion coming at them. *Impossible.*

More talk, sputtering, pointless chatter. The guard approached.

Closer . . . Closer . . .

Simon and Stewart locked their eyes on each other, uttered desperate words in low, grating voices. The guard still walked toward them. His lonely steps clicked on the cold concrete, echoing their terrifying countdown to an inevitable discovery, a certain, perhaps deadly reprisal. Simon's body stiffened; he clutched the bars, clammy hands wrapped around cold metal.

Distance closing . . . Nearly beside them . . . *Any minute now . . .*

Delbert walked right by Cell E-4.

Stewart cautiously followed the uniformed figure's every step, until he stopped about three cells away and cocked his arms behind his back, parade rest. The guard threw an expressionless glance in their direction, then resumed his stare at some object at the end of the hall. Stewart turned to Simon, blinked an okay.

Two long, controlled sighs.

Simon spoke first. "Problem is, he can see us better from where he's at."

"That may not matter," Stewart observed thoughtfully. "You can't get caught with that thing on you."

"Neither can you!"

Stewart shook his head, checked out the guard again, then looked intently at Simon. "I don't think that's their purpose. They want to find it on *you*, not *me*. Plus, I can hide it. Trust me."

Simon looked at Stewart as though accumulated jail house pressures had obliterated what little remained of his rationality. "I don't understand . . ."

"You will. First, put that note in a different place."

Simon considered this instruction. His last two visits to Boss Hogg's office involved the ritual of guards slapping his legs, torso, buttocks, arms, rummaging through pockets, checking for concealed apertures in his clothing. They did everything except force him to take off his clothes and stand naked before them. Very professional, very thorough, didn't miss a thing. No wonder you couldn't sneak anything out of this place. No wonder . . .

Simon's review stopped abruptly, settled on one point. They did everything except force him to take off his clothes. Of course. They wouldn't force him to do that!

Simon retrieved the note, inched aside his suit coat, pulled up a tuft of white shirt, and stuffed the rectangle of paper under his belt, inside his trousers. It clung to his damp skin as though he had pasted it on with a smear of glue. He shot a glance toward Ed, who remained standing there like a statue. Stewart's strange instructions, the guard's apparent indifference—none of it made any sense. Still, Stewart seemed to sense what was happening.

"Okay, now what?" Simon asked.

"Take out a twenty, wrap it around the knife, slip it into the broom," Stewart said.

Simon pulled out his wallet, retrieved a twenty dollar bill, inserted it into his suit coat pocket, and wrapped it around the knife. He lifted both out of his pocket. Another glance at the guard. Same studied aloofness. *Why isn't he watching more carefully?*

Simon leaned down, stuffed the twenty and knife into the bristles, and prayed that the heavy object wouldn't fall out and clatter on the floor. Stewart eased the broom inside the cell, quickly grasped the knife, tucked it inside his shirt. "Time for you to leave," he said.

"I couldn't agree more," Simon uttered. "What about the knife?"

"Don't worry about that," Stewart said. "Just leave quietly, act casual, *and don't come back!*"

"Not without the cavalry." Simon winked, and he walked away.

He took two steps, when he felt an iron fist clamp around his right arm. "I think you should come with me, Mr. Simon," Ed snarled, with a gleam of satisfaction.

"To the warden's office?"

"Yes."

"May I ask why?"

"New policy. Random checks of visitors leaving the facility. Consider yourself lucky," he chortled. "This is your third time."

And yours, too, Simon thought. *Three strikes and you're out.* His right hand inched up his thigh, probed his waist, patted his belt. Confidence flowed through Simon's body as he trotted before the prison official. *No way you'll locate this, Ed.*

Ten minutes later found Simon and his strutting chaperone standing before Boss Hogg, who sat behind his desk with the expression of a smug blowfish smeared on his flaccid countenance. A trim, athletic figure stood erect beside him: six-foot-two, Simon guessed, crisply uniformed, slivers of light bursting from the captain's bars on his shoulders. His sharp, lean features cut at right angles across his face, carving a menacing, hawk-like visage. A handlebar mustache curled up from his lips, spiraled across his taut cheeks. Grainy photographs of late nineteenth century baseball players strolled through Simon's thoughts. Except they looked quaint; this guy radiated cool, watchful malice.

Warden Kennedy cleared his throat. "Mr. Simon, let me indicate how much we appreciate the cooperation you've shown this office. Officer Delbert here"—he nodded toward the guard who took him in—"has probably informed you of our new policy. Checking visitors after they leave, as well as before they enter. Naturally, this is a random check . . ."

About as random as alphabetical order, Simon thought.

". . . but you happened to pick the lucky number again, anyway. So, with your indulgence," he motioned toward Ed Delbert, "I really doubt this will ever occur again, especially since your friend probably won't be here with us much longer."

Delbert, who was standing behind Simon, commenced his professional groping. "You should keep in mind," Kennedy continued, "that the possession of illegal objects in this facility constitutes a grave offense against our rules . . ."

Ankles slapped . . . then calves . . . thighs . . . waist . . .

Pause.

". . . but we could overlook such an infraction if . . ." his words trailed off.

Delbert's large hands groped around Simon's waist, his coat, his buttocks. Into pockets. Back to his waist. Under his arms. Frantic, desperate searching. *Nothing.* Simon observed Delbert's frustration register on the warden's face. Kennedy looked incredulous. He exchanged glances with Conner, whose icy blue eyes narrowed, bored on the man behind Simon.

"If what, Mr. Kennedy?" Simon inquired innocently.

"If, um . . ." he stammered. ". . . any such item should be discovered."

"You know me better than that by now, Warden," Simon stated coolly.

A rising tide of crimson flooded Gerald Kennedy's face. He shot furious glances over Simon's shoulder to his subordinate. "Well . . . it's not just that!" he blurted. Out came his cigar. An accusing jab. "Listen to me, Mr. Simon. We have reason to believe a few prisoners are plotting something against the rules, and that what they have in mind is connected to what you said to Stewart Lawrence!"

"What might that be?" Simon asked.

Kennedy gestured toward Delbert, who repeated the phrase. Simon merely shrugged. "It's a racing term. I place a few bets for Stewart now and then just to cheer him up, give him some news when we meet, and he happened to win that time, that's all. Now will there be anything else? I really must go."

Kennedy looked at Conner, who rolled his eyes. Simon thought he detected an I-told-you-so attitude in Conner's response.

"Yes, go! Get out of here!" Kennedy barked.

Relishing every second of Boss Hogg's discomfiture, Simon tucked his shirt, adjusted his trousers, and otherwise straightened his clothes in several theatrical gestures, then prepared to leave. *Someone's going to catch hell for this,* Simon thought gleefully. *Couldn't happen to a more deserving bunch of guys* . . . Conner stepped toward the door, and Simon followed him.

That's when he noticed it. Stewart's note had slipped down the inside of his trousers.

Simon stopped abruptly before the door. Conner swiveled around, shot him a look of irritation. "Anything wrong," he growled.

"No . . . no, nothing. Go on."

Door opened, Conner stepped through, then Simon. Conner closed it behind them. Down the stairs, two flights. Another door, this time with heavy, thick bars, flanked by uniformed figures who regarded Simon the way a pair of pit bulls slobbered at a hunk of raw meat passing beneath their noses. Stewart's note tumbled down a few more inches, like a spider crawling down his thigh.

I had to do it, Simon lamented. *A flash of bravado before making my last getaway.*

Last step, to the lobby, left leg planted, trousers shifted. Stewart's note dropped to knee level. Like some fiendish insect darting about his leg, taunting him before inflicting its fatal sting, Stewart Lawrence's devilish paper square pricked its corners into Simon's skin, finally lodging near the crook of his leg. One wrong step, and . . .

Just stay by my knee, Simon silently pleaded, as though his agonized entreaty somehow could affect the note's tortuous path. *Don't move.*

One more door opened to the lobby. Thick black bars, a single guard. Same malicious sneer. Conner still ahead of him, leading the way. The guard opened the door, inserted a key into a dark aperture with the outline of a miniature golf ball perched on a tee with a flat bottom. Metal clanked against metal, door opened, hinges squealed in protest, the lobby yawned before him and its door to the outside. The door leading to freedom, to safety, to the FBI, to the destruction of Boss Hogg's imperial domain. And Stewart Lawrence's emancipation from The Dungeon.

"After you, Mr. Simon," Conner gestured with his right arm.

The worst possible move. Conner now would be better able to observe him as he walked.

Simon nodded, Conner waited, cocked his head, curious. Simon's left arm moved down his leg, as though to scratch, clutched the pesky rectangle, shoved it up a few inches. Felt tighter now, a little better, more secure. A few more strides, through the lobby, out the door . . . *Don't move, you stupid thing!*

Simon took several long steps past the guard near the door, Conner right behind him. Middle of the room now, outside door no more than ten feet away. Simon riveted his gaze on that door. *One step at a time.* Note felt secure, glued by sweat to his thigh. Conner's black shoes clicked with authority, shadowed him closely. *Almost there.*

Suddenly the note tumbled down to Simon's ankle, stuck by his sock. Simon stopped. Conner bumped into him. He grunted, cursed.

"What's the matter with you?" Conner growled.

Beads of sweat clumped lines of hair in Simon's neck, trickled down his collar. The lobby was cool; chilly, even. Simon felt Conner's eyes bore on the back of his neck. *He must see me sweat.*

Simon bent over, flitted glances about him. All eyes in the room, guards', visitors', trained on his movements. He spied Conner's uniformed figure towering behind him.

"What is your problem, man?" he asked harshly.

Simon felt around his ankle, as though scratching again. The paper rectangle tumbled into his hand, just as Albert Conner stepped around his arched body and planted his feet by Simon's head. Simon stuffed the paper rectangle into his shoe, looked up to Conner, who had his hands planted on his waist.

The prison captain glared at him. "You're acting a bit peculiar, Mr. Simon," he said, a cutting edge to his words. "Maybe we should go to the warden's office for more discussion." He raised his right hand, thoughtfully fingered the tip of his mustache.

Simon stood up to his full height. "I'm not going anywhere but out of this jail, Captain Conner," he asserted, steel encasing each word. "Now, if you please . . ."

Icy glints of suspicion cracked from Conner's cold blue eyes, probing for weaknesses. Finding none, he stepped aside, let Simon pass. "See you next time you visit, Mr. Simon," he stated flatly.

Simon walked past him and strode toward the entrance. He opened the door to Jackson County Jail and breezed into the chilly winter evening. The massive door closed behind him with the finality of a boulder grinding across a tomb's aperture, thumping it shut. He took a deep draught of crisp air and hurried down the stairs toward his car two blocks away. Once safely inside his vehicle, Simon retrieved Stewart's incriminating letter and placed it inside his pocket. More than anything, he wanted to escape the area, fast.

Ted Simon darted his station wagon through the blighted streets surrounding the jail house and raced toward a major highway leading to New York City and to the Federal Building housing the FBI. Feelings of exhilaration and anxiety tumbled through his thoughts. Stewart's letter would give the FBI the evidence they needed to obliterate Boss Hogg's operation, no doubt about that. In the meantime, Stewart remained in jail, holding the knife Boss Hogg intended to use as blackmail against him. Simon shuddered. God knows what demonic retribution Gerald Kennedy would visit on Stewart and others in Cell E-4.

Simon stabbed the accelerator pedal. *Whatever the FBI has in mind,* he thought, *they had better act fast.*

Or Stewart Lawrence is a dead man.

Chapter Twenty-Nine

Captain Albert Conner placed his telephone receiver back on its cradle. His hand flopped over the phone like a wet rag; he slumped in his chair. Ed Delbert, seated across from him, noted his superior's uncharacteristic pose. "What's wrong?" he asked.

Conner studied his subordinate carefully, calculating the man's strengths and weaknesses and comparing them to the list in his private ledger of character attributes. "I have a task for you, Ed," he declared.

Delbert looked at him warily. "What is it?"

"I want you to move all of the inmates out of the infirmary."

"All of them? Why? What's up?"

"You'll see."

"Where shall I put them? There's not enough room on the fourth floor."

"Don't matter," Conner said. "Just do it."

Delbert regarded this order with suspicion. "What's going on, Albert?"

"I said, you'll find out," Conner replied in a harsh tone.

Delbert tried to digest this ambiguity. Finally, "Anything else?"

"Yes." Conner cleared his throat, mostly for effect. "This is what I want you to do next . . ."

The implications of Conner's words slowly registered in Delbert's thoughts, pushing a sly grin across his lips. "Another try, eh?" he ventured, probing for more. "Do I detect higher stakes?"

"Something like that," Conner answered cryptically. "Just be sure to send him to me, first. I want to speak to him alone."

"Why?" he asked, as though slighted.

"I have my reasons."

Delbert shrugged, got up, and stepped toward the door. He hurled an inquisitive glance over his shoulder. "You're sure there's nothing else you should tell me?"

"To repeat," Conner flared, "you'll find out."

"When?"

"Soon. Believe me."

Delbert stood by the door for a minute, searching for some hidden meaning lurking behind Conner's words, then squared his shoulders and marched out of the office.

Conner leaned back in his chair. He unsnapped his holster and lifted out his pistol. He examined the weapon, stroked its trigger, tested the gun's weight, savored its power. He checked the time. Any minute now, a knock on his door, a prisoner would be escorted inside. Then the door would shut, leaving the prisoner in his office. Alone, with him.

And his .38 caliber pistol.

The creaking groan of metal hinges grinding against each other pierced the low murmur of soft conversation in the cell block. Heavy doors opened and footsteps of a single man clicked through the hallway, flinging sharp echoes into the gloom. Soft swishing of inmates approaching their cell doors ruffled the air. The guard approached Cell E-4, stopped, faced a half-dozen curious faces. Key whipped out, metallic cylinder clanked into an aperture, shank twisted, double-barred door squealed open.

"Lawrence, Stewart," barked a voice. "Front and center."

Lawrence approached the guard. Pale light from the hallway glowed around the charcoal outline of Prison Guard Ed Delbert standing by his cell door.

"What is it?" Stewart asked.

"Come with me," Delbert ordered.

Stewart cautiously stepped forward. Delbert grabbed him by the arm, pulled him outside, and slammed his cell door shut with a loud clang.

"What's going on?" Stewart asked.

"That way!" Delbert commanded.

The prison guard shoved him down the hallway through several barred doors and up two flights of stairs. They stopped by the landing near a door with the word "Infirmary" printed on a Bakelite sign over a rectangular window. Delbert lifted a heavy metal ring jingling with keys and sorted through them. He offered several possibilities into the cone of light flowing from a single bulb hanging from the ceiling, tried some that didn't work, muttered a few obscenities, and resumed sorting.

Stewart observed this ritual with a sense of apprehension. The image of Roberto Lopez's maniacal visage flashed across his mind. But the Puerto Rican's assault on Stanton had occurred on the *fourth* floor, perhaps the only place the guards could orchestrate such an event. This was the third floor, the infirmary. Everyone knew a number of rooms had been converted to suites for the prisoner elite, but the floor still housed medical facilities. So, why was Delbert taking him there? Didn't make sense.

Another observation struck Stewart as even more bizarre. Where were the guards? Uniformed figures sprouted from every corner in The Dungeon like bats clustered throughout the crevices of a cave. But during their trek to the third floor, not a single guard appeared. No other prison officials, either. No one.

Delbert found the correct key, applied it to the door, cranked it open. "Get inside!" he snapped, gesturing toward the hallway.

Stewart took a few tentative steps. Suddenly, Delbert's fist thrust him in his back with the force of a battering ram, and he stumbled into the hallway. Door clumped shut behind him . . . Footsteps trailed away . . .

Silence.

Stewart scrambled to his feet, pounded on the door, shouted an obscenity. Echoes of his futile cries brushed against his ears, mocking his appeals. He was alone. Alone and trapped. But why?

A sound. Stewart swiveled around, backed up against the door, heart thumping in his throat. *Where did that come from?* He waited, listened. He heard it again. He peered down the hallway; nothing stood out. Looked like the hallway of any hotel. *This IS a hotel.* Maybe a half-dozen doors, each side. Every one, the same. Nothing to tell them apart, except . . .

Suddenly, the fiendish design became clear to him. Stewart was not alone. One other person shared the floor with him. And that person was a murderer.

Again, a muffled noise disturbed the empty silence. He couldn't determine its origin; one of the rooms obviously. Now what? With the force of a lightning bolt, the solution streaked through his thoughts. *Go to a room and hide before Roberto Lopez bursts into the hallway, brandishing his knife.* Stewart took three long strides toward the nearest door and twisted its knob.

Locked.

Of course! he thought, bitterly. What did he expect? A classic scenario, cat and mouse. No, not that. A different analogy ventured forth and paraded a fable so outrageously simple in outline that Stewart found a smile tugging at the corners of his mouth. Some story about a person facing two doors, one of which he must open. Behind one, a fabulous treasure; behind the other, a ferocious beast. And the choice *had* to be made. No other alternatives. Stewart comforted himself with the fact that at least he had more than two alternatives.

Ten, actually, he discovered after counting the doors. Probably all were locked; or, all but one, perhaps. Behind which lurked a killer, waiting for him. For a fleeting instant, Stewart's fright succumbed to a sliver of respect for the ingenuity behind it all. He concluded this scenario had to be Conner's doing; no one else could be as diabolically clever.

Which still didn't help him solve his problem. Stewart tried to fathom Conner's reasoning, Lopez's orders. Was the Puerto Rican supposed to wait for him? Did Conner expect him to go to his hit man, like a sheep to slaughter? Behind his immediate dilemma lurked a tangle of puzzles that assaulted his mind like a swirling throng of buzzing hornets. Where were the guards? The rest of the prisoners? Why did Conner single him out? Why didn't they rifle through his cell, search for the knife they knew he had hidden somewhere? What was his purpose?

Another sound, a faint knock escaped from the left portion of the hallway. *He's in a room on that side, no doubt about it.* Another scrutiny of the doors. Suddenly, a simple fact occurred to him, so obvious, Stewart wondered why he didn't think of it sooner. He had been in the infirmary a few times, to get medicine or something, and had made an observation that now assumed extraordinary importance. These doors had no bars. No special security. Just ordinary, locked doors, that's all. He should be able to break into the infirmary room. A determined kick, a single sharp thrust should smash that door open. Most important, the room was located on the side opposite to where he suspected Lopez was lurking. No way he could be in there . . . *Could he?*

Only one way to find out. Stewart walked toward the infirmary room, lifting his feet as though each step teetered on the edge of a precipice. *Don't make a sound, don't let him guess my location, anticipate my movements.* He stepped in front of the door. Arm raised . . . Hand placed on the knob . . . Turn, slowly . . .

Locked.

Stewart concluded that Lopez was not in that room. His thoughts raced through an inventory of the infirmary's contents. It was filled with tables, chairs, cabinets loaded with stuff—medicines, needles, first-aid equipment. He felt he would be better off in that room. Might even find something he could use as a weapon. Maybe even barricade the door, if Lopez didn't catch on quickly enough, which would give him time to defend himself. Then what? Stewart didn't know.

He retreated across the hallway, until his back touched the door to the room where he suspected Lopez was waiting. He had to crash through in a single lunge, no second chance. Stewart set his jaw, tightened every muscle in his body. He had four, maybe five steps. Take a deep breath . . . Aim for the dead bolt, four inches above the knob . . . Heels in front, like a battering ram . . . *NOW!*

He lurched forward, feet first . . . *THUD!* Stewart's right heel clipped the door knob, deflecting the force of his blow, and he collapsed on the floor. Stabbing pain. His foot twisted, broken, maybe. He grasped his right ankle.

Door didn't budge an inch.

Sounds behind him . . . A body getting up, moving . . . *Lopez is on to me.* On his feet, one more try, this time with the shoulder. Pain knifed through Stewart's ankle, as though a lance had speared into his foot. Hobble up to a standing position . . . Brace yourself . . . Ready to leap again . . . *GO!*

CRASH!

Stewart exploded into the infirmary, somersaulted across the floor, banged his head against a table sitting in the middle of the room. Stunned, he lay there for two, three seconds, then opened his eyes and looked at the door. The door jamb to the infirmary was pulverized in a gnarled mess of wood splinters and bent metal. Across the hall another door gaped open. Standing in the doorway, dressed in a T-shirt and jeans, every muscle on his wiry frame taut like a cougar ready to strike, was Roberto Lopez. His lean right hand wrapped around a knife. A crazed gleam of malice burned in his dark eyes, now narrowed, riveted on him. A contemptuous grin played across his lips.

Stewart scrambled to his feet, lunged for the infirmary door, heaved it shut with all his might. The door whacked against its frame, then sprang back, as though spitting vengeance into Stewart's face for the damage he inflicted on it. Lopez vaulted across the hall, filled the doorway. Stewart leaped backward, into the room, behind the table. Knuckles gripped wood, eyes trained on the attacker. Predator and prey locked on each other, waiting for the other to move first. With lightning quickness, Lopez pitched forward, whipped his blade across the table in a wide, sweeping arc. Icy heat sliced across Stewart's chest. He stumbled backward, looked down. Torn clothing, lacerated flesh . . . Blood blossoming on his shirt . . . *Nausea* . . . A single second, a grip on his thought . . . *Rage!*

Stewart seized the table, plunged it into Lopez's gut. The Puerto Rican jackknifed backward, crumpled to the floor, choked for air. He looked up, astonishment, wrath, flashed on his face. Seized by maniacal fury, he shrieked a cry in Spanish, sprang up, and leaped across the table. Stewart bolted away, back against the wall, next to a medicine chest. He gripped the wooden and glass cabinet, wrenched it from the wall, and sent it plummeting toward Lopez. The agile young man skipped to the side, the cabinet crashed to the floor in an explosion of glass, wood, and a melange of medical implements. Eyes blazing, Lopez hopped over the wreckage, charged toward Stewart, seized his crimson shirt. Blade whipped up to Stewart's throat . . . Bloody spittle frothing from Lopez's mouth . . . Madness cracking from every feature like sparks of electricity . . .

"*I ought to kill you, mahn!*" He spat out his words in heavily accented English.

Stewart gaped at the huge blade pressed against his throat, heart pounding inside his lacerated chest.

"You don't want to do that!" he cried. Stewart clawed for particles of rationality to counter Lopez's threat, for anything to save his life. "They'll execute you for sure."

"I'm already up for murder!" Lopez scoffed. "Don't matter. But Conner can help me. If I help him!" He drew his sweating head next to Stewart's face, squeezed his knife deeper against Stewart's flesh. Blood trickled from the slice across his throat, traced red paths down Lopez's merciless blade. "You tell me what racing words mean. Maybe then, I don't kill you." A wild, lunatic glint blazed in his eyes. "I teach you lesson, maybe, but still let you live. *Now*, gringo . . ."

A flash of comprehension exploded in Stewart's frenzied thoughts. *Conner set this up to discover the meaning of my clue!*

"Talk to me, mahn!" Knife cut deeper. Stewart inched his toes backward, toward the wall, strained his neck upward. Couldn't go any higher. A fraction of a second, one fast, deep slash . . . A severed jugular . . . Spurting blood . . . Life draining away . . .

Choked syllables sputtered from Stewart's throat. "I . . . don't . . . know . . ."

"I kill you anyway, *mahn!* I don't give a damn!"

Stewart coughed, terrified. Knife drawn back . . . Arm cocked . . . Blade flashing . . . "But you die the hard way!" Lopez shrieked. *"In your guts!"*

A stampede of footsteps rumbled down the hallway. Two men . . . Three . . . Four! Burst into the infirmary. Pistols whipped out, aimed at Lopez.

"HALT! FBI! Don't make a move!"

Doubt flickered in Roberto Lopez's eyes. A glance toward Stewart, ferocious. *He could still kill me,* Stewart thought. *What's he got to lose?*

"Drop it, Lopez! Let him *GO!*"

Back to the four guns aimed at his head. Lopez's eyes drifted to the side. His shoulders relaxed, he dropped the knife, it clattered on the wrecked cabinet at his feet. Four huge men swept across the room, descended on him. Handcuffs snapped on, Lopez was led away.

And Stewart Lawrence collapsed to the floor, barely conscious, a feeling of redemption flooding every ounce of his exhausted, wounded body.

God, that was close! Ted Simon mused, as he pondered the FBI's massive invasion of Jackson County Jail nearly five months ago, while observing the panorama of courtroom drama unfolding before his eyes. Agents flooding the jail house, securing the cell blocks, commanding every prison official to report to the lobby, immediately taking every guard into custody . . . And poor Stewart, stuck up on that third floor, a maniacal killer holding a knife to his throat. Simon remembered assuring him that he would bring the cavalry next time he visited. Like the cavalry, the FBI couldn't have shaved their timing any closer. A chill raced up Simon's spine as he contemplated the horrible possibilities. *In fact, if those agents had arrived a minute or two later . . .*

The judge's thunderous voice boomed across the courtroom, overwhelming his reveries. "And YOU, Mr. Gerald Kennedy," he intoned, a look of revulsion radiating from his stern countenance, "you have abused the public trust in a most reprehensible way . . ."

Simon had anticipated this moment with great relish. In the weeks following the FBI raid into the former warden's larcenous fiefdom, a score of prison officials had been arrested, and a federal grand jury handed down indictments stuffed with charges that seemed to exhaust the criminal code's list of egregious offenses: extortion, embezzlement, tax evasion, assault, and attempted murder, to cite a few. Unfortunately, sufficient evidence had accumulated to send only five men to trial, from which one had escaped by committing suicide—Edward Delbert. He unleashed a ferocious assault against two officers en route to his new maximum security residence, dented the skull of one agent, then somehow managed to hang himself. A bully and coward to the end.

". . . your *despicable* conduct against helpless inmates taxes the language of judicial discourse for words to convey the unbridled contempt felt for you by this court . . ."

That's telling him, judge, Simon thought, savoring vindication to an extent that surprised even himself. Kennedy did manage to garner a few defenders—mostly family members who conspicuously brandished handkerchiefs to absorb what struck Simon as well-orchestrated tears. No doubt their grief was sincere, Simon admitted to himself, as was that of the priest he had encountered during his first visit to the jail. The priest's presence still struck him as odd, though. A man of God festooned in garb that inspired an image of a fallen angel defending one of its own didn't exactly summon visions of sanctity in Simon's mind. Surpassing all was Kennedy's defense attorney, a suave character possessing slick black hair, a pleading countenance, and an oily tongue, which greased the warden's offenses with a thick lubrication of exonerating adjectives. Fortunately, the judge didn't buy any of it. Kennedy was going to get the ax, no doubt about it. But not until the judge finished expectorating his wrath.

Simon's thoughts drifted to an earlier trial, one he wished he hadn't attended. Albert A. Conner, Captain, head of the guard, and Kennedy's official second-in-command, his executive officer. Without question, his culpability ran as deeply as Kennedy's, but the prosecutor strained witnesses to attach responsibility for events in Jackson County Jail *directly* on him. Simon recalled fragments of testimony with chilling clarity.

Mr. Stanton, can you POSITIVELY identify Albert Conner as the man who threatened you in the back seat of your car?

Long pause. I think so, yes.

That's not enough! Can you positively identify THAT MAN, seated OVER THERE, as the man who threatened you . . .

A nervous cough. Well, when you put it that way . . .

And so it went. Even Stanton's inmate-brother, the accountant, couldn't establish beyond reasonable doubt that Conner *knew* Roberto Lopez was lurking in that bathroom on the fourth floor.

By the time I returned, it was too late, Conner had stated coolly. *I immediately apprehended Mr. Lopez and issued a call for assistance for his victim.*

Why, then, after this incident did you relocate Mr. Lopez to the so-called "prisoner-elite" quarters on the fourth floor? Wasn't that move to reward him for carrying out your orders?

Absolutely not! He was moved to protect the other prisoners, Conner replied.

Roberto Lopez admitted nothing, other than to boast about his own cleverness at being able to evade prison authorities and conveniently materialize in places where he found himself alone with another inmate. Against whom, of course, he found it necessary to defend himself.

Without doubt, Conner was dangerously shrewd, always working through others: Delbert, who was dead, and Lopez, who clamped his mouth shut. Other guards refused to implicate him. Never would Simon forget Conner's testimony, his cold aplomb, his brilliantly evasive answers. Worst of all, never could Simon forget . . .

". . . *and thus, I sentence you, Gerald R. Kennedy,*" the judge concluded in a roaring peroration, bringing Simon's thoughts back to the present, "to be incarcerated for a period of time no less than eighteen years. The only mercy this court extends is to permit your removal to a facility where you are not known, where you will be placed under an assumed name. Further mercies this humble court leaves to the infinite wisdom and grace of the Almighty God."

As Gerald Kennedy burst into a blubbering wail of tears and was led out of the courtroom, Simon's thoughts returned to a scene in that other trial, an image that spiked fear in his heart. Albert Conner's cold blue eyes radiating hatred, their intensity hurling across the courtroom a message that needed no words:

I'm going to get you for this, Ted Simon. I'm going to chase you down and kill you.

PART FIVE: THE GANDY DANCER

Chapter Thirty

August, 1969

Lori Armstrong squeezed a fist around her pencil and smashed it on a legal pad, bursting splinters of lead and wood across her kitchen table, gouging a small depression on its Formica top. *I'll never figure this miserable thing out, never!* she screeched inside. Not for lack of trying. She had endured dozens of visits to the trotters, which, in her opinion, swarmed with creatures who competed with one another for displaying the most outrageous garb, for exuding the most repulsive odor. And those were just the *spectators.* She could at least keep her distance from the other disgusting inhabitants at Lakewood Downs, ponderous quadrupeds that lumbered around the track, toting figures resembling oversized parakeets perched on tiny seats flanked by enormous bicycle wheels. Lori could not witness such organized lunacy without shaking her head. *They call this a sport?*

Her carefully planned accidental encounters with racetrack officials hadn't helped either; none had spawned a particle of insight into Stewart Lawrence's maddening clue. For all they knew, that standard phrase signified nothing more than exactly what it said. The number four horse came in first with a winning time of two minutes, two and three-fifths seconds. Problem was, Stewart's numbers did not match with this. His program contained data on fourteen races, not one of which had been won with that time.

Maybe that's not the operative part of his clue, Lori reasoned. *Work with number four first, then figure out the rest.* Here she had more luck. In one of the races, the number four horse won, a trotter called *The Gandy Dancer.* But it won at two minutes and three seconds. *Did Stewart have in mind the number four race?* Still didn't work. Aside from violating the plain meaning of the phrase, the number four race had been won by the number two horse at two-o-one-and-two. Back to *The Gandy*

Dancer, the number four winner. *But what do those incongruent figures mean?* Two years of feverish probing had not produced an answer to this question. Every time she hacked through the jungle of numbers blanketing Stewart's racing program like an impenetrable rain forest, she emerged exhausted, exasperated, and immersed in sweat. Sometimes with battle scars as well. She raised her arm, gently dabbed the fleshy part of her hand that had been stung by an errant sliver of pulverized pencil.

Lori swept away particles from the most recent casualty of her eruption of temper and reached for a box of saltines, still sprinkled with splinters of wood and pencil lead. She crunched on a cracker noisily, pondering her alternatives. What had begun as an exhilarating quest had deteriorated into repetitive slogging through a swamp of figures with no solution in sight. She kept hoping that eventually the key to Stewart's puzzle would leap from the pages, announce its presence with such blazing clarity that Lori would wonder why she hadn't stumbled on it earlier. Then she would race to the location indicated by his code, retrieve the bonds, *her bonds,* quit her job, and live without worry for the rest of her life.

The momentum of Lori's ruminations led her to consider Stewart's incarceration, the horrors he endured at Jackson County Jail, his narrow escape, his present circumstances. She marveled at the extraordinary risks taken by Ted Simon, how modestly he had explained to her his role in delivering his friend, a person to whom he owed nothing, from the clutches of that wretched place. A twinge of guilt slithered its way into Lori's thoughts. She tried to fend it off. She whipped open the racing program and concentrated on that same, unyielding quagmire of numbers. Finally, she looked up and stared blankly at some object at the end of the room.

Why should I worry about him? she mused, as if answering an accusation hurled at her from a part of her psyche she believed no longer existed. *He took my money, betrayed me, lied to me.* Lori reached for another cracker. *Whose money?* whispered a response from nowhere. *Well, Madison's money . . . But he owed it to me, the bastard!* Another crunch on the cracker. *But he also gave me my job back. Even got me a decent place to live near the beach. Any guesses about HIS ulterior motives?* Back to Stewart, sulking in a federal prison, waiting to get out, to race for his secret hiding place and escape with that money. Anger flared. *He's a rogue, like all the others!* Still . . . *Never did he hurt me, lay a hand on me, threaten me, or even utter an unkind word . . .* From these tangled musings emerged one salient fact. *Stewart's in prison for doing exactly what I did, except he got caught!*

After two years of futile mental assaults against a throng of numbers, Lori's thoughts finally converged on a conclusion. Two actually. *Plan A and Plan B,* she mused, relieved that at least temporarily she had settled on a course of action that involved more than her periodic confrontations with Stewart's obdurate data. *Plan A might work if Stewart trusts me, if he still loves me, as Ted has said he does.* Lori gathered the racing programs strewn across her desk, her mind skipping through the implications of what she wanted to do. She rummaged through related documents, re-examined sheets of paper filled with her scrawling trying to decipher Stewart's clue, put them down, and fussed with various objects in her kitchen. Aimless, nervous activity. Another sentiment hitched to her roving calculations, one she did her best to avoid facing. *Maybe I still love him, too . . .*

But Lori decided it didn't matter, one way or the other. *If Plan A doesn't work out,* she resolved, putting a grip on her emotions, *there's always Plan B . . .*

Great news, Ted! Just Great! Stewart had announced in his last letter. *Tell you all about it during your next visit . . .* Simon had written him back, cautioning his friend to rein in his optimism. He had been disappointed in the past, and deciphering the reasoning processes of parole boards was at best a precarious enterprise. In fact, Simon had little confidence in Stewart's powers of prognostication. He hoped this visit would enable him to check his friend's ardor with an injection of cold analysis. More than that, Simon carried news of his own that surely would spike Stewart's mood, regardless of what happened. But which way, up or down? He didn't know. *Maybe it's best not to say anything at all,* Simon wondered, as he turned toward the road leading to Stewart's new prison.

Simon wheeled into the parking lot of the Federal Penitentiary at Bluefield, Pennsylvania, located near a small town in the northeastern part of that state. He got out of his car and walked toward a stone wall, thirty feet high, studded with watchtowers and bulletproof glass booths, attended by guards whose uniforms sported a gaggle of military paraphernalia. He stopped by an electrically operated gate, recited his name, proceeded to another gate, answered a bevy of questions, and then walked into a yard area extending one hundred fifty feet from the main structure. Simon entered a clean, spartan building that could have passed for any government facility. An aura of competence and professionalism permeated the well-lit, smartly decked lobby. Crisply dressed prison officials marched him through another set of procedures, then led him down a long hallway and into the meeting room. A regiment of tables was mapped across the floor in precise, grid-like fashion, watched by guards standing at each end. Another remotely operated door opened across the room, and Stewart Lawrence stepped inside. He immediately spotted Simon and walked toward him in long strides.

"This is it, Ted!" Stewart gushed, as he sat down, his face bright, animated. "This time, there's no doubt."

Simon accepted his vigorous handshake and noted Stewart's improved appearance with relief. "No doubt about what?" he asked cautiously, fully aware of what his friend had in mind.

"My parole, of course! They'll grant it to me now; I feel it in my bones."

Simon struggled with how to respond and decided his honest, gut reaction was best. "Forgive me, Stewart, but that's what you said the last time. And the times before that. A year ago, Judge Chandler refused to reduce your sentence or even respond to your blizzard of letters. Then your case worker and parole board interviewer pumped you up for another review last November, which was again denied. More requests, more letters, more recommendations, still nothing. I think you should keep your head about this . . ."

"I tell you, things are different now!" Stewart insisted. "The parole board met with me a couple days ago. They got showered with positive stuff. Case workers, psychologists, they're all on my side. They tell me, thirty-six months, maximum. And I performed brilliantly—if I do say so myself—gave them all the right answers. Plus, I've been in group therapy to lick this gambling thing . . ." Stewart's words trailed off. His eyes wandered away.

Simon could understand why. The prognosis for compulsive gamblers usually looked dim, and knowledgeable persons had warned Simon that his former employee presented a most challenging case. In fact, Simon had learned more about Stewart Lawrence after his incarceration than he ever suspected while Stewart was just one of his salesmen. Successive revelations of Stewart's past showed that he had behaved as though some personal demon relentlessly goaded him to self-destruction, to sacrifice his soul on an altar of gambling. Thus, his repeated wagering binges at Roosevelt Raceway, at Lakewood Downs, at other places; his spectacular winnings, his calamitous losses. Yet he continued. Stewart's betting fortunes spiked and plunged like gyrations on a Richter scale monitoring erratic impulses of a severe earthquake. Seventy thousand won this week, a hundred thousand squandered on another; more borrowing, more losses, additional borrowing to cover greater losses.

And so it went. Stewart was obsessed, driven by a wicked temptress promising fabulous wealth, whispering from the dark recesses of his mind its depraved command: *Go on . . . Go on . . . Go on!* Stewart's defenses had always crumbled, his will always collapsed. Success ruined him as much as defeat, injecting ecstatic visions of ultimate victory into his calculations, prodding him to toss the dice one more time, to propitiate those deities of gambling until they hurled thunderbolts of triumph into his life. Defeat hollowed out his soul; desperation filled the void. Back to the betting booth he went, to recoup his losses, to make the world right again, or at least level, even. Goaded by pitiless taunts murmured by private demons, Stewart bet what he didn't have to win what he thought would make him happy, while murmurs of contemptuous laughter echoed through his mind. Stewart Lawrence was sick, and he knew it.

So did Judge Chandler, who reviewed his record carefully and sentenced him to ten years in prison, following a ninety day psychiatric examination at a Federal evaluation center after his trial. The judge felt that hope was justified, so he assigned Stewart an "A" rating, the highest possible category for parole possibilities. The fact that Stewart was a first offender helped; perhaps his sincere expression of remorse as well, but Judge Chandler reminded him that the bank teller he threatened remained traumatized by the experience. Still, with good behavior, Stewart could expect to be paroled after serving one-third of his sentence, which explained his present exuberance. Simon just hoped Stewart wasn't wrong. His track record hardly inspired confidence.

"So, how has that therapy been going?" Simon inquired. He felt like he was asking a wolf if it had cured its nasty habit of consuming delectable farm animals.

"I've read all the assignments; I'm working on it real hard. I can't say for sure I got it licked, but I'm working on it." His features tightened, an internal struggle played across his face, as though his fundamental instincts battled against a simple desire to state the truth.

An awkward pause; a change of subject. Simon quickly filled the time vacuum with inquiries about prison life, aspects of Stewart's job, high points, low points, things he wanted, and so forth, knowing the answers to all these questions from his previous visits. Simon knew life in prison didn't change much from day to day, week to week, from one month or year to another. The food was much better at this federal institution, visiting hours longer, more reasonable, and Stewart's prison duties enabled him to pass the hours about as tolerably as could be expected. His nimble intellect and ingratiating demeanor had also secured him tasks ranging from pleasant to gratifying. Stewart supplemented his office duties, his "day job," by working with other inmates to pilfer snacks for evening consumption in their cells. Simon was not surprised to learn that Stewart excelled at this, earning him the nickname, "sandwich man." An infraction of the rules, of course, but not too serious. And by criminal standards, his covert actions were negligible.

Beneath their ritualistic banter lurked a subject neither wanted to raise, one that inflicted pain on Stewart and that usually forced Simon to dissimulate. Simon hoped this time would be different. Still, he kept his silence. As time seeped away from their visiting period, he could see his friend summoning the courage again to venture the most important question of his life.

"Have you heard from Lori?" Stewart asked.

I was afraid of this, Simon moaned inside. "Yes, I have," he said.

Stewart's looked at him anxiously. "And?"

"She's coming to visit you, Stewart. At least, that's what she told me."

"That's fabulous!" Stewart exclaimed. "When?"

"Soon, I imagine. She didn't specify. Sometime next week, I think. When did the parole board say they would tell you their decision?"

"In the next two weeks," Stewart said, obviously trying to control his emotions. "Which is perfect, just perfect! I'll get my parole, get out of this place, Lori and I will visit, patch things up, I'll get back to where I was, with her, with you . . . *Perfect!* Only this time, everything will be better, Ted, much better! All this misery will be behind me, I'll be working for you just like before, and, best of all, Lori and I will be back together again!"

Simon nodded without further comment, pushing himself to share Stewart's happiness, but wondering if events would justify his exuberance.

Actually, neither could know that a joyful reunion with Stewart Lawrence was the last thing on Lori Armstrong's mind . . .

———

September, 1969

You need skin THIS THICK to do divorce cases, mused Carl Milliken, attorney-at-law, as he let his eyes roam across rows of legal tomes clustered on the walls of his Deer Park, Long Island office. *SHE CLAIMS he's a reprehensible pig who works all the time—that is, when he's not sleeping with his secretary—ignores the children, and slaps her face for not keeping him supplied with his favorite booze. HE CLAIMS she's a babbling trollop, whose slovenliness is surpassed only by her inability to form complete sentences.* And so it went in this profession. Milliken shook his head, jotted a few notes on a legal pad, and thanked God divorce cases comprised only a tiny percentage of his legal practice. He only did it for friends, and then only after they had exhausted other sources, often other relatives. He shook his head sadly as he signed his name to a document. *Former friends, now,* he concluded.

The intercom crackled. "Mr. Milliken?"

He pressed a button. "Yes."

"A person here to see you."

Milliken flipped through his appointment book, a meticulously maintained ledger administered by a person he believed was the most competent legal secretary in the country. *No, make that the world,* he thought as his eyes poured over jottings that could have been produced by a professional calligrapher.

"Eleanor, my book says nothing . . ."

"She just walked in. Says she has to see you. *Extremely* important."

Yeah, right, Milliken thought. He knew his secretary was communicating in that stilted tone especially reserved for awkward situations when the person in question was standing before her, waiting for a response. He scanned his afternoon schedule. A court appearance at ten—*that miserable witness had better show!*; a business lunch with an oleaginous rogue who believed every reprobate is a victim of unfortunate social circumstances; a conference with several indignant corporate lawyers, something about a conflict-of-interest case reeking with criminal implications and involving the State of New York, which they assumed he should understand since he once worked for the government. Milliken's cynicism about his government experience pushed a soft sigh past his lips. He belonged to what he regarded as a covert society of political geniuses, united only by a shared secret they dare not unleash to an unsuspecting citizenry: *at any given time, American government hasn't the faintest idea what it's doing.* Or *trying* to do, or *why*. His favorite response to sincere inquiries made by perplexed citizens: *there's no reason for it, it's just our policy.*

Milliken slapped his book shut. He marveled at the naiveté of ordinary folk who occasionally sauntered into his office, believing they could handle their problems by ordering a quick legal solution on rye, with a pickle on the side, hold the mayo. An ounce of hostility for the nameless patron standing outside disturbed his thoughts. *What does she think this is? A fast food restaurant?*

"Tell her to make an appointment, and we'll get back to her," he snapped.

"Yes sir."

A half minute, another buzz. "Mr. Milliken?"

"Now what is it?"

"She says it's about Stewart Lawrence. Extremely urgent."

Milliken's preoccupations vanished in a flash. "Send her in," he said.

A few seconds later, his door opened, and a young woman stepped through, then stopped. Hesitant, unsure, she scrutinized his office like an intelligent, captured jungle animal reviewing its new quarters before plunging inside. Her delay gave Milliken a few seconds to evaluate her. Dark brown hair highlighted skin possessing smooth, porcelain beauty, which covered well-proportioned features, as nearly as he could determine, that is. Her perfect nose emerged from enormous sunglasses that concealed much of her face. A scarf circled her neck and its loops trailed into her cleavage, which strained against a halter top clearly inadequate for its appointed task. Not that Milliken minded. A tight blue skirt wrapped around inviting hips, and inched a bit too high with her every step. She struck him as attractive, not gorgeous, but sexy, desirable, in ways that escaped other women her age who made more brazen attempts to look their best. Her figure captured Milliken's gaze, and he visually fondled its alluring outline, as she walked into his office. *Not a bad way to break up my day,* he mused. Except for the hateful words she uttered.

"Have a seat, please," he offered, gesturing toward a chair opposite his desk. She sat down, folded her legs, and cupped her hands over the small white purse on her lap. Milliken waited for her to broach the purpose of her visit. She remained silent.

Milliken cleared his throat. "May I ask who you are?" he inquired.

"I prefer not to reveal that," she said. "Not right now, at least."

Low, breathy voice. Milliken loved it. "Fine," he answered agreeably. He eased back in his large, leather chair. "You mentioned the name, Stewart Lawrence, so I imagine your coming here has something to do with him."

She acknowledged with a slight nod. "That's right."

"What about him?"

A slight pause. "I don't know exactly how to put this to you."

"Since I charge by the hour, might I suggest the most direct approach possible." He could see her twitch uncomfortably. Milliken waved his hand in a dismissing gesture. "Don't worry, Miss, this isn't costing you a dime. Not yet, anyway. But I am a busy man, and I would appreciate your getting to the point."

"Of course. I'm sorry." A few seconds . . . Thoughts collected . . . "You're his brother-in-law, is that right?"

"*Former* brother-in-law," Milliken corrected. "My sister divorced him several years ago. I've been helping her with her legal affairs on this matter ever since. Not that it's any of your business."

"You know that he's up for parole . . ."

"Yes, I'm aware of that," Milliken said. "What about it?"

"Isn't it also true that you used to be a prosecutor?"

"I once served as a United States Attorney," he corrected her.

"Do you know any of the people who are on his parole board?" came the next question.

Milliken inclined his head. "What if I do?"

"Well, I was wondering if there was any way you could talk to them, maybe give them advice. You know, your views on his parole . . ."

"And what do you think those views might be, Miss?" Milliken interrupted, now more intrigued than ever. He wasn't going to make this any easier for her.

"The same as mine, I believe."

"Which are . . . what?"

"I don't want Stewart to get his parole," she stated flatly. "I want him to stay in jail."

Milliken fiddled with his pen. "You referred to him by his first name. He's a friend?"

"A former boyfriend, yes," she admitted. "Mr. Milliken, this is terribly awkward for me, and I don't know how to say it. If Stewart gets out on parole, he'll go looking for me, and I'm afraid of him. I'm afraid of what he might do. But I feel helpless. That's why I'm here. To ask you if there's anything you can do to keep him in jail."

Milliken stared at her for a long moment. She didn't flinch. "Do you understand what you're asking me?"

"Yes."

"Well, you know, Miss, these things are usually more complicated than one might think. Parole boards have their own sources of information, their own ways of looking at things. Sometimes they act in unpredictable ways . . ."

"Anything you can do," she repeated, a cutting edge to her voice. "You know that several lives are affected and could be messed up by him being let out. His former wife, his son, even you, maybe. I'm just asking that you add me to your list of people you should think about. *Please."*

Milliken considered this. "Is that all you're asking?"

"That's all I'm asking."

"Then I believe we understand each other, Miss . . ." he groped for her name.

"Armstrong," came the reply. "Lori Armstrong. You'd find out sooner or later, I suppose."

Milliken resisted his urge to ask her to remove her sunglasses. Or other items on her body that restricted his view. "Very well," he said, as if to conclude their meeting. Lori got up, stepped toward the door. She placed her hand on the knob, turned toward him.

"I appreciate your time, Mr. Milliken," she said. "Is there any charge?"

"No charge," Milliken replied, flashing a grin. "Not all attorneys are money-grubbing bloodsuckers, Miss Armstrong. Sometimes we even talk to people for free." He tried to elicit a smile, but none was forthcoming.

"Thank you," was all she said, before closing the door behind her.

Milliken leaned over his desk and doodled on a legal pad. As a former prosecutor with a decade's worth of experience, and an attorney with an additional fifteen years practicing law, he had witnessed about every type of human reaction imaginable. Tearful women who trembled with fright over the prospect of an adverse court ruling; brutish husbands who insisted their thundering rage inflicted against helpless family members was completely justified; jittery witnesses whose selective memories wrecked carefully orchestrated cases; remorseless killers who dismissed their butchery with no more thought than that associated with slapping an errant pet; practiced liars whose earnest pleas squeezed sympathetic decisions from gullible juries; the categories marched on. And Lori Armstrong's reaction fit into none of them. Or, at least, not into the one she wanted him to believe.

That lady isn't scared of much, Milliken concluded. No doubt she had an agenda, but avoiding Stewart Lawrence's supposed violent proclivities was not on it. Lawrence might have been a skunk his whole life, but he was not a violent man; of that much, Milliken was sure. Clearly, she wasn't accustomed to dealing with lawyers, and venturing a suggestion that he influence the parole board's decision obviously made her uncomfortable. Still, she did it. But why? *She must have a very important reason,* Milliken thought.

He reached for his personal phone directory. *And I intend to find out what,* he concluded, as he dialed a number he was sure would make Lori Armstrong very pleased indeed. And himself, as well.

Stewart Lawrence hunched in his cubicle ensconced in a corner of the penitentiary's main office and stared blankly at the papers strewn across his small desk. He found it impossible to concentrate. Working with civilians imparted a sense of normality to his daily routine, but the impending decision on his parole application loomed over his thoughts like God's judgment on the destiny of his soul. Which was it to be? Heaven or Hell? Actually, Bluefield Penitentiary didn't qualify as hell—he'd already been there—but neither did it fall into a heavenly category. It was imprisonment, confinement. And Stewart smoldered every day he had to endure it, regardless of the nature of his duties, surely among the least unpleasant assignments in the entire facility.

Yet his mind wandered as he tried to make sense of his encounter with Lori a week ago, which left him devastated. His heart soared when he spied her gliding into the meeting room, taking a seat, and tossing him a warm, expectant smile. Hands grasped, bodies embraced, a fervent kiss; more fervent on his part, he now concluded in retrospect. Still, her lithe form eagerly melted into his—no way did she fake *that* reaction—and they had to be warned by a guard to keep their encounter within the bounds of prison civility.

It was her words that stung his heart, not her passionate greeting. A ritualistic exchange of news culminated with her gently prodding him about the meaning of his clue, the location of Madison's bonds. The passion glinting from Lori's eyes betrayed lust for something different from what Stewart had craved for the past two years. She wanted those bonds; she desired them more than a reconciliation with him. Stewart demurred, Lori flared, slung her handbag over her shoulder, and stomped out of the room. *Why can't you trust me!* she demanded, before slamming the door behind her. Then silence, nothing. Stewart sat there alone, pondering what his freedom would mean in a world without Lori. Still, every minute he contemplated her visit made him more determined to win her back after his release. That kept him going.

"Mr. Lawrence?"

Stewart jumped, his reverie broken. He looked up at the stern face of a middle-aged woman, a prison official to whom he reported. "I'm . . . sorry," he fumbled for words. "Kind of preoccupied today. I'll finish these reports."

"Don't worry about those right now. Your caseworker would like to see you," she said.

Stewart's heart leaped. "About my parole?"

"I think so."

He got up, followed her signal toward the door, where a guard was waiting. "Good luck," she said, a wan smile creasing her seasoned features.

Stewart preceded the guard down a long hallway, a flurry of conflicting scenarios raced through his thoughts. *Thirty-six months, max,* squeaked a voice of optimism. *Some guys on a twenty year sentence get out in less than two!* reminded another corner of his mind. But was Lori's stormy passage a bad omen? Stewart felt like a mystified shaman scrutinizing duck entrails supplied by Ted Simon, searching for the smallest clues that led to predictions of the future. Of one thing he was sure; his caseworker, a bookish, forty-year-old with a string of academic degrees trailing his name, displayed his mood with all the subtlety of a flashing traffic signal. One glance at his face would tell Stewart the decision of his parole board.

Stewart entered the lobby to his caseworker's office, sat down, and waited. Several minutes passed. Ten, maybe fifteen. Seemed like an eternity. Finally, a buzzer sounded, his guard got up, knocked on the office door, opened it. Stewart stood up, took four strides toward the open doorway. Caseworker seated behind his desk, looked up from a file, met his eyes . . .

Stewart was absolutely correct. His caseworker's expression said it all.

Chapter Thirty-One

September 30, 1971, 8:00 p.m.

Two men sat in rickety chairs constructed from scrap materials inside a ten-foot square hovel, hidden eight feet below ground level in a clearing surrounded by woods several hundred yards northwest of the main barracks. One of them, known by all inmates as The Speaker, let his eyes drift to shelves jutting out from the wall to his right, also constructed from discarded wood and insulated from the damp earth with mulched leaves and twigs. Pale light glowed from the cubicle's single bulb, which sat on a wooden bench that hosted two telephone sets and an assortment of pencils, note pads, and files. The Speaker shook his head, incredulous. He gaped at his companion, without question the most important prisoner ever housed at the United States Correctional Institution at Whitestone, located near Johnstown, Pennsylvania. James Riddle Hoffa.

"Actually, it was the Florida mob that organized the hit," the former Teamster boss clarified. "They hired three shooters. One was Oswald, who we thought would give the hit a political flavor. The other two were Cubans who waited on that grassy knoll everybody learned about from those films Zapruder made. Another one of our guys stood opposite the hill, carrying an umbrella to mark the spot, signal the shooters. Crazy thing was, somebody also got a picture of him, but the Feds never connected him to the hit. It's even in the Warren Commission reports. They're stupid. Why would a guy be carrying an umbrella in that weather? Good thing he got away, because he could've been connected to the Florida syndicate. He was our weak link, no question about it."

"I thought Oswald was the weak link," The Speaker inquired.

"Well, he was. I mean, he got caught and all. We figured he would blab, so we had to take him out fast. That was Ruby's job, and he did it good. Worked for the Chicago guys for years and was well-trusted. He was sick and dying, the perfect guy for the job. But it was one of those crazy things, you know. No hit is ever perfect, and this one had some close calls. Like that jacket for instance . . ."

"Jacket?"

"Yeah. One of the Cuban shooters ran away, bumped into that Dallas cop, Tippet, who didn't know who he had at the time. The Cuban dropped his jacket. Oswald had to take out the cop to protect the Cuban. The cops tried to track down the cleaners' tag number on the jacket, and they scoured the country, but never could find it. You know why?" Hoffa flashed his trademark, toothy grin.

"No, why?" The Speaker dutifully asked.

"It was cleaned in *Havana!*" he chortled. "I'll never forget that cleaning number tag, B-nine, seven-three-eight. The Cubans got away; they never found them. Ain't that rich?" Another satisfied smile broke across his lips. Hoffa let his gaze drift, took on a contemplative expression. "Kennedy had it coming."

"Why is that?"

"He didn't *stay* bought, for one thing," the Teamster boss huffed. "He double-crossed the Chicago people. They're the ones who put him into office! Stole two elections for him, the West Virginia primary and the Cook County vote in the presidential election, which put him over the top in electoral votes. Everyone figured he was now our guy, and for a while, it worked out that way. The Chicago mob supplied him with broads, but I guess everyone now knows that. Kennedy even slept with them in the same bed he and Jacqueline shared when she was out of town. He actually had meetings with some of the Chicago people in the White House. Can you believe that? Mobsters eating off gold china in the White House!"

The Speaker nodded, astonishment jolting his thoughts with each revelation.

"Kennedy got really fond of one of our broads, her name was Judy," Hoffa continued. "We had her wired, so we knew what he was saying when they were alone. J. Edgar tipped him off, told the President she slept around with mob figures, and that he should dump her. He was a little scared of Hoover—*everybody* feared Hoover!—so he dropped her. Then things got bad. That brother of his started poking into our affairs. Investigations and all, phone taps, FBI tracking our asses all over the country. Jack told the Chicago guys he couldn't control his brother, but nobody believed him. After the mob helped him to try to hit Castro, the stolen elections, a good supply of broads, and all . . . They felt *double-crossed.* That's about where I got into the picture. We figured that hitting Jack would get rid of Bobby, because Lyndon Johnson wouldn't keep him as Attorney General."

"Wouldn't Johnson give you as much trouble?" The Speaker asked.

Hoffa shook his head. "Not really. He was kind of, well, neutral. We figured, less of a threat. One thing for sure, he hated Bobby's guts."

The Speaker whistled softly. "So you pulled it off, almost without a hitch. Maybe a few close calls . . ."

"I didn't tell you about the closest one," Hoffa interrupted. "Remember that reporter? Dorothy Kilgallen, I think was her name?"

The Speaker hesitated. He rarely found it necessary to dredge his memory for newspaper headlines from a decade ago. "No, I don't think so," he admitted.

"Well, *I* do. She was a columnist, T.V. reporter, well-connected, too nosy for her own good. Somehow, she uncovered who had ordered the hit. She had three names. One of them was mine, and she was right on the money. Fingered one of the Cubans, too. Also said she had proof, so she called a press conference. One of our guys hit her the night before, made it look like a suicide. No one, not the police, the FBI, no one ever figured that out to this date. In fact, more than two dozen hits spun out of Kennedy's assassination."

Again, The Speaker slowly shook his head in surprise, taking it all in. Hoffa seemed finished with his explanation, and The Speaker had no more questions. None he dared to ask anyway, absent a specific lead-in.

Hoffa eyed him carefully. "You're wondering why I'm telling you this."

"Well, frankly, yes, I am."

"You've got the most trusted job of anyone in this whole prison. You know that." Hoffa stated the obvious, then continued. "I've been watching you. I like the way you operate. You're smooth, smart, don't interfere with other people, and are completely trustworthy. I need a man like you to work for me when we both get out. Which will be soon, otherwise neither of us would be here. So, do you want to work for me?"

"Doing what?" The Speaker asked.

"Damage control associate. Good job, pays great. I can't run my union and take care of all the bad publicity crap that lands in my lap. That's what I need you for. Damage control. I'll explain more when we're both on the outside."

"I'll do it," The Speaker said.

"Let's shake on it," Hoffa said, extending his hand. "From this point on, you are on the payroll." He checked his watch. "Time for me to turn in. Are you coming, too?"

The Speaker shook his head. "In a half an hour or so." He pointed to a stack of messages. "I've got a few phone calls to make."

Hoffa rose, offered his hand one more time. "See you tomorrow, Stewart."

"Tomorrow, Mr. Hoffa."

"Call me Jimmy."

Stewart Lawrence beamed with delight. "Okay, Jimmy." He pulled a rope connected to a counterweight that enabled him to lift the heavy, sod-covered door, which doubled as a their communication center's ceiling. Hoffa climbed out, scurried away, and Stewart Lawrence, alias The Speaker, got down to work.

Or tried to. Exhilaration flooded his thoughts at the prospect of working for one of the most powerful men in America, albeit one with mob connections. *Makes up for a lot of miserable disappointments,* he thought bitterly, as the list of parole denials marched through his mind like a regiment of storm troopers. In fact, his last turndown came at the same time another prisoner who had robbed nine banks received parole after only serving twenty-eight months. *Someone out there has it in for me,* Stewart groused. This time, however, would be different.

Stewart had no idea whether Hoffa was telling the truth about the facts of Kennedy's assassination, or his role in it. His explanation *sounded* logical; Stewart rarely gave the subject much thought. Like other inmates, he regarded the Teamster boss with a mixture of awe and fear, and serving time at Whitestone with this celebrity criminal in one's presence brushed every prisoner with a evanescent glow of fame. But he could do the others one step better: Jimmy Hoffa had actually offered him a job, and he had accepted.

None of which would have been possible, of course, if he hadn't been transferred to Whitestone after his last parole denial at Bluefield. He had his prison psychologist to thank for that. Apparently the man reasoned that serving his sentence in a minimum security facility, called "The Dairy" by knowledgeable inmates and resembling an army basic training camp, would make up at least somewhat for his repeated parole denials. And he was right, although Stewart's parole turndowns still clutched him like parasites, gnawing away at his spirit. Hoffa's offer thus came at exactly the right time, when he craved for a fresh injection of hope. *This will keep me going until I get out,* he reasoned.

In the meantime, he had work to do. The responsibility laid on Stewart's shoulders by his fellow inmates made him feel like royalty, the proud occupant of a throne passed down to him by distant forebears. Except one had to earn this position by gaining the trust of other prisoners, especially the small committee that selected him. Stewart's position as The Speaker imparted to him a unique privilege. He was the only prisoner allowed to send messages from their private communication center, whose existence had been kept secret from the authorities for over two decades. Stewart marveled at the ingenuity of those who had designed this brilliant subterfuge. He felt like the central character in a science fiction novel, taking advantage of the legacy bequeathed by a mysterious, distant civilization that had since vanished into the hazy mists of unrecorded history. Whenever Stewart contemplated the Com-Center's origins, an Old Testament voice rumbled through his imagination, reciting the words, *In the beginning, there was The Lineman* . . .

Actually, the beginning traced to the late forties, according to oral tradition, and the lineman was a communications repair specialist who had worked for a telephone company. He and his collaborators had succeeded over the years in scavenging supplies from prison scraps and smuggling equipment from the outside to construct their private communications complex. It allowed prisoners to circumvent burdensome telephone rules, which restricted their phone messages as to time and content. Instead, prisoners simply passed their messages to The Collector, who passed them along to The Speaker, whose identity, for security purposes, remained concealed from all but a handful of inmates. The rest only knew that sending messages to the outside was possible, nothing more.

The Speaker made collect or credit card calls, according to strictly observed rules posted in the bunker. By the time Stewart took the job, only credit cards were used, charged to a trusted person on the outside whom prisoners paid according to a fee structure established by a select committee. No one made any money from this scheme. It operated for the general welfare of all, and better-off inmates subsidized their poorer brethren. Not only did Com-Center function smoothly, it gave each participant the feeling that he was pulling one off on the authorities. And this made prison life a bit more bearable.

Stewart derived immense satisfaction from his duties. *Ed Sullivan should be so lucky,* he often mused. *And now, direct to you, from the secret prisoner Communications Center at Whitestone Federal Penitentiary, under the very noses of the unsuspecting klutzes who run this joint, the following message* . . . He checked the time again; 9:00 p.m. The center usually operated between 11:00 p.m. and 1:30 a.m., three or four nights a week, more frequently for emergencies. On occasion, like this evening, he began his duties after dinner, then hustled back to his barracks before bed check at 10:30 p.m., so guards didn't record him missing. He reckoned tonight's calls would take him about another half an hour. Plenty of time to complete them and return to his quarters.

Stewart lifted a file from a stack, pulled out its message, and held it next to the light bulb. The electricity drain from the prison only amounted to a hundred watts or so, virtually impossible to detect by analyzing utility statements. Physical inspection wouldn't turn up anything either; overlays of grass, sod, leaves, tree branches, all reduced leakage of light to practically nothing. And stumbling across the bunker by accident or design during the day was virtually impossible.

Stewart smiled as he examined the message. *If the original lineman only knew how many illegal activities would be directed from this center* . . . He dialed a number. Three rings later, an operator's voice crackled through his receiver.

"Credit card call, please." Stewart said.

"Your calling number, please."

Damn! Stewart quickly hung up. Try it again. Another number dialed, a different operator.

"Credit card call, please."

"Certainly. Your card number, sir?"

That's better. Stewart recited his card number, and a few seconds later, connected to a party on the other end.

"Hello?"

"Message for . . ."—Stewart glanced at his file—"Timothy Hansen."

His phone partner immediately recognized the source. "Speaking," came the reply. "What's the message?"

Stewart grinned as he recited the message. Seems one of the more clever inmates had in mind a questionable transaction involving municipal bonds. After conveying his written instructions, he chatted with the inmate's friend about recent events, bade him a congenial farewell until the next time, then hung up. Another number, another message, more instructions. One more phone call, and he was done.

Stewart dialed his last number, made the connection, waited. A quick identification, exchange of chitchat, messages briskly conveyed.

Then Stewart Lawrence heard a sound on the phone he had never heard before . . .

Dr. John Reynolds, staff psychologist for the United States Correctional Institution at Whitestone, muttered a light obscenity as he turned on the hallway light. *Blasted Congressmen,* he thought, marching toward his office. *Bad enough to work with inadequate funds without having to justify everything we do.* Three hours of wining and dining on his part generated little more than an identical amount of whining and crying on their part.

You have to understand the political climate, one of them had stated earnestly. Funds for correctional institutions apparently required greater justification than subsidies for the tobacco industry. Reynolds hated politics and politicians. He occasionally felt that dealing with his captive clientele produced more honest answers than what he received from Washington. Not always, but now and then. Especially during budget battles.

He reached into his pocket, fumbled for his office keys, isolated the correct one, and inserted it into the lock. He couldn't remember the last time he had returned to his office this late. Usually it stayed locked from 4:30 p.m. to 8:30 a.m. the following day. Filled with confidential files, the psychologist's quarters remained off-limits to all but a few selected prison officials. And Reynolds never used his office during evening hours, preferring instead to carry work home, if necessary. Tonight he only showed up to make a quick telephone call to his wife to explain his tardiness so she wouldn't worry.

He plunked his briefcase on his desk, plopped himself into his chair, and picked up the phone. He placed the receiver to his ear, reached for the dial, placed his finger against a number . . . Reynolds stopped.

Bzz . . . Right, me again . . . Static. Popping noises.

That's what he wants done, yes.

Bzz . . . Sound faded out. Long pause . . . Back again . . . Same voice punctuating the background of crackling electronic interference.

Highest price, of course.

Another fade-out. Then, like a distant echo whispering inside a cavernous building, *Can't tell you that, no.*

More static, weak, indistinct sounds. Finally, more loudly, *Leave it at Mill Street in the old farmhouse. One of our guys will pick it up.*

Reynolds sat up in his chair, fascinated, pondering the meaning of the sounds pattering his eardrums. *Crossed wires, perhaps?* Didn't seem logical; he wasn't aware of any work done on his phone system recently. *Listen for more.*

Scratchy noises, interference.

Right, gotcha Speaker Man . . .

More distinctly now . . . *Those are the last of his messages. Speaker out. Click.*

More dialing . . . Static, always static . . . Maddening! What's being said?

Fade-in . . . *Message for* . . . Fade out . . . Back in, now . . . *Yes, more money, he really needs it . . .*

On impulse, Reynolds tried an experiment. "Hello? Hello?" No response. Conversations continued with no acknowledgment of his voice.

He could hear whoever was talking, they couldn't hear him. But who were *they?* At length, the answer began to dawn on him. Each scratchy sound ignited another spark of recognition, finally assaulting his thoughts with a horrible realization. Those voices belonged to prisoners, to one of them, at least. *They tapped into this telephone line!*

Reynolds dialed another extension. Fifteen seconds passed. "Jack! Reynolds, here. Get over to my office right now!"

A few minutes later, the assistant warden burst into Reynolds's office, where the psychologist immediately directed him to pick up a phone on an extension. They both listened intently for ten minutes. The assistant warden's look of astonishment revealed the conclusion forming in his mind.

"Whose voice does that sound like to you?" he whispered.

"Stewart Lawrence," the psychologist stated.

"I can't believe it . . ." the assistant warden said. "They must have . . ."

"Tapped into this line," Reynolds completed the sentence. "But how?"

"We'll find out," came the firm response. "We'll act on this immediately! I'll call the warden from my office." He put his phone down and rushed out of the room.

Reynolds placed his receiver back on its cradle.

Click.

Stewart realized instantly that a third party had invaded his secure line. Never had he heard the sound of a distant receiver clicking off. He always hung up first; part of the rules. *I've got to get out of here, NOW!* He cut off his last message quickly, hung up, and switched off his light. Complete darkness. Stewart groped for the cord connected to the bunker's ceiling door, found it, and pulled it toward the floor. He climbed out, lowered the door, spread additional camouflage around its periphery, then began trotting through the woods toward his barracks eight hundred yards away. Darkness shrouded the path; he tripped several times, scuffed his clothes, got up, brushed them off, plodded on. Moist fingers from the damp evening penetrated his light clothing, giving him a chill while he sweated and trudged his way back.

Stewart replayed his two hours' worth of comments on the phone. *Everything I said was horribly revealing.* One statement in particular haunted him: *leave it at Mill Street in the old farmhouse, and one of the guys will pick it up.* The prisoner Drop Zone, a safe point established by a different generation of inmates, centered on an abandoned barn, sixty feet from a dirt road known as Mill Street. Non-federal property, outside the prison perimeter. Whitestone's lightly guarded border made it possible for inmates known as The Importers to scurry through the woods, scramble over the fence, and race to the barn where they retrieved contraband that had been deposited by prisoners' friends beneath a set of loose floorboards. The original telephone sets, electrical wire, other supplies, and an endless stream of creature comforts for inmates had passed through this Drop Route.

The Importers hid their collectibles at various drop zones in the woods; no "merchandise" ever made its way into the barracks. Far too dangerous, with huge penalties, especially if such goods included alcoholic beverages. Another group of prisoners, known as The Smugglers, took charge of retrieving and dispensing beer, wine, and hard liquor that traveled through the Drop Route. They deposited empty containers outside, where a trusted party got rid of them. Under Stewart's direction, the Bunker also served as a storage site for their drinks, because it possessed the right temperature for that task. All in all, a perfect scheme, which now would probably be uncovered, destroyed. *And its discovery occurred during my watch,* Stewart thought, miserably.

Only one thing remained for him to do. Hoffa had mentioned he needed someone for damage control. *No better time to start than the present,* Stewart thought. He approached the edge of the woods, about twenty feet from the building where the staff psychologist had his office. The Com-Center's founding fathers thought detection highly improbable, but as a precaution, inserted the last thirty feet of wire inside a pipe, the end of which was buried beneath the ground at the edge of the woods. Stewart plunged his fingers into the earth and groped for the pipe, found it, located the wire's disconnect point, pulled it out. He then yanked its other connection free from the inside edge of the building and coiled it up. He dashed back into the woods again, buried the incriminating wire at a drop point, and hurried back to his barracks.

Barely in time. A half an hour passed. Suddenly, lights switched on, orders bellowed from enraged prison officials, a troop of guards burst into his barracks and rumbled down the center aisle.

The shakedown had begun. It would get worse. And, for Stewart Lawrence, nearly unbearable.

———

Stewart sat limply on the edge of his bunk, shoulders slumped, unseeing gaze locked on a distant point, right hand clutching a sheet of paper. A sheen of moisture glazed his forehead, beads of sweat fell down his cheeks, neck, vanished into his damp collar. At length, desperation knifed into the gloom that paralyzed his thoughts, sending a tremor through his body, shaking his shoulders and arms. His hands balled into fists. Like a small marine animal retracting its tentacles around a much larger prey, his fingers clawed at the paper and slowly ingested it into the palm of his hand. He squeezed it into a tight, moist ball and shook his head.

A person approached, wearing a tan, army-style, zippered jump suit. A prisoner, like himself. He had an ordinary build, pleasant face, but easily forgettable, not distinguishable in a crowd. Totally average guy, nondescript, except he chewed gum noisily. His lack of distinction was one of his advantages. The other, more important one emerged after he sat down on the opposite bunk.

"You wanted to talk to me, Stewart?" the man asked.

"Yeah," Stewart said weakly.

"About what they're going to do to you?"

Stewart didn't answer. His eyes remained glassy, fixed in a visionless stare.

"Stewart . . . Are you all right?"

Finally, Stewart looked up. "You're getting released in a few days, aren't you?" he remarked in a hoarse voice.

"That's right."

"Bert, I'm wondering if you could do something for me."

"After all you've done for me, you just name it!"

"It's important. Might take some time now and then."

Bert leaned forward. "I've got a lot of time, Stewart. And if it's important to you, whatever it is, I'll do it!"

Stewart managed a wan smile. He opened his fist, carefully picked through the wrinkles of the soggy sheet of paper, flattened it on his leg. He scrutinized the sheet for a few seconds, then shoved it into his pocket. Eyes bored on his friend. "As soon as you get out, this is what I'd like you to do," he began. His instructions came in short, clipped sentences.

Bert nodded agreeably. His jaws casually moved in a slightly rotating fashion, manipulating his gum. "No problem," he assured.

The barracks door opened, several men entered, marched directly to his bunk. Grim faces aimed at Stewart. "Mr. Lawrence," one of them said. "Come with us . . ."

Chapter Thirty-Two

June, 1973

"I can't believe it!" exuded an incredulous reply. "Are you sure?"

The figure seated across the desk nodded his head. "This is not something one gets wrong, my friend," he replied, trying to assuage the shock of the revelation he had just imparted.

"How long ago?"

"About three weeks ago, I think."

"Any details?"

The bearer of bad news shook his head. "Very few, I'm afraid. What I could tell you I'm not sure you want to know. Certainly it makes little difference."

The person who had resided for thirty years in the quiet office hosting this conversation leaned over his desk, trained his eyes on his companion. "Anything you could tell me might be helpful."

A sigh hushed out, signaling reticence. In carefully selected words, an explanation followed. A string of punishing syllables flowed across the desk, hitting its recipient like a succession of slaps to the face. At length, he held up his left hand, planted his right elbow on his desk, and rested the bridge of his nose on the forefinger and thumb of his right hand. "Where did you learn this?" he asked, closing his eyes.

From across the desk, "Judicial authorities, who told me to present it to you personally. They also insisted that strict confidence be maintained."

"Wise decisions. Who else knows?"

"No one."

"How much time do we have?"

A pocket calendar materialized. A forefinger glided across rectangles of dates. "A week, I'd say. Maybe less, depending."

"Depending on what?"

"On how fast information travels."

Eyes shifted to stained glass windows flanked by an elegant sculpture of the Madonna and a portrait of Jesus Christ. "That is all, you may go now. Thank you."

A polite nod, a quiet departure. Solitude. He buried his head into his hands. *Never did I think I would have to face this again, NEVER!* Up from the desk, toward the window, an aimless gaze outside. Pitiless moral commands marched to the forefront of his thoughts and silenced objections offered by that part of his soul seeking escape from responsibility. His judgment clarified, and like a spear of light, pointed to the only decision he could make. The direction was clear, the path, dangerous, unfamiliar. Yet it was a path he had to take.

That still left a lot for details. *Innocent inquiries will get me nowhere,* he quickly concluded. *I could protect myself, but I would be useless.* Other methods came to mind, none of which offered the slightest opportunity for success. Finally, a solution emerged, one that made him feel ridiculous, out of sorts. *Maybe if I don't go as myself . . .* Inspired by that notion, he returned to his desk, pulled out a list of appointments, and started jotting down instructions. Satisfied he had done all he could to cover his absence, he pushed his work aside, rested his chin on the heel of his hand, gazed at some object on the wall. Wretched scenarios paraded through his mind, heaving before him a single, deadly conclusion.

I've got to get to him before it's too late.

His belt buckle felt more like a noose strapped around his waist, his red plaid shirt draped over his skinny torso like a rain poncho, and his shoes . . . *Well, no one looks at shoes, do they?* He snuggled his modest sedan into a clump of imposing pickup trucks, glanced at a tangle of antlers perched on the hood of an enormous flatbed, took a deep breath, and walked toward the entrance of *Kelly's Bar and Grill.* Neon script flashed above the ramshackle structure, minus a few blinking letters, which accented the sign's absurd penmanship with ridiculous spelling. Not that its patrons seemed to mind. Vehicles of every description, all adorned with a gaggle of bumps and scraps detailing their personal histories, blanketed the parking lot. Several tractor-trailer rigs loomed in the background, saturnine behemoths keeping watch over a brood of lesser creatures. Random whoops and cries from raucous country music within the building leaked outside. Hardly his kind of place.

He reached the bar's entrance. He took a few seconds to gape at the double doors, which were emblazoned with a garish display of a barmaid hoisting a huge platter filled with beer mugs. A man the size of a buffalo with tattoos sprawled across his arms brushed by him as he stepped inside. Screeching sounds of an adjacent jukebox assaulted his ears, while he scanned murky chambers jutting off from the central restaurant area. Weak illumination suffused the interior, glowing in patches amidst groups of people engaged in a cacophony of unnaturally loud conversation. Booths shrouded by smoke and dull light lined the wall to his right; a pool room announced its presence with a familiar chatter of colliding spheres and stabbing cue sticks. A row of stools was propped beneath a huge bar that ran across the central length of the room. Most of the stools were filled. Several bartenders scurried back and forth in the narrow rectangle between the long mahogany counter hosting their customers and a wall covered by a hive of liquor bottles.

He rubbed his stinging eyes. *At least no one seems to notice me,* he comforted himself. *In this menagerie, hardly anyone stands out.* A long walk to the bar . . . Plunk on a stool . . . Blend in . . .

"What'll it be, Slim?" boomed a voice. A man built like a beer barrel with ham-hock arms shot him a friendly look.

"Um . . . I don't know. Something sweet, I guess."

The bartender aimed his moon face at him and grinned widely. "We got lots of sweet stuff, man. Whaddaya want?"

"How about a martini?" cracked the guy beside him. Looked like a truck driver. They all looked like truck drivers to him. He felt like a pigeon surrounded by hawks whose intentions were unclear.

"Is that sweet?" he asked innocently.

Laughter erupted about him. "It'll give you a real sweet sleep if you drink enough of them," cackled a voice from a different direction.

The bartender took a more sympathetic tone. He leaned forward. "I'll get you a whiskey sour, okay? Real sweet, slides right down, easy on the belly."

"Look, mister," he said. "I really don't want anything to drink . . ." The bartender immediately took a less friendly expression. "Actually, I'm looking for a man."

The bartender approached him again, his face close, as if to impart some confidential point. "In that case, you've come to the wrong place. You see, we don't cater to those types"

Chortles again rumbled across the bar. Clearly, a more direct method of inquiry seemed appropriate. He plunged his hand into his shirt pocket, pulled out a picture, placed it before the bartender's eyes.

"Have you seen this man? I mean, recently?"

A quick scrutiny, a stone face. "No," he said.

"Are you sure? I was told that a lot of people around here knew him, and . . ."

"*Listen, buddy,*" the bartender growled, planting his huge hands on the counter. "If I said I didn't see him, I didn't see him. You get my drift?"

Picture lowered, nervous glances about the bar. "Well, perhaps others . . ."

"*Nobody's* seen him," came the gruff response. "Cause nobody *knows* him. Someone gave you the wrong information, Slim. Now, if you're not drinking, do you mind? I only serve paying customers."

Hostile glares bored on his small frame from every angle. Time to leave. "Thank you, then," he muttered. He slid off the stool, walked quickly across the room, passed through the doors, and took a long draught of refreshing night air. He trotted into the parking lot.

Once inside his car, doors locked, a sense of relief flowed through his body. He took a few minutes to settle his thoughts and assess his situation, to figure out what their response meant, what to do next. Obviously, the bartender and his group of familiar lovelies recognized the person in the photograph. They either were trying to protect him, or they were afraid of him; perhaps a bit of both. Either way, the alarm had been sounded. *What indeed was I trying to accomplish?* whispered an anguished question from a corner of his mind. *An announcement of present whereabouts? A phone number? An address?* Actually, those were precisely his expectations, though now it was clear this expedition had not been carefully thought through. He lamented his own naiveté and lingered on the consequences of this visit. A dreadful conclusion weighed on his mind: *certainly a warning will be flashed; I'll never catch him by surprise now.*

Car started, backed up, squealed onto the road, accelerator floored. A succession of screeching turns, onto the ramp, roar down the interstate through New York City, toward eastern Long Island. As the implications of a horrible realization flooded his thoughts, he prayed desperately that he could locate his target before it was too late.

At the same time, he scolded himself bitterly: *God help me, I've been chasing after the wrong person!*

The gunman peered through his slender, exquisitely designed, ten-power Unertl scope perched on his Model 70 Winchester .30-06 rifle and picked out his target with ease. Accurate beyond 1,125 yards, with an effective range far exceeding that, his Winchester had served him well during his tours of duty as a Marine sniper stationed near the DMZ in Viet

Nam. And his present location, a sandy bluff overlooking beachfront terrain off the southern coast of Long Island, presented none of the difficulties he wrestled with in the jungle. The weather was perfect, the air, crisp, cool, his view unobstructed. The sun descended at his back, a reddish-orange ball smoldering through hazy mist, rewarding his vision with exactly the right amount of light. Most important, no one would be shooting back or trying to isolate his firing position. Just as a precaution, however, and perhaps for superstitious reasons as well, he whipped out a handkerchief and placed it beneath the muzzle of his rifle. That way, gasses expelled by the bullet when it shot from the barrel would not kick up any sand and unmask his position. A meaningless gesture in these circumstances. Still, years of military training retained their grip on his mind. Never depart from sound infantry tactics.

Every bodily sense snapped to attention, focused on those elements of his environment appropriate to its function. Odors, temperature, wind velocity, distance to target, light, humidity, air density—all recorded with precision and factored into calculations with computer-like accuracy. His trained eyes determined a six hundred yard distance from position to target. An easy kill. Still, very satisfying, and practically risk-free.

A few last minute adjustments. Fine tuning. Heat played no factor in the round's trajectory, so he wouldn't have to adapt for elevation based on more rapidly burning powder when he fired the round. A slight breeze from the ocean advised a few clicks of angle to compensate for windage. He checked his target again. The object of his concentration moved to a different location on the patio, relaxed on a chaise longue, lifted a newspaper, frontal position toward him. *Incredible.* Couldn't ask for a better angle.

Rifle raised, scope aligned, cross hairs fixed on target's chest . . .

The assassin's mind ticked through a phalanx of marksmanship principles with exact, military precision. Firm grip, steely concentration, intake of breath, not held too long, exhale and relax, *naturally,* focus on crosshairs . . .

Perfect.

Confident anticipation flowed through the killer's body, as he slowly squeezed the trigger . . .

Chapter Thirty-Three

As the sun's retreating glow surrendered to the advancing twilight, Ted Simon planted his New York Times on his lap and reached for a last sip of coffee. Streaks of light peeked over the top of his newspaper, tingeing its edges with a soft yellow glimmer. He shifted positions in his chaise longue, giving him a better view of distant sand dunes, glistening folds of light brown patched by flowing whiskers of tall grass. He let his gaze drift toward sparkles of blue, green, and yellow that danced on the ocean's surface and played across shimmering sands on the beach. A few paragraphs of reading, a glance toward the horizon, amidst sounds of lapping waters caressing his ears . . . *Relaxing.* He felt at ease, comfortable.

The faint rumble of an approaching vehicle caught his attention. Louder, now, into the driveway. Screeched to a halt . . . Door opened, slammed shut . . . Hurried footsteps . . . Furious banging on his front door . . . *What's going on?* He heard the soft rustle of his wife, Beth, as she negotiated her way around boxes cluttering the hallway toward the entrance. Simon mentally thumbed through his personal inventory of urgent matters and came up with nothing. His builder promised to drop off plans to modify the family room of their new house sometime this day or the next, but, *right now?*

"TED!" shrieked a voice.

A surge of adrenaline spiked through Simon's chest. *God, that's Beth!* Instant conclusion: *She's being assaulted!*

Paper heaved aside . . . Lurch to one's feet . . .

SLAM!

Before Simon could stand up, race to her rescue, someone burst through a patio door, vaulted through the air, crashed against him and bowled him over. The two bodies rolled, tumbled across the wooden planks. Simon wrestled with his assailant, freed his hands, reached for the man's throat . . .

Thunk!

"GET DOWN!" the man screeched, sputtering in his face. He wrapped his arms around Simon, cut his eyes toward the sand dunes, face blazing terror. Time froze. Simon stopped struggling. *What's going on?*

Thunk! Thunk!

Splinters of wood spit near their heads. A sudden grasp of what was happening sped through Simon's mind like a bolt of lightning. Those were bullets. Someone was firing at them.

"Into the house, fast!" he cried.

The two men stumbled over each other, crawled to safety inside the house, hugged the floor, waited. *Silence.* Heaving breaths. Hearts pounding against freshly installed carpet. Simon's eyes darted toward Beth. She was cowering near the refrigerator, fright clamped on her face. *She's okay.* A quick review of body parts. Nothing damaged, everything felt fine. Simon spied a smear of blood on the carpet. *Did he clip me with a round?* Another check. Don't think so. *What about the other guy?*

"I think he's gone, now," his intruder muttered. He crawled toward a window, cautiously raised his head, peered outside. "I doubt if he'd stick around after a failed mission," he observed. "I'm sure he's left. You won't see him again. Not right away, at least."

Simon and Beth didn't move. *"Who's* gone?" he demanded. *"What* mission? And who are *you?"*

The man stood up and swept the sleeve of a ridiculously oversized plaid shirt across his brow. Simon struggled to his feet, waved his wife toward another corner out of harm's way, and studied the person who saved his life. A full day's beard darkened his gaunt face, which struck Simon as too thin to accommodate his prominent features, especially his large brown eyes. He looked vaguely familiar, but Simon couldn't immediately place him. Small person, actually. Gangly limbs, slender build. Certainly didn't look threatening.

A welter of images flashed across Simon's mind. Nothing about the man's demeanor matched his attire. Looked ridiculously put together, in fact. Simon probed his memory, put him in a different time, at a different location, other circumstances . . . Suddenly it came to him. "You're that priest!" he exclaimed. "Jackson County Jail, right?"

The priest slowly nodded. "Raymond Holton, to be exact," he confirmed. "At your service." A wan smile touched his lips. "You'd better contact the police right away, Mr. Simon. Then let's sit down and talk."

"I'll do it," Beth offered in a strong voice. "Then let's get to the bottom of this." She strode out of the room, picked up the phone, and dialed a number. A short wait. Then, words from her assertive tongue

intermittently floated across the room, as Simon and Father Raymond Holton sat down at the kitchen table.

"Can I get you some coffee or something?" Simon offered.

"I prefer a stiff drink," the priest responded.

Simon arched his eyebrows. "I didn't realize priests drank."

"Some do, some don't. I'm starting right now."

"In that case, do you have any preferences?"

"Yes. How about a whiskey sour?"

Simon pursed his lips in a noiseless whistle. "Well, I suppose I can make that, yes."

"Good. Make it a double. Whatever that means," Holton instructed.

A few minutes later found both men slumped in their chairs, cradling their drinks, letting the alcohol seep into the farther reaches of their bodies. Simon gently dappled at the bruise on his forehead, which he discovered was the source of the stain on his new carpet.

Holton twirled the liquid around his glass, lifted it to his mouth, and threw his head back. He swept his blanket-like sleeve across his face again and let a breath of relief brush past his lips. "That bartender was right," he observed. "Real sweet, slides right down, easy on the belly. Remind me sometime to try a martini." He hoisted his glass toward Simon. "I'll take another. If you don't mind, that is."

Simon grinned. "Coming right up."

Beth strode into the kitchen, pulled out a chair and sat down. "The police are on their way," she said. "I told them as much as I could. They're sending out a squad of detectives." She turned toward Ted. "I'll take something to drink, too, darling."

Raymond Holton's countenance turned grave. "Mrs. Simon, I do not think you should be in this room with us. What I am about to say involves matters that would be best for you not to know."

"If it concerns Ted, it concerns *me,* thank you!" she bristled. "We've only been married a year, Mr. Holton. I refuse to be excluded."

The look on the priest's face suggested that Beth was not a person to trifle with. "Believe me, Mrs. Simon, it would be best if you did not know anything," Holton insisted gently. He appealed to Ted for support and received it.

"Perhaps he's right," Ted stated. "If this is what I think it's about, you already don't know a great deal. I prefer we keep it that way."

Beth Simon shifted her gaze from one man to the other, saw no break in their resolve, then quietly left the room. When assured they were alone, Father Holton spoke. "Gerald Kennedy is dead," he announced.

"Gerald Kennedy? You mean, that warden?"

Holton nodded.

"He was . . . what? Sixty-five or something? Must have been close to seventy, now. What did he die of, a heart attack?"

"No, he was murdered."

"Murdered?" Simon exclaimed. "How is that possible? Wasn't he going under an assumed name, a different identity, at a remote prison?"

"None of that made any difference. As soon as the wrong people learned his real identity, Kennedy's death was assured."

"But how?" Simon asked.

Ray Holton took another sip of his drink and looked at Simon in that distinctive way that presages a horrible revelation. "Albert Conner had him killed."

Simon flinched. "Conner's out of prison?"

"For good behavior, no less," Holton commented acidly. "They never did pin much on him at his trial, you'll recall." Another sip of whiskey sour. "Conner got out of prison a few weeks ago, and I was immediately notified by one of my friends at the court. I knew he would be prowling for revenge, settling old scores. He also managed to slip information that got Roberto Lopez killed, that young man who did his dirty work at Jackson County Jail. He was killed in prison, of course. My first thought was to warn others on Conner's hit list, other prisoners first, then Conner's fellow guards. I visited Stewart Lawrence . . ."

"You did?" Simon interjected. "At Ambrose?"

"Yes. A foolish move on my part, I concluded as soon as I was led into the facility he was in. There's nothing I can do to help him. After the prison approved me—a laborious process, by the way—I couldn't bring myself to state the real reason for seeing him. So I hemmed and hawed for fifteen or twenty minutes, wished him well, then left. I'm sure he thinks I'm crazy. Probably he's right. I accomplished *nothing.*" He looked at Simon sheepishly. "Sorry."

Simon dismissed his last word with a quick shake of his head. Holton continued. "Then I thought that if maybe I could find Conner, talk to him, reason with him, I could make a difference. I made inquiries, questioned his former associates, even took a chance that I might bump into him at a bar he used to frequent, but I just made a fool of myself and that got me nowhere. Might have even hurt, I'm afraid. The man is well protected, believe me . . ." His words trailed off, his face took on a contemplative look. "In fact, he's quite extraordinary. And *evil.*" The priest shuddered. "More evil than the warden he worked for and twice as smart."

"What made you come here?" Simon asked.

"I should have notified you first," Holton confessed. "Considering your role in breaking up that extortion ring at Jackson County Jail, you had to be high on his agenda for revenge. Since Conner seemed to be going after his collaborators and former inmates, it just didn't occur to me right away. Finally, I tried to call you, but there was no answer . . ."

"Our phone was just installed today," Simon interjected.

Holton nodded. "So I decided to race over here to warn you, personally. Got directions to your house from someone in that small town nearby—whatever it's called—who seemed to know everything, then drove here as fast as I could. On the way, I spied a truck tucked into a gully off the road. That sight nearly gave me a heart attack. *Mother of God!* It *had* to be Conner's truck. But the sand dunes surrounding this place . . ."—Holton shook his head— "I didn't think I could find him by trudging through all that, not in time, at least. Plus, I was exhausted. And if my directions were correct, all I had to do was to zip down your road, which I was told would lead me directly to your new house. It did. *Thank God!* And not a second too soon."

Holton downed the last drops of his drink. Simon marveled at his ability to withstand the alcohol's sedative effects, particularly since he indicated he was not accustomed to drinking. *Maybe the effects of all that communion wine over the years,* Simon mused.

"Mr. Holton, a few things puzzle me. When I visited Stewart at Jackson County Jail, I saw you many times. I also saw you at Boss Hogg's trial. Tell me this. How much were you aware of what was going on?"

"I suspected they were taking advantage of the inmates, but I never looked into it. Not seriously, anyway."

"Why not?"

"Because doing so would have jeopardized my freedom to work with the prisoners. Kennedy would have found ways to prevent me from seeing them, I'm sure. Their spiritual needs constituted my primary responsibility." His eyes fell to the table. "Plus I do not possess your courage, Mr. Simon," he uttered, like a confession. Holton buried his head in his hands. "I've been doing penance for my sins of omission ever since."

Simon extended his arm over the table and patted the priest on his shoulder. "You showed remarkable courage tonight," he stated firmly. "You saved my life."

"For *now,* at least," Holton said. "As I said, I don't think he will bother you, not for a while. Maybe not for a year, even, or longer."

"I guess I should feel comforted, but why do you say that?"

"Because of what I've learned about Conner's methods. He's incredibly patient, shrewd, rarely takes chances or makes mistakes, and usually works through others. Everyone I spoke to about him respected him, feared him. No one *dared* to provoke him. More than a few regarded Conner as invincible, like some kind of god."

Simon's thoughts flashed back to Conner's trial two years ago. Those razor eyes, that chilling gaze, his mordant expression blazed before Simon's mental vision. Albert Conner was not a man anyone would want as an enemy. Which is exactly how he regarded Ted Simon.

"Conner was in the Marine Corps, served in Vietnam as a sniper," Holton continued. "The rest I only know in fragments, as though nobody really dared to reveal the whole story. Apparently, snipers work with one other Marine as a two-man team. The other Marine is called a spotter . . ."

Simon's military experience immediately confirmed the priest's explanation. "That's correct," he said.

"Conner once accused his spotter of nearly getting them both killed, apparently for doing something he thought was stupid. Conner tried to get him replaced, failed, and, the accusations say, finally killed him. But not right away. A year and a half or so later. He forgives no one and forgets nothing. The Marine Corps could never prove Conner did it . . ." Holton paused, as though toying with a thought. "How can you prove *murder* in such a place?" he exclaimed. "Anyway, Conner was given the choice of a General Discharge or a murder investigation. He chose the General Discharge, which is less than honorable, I've learned. That ended his military career. A few years after he left the Marines, he joined up with Gerald Kennedy's nest of vipers, and with Conner's intelligence and experience, immediately rose to the top. The rest you know."

Sounds of approaching vehicles filtered through the windows, and in a few minutes, heavy knuckles pounded the front door with authority. Beth rushed toward the entrance; police officers announced their presence and stepped into the house. Simon glimpsed several uniforms darting about the grounds, stabbing beams from their flashlights poking into every corner, every ravine, any place that offered concealment. Detectives then spread out from the house, fanned the area. While Simon answered questions about the evening's events, he caught sight of several men clambering up the dunes, like large black ants crawling up distant mounds of sand and vanishing into the invading murkiness of twilight. In a half an hour they returned with nothing to report and a host of pointed questions.

Neither Holton nor Simon provided much help. Simon, of course, saw nothing, and Holton remembered little about the truck he passed on the way to the house.

Color of the vehicle?
Brown, I think. Or black. Maybe dark brown.
Make? Model? Year?
No idea.
Don't suppose you noticed the plate number . . .
No, I don't suppose I did. Sorry.

The exasperated officers took down as much information as they could and promised to look into the matter. Warnings for caution were followed by effusive thanks, and by midnight all but one had left. The police assured the Simons they would pursue any leads on a black or brown pickup truck, five, ten, or fifteen years old, no make, model, or plate number, just to see what turned up. But they made no promises. *Keep us informed; we'll do our best,* they said.

Beth offered Holton an extra room for the night, which the priest graciously accepted. He collapsed on the bed, and in five minutes fell fast asleep. Ted and Beth gathered in the privacy of their own bedroom, while their lone sentry roamed around the house, until finally taking a position in the living room.

An hour later, the two faced each other across the bed, a stack of documents between them. Ted stared at his wife's attractive face, now creased with worry. Beautiful brown eyes, long, dark eyelashes, perfectly proportioned features, all set against flawless olive-toned skin . . . *A single bullet to my head, a blinding crack, my life snuffed out, and I'd never see her again,* he thought with a tremor.

He could wait no longer. "Beth, please listen carefully. If anything ever happens to me, this is what I want you to do . . ."

Albert Conner could not believe what he saw. He spat out a profanity, squeezed the trigger twice again, and watched helplessly as his target, now entangled with another body, rolled inside the house, out of sight. *Time to get out of here, FAST!*

Conner grasped his weapon, moved across several mounds of sand, darted through winding crevices, and ran toward his truck. He heaved his Winchester inside the cab, climbed into the driver's seat, started his engine. A few grinding gear shifts, churning wheels, and he squealed onto the road that led away from Ted Simon's beachfront house. Exasperation stormed through his mind as he raced toward the Long Island Expressway. After reaching it and consuming an hour's worth of traveling time toward New York City, he had settled down sufficiently to take stock of what happened.

That miserable priest! he finally concluded. Conner had received warning that Father Holton was looking for him, but he regarded the diminutive character as little more than an irrelevant religious artifact, certainly not a threat to his plans. The last thing he expected was to see the little monkey vault across his line of vision when Conner had his target sighted perfectly. He considered teaching a lesson to the meddlesome fool, maybe even wasting him. But the sheer wickedness of the act expired under the weight of other considerations. *Good lord, I can't kill a priest!* Conner told himself, although unable to explain to himself why he couldn't. He just knew he couldn't.

Didn't matter. *I'll get to Simon in due course,* Conner concluded. In the meantime, he would lay low for a while, as long as it took, wait, and see what happened. Plus, he had stumbled on some intriguing information in recent weeks, really interesting events surrounding certain people several years ago.

Things that had Stewart Lawrence's fingerprints all over them.

Chapter Thirty-Four

August, 1973

Ted Simon gawked at the entrance of the United States Penitentiary at Ambrose, Georgia. He knew seasoned inmates referred to Bluefield, where Whitestone authorities initially reassigned Stewart for the first stage of his punishment, as "The Wall," because of its distinguishing characteristic. Undoubtedly, long-term prisoners exhausted their metaphors before concocting a striking phrase to depict the facility that loomed before him now. Ghastly images of Nazi concentration camps flickered in his thoughts, sending a chill up his spine. *Good grief, it's just an American prison!* he reminded himself. But Simon quickly discovered that maximum security meant precisely that: *maximum* security.

Bluefield had one wall; Ambrose boasted two, separated by a twenty foot space. Multiple guard towers protruded from both high barriers, attended by uniformed figures clutching semiautomatic rifles, which appeared to Simon like U.S. Army M-16's. Television surveillance cameras clung to concrete facades, like black vultures hovering over the landscape, sweeping the grounds with their slow, ominous gaze. Deadly spikes jutting from concertina rolls perched on top of a barbed wire fence clawed the air. Between that coiled death trap and the second wall stretched the most desolate, forbidding strip of land on the planet. Simon remembered reading about this formidable complex, the impossibility of escape from it. After following guards past several ponderous steel doors, walking through multiple security points, and raising his arms, spreading his legs for a thorough pat-down before entering the visiting room, he believed it. *An invisible man couldn't escape from this place,* he concluded. *Nor get into it.*

Posted rules glared at him from every wall: *Correspondence Regulations,* read one; it cited rules for writing letters. *Visitation Regulations,* stated another, which hurled a warning with each precisely stated rule.

Severity gripped every command like a cold fist; threats clamped to each word. Phrases like, *strictly prohibited, absolutely forbidden, prosecution for violations,* studded the edicts like spears thrusting from a field of bayonets, all pointed at your heart. Again, Simon felt a chill. He knew that this would be the first and probably the only time he would ever visit the United States Penitentiary at Ambrose, Georgia. And its distance from his Long Island home had nothing to do with this conclusion.

Simon proceeded to the visiting room with a half-dozen other people, who were led and followed by guards. Their route passed through long rows of cell blocks, sparking grim memories of his excursions to the Jackson County Jail. Depressing. One of the visitors in his group struck Simon as familiar, but he couldn't immediately place him. He reasoned that the trauma of first encountering Ambrose Penitentiary had temporarily paralyzed his powers of recall. *It'll come to me later,* he thought. In the meantime, the gap in his memory gnawed at his thoughts, as though somehow his failure to recognize the man might be important. And he didn't know why. That bothered him as well.

Ambrose's visiting room stood out in the facility's overbearing atmosphere like an oasis. A well-guarded oasis; at least a half-dozen or so armed men stood at various points in the room. One in each corner, two by the prisoner door on the opposite side, one by a gray desk near the visitor's entrance. A brightly illuminated interior containing a bevy of round tables greeted his eyes; three to five chairs circled each table. Prison visitors fanned out and claimed tables to wait for their men. Simon took a chair, scanned the room, let his eyes drift to that puzzling companion who took a chair near a table to his right. The man glanced at him, then rested his forearms on the table and looked straight ahead. While Simon groped his memory for place, context, and face, an electronic buzzer sounded, and Stewart Lawrence stepped into the room.

He strode toward Simon's table, pulled out a chair, and extended his hand. "Hi, Ted. Welcome to Ambrose, Georgia." Stewart wore a bluish-gray jump suit, which, Simon noticed by observing another inmate from a different angle, had the word Prisoner and a number printed on the back.

"How are you doing?" Simon asked, comforted by his friend's apparently well-adjusted demeanor. That impression soon changed.

"About as well as can be expected for doing time in another chamber of hell," Stewart said, his expression immediately transformed to a scowl.

Before Simon could ask any questions, Stewart launched into his favorite topic. Simon patiently waited for him to expend his energies before broaching a different subject.

"... so I figure that if you write that letter to the Chief Justice of the United States Supreme Court outlining the facts of my case, we're sure to get some kind of reply. If that idiot in Florida—what was his name? Clarence Gideon?—can petition by writing a letter to the Supreme Court, someone like *you* should be able to get their attention!" His eyes burned with intensity, his visage radiated bitterness.

"Um . . . Stewart," Simon ventured, "you *did* break the rules there, you know . . ."

"Not enough to deserve this!" he snapped. "They had no proof against me, only *suspicions.* Just for that, they sent me to Bluefield, thinking that would make me confess. When I still didn't say anything, you'd think they would figure I was innocent and return me to Whitestone. *But no,* instead they sent me here."

"Did they ever find anything?" Simon inquired.

Stewart shook his head. "Nope. The line ended inside the building. They figured that somehow a prisoner, presumably *me,* had smuggled a phone into the recreation center below the psychologist's office, hooked it into his telephone line, and made the calls from there. The fact that the room was locked and that they never found any electronic equipment, didn't matter to them. You know another thing: Lots of guys actually get caught breaking the rules, but that doesn't affect their parole chances. They still get out early!" Rancor now crackled from each syllable. Simon tried to change the subject.

"Ever hear from Hoffa?"

"Not since I came here. I don't know if his offer is still good or not." A weak smile. "Pretty interesting stuff he told me, though. About Kennedy's assassination, and all."

Simon responded as carefully as he could. "Stew, be careful about what he told you. He's boasted a lot about his role in the assassination. Don't you think he would have gotten nailed by this time if there were any truth to his story?"

That additional jab at Stewart's private world of events and expectations registered immediately on his face. "Guess I'll have to get another job, then," he sighed. A roguish grin angled across his lips. "Maybe like robbing banks."

"You can't be serious!" Simon exclaimed.

"Twenty thousand dollars for fifteen minutes' work? Beats minimum wage."

"For God's sake, Stewart! You'd get caught *instantly.* The world's different out there, now. Banks are better protected, a lot more precautions, warning devices, TV monitors . . ."

Stewart dismissed Simon's protests with a shrug. "I can't say definitely I would do it. Sometimes, I think it's the last thing I would do. Sometimes, all I want is to be left alone, somewhere, in a mountain cabin, maybe, sipping a drink, Lori at my side . . ." His words trailed off, a wistful look calmed his face, as if in a trance. Then, more forcefully, "Anyway if I did rob banks, I'd be much smarter at it. Avoid that one big mistake."

Simon felt that six years of wasted life had labored to produce nothing more but another looming disaster. "You don't know what you're saying. I can't believe that you would . . . would . . ." His words collapsed in a heap of incredulity.

Stewart leaned forward. *"Ted!* Do you know what prison is? *Do you?* I'll tell you. It's a convention of criminals searching for the perfect crime. In here, we analyze our crimes, Ted. I mean, we put them under a microscope, pick them apart, probe for that single mistake that landed us here. Then we pool our talents, figure out how to avoid that fatal mistake." He leaned back, took the measure of Simon's reaction. "It's no different from any other group of professionals who get together to talk business."

Simon sat there, stone-faced. Stewart checked his watch. "My God! Time for you to go. I only get four hours a month for outside visitors, and we've used up almost three of them. I have to keep at least one in reserve. Never can tell who might show up."

Simon acknowledged with a weak nod. "Like the priest from Jackson County Jail, for instance?"

Stewart looked surprised. "You know about that?"

Simon nodded. "He stopped by to see me, too."

"That idiot took up a half an hour of precious time just with aimless chatter. If I hadn't been so desperate for outside contact, I would have refused to see him. Why do you think he stopped by?"

Simon wrestled with his thoughts before answering. "Doing penance, maybe. For past misdeeds." He could see that his answer connected with nothing in Stewart's moral architecture; he remained expressionless, and finally just shrugged.

"I'll try to forget him," he sneered.

And I'll try to forget that I've been sleeping with a pistol beneath my pillow every night because of you, Simon thought with a trace of bitterness.

The two shook hands, and Simon caught sight of the man whose face had been taunting his memory. Really odd. The stranger remained there by himself the whole time he and Stewart had been conversing. Just sat there, chewing gum. On a whim, Simon turned to Stewart. "By the way, Stewart, do you have any idea who that guy is over there?"

Stewart glanced to his left. "No . . . No idea." Back to Simon, a warmer expression. "Please stay in touch, Ted. You're one of the few people authorized to send me letters. Please don't stop."

Simon forced a reassuring smile across his lips. "Don't worry, I won't." Simon turned and walked toward the door. A guard nearby opened it for him. Thinking again that he would probably never visit the place, Simon threw one last look over his shoulder.

He saw something very strange.

The man who had been sitting alone pulled up a chair by Stewart's table. Stewart remained there, trained his eyes on his new visitor.

"Once you get up, you have to leave," cautioned the guard by his side.

"A few seconds. *Please!*" Simon pleaded.

Stewart's attention was riveted on the man across his table, and he was completely unaware that Simon remained in the room by the good graces of the guard. Simon observed the man's lips moving, but his words evaporated into the din of quiet conversation pervading the room. A pained expression passed across Stewart's face; he buried his head into his hands. His friend extended an arm in a consoling gesture. Finally, Stewart got up, nodded curtly at the man across the table, and walked toward the prisoner door in the back of the room. Simon quickly slipped through the visitor's door, so Stewart wouldn't notice he had lingered.

Simon trudged his way back through the depressing chambers and checkpoints of Ambrose Penitentiary. Although Simon believed the matter had nothing to do with him, Stewart's lie about not knowing that mystery guest augmented the importance of recalling his visitor's identity. A shroud of distress darkened Simon's speculations about this enigma. It issued from Stewart's parting words, which now echoed through his mind.

Do you know what prison is, Ted? It's a convention of criminals searching for the perfect crime . . .

―――

The withering Georgia sun encased each body inside a personal cocoon of sweltering misery. Thick, inescapable, relentless, the afternoon heat saturated clothing and occasionally ignited tempers. As Stewart Lawrence walked through Ambrose Prison's yard to meet his friends who gathered by a bench near one of the interior walls, he felt more like an marine animal crawling across the sea bottom through liquid heated by a submerged crack in the earth's crust. He nodded his greetings and plunked his wet hulk on the bench. Stewart swept a sopping forearm across his face. Hopeless. New sweat immediately blossomed to replace the old.

"The Lobster Day session of the STP Club is now in order," he announced, drawing grins from his two fellow sufferers.

"Lobsters have it easy compared to this wet mush," commented Terrence Daly, who represented the "T" part of their small group. "At least they die in the pot *quickly*. Has to be better than putting up with this."

"Speaking of pots, just what did we settle on as the goal of our business venture," asked Peter Radius, the "P" member of their trio. "You know, the total pot."

Stewart considered the question, as he stared at the throng of inmates clustered throughout the prison's stuffy interior courtyard. "A million-five," he declared. "That's a half million per person. Once we reach that figure, we stop, disband, and disappear."

Terrence, a balding, fifty-five year old possessing brown eyes, a tawny complexion, and a Kirk Douglas dimple, nodded in agreement. "That division sounds right to me," he said, "although we should confirm it with a calculating machine." His comment drew smiles. Terrence never challenged Stewart; or anyone else for that matter. Except, of course, the last eyewitness who claimed to spot a traceable license plate number on the car he used in his last robbery. That challenge he lost.

"Anything particularly significant about your figure?" Peter Radius inquired.

"Yes, it has special meaning to me," Stewart said. "My personal mission in life is to acquire that amount one way or another. I would prefer getting it another way, but if that doesn't work out, then STP goes into business." He stared into the yard, leaving his friends with the task of deciphering this cryptic remark.

Neither decided to pursue the matter. Peter Radius, a forty-year old with brown hair, blue eyes, and lips angled in a permanent frown, pulled out a Winston and snapped a Zippo flame on it. "I've got the car angle figured out," he said, taking a deep drag of the hot smoke. This attracted interested looks. "A master key," he announced with a flourish. "Saves time, trouble, suspicious glances, and gives us an automatic supply of cars. The only drawback is that master keys only fit particular models. Still, it beats trying to break into a car for each robbery. Especially, considering the number of cars we'd need."

"More than one is always advisable," cautioned Terrence. "Believe me, I know."

"Then this is how we do it," Stewart stated, taking charge. He picked up a twig, started drawing in the dirt. "Say, here's the bank. A small, branch bank, easily accessible. We already agreed on that point, right?"

His partners nodded.

Stewart continued. "Then Car One we park three to six blocks from the bank. After the job, we drive it to Car Two, which is parked at a shopping center. We drive it three or four miles to Car Three, which is, say, *here.*" He stabbed the ground. "Car Three should be legally owned by people we trust. Like family members, for instance. We drive it to our temporary headquarters, an apartment or house, but we never park the car directly in front of it," he emphasized. "A few blocks away, at least. Then we divide our earnings, settle ourselves, prepare for the next job."

His partners studied the ground, appreciating his outline and the principle it demonstrated: successful missions leave not a trace of those who carried them out. Like scratches in the sand, which easily vanish with a sweep of the foot.

"Looks good to me, General," Terrence commented.

"Admiral," Stewart corrected. "I was in the Navy, remember? But as long as you bring it up, remember Sun Tzu's comment that all warfare is based on deception. Which brings me to our next point. Camouflage."

"We should talk about guns, first," Peter interjected. "I don't care about your Soon Chop Suey crap. What guns are we going to use?"

"We're not going to *use* any weapon," Terrence emphasized, in a scolding voice. "Except as an absolute, last resort. If you mean, what are we going to *carry* into the bank, what are we going to *show,* I recommend a pistol and a sawed-off shotgun."

"Why the heavy artillery?" Stewart inquired. "I never used more than a pistol. And that I never even had loaded."

"Psychological effect," Terrence explained. "People obey instructions faster because they're more scared. Time is of the essence. Cops take six to ten minutes to reach the bank after they're alerted, which means we have no more than five minutes to complete the job. Plus, nothing else will bring the heat down on us faster than actually shooting someone. Could destroy our business real fast."

Stewart and Peter grasped his point instantly, demonstrating another advantage of their STP club meetings. All three had served time at Bluefield, endured the best and the worst of prison life at three federal facilities, drew extensively from their experiences inside and outside of prison, and trusted each other completely.

"Which brings us back to camouflage," Stewart continued. He launched into a discussion of clothing, which included detailed procedures for the wearing of ski masks, hats, gloves, sunglasses, shoes, and the use of shopping bags to transport such things, including stolen cash. Rules snapped off his tongue with military precision, and he concluded with a flourish. "Remember, we're never more than one error away from perfection, but that single error could be fatal. Thus, if anyone has a bad feeling about a job, for whatever reason, we abort, period. No questions asked. Casing a bank for three or four days and rehearsing our moves a couple of times beforehand means nothing, if we trip up on something simple, something stupid . . ."

"Like speeding, or getting a parking ticket," Peter commented acidly, as though recalling a bitter experience.

"Exactly," Stewart agreed. "And we obey these rules *to the letter.* No deviations. Agreed?"

His partners acknowledged, this time with handshakes. "We ought to put together a field manual," Terrence suggested. "Beats the years I spent poring over volumes of Army Regulations."

"I'd prefer that we keep all this in our heads," Stewart stated firmly.

A gust of hot air flowed through Ambrose Prison's yard, penetrating their bodies like steaming gelatin pouring into a mold and spreading throughout its contours, filling every crevice.

Peter dappled a wet handkerchief across his forehead. "We start as soon as we all get out of this hellhole, right?" he proposed.

Stewart remained silent, drawing their quizzical stares. "What about it, Stewart," Terrence asked. "We did elect you leader, you know. We can't very well begin without you."

"Let him alone. He's thinking up another quote from Chop Suey," Peter cracked, which drew a sharp look of rebuke from Stewart. Peter immediately backed off. "Hey, I'm sorry, man," he apologized. "You got something else on your mind?"

Stewart dismissed Peter's comment with a shrug. "Let's leave it this way. At the rate I'm going, you guys will probably get out before I do. As soon as I get paroled or finish my sentence, I'll call you, let you know. I have a few things on the outside. I'm waiting to see what happens. If we start our business, I'll say these words: *The Three Musketeers Ride!* Then we meet at where we agreed. Okay?"

The two nodded in assent. With nothing more to discuss, Peter and Terrence sauntered away, mingled with other prisoners. Stewart stayed for a moment in deep thought. Finally, he got up, glanced at the diagrams etched in the dirt, swept a foot across his handiwork, and walked away.

Chapter Thirty-Five

February 1974

If I can just make it to the tree line, he thought, blood pounding against ears bit by the frigid air. He peered around the giant boulder and spied the trail that snaked through towering conifers, whose more distant outreaches clawed the back of a soaring mountain like a smattering of jagged green arrowheads. Bottoms of great hammerhead clouds scraped against the peak's bold thrust into the sky, shrouding its top with hazy white mist. Closer to earth, the twisting path behind him relinquished nothing about his mysterious pursuer. He turned around, collapsed against the rock's craggy hardness, his aching chest snatching oxygen from slices of cold that knifed into his lungs with each heaving intake.

Puffs of breathy crystals shot past his lips pummeled the air, as he squeezed his eyes toward the tree line, no more than a hundred yards ahead. A barren stretch littered with boulders and scoured free by whipping blades of wind greeted his scrutiny. This residue of nature's battlefield, casualties from a glacier's grinding passage, offered little concealment along the way. He either made it in a single, frenzied lunge, or he didn't make it at all. Another stolen glance around his massive cover. Nothing appeared. *Maybe he lost me,* he thought, grasping for hope. He cupped his gloved hands over his mouth in a futile attempt to offer reprieve from the punishing air. *A quick sprint, I can make it,* he concluded. *I know where to hide in there, he'll never find me!*

Garnering his strength for one last dash to safety, the small man struggled to his feet, scooped more lungfuls of oxygen, then crouched as though preparing for a marathon run. As if on instinct, part of his mind summoned an extra measure of strength from a well of discipline formed by decades of severe training in his former profession. An internal countdown ticked off seconds, priming him for the single furious dash toward the wooded sanctuary that beckoned ahead. Five . . . four . . . three . . . two . . . one . . . *GO!*

He leaped forward, across the exposed landscape, running as fast as he could. Legs pumping, pulse pounding against eardrums, lungs smashing brittle air, he sprinted across and weaved through the field of rocks toward that protective thicket of trees.

Twenty yards . . . Thirty . . . Fifty . . . *Halfway!*

Vault over that rock, *skip* past that boulder, *dart* around that treacherous gully . . . *Almost there!*

WHAM!

His assailant sprang over a boulder as if launched by a catapult, crashed into him, and strapped his flailing limbs to the ground with powerful hands.

"Stop it, you idiot!" shrieked his attacker. "Stop struggling, for God's sake!"

Pinned on his back by hands that felt like vise grips, the smaller man whipped his arms back and forth, pounding his foe on the shoulders with his soft fists. He might as well have tried to pummel a mountain lion in the flanks with wooden spoons. Ridiculous, futile resistance.

"If you don't stop, you little bastard, I'll smash your face in! Now, cut it out!"

He ceased fighting. His victorious opponent relaxed his grip a bit and let him catch his breath. Vanquished and helpless, the smaller man blinked hard, stared at the figure hovering above him. Razor blue eyes cracked an icy gleam from his taut, white features, braced by cold. Flecks of snow salted his stocking cap; ice crystals clung to his sweeping, frozen mustache. His attacker's cruel good looks fixed on him.

The larger man eased backward, stood up, leaned against a boulder, keeping his eye on his prey's every move. The smaller man hoisted himself to a sitting position. He glanced toward his opponent and flinched.

"If you try to run away again," the man sputtered, "I'll blow your brains out!" The muzzle of the pistol pointed at his head.

A slice of frigid wind cut across their dangerously moist bodies, sweeping away this unnecessary threat. The smaller man quickly scrambled to the protection of the closest boulder and crouched near the feet of his assailant. By this time, the pistol had vanished beneath folds of winter clothing that protected exposed skin. Howling breezes finally whimpered to sporadic gusts that whipped across their faces. Composure restored, an audible question crept from a scratchy throat. "Who are you and what do you want?"

Albert Conner sneered. "I want YOU, *you idiot!* I've been chasing you off and on for the past eight months through this godforsaken wilderness." His eyes swept across the forbidding horizon. He sniffled, shook his head, coughed.

"Most people think it's beautiful."

"Beautiful?" came Conner's scoffing reply. "I once thought the jungle was beautiful. Until I had to fight in it. Now, I think it's *hell.* And so is this! Just colder, that's all. One hell of a cold, miserable place." Conner bent over, planted his face a foot away from the crouched figure. "I started out up north, by the Canadian border. I figured that made sense, because it was summer. That's where people go that time of the year. Right? *Wrong!* I drove, then hiked, drove some more, hiked God knows how many more miles. I couldn't get through. You know why? *Snow!* They were still clearing away the goddamned snow! *In June!"*

Conner's indignation in a strange way offered comfort to the smaller man. Maybe it was just the sound of another human voice in the wilderness. Or the fact that the weapon had disappeared. Or a reaction to the ridiculous nature of his adversary's utterances. He couldn't tell.

"Then I went south. Scorched my ass on the paths near San Diego, then froze it whenever I went into one of those fifty national forests between Canada and Mexico!" Conner's tone suggested that blame for his frustration should fall on the shoulders of his victim.

"Twenty-three, actually."

"What!"

"There are twenty-three national forests on the Pacific Crest Trail between Canada and Mexico." He had no idea why he said that. The training, perhaps, prodded him to hurl corrective information toward ignorant minds, regardless of the circumstances. It suddenly occurred to him that his instructors probably did not have the current situation in mind, however.

Conner just glared at him. "What motivated you to go up here?" he shouted, straightening up. "At this time of year?"

"I heard someone was looking for me, someone who wouldn't reveal his name. I got scared, decided to hide out in the Sierra Nevada's, the part of this trail I know best. I figured only a fool would follow me up here." *Definitely* not a smart thing to say. Nervous eyes flickered upward.

Conner burst out in derisive laughter. "You got *that* part right! Only a fool would come up here now. But this fool knows what he wants. And you're going to tell him. In fact, you're the only person who can tell me what I need to know." Conner squatted in front of his quarry, seized the smaller man's shoulders.

"I'm just a tour guide," came the stammering response.

"Right!" Conner sneered. "And I'm Teddy Roosevelt on a nature tour."

"What can you possibly want from me?"

"YOU are *Morris Courtney!*" Conner shouted triumphantly. "And *you* are going to tell me *everything* I want to know!"

Morris Courtney's shoulders sagged. He closed his eyes, stricken, defeated. "I couldn't get a job after my conviction for race fixing. No one would touch me. I've got a cousin in the Forest Service, he made arrangements . . ."

"I don't give a *damn* about your personal history!" Conner boomed.

Courtney studied his adversary's intense countenance. "What, then?"

Steely grip tighter, cold eyes gleaming, "You will tell me *everything* you know about Stewart Lawrence," Conner ordered. "Everything!"

Conner's powerful hands knifed into Courtney like talons of a giant bird of prey. Pain stabbed Courtney's shoulders, down his arms. "You don't have to get rough. I'll tell you whatever you want to know."

"Good!" Conner affirmed through clenched teeth. "That will save us both a great deal of trouble."

Judge Harvey Walton, United States District Court Judge, New York City, removed his glasses, rubbed the bridge of his nose, and stared at the file on his desk. The prisoner's name was clear to him, even through his blurred vision: Stewart G. Lawrence. The sheer volume of the stack of letters laid before him pointed an accusing finger at the American judicial system. He reached forward, picked up the top sheet of paper and scanned its contents for perhaps the fourth time. *I still can't believe it,* he thought, placing it back on the pile. He had recently decided a case very similar to the one argued by this inmate. Same judge, too. Chandler, his name; died a year after sentencing this guy. After that, Lawrence's letters of appeal vanished into the labyrinth of judicial bureaucracy, never saw the light of day. Procedures weren't followed; documents got misplaced; inmates were transferred by questionable authority; parole boards received suspicious recommendations from unnamed sources.

He couldn't prove this last circumstance. Didn't have to; the other three stirred his judicial conscience sufficiently to motivate his actions. He placed his reading glasses back on his face, reached for a pen, and pulled out a form. He affixed his signature on a legal order. *This ought to brighten his day,* Walton thought, as he stared at one of the lines on the legal document:

"I hereby order the above sentence of (Mr. ~~Mrs.~~ ~~Miss~~) STEWART G. LAWRENCE, Federal Prisoner Number(597-334-8889)—VACATED . . ."

His next judicial command advanced procedures by one more step.

Stated prisoner shall be TRANSPORTED to North Road Federal Holding Center, Queens County, New York, NO LATER THAN 28 February 1974, for a re-sentencing hearing at said premises of this court . . .

Walton placed both documents into his OUT file, for immediate mailing. He leaned back and let his gaze drift to a Scales of Justice statue that he had carried with him since his days in law school. This bronze figurine, only six inches high, including pedestal, had served as a mute but effective reminder of the sacred trust placed in him by the President of the United States, with the Advice and Consent of the Senate. Justice, pure and simple. Walton noticed the scales tilted slightly, off balance. He reached forward, set them right.

If only the rest of this job were so simple, he mused, as he picked up another document.

March, 1974, North Road Federal Holding Center, New York

Stewart Lawrence glared at the most reliable friend he had ever known during his years in three Federal prisons. The man seated on the opposite side of a wire-mesh barrier tried to mollify his grim news with a wan smile.

"You shouldn't be that surprised, Stewart. I've kept you up to date over the years," he said, jaws exercising on a piece of gum.

Stewart tried to control his exasperation. *"But why now?"* he cried. "Why not a *year* from now, or even a *month?* Why does all this have to happen *exactly* the time I might get out of prison?" He balled his fists, pounded the counter, drawing a cross look from a nearby guard. Stewart gave him an ingratiating smile and what he hoped the guard would understand as a nod of apology for the slight commotion.

"Or, this could have happened last year, or the year before that, Stewart. Paroles are unpredictable events. No one knows that better than you."

Stewart folded his hands together in front of his face in a tight grip. "Are you still willing to help me out?"

"Of course."

"I really appreciate this, Bert, and I promise to make this worth your while." He glanced at a wall calendar, closed his eyes, made some silent computations. "The timing on this could be crucial. That's why I'd like to employ your services full-time. There's money in this for you when I get out. I promise."

"I could always use the money. What do you want me to do?"

Stewart gestured Bert to lean forward; he uttered his instructions in a low voice. When he finished, Bert arched his eyebrows, impressed.

"Really?" he exclaimed.

Stewart nodded. "You are the only other person I have ever told this to, Bert. I trust you completely. Your reward will be substantial. You can count on it."

"You can count on me, too," Bert affirmed.

"You retain your old skills, I presume?" Stewart ventured.

Bert's jaws ceased working. He looked slightly offended. "Those skills never left me, Stewart. That sort of training stays with you forever. In fact, I'm better now than I ever was."

"Good! Then it's settled. You'll keep me informed on a daily basis."

"Hourly, if necessary," Bert rejoined.

"That won't be possible here, but maybe you can . . ."

"TIME!" the guard snapped. Visiting hours had expired.

Bert got up, signaled his good-bye with a curt nod and a look of determination.

"Good luck," Stewart said, as he watched his friend depart. He had placed his destiny into the hands of a man who he had no choice but to trust wholeheartedly. Stewart thought about the hearing scheduled two days from now. He had done everything he could to prepare for it and for the unknown events that might occur outside the courtroom as well. All he could do now was wait.

Wait and brace himself for whatever might happen within the next week or so.

"Stewart's probably getting out of prison," Lori stated, glaring at the attorney seated behind his desk. "Real soon, too."

"Yes, I know," Milliken replied.

"How did you find out?" Lori asked.

"I first heard from my sister. Stewart has kept in regular correspondence with his son. Scores of letters over the years about name changes, legal adoption, and whatnot. Complicated legal stuff," he added with a hint of condescension. "Plus, of course, other sources I consulted over the years. Who told you?"

"Ted Simon. He called me, said Stewart wrote him all excited about a re-sentencing hearing. Same old stuff, except this time, he's actually being moved to New York City. In fact, he might be there right now."

"Given the long time he served on his sentence, this was inevitable," Milliken observed.

"Isn't there *anything* more you can do?"

Milliken looked at her intently. "Listen, Lori. You've not been completely honest with me. I know Stewart Lawrence. He's a thief and a liar, but he's not violent. Whatever reasons you have for wanting him to stay in jail, I doubt that fear of being physically assaulted by him is one of them. Now, you've consulted with me for . . . what? A dozen meetings over the past five years or so? Don't you think it's time you told me the truth?"

Lori bit her lip, said nothing, her thoughts paralyzed by the dilemma that had dominated her life since Lawrence's arrest. Sharing her secret with Milliken meant confessing her guilt. *He's a former prosecutor, for God's sake! How would he react?* On the other hand, Stewart would certainly be released, within weeks, perhaps. No question that he would retrieve those bonds the minute he stepped outside prison walls. She concluded that she had one hope. Milliken's desire to prevent that from happening might outweigh whatever compulsion he'd feel to pursue her crime in taking them.

"Okay," she said. "Only if you promise not to do anything that would put me in trouble."

"Consider me your attorney," Milliken said unctuously. "A lawyer-client relationship is sacrosanct."

Lori shot him a puzzled look. "What?"

"Nothing you say leaves this office, and I promise you I will do nothing that would put you in legal jeopardy," he clarified.

Lori nodded her acknowledgment, uncertainly. She told him her story, embellishing it with editorial comment about the wretchedness of Jeremy Madison, Stewart Lawrence, and other heels she had known. She finished, awaiting Milliken's reaction with apprehension.

The former United States Attorney responded with a look of respect. He issued a soft whistle. "A half million dollars worth of bearer bonds?" he repeated.

Lori nodded.

"Wow! And you never figured out the meaning of his clue?"

"I don't think it means a damn thing!" Lori snapped. "He just put those words together to poke fun at me, to torture me. So I tortured him back. I kept him in jail as long as possible." Pride surged through her voice. "With your help, of course," she added.

Still marveling at her story, Milliken groped for a new way to repeat what they both knew. "He's getting out now, Lori. You have to accept that."

"I know. But in the meantime, I did my best to make him miserable. I've been working for Jeremy Madison again, and I know he knows that."

"How does he know that?"

"I told him myself. I wrote him."

Again, Milliken fumbled for the right words. "Are you sleeping with Madison as well?"

Lori scowled. "Occasionally," she admitted. "Another way to get revenge. On them both!"

"What do you mean?"

"Every once in a while when Jeremy and I are having sex, and I know he's really into it, I whisper Stewart's name in his ear."

Milliken could not suppress a chuckle. "That must have an interesting effect on him," he observed.

"You never saw a man go limp so fast in your entire life," Lori giggled.

"I guess I won't argue with that."

"He still returns for more, and, anyway, I've had my fun."

"Sounds like you've wanted to torture both men."

"Exactly," Lori stated firmly. She found that venting years of exasperation while impressing a high-priced lawyer was an exhilarating experience. Lori detected no phony outrage in Milliken's reaction to her account; if he was offended by her crime, he certainly didn't show it. On the contrary, every inflection in his words sparkled new respect. She liked that.

"Which still leaves us back at square one as far as locating those bonds," Milliken said. "That program he gave you—do you still have it?"

"I keep it with me all the time. It's in my purse."

"Do you mind if I take a look at it."

Although the Lakewood Downs racing program had taunted her for the past half decade, Lori still found it difficult to relinquish. It was her talisman; didn't bring her good luck, but it remained her only possible link to Madison's bonds. She snapped her purse open, fumbled through a menagerie of items, lifted out a twice-folded, worn rectangle of papers, and handed it to Milliken.

Milliken manipulated the pamphlet into readable form. He started paging through it, then looked up. "Do you mind if I study this a little while? Never know what might come up."

"Go ahead," Lori said. "Just keep it safe. I want it back when you're done."

"Of course."

"I guess I should go now," she said, getting up to leave. She stopped by the door, creased a worried look toward Carl Adolphus Milliken, attorney at law. "Mr. Milliken," she started, paused. *"Carl . . ."*

Milliken perked up.

"If you should somehow come up with something, by accident, or whatever, you *promise* to let me know, won't you?"

Milliken set his jaw and looked at her intently. "Lori, if I manage somehow to stumble over something you didn't, I promise I'll let you know *immediately.*"

Lori pondered this. "We could split it, you know," she ventured. "Fifty-fifty. Just so Stewart doesn't get any of it."

"My thoughts exactly," Milliken agreed. "And I'd quickly turn over my half to my sister. Final payment from her former husband. She deserves it."

That made Lori smile. She glided through the doorway and left. A quick departure from his professional building, across the parking lot, into her trusty Volkswagen, another talisman from her distant past, except this one worked. That's why she had kept it so long. Madison had offered to buy her a new car but she refused. Enough that he had supplied her with an apartment close to the beach, although she had to admit, that was as much for his convenience as it was to improve her living standards. No matter, Lori thought, as she pulled out of the parking lot toward the Long Island Expressway. She enjoyed her lavish quarters just the same.

She glanced out of her rear view mirror. Now, if she could only conquer the fear that she was being followed . . .

Oliver choked for breath while ghastly powerful fingers clutched at his throat, pinning him against the wall. Eyes bulging with terror, he caught sight of his attacker's pistol rising to his temple.

Steel against bone . . . Hammer pulled back . . .

Click!

Assailant's face two inches away, blazing fury, madness . . .

"Oh, God!" Oliver croaked.

"If you EVER," Albert Conner hissed, "breathe a word of this to *anyone . . .*" His deadly grip tightened around Oliver's throat. "I will kill you!"

The former Marine let his hand relax but kept his forty-five pistol in place. Oliver collapsed to the floor and rested in a sitting position against the wall. Conner waited for him to recover, then crouched and jammed his weapon's muzzle against Oliver's nose.

The former security man's whole body trembled, as if preparing to shut off in a final convulsion before death relieved his anguish. Conner quickly removed the pistol. Oliver fell to the side, his flaccid body still partially supported by the wall. His chest heaved, his eyes quivered, unseeing, glassy.

"Do you understand me?" Conner demanded, wondering if additional threats made any difference. *The guy's almost dead, anyway.*

"Yes . . ." Oliver gasped. "Please . . . don't . . . hurt the lady. *Please!"*

Conner leaned over him. "What happens to the lady depends on you. A single word from you, and you both die. You got that?"

Oliver nodded weakly.

"Good!" Conner shoved his pistol into his belt, stepped past Oliver toward the door, threw one last glance toward his pitiful victim. "By the way, thanks for the information," Conner cracked. "It was helpful." Then he slipped out the door of Oliver's house, and trotted toward his truck.

Very helpful, Conner repeated to himself as his pickup roared away. In fact, his nimble mind had quickly interwoven the elements of Courtney's detailed account with Oliver's revelations, as they tumbled from the old man's sputtering lips. Oliver had barely finished speaking when the solution to Lawrence's puzzle exploded in Conner's mind. For a fraction of a second, Conner's pistol drooped from his hand, while the befuddled Oliver gaped at what must have been a look of astonishment on his intruder's face. Conner quickly recovered, thoughts racing, and threatened Oliver nearly to death. *Got a little excited and probably overdid it,* he thought, taking a turn. *No matter. I'll still get those bonds.*

Conner turned his truck toward the road leading to Lakewood Downs, pondering the simple genius of Stewart Lawrence's clue. He thought about Lori and found himself shaking his head. *Sounds like a really gutsy broad,* he mused. *But considering the number of years she had to think about this, not all that bright.*

Which was the same unflattering conclusion arrived at by Carl Milliken. Unfortunately, however, several days later.

The phone rang its customary three times before the receptionist picked it up. "Sweets Ahoy. May I help you?"

"Lori Armstrong, please," Milliken said.

Fifteen seconds passed. Lori's sultry voice crept into his ear.

She sounds even sexier on the phone, Milliken thought. "Yes, Lori, Carl Milliken here. Listen, I've been mulling over this clue Stewart gave you, and I've studied the program, too. Probably I went through all the same mental gymnastics you did, but something kind of interesting occurred to me. Have you ever thought of looking through the *stable* that the Gandy Dancer came from?"

Silence.

"Um . . . Lori? Lori? Are you still there?"

Then Carl Milliken thought he heard the sound of the telephone receiver slipping from her hand and clattering to the floor.

Chapter Thirty-Six

". . . and that over there is the tack room," explained Timothy Dornan, owner and manager of Dornan Stables. "Actually, I've found that a tack box by each stall is more convenient, especially since I've gotten into the habit of keeping my horses in their own, special stalls. Now if you look over here . . ."

Albert Conner listened carefully, doing his best to separate useful items of information from the stream of drivel that poured endlessly from the mouth of his septuagenarian guide. Nuggets of data had to be mined from each laborious sentence. *Insufferable old coot,* Conner thought, as he glanced at a face that seemed carved out of a walnut shell. The old man topped his wizened visage with a Washington Senators baseball cap, which sprouted shocks of gray hair like bundled shoots of straw. Blue jeans and plaid complemented this loquacious apparition, who might have tumbled from the pages of *Field & Stream.* Conner groaned inwardly, trying to follow Dornan's meandering explanations. Every point had an anecdote; every horse, its own story; every digression, its personal set of irrelevancies. But nothing the old man uttered ever seemed to possess an end, because everything he said reminded him of something else. *Even horses have to cross finish lines,* Conner groused. Apparently not this one.

While Dornan babbled away, pleased to share his three-quarter-century's worth of experience raising and driving standardbred horses, Conner filled gaps in his knowledge by scrutinizing the ten-horse stable. A few cats scurried about; a huge black dog of unknown pedigree eyed him warily; paraphernalia of all descriptions filled every corner.

"Each stall contains three to five inches of clay, covered by fresh straw. Now that big one over there"—he pointed toward what appeared a double-sized stall—"that's for foaling. Most mares foal in March or April."

Conner nodded, pushed a smile into his handlebar mustache, and continued scanning the stable.

Dornan didn't miss a beat. "Of course, I make that floor especially thick, up to eighteen inches. Never can be too careful, and . . . You know, that reminds me of the time some years ago, actually, 1945, just after my boys got back from the war . . ."

And on he went. Conner noticed a half-dozen sulkies lined up against the wall next to a stall, fitting into each other like a series of collapsible boxes. A multitude of implements hung from every available hook: bridles, whips, tangles of straps, and a plethora of other equipment whose purpose Conner could only guess. *If all that stuff is hanging up, what does he keep in the tack boxes?* he wondered. One thing in particular, however, caught his attention.

"Those names," Conner asked.

Dornan stopped. "Eh?"

"I see you have horse's names hanging next to each stall."

Dornan stepped up to a wooden nameplate and lovingly fondled its letters. "Yep," he said. "Kept 'em all, over the years. Every horse I ever owned. I figured I owed them that, you know, to remember what they did for me, the money they made me. Kind of a hobby of mine." His ruddy features cracked into a toothy, tobacco-stained grin.

Conner scanned columns of names routed out on wooden paddle boards attached to each stall. He marveled at the ridiculous appellations he encountered, wondering how much ingenuity had been wasted over the decades in attempts to concoct a horse name no one had ever heard before. His eyes roamed over the engravings etched near each stall. Finally, he stopped.

There it is. The Gandy Dancer.

Except its name plate didn't attach to a post near a stall. Instead, it was listed with a dozen other names enclosed by a frame jutting out from a wall of a small room. Conner stepped closer for a better look. Suddenly, an enormous black dog lunged toward him, barked ferociously, then got yanked backward by a thick chain. He collapsed on the dirt, sprang to its feet, and snarled at him in a low, rumbling growl as it strained against its leash.

Conner jumped backward. He glowered at the menacing beast and it glowered back, sniping at him, baring its teeth. Dornan clapped Conner on the shoulder, reassuringly.

"Don't worry about Old Smoky," he said. "He can't reach you. Just pray that he doesn't pull out that iron spike we got his chain attached to," he cautioned. "But that's only happened once."

Conner nodded, keeping his eye on the dog. "You keep him chained here all the time?"

"Yep. Best security ever invented—guard dogs. He sleeps outside the whole year, even in winters, like now. We got a light out there too, keep it on all night. You know, just in case. Don't know what works better, the light or the dog."

The dog! Conner concluded instantly. *Definitely, the dog. And by this time tomorrow, a DEAD dog.*

He turned his attention to the room. "What's in there?"

"Used to be the tack room," Dornan explained. "I still call it that, but I use it to store all sorts of special things."

"Like what?"

"Oh, you know, stuff that goes with each horse. You see, I figured that their prizes and such were earned by them training out here, and belong out here, not in some dusty glass case inside my house. My wife, my kids, think I'm nuts, but you know, at my age, I think I'm entitled to put special stuff where I want to. Plus it gives me a chance to take visitors, like you, for instance, to the stable."

Conner felt his pulse quickening. "Like *what* things?" he asked earnestly.

"Prizes, memory-type stuff. Things previous drivers have given me. Letters and such. Lucky charms. I just plunk stuff in the bench below the horses' names. Makes it all very special. You know, at my age . . ."

"May I see what you've got?" Conner snapped, losing patience.

A flicker of irritation passed across Dornan's cragged features. He did not like to be interrupted. It passed quickly. "I suppose so," he said. He reached into his pocket, pulled out a large ring filled with keys, and sorted through them. Finally, he isolated the right one, inserted it into a padlock, and swung the door open. He reached around the corner and switched on a light.

Conner studied the room. It resembled private quarters found in railway cars of a passenger train. A dozen pictures, six on each side, lined the walls. Beneath them, a bench. Dornan stepped up to one of the pictures, cocked his head back to peer at it with the bottom portion of his bifocal glasses.

"A driver and his horse," he muttered wistfully. "You have no idea . . ."

Conner ignored him. He stared at a photograph of a driver standing next to a horse in the winner's circle. *The Gandy Dancer.* Excitement surged through his body. He looked down at the bench, tried to lift its cover.

Locked.

Dornan ceased talking, turned toward him. "Oh, you can't get into that," he said.

"Why not? I'm interested in *The Gandy Dancer* and wanted to look at some of the awards you were talking about."

"A lot of that is personal stuff. This is like my private storage space, private trophy room. For drivers, trainers, special folks I've known over the years."

Conner nodded as though he understood, thinking that Lawrence's clue made more sense with each revelation. He still didn't know the numbers' significance, but those seemed to make less difference. Perhaps he'd stumble on their meaning in the process of exploring the contents of the bench. "I guess I see what you mean," he said.

"In fact, I don't even know what some of that stuff is!" Dornan added, as though proud of his ignorance. "I just know it's special. Just for those special folks who want to see it now and then. I've kept this room for them," he repeated.

Conner looked away, rolled his eyes. *This old fool has no idea what a setup this is!* he mused, incredulous. Back to Dornan. "Well, Mr. Dornan, I think I've seen enough. Thank you very much." Conner shook his hand appreciatively. "You've told me a lot that I can use for my article."

"What magazine was that, did you say?"

Conner paused, trying to think of an answer. *"Top Trotter."* He didn't know if such a publication existed. Or, if it mattered. But it sounded good. "I really have to go now. Deadlines, and all."

"But I've hardly told you anything!" Dornan protested.

You've told me enough, Conner thought. He stepped out the room into the stable and immediately jerked backward. Old Smoky leaped at him again, then stood there, flaring his teeth, salivating, growling.

A VERY dead dog, Conner repeated to himself.

"You know, these horses have their own quirks," Dornan continued to explain, running up behind Conner as he walked toward the stable's front entrance. "Like *Raising Cain,* over there, for instance . . ."

Conner walked outside, studied the landscape. He had traveled through this part of northern New Jersey but wanted to familiarize himself with the immediate surroundings. Rolling hills dusted with a light covering of snow and scarred by winding lines of wooden fences greeted his eyes. He spied Dornan's house, its back porch, the line of vision to the rear of the stable. Back to the horizon . . .

That bluff over there, Conner concluded quickly. Sixty, maybe seventy yards away, maximum. *Perfect.*

"... whenever he's curious, he just flips that switch on by his stall. Isn't that something? One smart horse, I tell you. My wife says, why don't you just move the stupid switch, so you don't have to come out here every time he switches the light on, but you know, I just can't..."

Conner faced his aged host, cutting off his monologue. "Let me thank you again, Mr. Dornan," he said, shaking the old man's hand. "I promise to mention you in my article."

Dornan's grizzled features lit up. "That would be nice of you, thanks."

Conner climbed into his truck, paused, then called out the window. "By the way, when did you say your feeding times were?"

"Eleven in the morning, four in the afternoon, and eleven o'clock in the evening," he answered. "Why do you ask?"

"Just curious," Conner said. "You know, to compare it with other stables."

"Oh, right."

"Thanks, again." Conner rolled his window up, started his engine, backed up, and rumbled away on the long driveway that snaked around the buildings of Dornan Stables. He could not hear Tim Dornan say to himself, aloud, "Right nice fellow. Wished he could've stayed longer..."

Crisp breezes cut across Albert Conner's face as he scrutinized the rear entrance of Dornan Stables from his hillside perch approximately fifty yards away. Sporadic winds chased away wispy clouds, leaving a dark canopy flecked with sparkling stars above his head. The cold ground beneath him and the frigid air that occasionally whipped through the hills affected him not one bit. He wore a body-length hunting jacket, profusely insulated, replete with zippered compartments and a bevy of accessible pockets to stuff every imaginable accoutrement. It contained only a few implements for this mission: night-vision binoculars; a twenty-two caliber silenced rifle; and a Walther P-38 automatic pistol, complete with a sound-suppresser kit in a different case. He would have preferred to carry just the Walther, but he felt it impossible to creep up on that dog close enough for a killing shot without alerting the animal, who would then arouse the rest of the Dornan household and raise all sorts of havoc.

Thus, the Winchester. A drastically modified version of the Model-74 and fourteen inches shorter, this rifle contained a fatter barrel with an internal sound suppresser. It fired subsonic ammunition whose sound signature could easily be swallowed by chatter coming from a television or radio operating at normal volume. His Walther had similar characteristics, except its sound moderator attached to it separately, in an operation that took about a minute. Its discharge could barely be detected in the din of normal conversation. Together, these weapons hardly constituted heavy armament, but then Conner only intended to raid a stable, not assault a beach.

Conner's unobstructed line of vision revealed a bright island of illumination blazing from a cluster of high-wattage lamps attached near the crown of the building. He could easily destroy the lights, but that would signal an alarm as quickly as a frantically barking dog. *Probably intended for stupid intruders,* he reasoned. Absent the dog, one could conduct a rain dance behind that barn and not be detected by anyone in the house, because the stable's rear entrance could not be seen from that angle. The dog posed the problem. One he intended to solve right now.

Except Old Smoky was nowhere in sight. Conner spied his chain attached to a metal spike thrusting up from the dirt and leading to an aperture in the building. *A dog house?* Probably. *How do I get him out?* Conner mulled over that problem, finally came up with a solution. A *possible* solution. *Fire one round, catch his attention, draw him into the light, fire another round, kill him.* No room for mistakes.

Conner lifted his Winchester, peered through a telescopic sight he had rigged specially to fit this weapon, bored on that dark aperture. A whisper of doubt nudged his thoughts. *What if that dog barks his fool head off at just a minor disturbance, then what?* He paused, unsure, mentally chewing over alternatives. Couldn't come up with anything. He looked through his sight again and caught something he hadn't noticed before. The edge of the light cut a hazy border across the dog's snout, which protruded slightly from that hole in the side of the stable. *Can I make it that close?* Conner adjusted his body position, internally ticked off his list of marksmanship rules, prepared himself to squeeze one, fatal shot.

Body relaxed, crosshairs steady, grip firm . . . Trigger slowly squeezed . . .

Thunt!

Silence.

Conner's eyes scoured the dog house. No movement. *Must have got him.* He slung his rifle over his shoulder, on his back, strapped it tight to his body, immobile, but accessible, if necessary. He unzipped another compartment, retrieved a hard-shelled camera case, removed the sound moderator for the pistol. Then he pulled out his Walther from an unzipped pocket and assembled the two instruments. Finally, he patted a small mound bulging from his right pocket. A ski cap. Probably not necessary, but you never know. He checked the fluorescent dial on his watch.

One-twenty. Two hours since the last feeding. The last light glowing from the farmhouse had turned off an hour and a half ago. Now he was ready.

Conner slipped down the hillside quickly, with a minimum of sound. He skirted behind available shadows formed by unevenness in the terrain—his hill was still visible from the house—dashed to level ground, skidded to the rear entrance of the stable, and hugged its side. He peered across the wall, toward the dark aperture. Nothing moved. No sounds, even. Out with a small flashlight. Walther cocked, flashlight in hand. Walk toward the dog house . . . Still no sound. Aim the beam inside . . . *What's there?* The dog's pulverized head lay in a glistening splotch of blood that trickled through the damp dirt.

Good shot, Albert, Conner complimented himself. Now, the padlock. Pistol raised, aimed at the lock, eyes to the side, trigger squeezed . . .

Thunt—*ti-i-i-ng!*

Damn that sound!

A quick look about. Nothing.

Conner removed the demolished lock, slid the heavy door aside, entered the stable, kept the door open. He took out his flashlight, switched it on, and swept its narrow beam about the cavernous structure. Light sparkled from a few horses' eyes. A little rustling here and there, nothing serious. Dornan's "trophy room" loomed to his right. Several quick steps brought him to its door. He aimed his flashlight at the lock, raised his pistol, prayed the stupid metal wouldn't shriek when the round hit it. Eyes covered . . . Trigger squeezed . . .

Thunt!

That's better. One more lock to go. The one that counts!

Conner twisted off the blasted metal, tossed it aside, walked inside the small room. His flashlight beam skittered past rough wood panels, probed corners, glided across the bench beneath *The Gandy Dancer,* isolated the last lock to fall victim to his Walther. *Found it.* He crouched, placed his pistol on top of the bench, examined the large metal fastener. A combination lock. *Of course!* A sense of intellectual satisfaction flowed through him, pushing a broad smile across his lips. The numbers in Stewart Lawrence's clue reeled before his mind's eye in ticker-tape fashion, with robust clarity. *Two-o-two-and-three.* Conner nearly laughed out loud. A mischievous notion tantalized his imagination, defied his usual caution. *I can't destroy this thing; I've got to keep it as a souvenir.* How long could it take to figure out the combination, based on the few variations spun out by Lawrence's numbers? The ends of Conner's handlebar mustache again probed the limits of his grinning face, as he applied his fingers to the large, easily readable dial. Then the unexpected happened.

Illumination flooded the stable. Conner leaped up, grabbed his Walther. He stepped cautiously toward the trophy room door. A shaft of brilliance carved a yellow rectangle into the small room, assaulting his unshielded eyes with stinging slivers of light. He blinked, adjusted, approached the bright exterior, and peered outside. The usual display greeted his wincing scrutiny. Back door still open, front, still shut. Rustling sounds of a few eight hundred pound hulks brushing against the sides of stalls floated through the building. Conner whipped his pistol chest high, gripped his right wrist with his left, stepped into the stable, eyes aimed at the dark slit formed by the partially opened rear door. He walked backwards, toward the closed front doors, one wary step at a time. Eyes darted about, his Walther signaling each probing glance, as its silencer, a fat cylindrical shaft jutting from the muzzle, jerked around the room.

Nothing.

Conner finally stopped, his back to the front entrance, and lowered his pistol. He scanned the stable again, this time, more puzzled than alarmed. Then he saw it.

The horse to his immediate right, first stall as one entered the stable from its front door, bobbed its head, made low, grunting sounds. Above the stall attached to a post, a paddle board that read, *Raising Cain.* To the side, a light switch, easily reachable from the stall. Conner couldn't believe it. *That horse had switched on the light with its nose!* Then a few lines from Tim Dornan's incessant babbling trickled into his thoughts, offering an explanation. *The old coot actually warned me about this, I just didn't pay any attention.* More grunting, horsy noises from his right. *Damned beast is laughing at me,* Conner thought. He shoved his Walther into a deep, unzipped pocket, headed back toward the trophy room.

Sounds of approaching footsteps crept through the doors behind him. Someone was coming.

Conner plunged his hand into a pocket, pulled out his Walther again, then scooted to his left, back against the wall. Clinking sounds of a key into a padlock . . . Door rumbling open . . . Pistol raised, chest high . . .

A deadly realization spiked Conner's thoughts. *Good God, he'll recognize me!*

Left hand into pocket, ski mask whipped out, pulled over head, hot breath against scratchy cloth. Tim Dornan emerged into the light. Conner aimed his pistol at the man's head.

"*Raising Cain,*" Dornan muttered, "you're raising Cain, again, you silly . . ." He stopped. Conner followed his vision as the old man spied the open rear door, the trophy room, then jerked his eyes to his left, and gasped.

Conner gestured Dornan to walk farther into the stable, which he did.

"What . . . do you want?" Dornan asked in a shaky voice. Conner's thoughts raced. He could immobilize the old man, blast the lock open—*forget this souvenir bit*—and scurry away. Except he really didn't want to hurt him, because that would complicate matters. A horrible thought knifed into his guts. It would take little brains for Dornan to figure out who broke into his trophy room and inform the police accordingly. A phalanx of criminal charges with likely sentences marched through Conner's mind. *This is one job I can't pin on others,* he concluded. *Make it simple, leave, then get out of the country.*

"Over there!" Conner ordered, gesturing toward the trophy room. Dornan understood, started walking before him, hesitated, then shuffled to a stop.

More footsteps. Heavy feet. Men, obviously, a number of them, approaching the stable.

"Over here, FAST!" Conner commanded. He wrapped a steely arm around his small captive, planted the fat barrel of his pistol at Dornan's temple, and dragged him back against the wall parallel to the front entrance. Three men burst into the stable, young, strong-looking. One carried a shotgun.

"Dad?" called a voice.

They all caught sight of their father's small frame grappled by an intruder about the same time.

"Drop it!" Conner bellowed.

The lad gripping the long firearm complied instantly. Stunned expressions gaped at Conner and their helpless father.

Exasperation shrieked through Conner's thoughts, barely able to comprehend another botched mission. A priest swooping out of nowhere to rescue his target, and now a horse switching on a light with its *nose,* no less . . . Incredible! *Good God, I had more luck in Vietnam!* he thundered inside. Conner tried furiously to sort out what to do. He scanned the walls, bursting with stable implements. A plan collected. He aimed his pistol at one of the men before him.

"Get that padlock from the front door, put the key in it, throw it over here." The one closest to the door did as he was told. Conner scooped it up, stuffed it into a pocket. "That metal hook hanging there, get it and throw it at my feet." Instant compliance. He plunged the hook through a loop jutting from his jacket. "Close the door," he ordered. The three exchanged puzzled looks, but obeyed his command. "Stay there, don't move!" Conner ordered with frightening authority.

The former Marine then hoisted Tim Dornan under his arm like a bundle of tree branches, backed toward the rear doors, stepped outside, dropped Dornan to the ground. The old man stayed there, didn't move. Conner shut the doors, spiked the hook's shaft into overlapping metal loops, which had not been damaged by his pistol shot, and secured the rear doors tight. He signaled Dornan to stand up, then trotted him around the building, and stopped by the entrance. The three men were still there, puzzled but compliant. Dornan shoved inside . . . Door scraped closed . . . Padlock affixed, snapped shut . . .

There!

Conner whipped off his mask, now damp with cold sweat. Cursing vehemently, he buried his pistol into his jacket, dashed into the hills, and sprinted toward his truck, which he had parked in a protective copse of sprawling maple trees on a dirt road nearby. Conner screeched away, taking roads that led to Interstate 80 toward New York City, and, beyond that, Long Island.

His thoughts concentrated with devastating clarity, as his pickup roared across northern New Jersey. He concluded that only one person could retrieve those bonds now—Lori Armstrong. *I think it's about time I make her acquaintance,* Conner thought with savage determination.

Chapter Thirty-Seven

"If this is what you want, here it is, take it!" Timothy Dornan snapped, thrusting a package into the arms of Carl Milliken. The attorney exchanged a puzzled look with Lori, then nervously eyed the three stout men huddled about the owner of Dornan Stables, shielding him with their bodies. All carried hunting rifles, held in a fashion showing readiness for instant use. They stared at Milliken and Lori with antagonism.

Neither had any idea what provoked such bellicose caution. No sooner had he and Lori pulled up to Dornan's residence and gently inquired about *The Gandy Dancer,* than three men armed with rifles burst from various parts of the grounds, ran toward them, and surrounded their car. Tim Dornan studied the pair carefully, nodded to himself as though arriving at some conclusion, then trotted to the stable and returned with a package he seemed eager to get rid of. Which left Milliken and Lori standing by the attorney's Cadillac, hoping neither would do anything unnecessarily to anger them.

Milliken accepted the package he hadn't requested, then raised his hands in a disarming gesture. "Gentlemen, please forgive our intrusion. Is there something wrong?"

"You tell me!" Dornan flared. "Call it a sudden, unnatural interest in *The Gandy Dancer.*" He quickly explained events of the previous evening. Milliken and Lori listened, noting with relief that the elderly man's personal guard gradually relaxed their vigil. One of them even cast an interested glance at Lori, who smiled in return. That simple gesture melted his suspicion.

"Did you call the police?" Milliken inquired, knowing this question immediately put him on the right side of the law.

"I can take care of my own affairs!" Dornan stated indignantly. "Plus, he didn't get what he wanted, and if he comes back, I'll be ready for him." A pained expression twitched his ruddy features. "He killed my dog!" The man closest to him patted his shoulder.

"I'm sorry about that," Milliken said.

"You got any idea who this fella might be?" asked one of Dornan's protectors.

Milliken looked at Lori, who shook her head. "I'm afraid not. Not yet, anyway. This much I can tell you, Mr. Dornan. The contents of this package belong to a private estate, which currently is being legally contested. I represent one of the parties who possesses a legitimate claim to it. As you can figure out, some of the other parties do not." He hoped this sanctimonious response would satisfy their curiosity.

It did. Almost, that is. "What's in the package?" the huskiest guard asked.

"I honestly am not sure," Milliken said. "Its contents will be revealed at the reading of the will." His questioner seemed satisfied with that answer.

"Whatever it is, you're welcome to it," Dornan stated firmly. "And if you finger that guy who busted into my stable and killed my dog, you tell him just to try that one more time!"

"The last thing I can do is to advise someone to break the law or to put oneself in personal danger," Milliken stated smoothly. "But in this case, Mr. Dornan, I'll make an exception." That response pleased everyone.

Thunderclouds rumbled above them, drawing everyone's glance upward. Sprinkling rain offered a perfect excuse to terminate their encounter and leave the premises. They shook hands, Milliken trotted around to the driver's side, threw a glance at Lori, who gave him a look as though she were mentally gagging. Engine turned over, a last wave of departure, and Milliken's Cadillac rumbled away.

"All right, Lori, *the truth!*" Milliken bellowed as he drove toward the interstate. "Who else knows about this besides you, me, and Stewart Lawrence?"

In his haste to leave, Milliken directed the wrong question at the wrong person. He would have found a few more inquiries at Dornan stables immensely informative.

———

Albert Conner's high-powered binoculars enabled him to catch every gesture and facial nuance of those huddled about that stranger's Cadillac parked by Dornan's house. With a minor adjustment of the dial on Conner's glasses, the road map of wrinkles splayed across Dornan's cragged features burst into clarity and highlighted his anger, which motivated the fellow next to him to place a hand on his shoulder. *Probably blubbering about that stupid dog,* Conner reasoned. He couldn't guess the identity of the guy draped in Brooks Brothers' finest, but based on his jailhouse experience, Conner pegged him as an attorney. He could detect a lawyer's presence in any situation; he could *smell* them, even at this distance. The lady standing next to him had to be Lori. He let his eyes roam over her provocative figure, wishing he had time to pursue her for himself. *Lawrence is one lucky son of a bitch,* Conner mused.

Especially if Lori Armstrong were acting on what Conner had deduced must be Lawrence's instructions. Sources informed him that Lawrence had been transferred to New York City for a re-sentencing hearing, which almost certainly would result in his release. How they could keep a guy in prison for seven and a half years just for robbing a few banks he didn't know. Not that he cared. Conner figured that Lawrence had directed Lori to get the bonds, meet him at some secret location, then vanish and live like royalty for as long as the money held out. He pondered the lawyer's presence. Maybe Lori had gotten herself a new lover, decided to collect those bonds early, skip town, and leave Lawrence with nothing. Anything was possible, and none of it mattered. All Conner knew was that in a few hours the contents of that abundantly wrapped shoe box would be in his hands. He would do anything necessary to achieve that goal.

Conner rubbed his beard with cold, dirty fingers. He hadn't shaved, showered, or slept for twenty-four hours. Mostly he drove, first to Long Island where Lori worked, then back to his present location, about eight hours in all. That pathetic former security guard had given him precise directions to Sweets Ahoy, along with a wrinkled photograph of Lori Armstrong, bearing evidence of many years' unsatisfied lust for her on his part. Thus, Conner recognized her instantly when Lori's vivacious form burst from the exit door at Sweets Ahoy, sprinted across the parking lot, and stormed off in her Volkswagen. Her eyes blazed with exhilaration, excitement bounced in each step. Whatever had seized Lori's attention prevented her from noticing anyone following her car.

The man who picked her up at Deer Park seemed equally oblivious. He drove fast, desperately, it seemed, through New York City and across northern New Jersey to Dornan Stables. Still, Conner found him easy enough to track and detected nothing on their part to suggest they knew he was behind them. *A freight train could have tailed that couple without their noticing,* he concluded with confidence.

Nor did Conner believe he would have difficulty following them back. He had borrowed a friend's car, much faster, and parked it off the road twenty feet or so behind him. *I'll be on them like an invisible coat of paint,* Conner thought, *as soon as they leave Dornan Stables.*

Which was about to happen. He kept his binoculars trained on Lori's fluid motions, as she and her companion signaled their departure and climbed into the attorney's car. Conner crawled away and climbed into a dark blue supercharged Mustang, compliments of an acquaintance at *Kelly's Bar and Grill* who yearned to court his favor. Conner squealed his speedy machine down a road leading to the only intercept point between Dornan Stables and the highway. He dreaded the trip back to Long Island, but the prospect of a huge payoff overcame his fatigue and goaded him forward. Tracking them would be tedious, not difficult.

Provided the gentle mist spraying on his windshield on this quirky spring day didn't turn into freezing rain.

"I knew it! I knew it! I knew it all along!" Lori shrieked, passing her inflamed visage one last time across the shoe box's contents. She whipped her left arm across the expansive plateau of Carl Milliken's mahogany desk. A confetti of pens, pencils, legal pads, documents, and one helpless globe sprayed across his office. She kicked, stomped, pounded her delicate fists against impassive legal tomes lining the walls, and otherwise exploded in a full-fledged, adult strength temper tantrum. Profanity sputtered from her lips like rounds of machine-gun fire, even causing her seasoned companion, who thought he had heard it all, to arch an eyebrow. Milliken sat at his desk like a concrete pillar facing the ravages of a hurricane, cradled the shoe box to protect it, and waited for the storm to pass.

Finally, it did. Lori collapsed into a chair, buried her head in her hands, and sobbed bitterly. Milliken groped for consoling words.

"Lori . . ."

Her head snapped up. "That lying bastard!" she shouted. *"Toying with me for all these years!"*

"Lori . . ."

"*'Sure, Lori,'*" she mocked. "*'The answer's in the racing program. Figure out the clue and you'll find the bonds.'* That miserable, lying bastard!" Then she started all over again.

When the soaring decibels of Lori's raving had subsided to an acceptable level, Milliken tried to sneak in a few syllables of encouragement. "Maybe there's another clue . . ."

"No!" she screeched. "No more clues, Carl! What we see is what we got. Pictures, letters, and bunches of stupid leather what-cha-ma-callits. *That's it!"*

Lori bolted up from her chair, paced the room, faced Carl Milliken.

"I'm done. I'm through. *Stewart!*"—she hurled her eyes toward the ceiling—"congratulations! You've won. You've beaten me!" She retreated to her chair, sprawled her limbs across it at crazy angles, and stared ahead blankly with red-rimmed eyes.

Milliken took a moment to return articles to the shoe box, which he then covered and proceeded to wrap shut. He saw no reason to keep the useless container, especially if an armed madman lurked out there somewhere and seemed willing to kill to retrieve it. Of course, that possibility triggered a suspicion that the box's items possessed more importance than met the eye, but he decided not to pursue the matter presently. He completed his task, shoved the box aside, and folded his hands on the naked surface of his desk. He let his eyes rest on the distraught woman heaped across the well-stuffed leather chair across the room. Milliken plunged into the reservoir of consoling comments he had accumulated over the decades, found nothing adequate to the situation, or even close, and remained silent. Lori would have to bear the pain herself. *Thank God, we waited until we got back to my office to open this thing,* he thought. *An outburst like that in the car would have killed us both.* Although the shoe box's contents had unquestionably devastated her—no one could act *that* convincingly—Milliken still wondered if she were being completely honest with him.

"It just isn't fair," Lori whimpered. "Not fair at all. Those were *my* bonds. *I* risked myself to get them." She reached for her purse, pulled out a small wax paper wrapping, noisily fumbled it open, and started munching on a saltine cracker.

Milliken felt genuinely sorry for her, even though the bonds in question constituted stolen goods, and Lori had committed grand larceny. But those stunning facts seemed little more than minor legal technicalities to him at the moment. All he saw before him now was a beautiful, distraught, teary-eyed woman. Who could resist that? He felt like the most gullible member of an easily swayed jury, letting emotional heartstrings overwhelm his rational faculties.

Lori got up, straightened her clothes. "I'm going home, now," she announced.

"Now? In this weather? Are you crazy?" Milliken glanced behind him at the freezing rain pummeling his office windows. "Why don't you sleep here tonight, Lori, on the couch in the lobby. It's comfortable, private, and I've got some blankets . . ."

"No!" she snapped. "I'm getting out of here now!" She groped for her keys.

"Lori, *please.* You're not thinking straight. You'll feel much better after a good night's sleep. Don't risk driving all the way to the coast in this weather."

She eyed him coldly. "I'll feel much better," she countered in a sharp voice, "after I drink myself into a coma and fall asleep in Jeremy Madison's arms. I'll get someone to take pictures of us and send them to Stewart." She twirled toward the door, opened it, passed through, and slammed it shut.

For a long moment, Milliken stared at the door, sounds of punishing rain playing havoc with his windows. Traveling any distance in this weather was insane. An image of her ridiculous Volkswagen, battered beyond recognition and heaped upside down in a muddy ditch, flashed in his mind. He shuddered.

God help that poor lady make it home alive, he thought.

Actually, it took Lori about a half an hour of white-knuckled driving before concluding that she should have taken Carl Milliken's advice. Howling sheets of rain whipped across the road, freezing instantly on contact with the pavement. Treacherous patches of glazed ice humbled the most formidable vehicles to sliding hulks of defenseless metal. Lori drove by cars strewn into ditches, pitched at grotesque angles, as though tossed there by a cruel, playful giant. Her Volkswagen crawled along at a pitiful rate, often gliding across mirror-like surfaces with heart-thumping helplessness. At her rate of progress, she would reach her beachfront address by the middle of the night, if not detained interminably by an accident.

Still, she plunged forward. Highway officials wrapped in bright yellow rubber coats flickered in front of her rain-spattered windshield, frantically signaling anyone caught on the road to avoid this route, that route, and take another. Other detours announced by flashing yellow lights and orange cones diverted her path. Two hours of this left Lori confused and hopelessly lost. She squeezed her eyes, tried to cut through the blinding sheets of pounding rain to get her bearings, or at least spy an underpass where she could stop and study her map. Nothing appeared. Sheets of rain assaulted her view like hosts of dull, gray blades, plunging toward the earth, obliterating any sight of road signs. *I'll never get out of this soup,* she lamented.

A brief respite, a sign materialized. *25 Spur,* it read, with an arrow pointing to her right. Lori groaned inside. *That's nowhere near where I want to be!* Still, if she recalled correctly, that offshoot would lead her to a wider, presumably safer, north-south route, which would then take her back to the expressway and to points south. Lori cautiously angled her car toward *25 Spur,* and gritted her teeth as she negotiated its narrow width.

A half an hour of anxious driving passed. The rain subsided, offering her better vision and her wipers a rest from their frantic whipping back and forth across the windshield. Relief from the rain's merciless clamor also made her relax a bit. She came to a stop, a crossroads. A few stores materialized, clustered about the corners. A grocery store, what looked like a hardware store, a couple of gas stations, and a . . .

Lori's breath stopped. Her heart leaped to her throat. She swallowed hard. She blinked. Then she blinked again, to make sure the weather wasn't playing tricks with her, teasing her addled imagination. But there could be no doubt about it. Flickering before her dumbfounded eyes, perched on top of what seemed a restaurant and bar, was a sign that read, *The Gandy Dancer.*

PART SIX: THE PERFECT CRIME

Chapter Thirty-Eight

Ted Simon trotted up an avalanche of worn marble steps that flowed past massive columns supporting the Federal Building. Capped by a gold dome and possessing design features borrowed from a variety of architectural traditions, this ornate structure sprawled along a wide avenue located in the Manhattan district of New York City. The building evoked vivid memories for Simon. He recalled the elaborate stakeouts concocted by FBI agents to lure Stewart into custody over seven years ago, how Stewart cleverly eluded federal authorities and finally turned himself in, under his own conditions. *What a mind that man has!* Simon mused. Brilliant, adaptive, possessing analytical abilities honed by years of military training, but deficient in one critical element: a moral sense. Simon thought with a shudder how well the military component of Lawrence's mental architecture still functioned. But he feared that years of bitterness had expunged any trace of morality that might have lingered in his psyche. *Perhaps today will offer hope,* Simon thought, as his feet clicked down the marble hallway toward an elevator.

Stewart's frantic telephone call at 9:20 this morning had prompted Simon to cancel all his appointments and race downtown for the re-sentencing hearing, which had been earlier twice postponed. Suddenly, it burst into everyone's schedule with unexplained urgency, and Simon had to rush to make it in time. He emerged on the second floor of the building, spied a row of courtroom doors lining the hallway, and entered the one presided over by Judge Walton. Empty. *Not another crushing disappointment!* he thought, alarmed.

Simon paced, waiting for something to happen. Images of past visits to courtrooms in this building rolled before his mind's eye: Stewart's original sentencing; Boss Hogg's sickening emotional breakdown; Albert Conner's terrifying last look. Simon felt a chill, then fretted. *Where is everybody?* Commotion across the hall caught his attention. Police, spectators, and newspaper reporters clustered by a courtroom hosting an explosive rape-murder trial. *Really dramatic stuff,* Simon thought, comparing it to what he anticipated he would encounter, if the judge and principal parties ever showed up. This judgment was premature. Simon had no idea what drama awaited him.

Finally, people filtered into Judge Walton's courtroom, and Simon pulled its heavy doors open and entered again. The room exuded a solemn atmosphere. White marble pillars rose from each corner, looming over rows of wooden benches lined up to a railing, about ten feet from the judge's stand. His bench stood four feet above the floor; the jury box sat to the right. Other than Simon, only two people were in the room, an Assistant U.S. Attorney and a law clerk. Fifteen minutes passed, then Judge Walton entered from a side door, wearing a flowing black judicial cloak. He had gray hair, bristling eyebrows, and a severe countenance. The judge and his associates chatted in low voices. Finally, Stewart emerged from the rear of the courtroom, flanked by a guard and his court-appointed attorney. They sat down by a bench. Stewart waved; Simon waved back, just as his heart sank.

Stewart's court-appointed attorney possessed the well-scrubbed look of a high school student body president, and appeared to belong to that age category as well. Simon feared that his friend's destiny rested in the hands of someone whose main accomplishment in life had been to chair the prom committee. Unfortunately, this young lawyer's utterances failed to dispel such notions. Bland, monotonous, lacking passion, his sentences restated what everyone knew. Judge Walton looked bored. He mumbled a few questions to the U.S. Attorney, put on his reading glasses, then paged through some documents laid before him. Simon and Stewart exchanged worried looks. After all these years, to have soaring hopes dissipate in a banal fog of legal jargon . . .

Suddenly, Stewart rose from his chair. "Your Honor, may I address the court?" he blurted. All eyes in the room shifted toward him. Judge Walton arched his eyebrows; Stewart's attorney flashed alarm. He quickly conferred with his client, muttered something in his ear, then approached the bench. Whispers floated across the room, the judge nodded, and Stewart's attorney returned to his seat.

"This is highly unusual," Walton intoned, "but if you have something you wish to say, this court is prepared to listen."

"Thank you, your Honor," Stewart said. He threw a nervous glance toward Simon, cleared his throat, and began to speak.

Carl Milliken paced before Lori Armstrong's anxious stare, quickly flipping through documents that had been placed in his hands by a breathless messenger a half an hour earlier. He muttered under his breath, nodded occasionally, as though recognizing something familiar, flipped a glance toward her impatient eyes, then continued pacing.

"What is it?" Lori demanded. "What did you learn?"

Milliken circled his desk, then sat in his chair, gaze still locked on his folder. He peered over the file toward Lori, who seemed ready to say something, but he waved her off.

"Come on, Carl, talk to me!" Lori snapped.

Milliken spoke slowly as he continued to read, clumps of words floating over the file perched beneath his nose. "Resided in Michigan, New Jersey, upstate New York—that's probably where Stewart met him—divorced, two children, remarried, relocated . . . Um . . . let's see here . . ." More pages flipped. "Hmm . . . *That's* interesting." He looked up, digesting a piece of information. "Makes sense, too."

"What's interesting? What makes sense?" Lori asked, exasperated.

Milliken placed the file on his desk. "It seems the present owner of *The Gandy Dancer* used to be a high roller himself, like Stewart. A guy by the name of Axel Thomas."

"Strange name," Lori observed.

"A strange guy," Milliken agreed. "Apparently, he ran up some debts he couldn't pay . . ."

"Like Stewart," Lori interjected.

"Correct. Anyway, his bookie hired a thug to teach him a lesson about the proper protocol for debt retirement. But instead of breaking his legs, the thug burned his house down. Thomas lost everything. He moved to Long Island, won some big bucks on a horse called *The Gandy Dancer,* and, unlike Stewart, decided to quit while he was ahead. He used his earnings to open this bar and gave it the same name of the horse that enabled him to do it. Seems to be thriving, too, according to my information." Milliken chuckled, shook his head. "He's even in the yellow pages. Would you believe that? The yellow pages!"

"What about the shoe box filled with that stuff?" Lori inquired.

Milliken smiled. "This is a case where the simplest explanation is also true. After you called me, I called Dornan Stables. They explained the use of a special room they keep in the back of their stable for memorabilia. My guess is that he stored this stuff there to protect it in case his old friends showed up. Apparently, he didn't want to take the chance of losing things important to him again."

"Those pictures inside . . ."

"That's Thomas, of course. The owner of *The Gandy Dancer* bar.

Him and some of his winning horses. Along with other things that meant something special to him."

Lori pondered this information. "Carl, do you think this place is what Stewart had in mind when he gave me that clue?"

Milliken rubbed his chin thoughtfully. "There's a good chance of that. We know they borrowed from the same bookie. We know they fled upstate New York about the same time and for the same reasons. Apparently Stewart skipped town before he did, which was a mistake for Thomas. Maybe he didn't want to run anymore. He waited too long, then he got burned out, literally. In fact,"—Milliken pulled a photograph from the file—"we have a good idea who burned his house down. A guy by the name of Alfred W. Schultz. Very adept arsonist, never got convicted, not for that, anyway. His nickname was Bernie. Get it? He burned things, so they called him Bernie! That's about as clever as a gangster can get. He was pretty good with a knife, too. He and a muscleman worked for a bookie named Arnoldi, and . . ." Milliken paused, observing a shocked expression spreading across Lori Armstrong's face.

"Oh my God!" she gasped. "Do you have Bernie's picture?"

"I've got *everything,*" Milliken said confidently, passing it across his desk.

Lori's eyes nearly leaped from her face. "That's him! That's him!" she exclaimed.

"You *know* him?" Milliken asked, surprised.

"I'm afraid I do," Lori said. "He held me captive in my apartment one time. That was years ago, when Stewart and I were dating. He and his friend were using me to get to Stewart." She handed the picture back. "But we finally got to them!"

Milliken's fears that Lori had been holding out on him seemed confirmed. "Would you care to explain all that?"

"Yes, but not now. What about the numbers in Stewart's clue? Did you learn anything about those?"

"I'm afraid not." Milliken glanced at his file. "Doesn't even correspond to his street address." Lori looked disconsolate. "Don't worry," Milliken assured, "we'll find out everything we need to know when we pay Axel Thomas a little visit."

"How?" Lori asked. "You said he probably was a friend of Stewart."

"*I have my ways,*" Milliken retorted smugly. "If he's the real reference behind Stewart's clue, I'll be able to wring it out of him. Remember, he's a runaway. Left a wife and two kids in another state, and my records here show that he's behind in his alimony payments."

"I thought you said his business was doing well," Lori reminded.

"It is. He's still not paying."

"All men are pigs," Lori commented bitterly.

Milliken ignored her remark. "He's also got a few priors . . ."

Lori looked puzzled.

"Prior convictions. And some other questionable legal dealings that are hanging over his head. I don't think he'd want to risk everything he's got for a guy who's been in prison for the past seven and a half years. I've been in this business a long time, Lori. I know how to apply pressure, believe me." He looked down at his file. "Particularly armed with the information in this file."

Although Lori nodded slowly, her opaque expression implied lack of comprehension. Not that it mattered to Milliken.

He gathered documents scattered on his desk, put them in order, and plopped them into their file. "What I have here ought to do it," he repeated firmly. "So, let's go." Milliken got up and Lori followed him out of his office. He paused by his secretary, leaned by her desk, spoke in a low voice.

Eleanor gave him a quizzical look. *"All* of your appointments?"

"All of them," Milliken confirmed.

She shook her head disdainfully. "Mr. Milliken, the last time you left like this, I had to field a lot of angry questions," she said in a scolding voice. Extremely competent executive secretaries could speak their minds with impunity. Milliken quickly accommodated her.

"Okay, look. This is where I'll be," he said, scrawling on a piece of paper. "Satisfied?"

Eleanor pursed her lips in an expression suggesting that it would have to do. Neither gave a thought to the possibility that the information Milliken gave her might prove to be fatal.

———

Albert Conner regarded his six-foot-two frame as a piece of equipment that required regular maintenance by a trained expert. Thus, when his Mustang slid across a glassy patch that hurled it onto the slick expanse separating east-west traffic on Interstate 80, he concluded that this otherwise wasted time should be put to good use by resuscitating depleted body parts. A four-wheel-drive truck wearing chains clattered by, offered him a lift, and deposited him at a motel fifty miles west of Deer Park. He dragged his weary body into a room, plopped his duffel bag on the floor, and collapsed on the bed. Ten hours of undisturbed sleep produced exactly the invigoration he needed. An hour later found him clean and alert, razor-blue eyes darting above lean cheeks and his sprightly curled mustache, his taut outline sporting a dapper, herringbone jacket, dark green slacks. *I even smell like a lawyer myself,* he silently boasted, as he drove his rented vehicle toward Deer Park.

Conner's refreshed determination confirmed the decision he made last night. After throttling a spike of rage that propelled his fist against the hood of his friend's car, he settled down and took cool measure of his situation. It became clear that attempting to track the Cadillac no longer made sense. For all he knew, Lori and her friend had tumbled into a ditch as well or had stopped someplace to wait out the weather; the next day promised sunshine and warmer temperatures. No matter; Conner knew where to look, he would find them. Starting at that place where Mr. Brooks Brothers picked up Lori struck him as most prudent. He pulled into the parking lot, scanned the four-story professional building looming above him, and trotted toward its entrance.

After passing through heavy glass doors, Conner's hopes for making quick contact instantly plunged. Lists of attorneys' names embossed on metallic plates lined each wall in the lobby. Closer examination revealed that most of these pompous pewter letters attached to practitioners of other devious crafts; like accounting, for instance—*does that include counterfeiting?* he wondered—insurance consulting, financial planning, whatever that term meant, and dentistry, a single office. The notion of blowing up the whole building as a service to humanity flickered in his thoughts. He noted that most lawyers clustered on the fourth floor. *Like a wriggling hive of maggots,* he thought acidly. *Now to pluck out the right one . . .*

A quick dash up four flights of stairs brought him there quickly and hardly challenged his breath. A long hallway stretched before him, heavy wood doors hosting black letters lined each wall. Like a predator cat stalking his prey, Conner began his deadly, systematic hunt.

He walked up to the first door to his right, knocked, then entered a small waiting room. A young lady sitting behind a desk covered with neatly stacked folders, an In-Out box, a pen holder, and a phone sprouting a row of buttons at the bottom, looked up and smiled.

"Excuse me, Miss, but I have an appointment with the attorney representing Miss Lori Armstrong. I'm afraid I've lost the business card that had all the information on it, but I think it was this week. I really feel foolish about this, and . . ."

"Oh, sir, please let me check for you!" came the ingratiating response. Appointment book flipped open . . . Eyes darting across dates . . . Shaking head . . . She looked up, apologetic. "I'm sorry, sir, I don't seem to have a Miss Armstrong listed for Attorney Bendix. Are you sure you have the correct week? I can check other times . . ."

"I'm not sure I have the correct *anything*, Miss," Conner interrupted, feigning his best impression of a good ole' boy who had lost his way.

"Let me look some more," the receptionist offered.

Conner shook his head and backed away. "No, that's not necessary. You've been very helpful, thank you." He hurried out of the office.

Conner found it necessary to subject his ego to this self-effacing charade only one more time before approaching the legal offices of Milliken, Askew, Brady, and Donovich. Below this list one name stood out separately: Carl J. Milliken. Conner knocked twice, waited, then opened the door.

He stepped into the largest reception room he had yet encountered on this excursion. Richly paneled walls hosted large, gold-trimmed frames, which enclosed portraits of old men with haughty expressions smeared on their pasty faces. Glossy wooden floors etched a purple rug bursting with at least a two inch pile. Elegant Victorian sofas with elaborate designs sat by each wall. Presiding over this domain stood a portly, gray-haired lady, maybe about sixty, holding a legal tome the size of a foundation brick. Conner spied the nameplate on her desk: Eleanor D. Pettigrew, it read. He quickly evaluated this sole occupant of Carl J. Milliken's reception room. Possessing a severe countenance and exuding a no-nonsense air, she struck him as a cross between Brunnhild and a Marine drill sergeant. She turned in his direction, regarded him coolly, no smile.

"May I help you?" she asked in a husky voice.

Conner plunged into his routine. She inclined her head and looked at him sharply. Suspicion flowed across the room. "Offhand, I don't know if I can say that I recognize that name," she said.

I've found the right guy, Conner concluded instantly. He stepped up to her desk, stood before her.

"Pardon me, ma'am, are you sure?" he pressed, a harder edge to his voice. "Don't you want to check your appointment book or something?"

She plunked the imposing volume on her desk with a heavy thud, as if to accent her next words. "I don't have to check, young man," she huffed. "If Attorney Milliken were representing a person whose affairs involved you, I would know it. Now, is there anything else I can help you with?" She uttered this last sentence in a tone suggesting dismissal.

Conner turned toward the door, spied a dead-bolt lock, then strode toward it and twisted its knob shut. He walked back toward Brunnhild, this time stepping around her desk, and faced her squarely.

"See here, young man!" she bristled. "Just what do you think you're do . . ."

Conner's left arm whipped out with the speed of a rattlesnake attack, clutched her throat, and pinned her against the wall. He moved his face a few inches from hers.

"All right, you old bitch!" he hissed through clenched teeth. "You listen to me good. You tell me exactly what I want to know, and I won't hurt you. Got that?"

Choking, eyes ablaze with terror, Eleanor Pettigrew jerked her head, yes.

"Where did Milliken go with Lori Armstrong?"

Eleanor blinked hard, tried to swallow. Conner relaxed his grip. "I . . . don't know," she gasped.

Fingers jabbed deep into her neck, like talons. Eleanor's big chest thumped for air, got nothing. Her eyes floated, then rolled backward.

"Wrong answer!" Conner roared. He glanced over her shoulder. "That's his office?" Grip abated, just slightly.

Eleanor nodded, yes.

Before she fainted, Conner removed his fingers from her neck, grasped the top part of her dress. Eleanor responded with a shrieking intake of breath. He dragged her toward the door. With his free hand he twisted its knob. Locked. Rage surged through Conner's body. With his victim clutched in one hand, he balanced himself, then propelled his right foot against the door like a battering ram.

CRASH!

Victim dragged in, heaved into a chair. Door slammed against a pulverized lock. Feet planted, Conner scrutinized Milliken's office.

He saw it instantly.

Conner leaped toward the desk, grasped the shoe box, clawed at its wrapping. Reinforced tape frustrated his efforts. He spit out another curse, whipped open the top drawer of Milliken's desk. Furious rummaging. Another curse. Suddenly, he grappled the sides of the drawer, wrenched it free from its enclosure, dumped its contents on the burnished mahogany surface. More frantic shoving, poking, searching. Hand swept across the desk. A letter opener skidded off, tumbled on the floor. Conner grabbed it, plunged it into the box, ripped the container open. He turned the shoe box over. Its contents tumbled out. He studied them.

Nothing but a bunch of worthless junk.

Conner cut his eyes toward Eleanor, still in the chair, quivering in fear. He stepped toward her. Chair gripped, Eleanor shaking, trying to back away, escape. Impossible. Conner's face two inches from hers . . .

"They took the answer *with* them, didn't they, *Miss Pettigrew!*" Conner hissed. "Where did they go, Miss Pettigrew? *Tell me!*"

Fright she had never known in her life paralyzed Eleanor Pettigrew's vocal chords. Her eyes bulged from their sockets as she watched Conner's next move. Like a hideous little animal with five deadly claws, Conner's right hand crept up her chest, groped toward her throat. Her trembling now nearly uncontrollable. Then, as if instinctively acting in a way that would save her life, she cast a long look toward her own desk, visible from where she sat.

Conner caught it instantly. He released his grasp, dashed through the open door, and stopped by her desk.

There it was.

Conner scooped up a sheet of paper, studied it. He smiled in satisfaction. He walked into Milliken's office, grabbed a map of Long Island from the floor, scrutinized it with burning intensity. He had found what he wanted. A glance toward Eleanor. He searched for the letter opener, spied it on the floor, picked it up, walked toward her.

He whipped the cruel instrument up to her face, six inches from her eyes. Eleanor gaped at the flickering blade. Then he pressed it against her throat. "I'm going now, Miss Pettigrew," Conner snarled. "If you call anyone—do you hear me? *Anyone!* I will come back here, carve out your liver, and stuff it down your fat throat. Do you understand, *Miss Pettigrew?*"

A jerky nod, yes.

"Good! Just to be sure, keep this in mind: Police don't hunt me. *I hunt them!* And I'll hunt you, if you call them. Or anyone else. Got that?"

A barely perceptible acknowledgment. Conner got up. "When did they leave?" he snapped.

Eleanor swallowed hard. "About a half an hour ago," she whispered.

Another quick look at the map. *I can make that,* Conner concluded. He stuffed the map into his shirt, strode toward the door. Then he turned, faced her.

"By the way. You ought to tell your boss to keep a neater office," Conner chortled. And off he went.

Eleanor Pettigrew remained in her chair for a long time before getting up. It would be an hour before she garnered sufficient courage to place a single telephone call.

A call she should have made sooner.

Chapter Thirty-Nine

Milliken and Lori zoomed across the Long Island Expressway, its once treacherous surface having transformed overnight to a shimmering glaze of wet pavement. Wet patches assaulted by the Cadillac's big, all-weather tires occasionally roared inside the wheel wells, displacing the constant hissing emitted by the sloppy road's protest against rolling rubber. Lori rested her arm on Milliken's briefcase, which sat between them, and studied a map while he gripped the steering wheel, driving much too fast, in her opinion.

"Do you remember the turns you took?" Milliken asked in a sharp voice. "That might save us a little time."

"I doubt it," Lori said. "It was dark, stormy. I drove as though my life depended on it, then found *The Gandy Dancer* after a detour. Anyway, you have the address."

"You could have been more observant," Milliken groused, wheeling around a slower car.

"More observant?" she responded irritably. "You knew what the weather was like! You tried to get me to stay at your office, for God's sake. You should *thank* me for finding the place."

"Stumbled on it, you mean," he muttered.

Lori cast a long, studied look at Carl Milliken. His jawbone flexed and twitched; his eyes riveted on the road as though he were fixing a shotgun sight on a target. Determination bristled from every feature. *No, not only determination,* she sensed. Not merely eagerness, either, which she could understand. More than that. *Greed.* The fever of avarice. It crackled from every pore on his countenance, as though some demon had seized his soul and now controlled his actions and spoke through his voice. Burning intensity consumed what earlier had been a mutual interest, a shared goal. Now he seemed a different person, an alien, driven creature.

Unease crept into Lori's thoughts. Some reflex action inspired her to pull down the visor and glance at the vanity mirror. Lori looked and gasped. The image that ricocheted from the mirror belonged not to her, but to Stewart, a haunting reminder of his reaction to her shrieking demand for these very same bonds. Although their present quest rekindled her sense of urgency, Lori still sensed that the devils firing her soul had now drifted over to her companion, taken possession of him as well. She found this frightening. She also caught sight of something else in her mirror, which scared her even more.

Lori turned her head around and looked behind them.

"Carl, I think we're being followed."

"What?"

"That car behind us, I think it's following us."

Milliken snorted. "Why do you think that?"

"That car's been behind us too long. In fact, I've felt that someone has been following me for some time, now. I just never told you that."

"Lori," Milliken said, as though addressing a child with an overactive imagination. "If you were truly being followed by a professional, you wouldn't know it. Believe me, they're too good to be detected."

"Oh, really?" Lori retorted. "Then what do you call that car behind us?"

Milliken glanced at his rear view mirror. "I'd say a brown Chevy."

"And what do you call it if it's following us?" she pressed.

"Unprofessional. Look, Lori, we're *not* being followed. Just settle down. We'll go to *The Gandy Dancer,* I'll have a few choice words with the owner, and if there's anything to Stewart's clue, Axel Thomas will give us what we want. Trust me." He took his eyes off the road for the first time, glanced at her and pushed out a condescending grin. Lori felt repulsed.

An hour and a half after they left Deer Park, Milliken pulled his car into the parking lot of *The Gandy Dancer.* He locked his vision on the garish, dancing letters on the sign and sat for a long moment.

"I can't believe it," he muttered, as though he had never quite taken Lori seriously, but now confronted the undeniable truth of her account. "I'll be back, stay in the car," Milliken ordered, opening his door.

"Not on your life!" Lori fired back. "I'm going in there with you, Carl. I intend to be there every step of the way."

Milliken paused, regarded her agitation, then shrugged. "All right, but stay in the background, Okay? Sit someplace else and watch from a distance. *I'll* do the talking."

Lori accepted this compromise. He grabbed his briefcase; they climbed out of his car and walked toward the entrance of *The Gandy Dancer.* Mid-afternoon produced desultory business, leaving only a few cars sprinkled around the parking lot. Tantalizing aromas floated across their path, and for the first time all day, Lori realized she was hungry. Famished, in fact. *When this is all done, I'll celebrate and eat myself into a coma,* she resolved.

Only a few customers scattered about the restaurant, one of whom trained his eyes on her, but Lori was used to that. *The Gandy Dancer* appeared a thriving establishment. The one-story structure hosted a high-beamed ceiling that looked over a floor plan dominated by a harness racing motif. A sulky pulled by an enormous stuffed horse sat in the middle of the floor. Stable implements of all descriptions—bridles, drivers' uniforms, leather straps, and a host of other paraphernalia—sprouted from walls, hovered over booths. In fact, one got the impression of entering a spotlessly maintained stable whose patrons happened to be people. Lori never felt infatuated by Lakewood Downs, but this place impressed her. She glanced at Milliken, who also looked impressed.

"I'll ask for the owner. Why don't you take a seat by a booth," he instructed, gesturing toward the wall to their right.

"I'll figure out where I want to sit after I see where you end up," she countered.

Milliken shrugged, then walked up to the bar, where a man decked out as a driver was drying shot glasses with a towel. Lori took a seat in a nearby booth where she could observe Milliken's actions. Conversation and soft music hummed in the background, making it difficult for her to hear. She contented herself with watching. Milliken said something to the bartender, who nodded, then vanished past swinging bar doors behind him. About a minute later, another man emerged, who took one look at Carl Milliken, spied his briefcase, and stiffened. Tall, gaunt, very homely, Axel Thomas struck Lori as someone she had seen before, but couldn't place. He motioned toward a table twenty feet away and situated perpendicular to where she sat, giving Lori an unobstructed line of vision. The two men slid into the booth. Lori could see Axel Thomas's face clearly, but Milliken was partially obscured by the booth's high back. However, she could catch his hand gestures, and as soon as they sat down, Milliken started talking.

It did not go well. Lori saw Thomas's expression harden, his large brown eyes flickering contempt. He shook his head several times, vigorously. More arm waving on Milliken's part, followed by additional denials. Lori's heart sank. *This whole thing is probably a crock,* she lamented. Or simply a meaningless coincidence involving identical names. However, if any truth clung to their speculation, then Axel

Thomas's reaction deserved respect. No one wanted to be confronted by a well-dressed attorney armed with a briefcase, and Axel Thomas seemed to be holding his ground. Milliken posed a formidable adversary, she knew. And he was about to play hardball.

"May I interest you in our special today?" came a voice from nowhere. Lori jerked, looked up at the eager face of a waitress, holding a small tablet and a pencil. She placed a menu on the table. "The roast beef is very good . . ."

"Fine! I'll take that! Leave me alone, please!" she snapped.

The waitress quickly collected the menu and walked away, sauntering in front of Lori's view of the two men. Lori stretched left and right to peer around her.

Her next visual shot caught Milliken reaching for his briefcase. He pulled out a file and splayed its contents on the table before Axel Thomas's eyes. *Time for the heavy artillery,* Lori thought. She leaned forward intently, as though her aching desire to hear their words could slice through the room's irrelevant sounds and pick up the conversation. Thomas's next reaction did much to obviate this yearning. Milliken placed a document before him. A careful scrutiny . . . A crack in his demeanor . . . A resigned look into the distance . . .

Scored a hit, Lori thought, heart pounding with anticipation. Her stomach began to churn, stirred by seven years of frustrated searching, now building up to a crescendo.

"Here's your meal, ma'am," and the smell of roast beef placed before her instantly assaulted her nostrils. Nausea welled up her chest in lunging, punishing waves. She abruptly shoved the plate away.

Faint sounds of a ringing telephone trickled through the din of muted rock music and quiet chatter pervading the room. A man emerged from another set of swinging bar doors behind their booth, planted a telephone with a very long cable directly in front of Axel Thomas. Thomas picked up the receiver, turned his head to the side, and listened. Lori studied him carefully, thought she spied movements suggesting the words *May I take a message?* twittering on his lips, but couldn't be sure. Suddenly, Thomas jerked his eyes toward Milliken, as though prodded by recognition. Milliken got impatient. Lori saw his fingers drumming the table. Finally, Thomas placed the receiver down, and his employee, who stood nearby, quickly removed it. Thomas now seemed to stare at Milliken in a different way, which Lori found impossible to decipher. She didn't like it, though; made her feel uncomfortable.

Lori bit her lip. Eager anticipation she felt for this moment seeped away, replaced by a welling sense of apprehension. *Something's wrong, I feel it in my guts.* A stomach in turmoil clawed the lower reaches of her neck, taunted her self-control. Fingers of acid crept up her throat. *Crackers.* Small packages of saltines encased in cellophane sat in a container next to the salt and pepper. She grabbed for them, noisily tore a package open, stuffed a cracker into her mouth. Back to Axel Thomas, eyes locked on his next move.

The owner of *The Gandy Dancer* slowly shook his head in a gesture that implied indifference. Lori swallowed hard, crunched another cracker, and continued to watch him carefully. No question that Thomas's expression had changed, in a way she found impossible to penetrate. Somehow, he looked less intimidated, more confident. But with a face like that, who could tell?

Finally, he muttered something to Carl Milliken, slid out of the booth, and vanished into the back of the restaurant. An eternity passed. Lori kept looking at her lone partner, who whiled away the time by casually flipping through documents, as if putting them into order. Random whiffs of roast beef floated up to her nose, triggering a gagging reflex. Lori caught a flood of bile just in time, wondering how she ever could have felt hungry. *That's all I need to do now,* she groaned. *Throw up in a restaurant.*

Thomas's continued absence spawned a multitude of tortured thoughts. *He's calling the police,* Lori speculated, a prospect that nearly overpowered the tenuous grip she struggled to maintain over her stomach. Rationality squeaked in a more encouraging note: *Why would he do that?* she wondered. Her mind then oscillated to the opposite conjecture, trumpeted it before her with breathtaking boldness. *He'll return with a shoe box filled with bonds,* she ventured. *Which Milliken and I will immediately split, and I'll take off with a quarter million dollars, and . . .*

Neither alternative materialized. Axel Thomas emerged from the rear of the restaurant grasping a sealed manila envelope, which he handed over to Carl Milliken. Lori's hopes soared. *Is that the same envelope I turned over to Stewart years ago?* She couldn't tell. The two men chatted a bit longer, Thomas again shaking his head, firmly. He nodded toward the envelope held by Milliken, and seemed to mouth the words, *that's it.* Milliken appeared satisfied. He got up, offered his hand to *The Gandy Dancer's* owner, who responded only with a sly, unsmiling look.

Milliken strode toward Lori, envelope grasped beneath his right arm, an ambivalent expression on his face. Lori quickly got up, joined him, and walked toward the entrance.

Just as they opened the door, a voice called out. "Hey lady! You didn't pay . . ."

Axel Thomas quickly stepped up to his indignant employee, and placed a hand on her shoulder. "It's on the house," he said, with that same, inscrutable look. Milliken and Lori nodded, then turned and left.

They trotted into the parking lot, Milliken unlocked the doors to his car, tossed in his briefcase, climbed into the driver's seat. Lori jumped into the car after him and watched Milliken's fingers immediately attack the envelope, slightly faded by age. She didn't spy the *Sweets Ahoy* label. Sealed with postal-strength tape, it resisted his frantic efforts for a few seconds, then finally succumbed to a pair of teeth gripping the top edge and ferociously ripping it apart. Milliken blew into the ragged tear, creating a yawning aperture. He peered inside. Lori watched anxiously, swallowing to keep her thumping heart from ramming her guts up her throat.

Milliken tilted the large envelope so its contents would spill out. A smaller envelope, about one inch by three inches, tumbled into his palm. Another check into the larger container. He reached inside, grasped what appeared a business card. Milliken examined it carefully. Lori moved over to his side as close as she could, to see what he was holding. The words, *Deer Park, County First Federal Bank of Nassau County,* were printed on the small piece of paper. The two exchanged looks. Recognition gradually flooded Milliken's face, but Lori remained perplexed.

Milliken ripped open the sealed flap of the smaller envelope, squeezed the edges, then tipped it above his open palm. A key fell out. Milliken picked it up by the shank and peered at it. Lori planted her head two inches away from his, and they both stared at the small piece of metal. Numbers were embossed on its handle. They read: *202-3.*

Milliken slowly lowered the key toward his lap. Lori moved back a few inches, inclined her head, and the two looked at each other with gaping expressions. Then, as though moved by a common spirit issuing instructions to their flabbergasted minds, they recited aloud to each other, at exactly the same time, these words: *two-o-two-and-three.*

Lori sat upright, slapped her forehead with her right hand, and threw her head back, grinning broadly. Milliken erupted in laughter, pounding the thick, padded dashboard of his Cadillac with his right fist.

"Brilliant!" he proclaimed. "Absolutely brilliant! And so simple, too! *A safety-deposit box key.* What else?" Lori remained speechless. "Not only that," he chortled. "It opens a box in one of the banks he held up!" Raucous, leather-pounding merriment. "I'll say this about Stewart," Milliken added, wiping tears from his eyes, "he's got *style!*" He plunked the key into its container and inserted the small envelope into his left breast pocket. Then he plunged his car key into the ignition. "Okay, gorgeous, let's get out of here," he said, starting the engine.

Milliken backed up, scooted free from *The Gandy Dancer's* parking lot, and revved his Cadillac's powerful engine down the road toward the Long Island Expressway. A strange mix of emotional exhaustion, contentment, and excitement flowed through Lori's body, while Milliken continued to burble like a schoolboy. They had not traveled two miles, when a head rose from the back seat behind them.

"I'll take that, thank you," came a voice.

Lori's heart leaped, Milliken jumped, his hands lurched the steering wheel to the left, nearly colliding with an oncoming vehicle, then to the right, toward the road's shoulder. Swerve . . . Skid . . . Control regained . . . *Steady,* now, straight ahead. From the corner of her eye, Lori spied the black muzzle of a pistol pressed against Carl Milliken's head.

"Now that you've dazzled me with your driving, *Attorney Milliken,* let me repeat: hand it over!"

Carl Milliken's trembling fingers groped for the safety-deposit key envelope. Keeping his eyes on the road, he reached across his chest holding it between him and Lori. The man behind them quickly snatched the small article.

"You know, you ought to pay more attention to what's in your back seat," the man said in a flippant tone. "Broad daylight, even. You make it too easy. Reminds me of the good old days," he cackled, as though enjoying some private joke.

"Who . . . who are you?" Milliken asked, his voice quavering.

"Robin Hood. Now, stop and turn this heap around," their captor ordered. Milliken slowed his Cadillac, obeyed the command. Soon they glided down the road in the opposite direction.

Lori ratcheted up her courage, blurted a question. "Where are we going?"

"Not that it's going to matter much to you, but if you must know, a little road off this one called *25 Spur.*"

Lori's thundering heart skipped a beat. She moved her head in tiny jerks to her left, saw his pistol planted behind Milliken's right ear, caught sight of a feral look glinting from cold, blue eyes, over taut features and a big, handlebar mustache.

"Eyes front and center, lady!" he snarled.

Lori snapped her head forward. "What . . . are you going to do with us?" came her next, unnecessary question.

The man in the back seat didn't answer. He didn't have to. Silence conveyed his intentions with devastating clarity. He had gotten what he wanted; he knew exactly what it meant.

And he planned to kill them both.

Chapter Forty

Stewart Lawrence choked on his last word, then sputtered to a halt. He hoisted his arm, swept the sleeve from his prisoner's uniform across his face, dappled his eyes. He tried again to speak, scooping words from a deep well of despair. He prodded them to cohere, to form his next utterance. Impossible. Words collapsed before reaching his lips. Hard swallows pressed veins through the skin on his neck. Finally, a sentence wriggled through his throat, thickened by emotion.

"I beg your pardon, your Honor. Am . . . I presenting my case properly?" Glassy eyes shimmered, appealed to the bench.

Judge Walton leaned forward and planted his elbows before him. Severity drained from his countenance. "You are doing an outstanding job," he stated in a soft voice. "You may continue."

"Thank you, your Honor." Stewart swallowed, snatched a quick breath, reclaimed his composure. All eyes riveted on him, as his words flowed across the yawning courtroom, whose expansive walls and haughty pillars seemed diminished by the arguments hurled before them.

"Thus, if it please the court," Stewart concluded, "I respectfully ask that the following document, which summarizes my case, be presented as my final exhibit." Judge Walton nodded. Lawrence handed a two-page letter to the clerk and sat down.

For a long moment, stone silence. Finally, Judge Walton turned to his right and looked at the official representing the government. "Well, Mr. United States Attorney, what do you suggest we do at this incredible juncture?"

"The government has no objection to reopening this case for retrial, your Honor," came the response.

The judge sat back in his huge leather chair, a look of astonishment clutching every feature. *"Reopen* this case, did you say? *Retrial?* Did we both listen to the same story, *Mr. United States Attorney?"* Hands clasped before him, eyes burning with intensity, Judge Walton issued a withering look. "Let me ask you this, sir! Is this account, as you know it, essentially accurate?"

The United States Attorney gulped. "Yes, sir."

"Then this defendant should be released!" the judge snapped. "Immediately!"

Silence again fell on the courtroom. Then murmurs rippled among the few individuals present who had witnessed Stewart Lawrence's stirring presentation.

BANG!

Instant quiet. All eyes toward the bench. Judge Walton wielded his gavel as though brandishing a sword. His overpowering gaze roamed the courtroom, confronting each person with a look that would have scorched asbestos. Absolute, complete control.

"It is so ordered," he proclaimed.

Like a mouse squeaking in a forest, a voice floated up to the bench. "Um . . . I'm sorry, your Honor, but you can't do that."

Walton glared at the source, the government attorney. "Why not?" he demanded.

"Well, paperwork, actually. You see, paperwork must be processed through normal channels. The defendant's file is still at the Federal Penitentiary at Ambrose, Georgia. Signatures are needed, processing required."

"How long will this so-called processing take?"

"I would say four or five weeks."

"Are you telling me to extend this defendant's incarceration for another five weeks merely to satisfy some pencil pushers at Ambrose?" He raised his arms, palms toward the ceiling, and lifted his eyes, like Moses appealing to the heavens. "Am I talking to myself here? I just ordered this man released!" Back to the government attorney: "Mr. Lawrence has already served far more than his intended sentence. I refuse to allow another minute of it, *not another second!* Is that clear?"

"Yes, your Honor. But this is standard procedure. Out-processing rules stipulate that . . ."

Walton's cloaked arm sliced the air, cutting him off. He turned to a person seated below him to his right. "Miss Wells, get me the warden at Ambrose Penitentiary immediately. I'll take the call in my chambers." Gavel lifted . . . *BANG!* "This court stands adjourned for forty-five minutes!" Walton bolted up, began striding toward the door leading to his office, and caught a sight that made him stop.

He spun around, planted his hands on his hips. "What are you doing?" he demanded in a sharp tone.

The guard adjacent to Stewart looked up. "Applying handcuffs to the prisoner, your Honor," he replied, a bit apologetically. "Standard procedure."

"If I hear that term one more time, I'll throw up!" Walton snapped. "Perhaps you would care to explain, along with the United States Attorney there"—he gestured to his left—"just *where* all these standard procedures have been *hiding* for the past five years." The guard flinched and retracted the cuffs. The government attorney looked like a chastised puppy.

Walton locked on Stewart. "Young man, I'm trying to free you. You promise to stick around for the next forty-five minutes?"

Stewart's answer burst from his mouth. "Yes, sir."

"I thought so." The judge turned and vanished from the courtroom.

While Judge Harvey Walton wrestled long-distance with the potentates of paperdom, another, more deadly drama was unfolding outside his domain, at a remote location in Long Island.

"There, over there," Albert Conner ordered, signaling Milliken toward a dirt road jutting off *25 Spur.* Milliken slowed, lurched his huge car on what appeared little more than a pathway for utility vehicles. Undoubtedly, the sloppy, rock-strewn passage had hosted a goodly share of private trysts involving high school lovers. Their captor intended an entirely different use.

"Stop here," Conner said. Milliken complied, plunging his Cadillac into a peninsula of tall grass, flanked by trees on one side and what appeared a deep gully on the other. A ridge loomed beyond the gully to their right, shielding their eyes from retreating streaks of yellow flung across the horizon by the setting sun.

"Turn off the engine," Conner snapped. Milliken did as he was told. He and Lori kept looking straight ahead, too frightened to move. Ten seconds passed. Lori caught sight of their captor from the outside mirror. He sat directly behind her, eyes scanning the outdoors, craning his neck to see what apparently lay beyond his vision. He swore. Lori began to sob, quietly.

"Shut up!" Conner growled. He grunted, as though disgusted. "All right, get out of the car, both of you. Milliken, you first. Then you, lady. Both of you walk to the passenger side. If you try to run away, I'll cut you down in an instant!"

They needed no warning. Milliken climbed out of the car, walked around the front, and stood by the right fender, feet planted on the soggy ground. Lori got out, shut the door, stayed put. Conner quickly emerged from the back seat, walked in front of them, then peered over his shoulder to the crevice at his back. He swore again, as though confirming a disappointment.

"Not as clean as I wanted, but it will have to do," he remarked, talking mostly to himself. He fixed a murderous gaze on them both. He raised his weapon.

Panic shrieked through every fiber in Lori's body. She started shaking, uncontrollably, whimpering, sobbing. *"No, no, no,"* she repeated, as though her brain, sensing imminent death, threw its last, helpless protest at the feet of the unspeakable evil standing before it.

Milliken took a half step forward, hands raised. *"Look, mister,"* he croaked, "you don't have to do this. You can have the bonds, they're yours . . ."

A wicked chortle erupted from Albert Conner's throat. "Of course they're mine!" He patted his left breast pocket. "You think you needed to tell me that?" More demonic laughter.

The fiendish smirk lurking beneath his handlebar mustache suddenly evaporated. Conner's eyes narrowed. He aimed his pistol, slowly, savoring each second. Killing lust glinted from his cruel blue eyes . . .

Crack!

Lori collapsed against the car. She fell to her knees. A voice whispered from deep within her: *Expect a spike of pain, then a death gasp . . . Followed by eternal peace . . .*

She felt no pain. Lori raised her eyelids a sliver, looked down. Blood spattered her clothes. She glanced up. The killer stood before her, eyes bursting with shock, mouth gaping open. Blood blossomed from a two inch gash in his right shoulder. His gun hand wilted, he stumbled two steps forward, jerked his head around, looked behind him . . .

Crack!

Conner's body lurched toward the car, crashed against the Cadillac's fender between Lori and Milliken, his gun hand clanked against the metal. The pistol slapped free from his hand, clattered across the hood, then slid to the ground. He crumpled to the wet earth, blood gushing from a savage wound ripped through the middle of his chest. He sprawled before them, head cocked at a grotesque angle against the car. Dead.

Lori and Milliken gawked at this apparition. Their breath escaped in stuttering gasps.

Rustling noises floated through the crisp air. They came from the gully. Lori and Milliken spun around and saw a figure rising from the crevice, a trim physique outlined against the daylight's receding glow.

The man clambered up to a standing position on the edge of the crevice and rested the butt of his rifle on his hip. He chewed gum and regarded them without expression.

"Who . . . who are you?" Milliken asked.

"My name's Bert," came the response. "I'm a friend of Stewart."

Lori and Milliken exchanged uncomprehending looks. Bert took a couple of steps forward, stopped, and eyed them intently. "I think it's time the three of us had a little chat," he said.

Judge Walton's forty-five minute adjournment stretched into two hours. Each extra minute beyond the time he designated crawled along at an agonizing pace toward an unknown ending point. Finally, he swept into the courtroom, his flowing robe rippling with each step. He took his seat and raised his gavel.

BANG!

"It appears that authorities at Ambrose Penitentiary and their soul mates in the Department of Justice strongly object to deviations from procedures that require the detention of this prisoner for an additional four to five weeks," he intoned in a strong voice. "Which is why I have decided to release the defendant under the direct probation of this court, immediately. The officials I have spoken to strongly objected to this course of action, and I want their names and objections duly noted in the court record. Nonetheless, their comments leave me unconvinced. Therefore, I am ordering the United States Probation Department to work on the defendant's papers on an emergency basis." He looked sharply at the defense table.

"Mr. Lawrence, will you rise?" Walton commanded.

Stewart stood up obediently.

"Mr. Lawrence, do you solemnly pledge to remain within this jurisdiction for six to eight weeks, pending administrative completion of your case?"

"You have my word, your Honor," Stewart stated solemnly.

"Good. You are to report to the fourth floor of this building to the probation office, which will require your presence for about another hour. Mr. Lawrence, starting right now, *you are a free man!*"

A tear trickled down Stewart Lawrence's cheek, got caught near a crease formed by his wide, smiling lips, then raced down his neck. "Thank you, your Honor. Thank You."

Judge Walton leaned back in his chair, a smile tugging at the corners of his mouth. "You're welcome," he said. Gavel lifted, cocked in the air . . .

"This court is adjourned!"

BANG!

The judge stood up, strode from the courtroom, his task completed. The dozen people who remained, court officials and spectators, slowly filed out.

Ted Simon witnessed this spectacle in a state of what he believed constituted vicarious shock. Seven and a half years of anguished pleadings and justice denied had finally come to an end, producing one more free human being and a courtroom engulfed in silence. Although hardly an event to rival extravagant celebrations following a Super Bowl victory, Stewart's release warranted at least a few cheers, Simon thought. Maybe a banner waved, a trumpet blaring victory, even a single hurrah would do. *Maybe that's not what justice really is,* Simon mused. *No huge clapping or raucous celebrations, just a myriad of small victories for the human spirit.*

He met Stewart by the door, and they clasped hands warmly. "Hey, mister, can I treat you to dinner," Simon asked. "After you're finished upstairs, of course."

Stewart beamed and rolled his eyes about, as though he had entered a different dimension of reality. Still, his response puzzled Simon.

"I'd love to. I've got to make a few phone calls, first."

"Fine with me," Simon said agreeably. "I'll pick you up after you're done with that and your business on the fourth floor."

"Great. I'll see you then." Stewart turned around, walked briskly down the hallway, spied a phone booth tucked into a corner, and vanished inside.

Simon dismissed Stewart's peculiar behavior as the result of a temporary, delirious state of mind, exhilaration resulting from his first breath of freedom. He did not know that Stewart tried to contact three people: Lori Armstrong, Axel Thomas, and Bert.

He only reached one, who immediately hung up.

Bert kicked out his foot and shoved his victim's head from the car, where it flopped back on the ground, face toward the sky. He regarded the dead body with detachment.

"Friend of yours?" he asked.

"I have no idea who he is," Milliken said. He turned his ashen countenance toward Bert and looked at him with anxious, fearful eyes. "Are you going to kill us, too?"

Bert drew back, seemed offended. "If I intended to do that, you'd both be dead now, wouldn't you?" he said with professional aplomb.

"Yes, I guess we would," Milliken said, leaning back against his car. He appeared to remain on his feet only by the accidental locking of his knees in a standing position.

Relief flooded through Lori's body like a sedative. Soothing laps of wooziness flowed through her head, melting her limbs. Lori swooned. Then words sneaked through waves of relief washing across her thoughts.

"Hey, careful there, lady!"

A firm but gentle grip hoisted her upward. Her legs still felt like gelatin, and she struggled to her feet only with the help of Bert's careful assistance.

"Thank you," she whispered. Strands of dizziness still clung to her like wisps of lingering fog, then retreated as awareness gradually reclaimed her mind. She steadied herself, instinctively brushed down her clothes, then let her eyes drift toward the man who had saved their lives. Bert retained his impassive look, making Lori wonder how a person who had just killed someone could remain so calm. "Do . . . you know who this is?" she ventured.

"Yeah, I do," Bert said. "Though I never met him. His name's Albert Conner. Used to be a guard at a jail where Stewart stayed for five or six months. Got nailed on extortion charges while he was there, served time, then got out about, oh, a year or so ago, I guess. Been on a rampage ever since. A priest who knew this guy visited Stewart a few times, finally warned him to keep a look out while he was at Ambrose, to be careful, some guys might try to do him in. Conner's got a long reach. Lots of connections all over, with prisoners and other guards. Incredible." Bert snapped his gum, tossed another look toward Conner. "After I got paroled, I looked up that priest myself and he filled me in some more. Believe me, this is one tough son of a bitch." His eyes flickered toward Lori. "Sorry about the lady," he added, sheepishly.

A killer and a gentleman, Lori thought. "How did you know where he was taking us? How did you happen to be here?"

Bert rubbed the back of his neck and casually surveyed their surroundings. "I grew up in these parts. I know every road, every hideaway. My girlfriend and I used to neck over there." He pointed toward a clump of trees about forty feet away.

"How did you know he was taking us here?" Milliken asked.

"I followed you, of course. I spotted you in Axel's bar . . ."

Lori immediately placed Bert's face. "That was *you* in there!" she exclaimed. "I thought you were just ogling me."

"Well, I was doing that, too," he confessed. "But I was also sort of waiting for you to show up, because Stewart confided in me after I gave him the rundown on you two. He thought you might find that place before he got out. After you left Axel Thomas's place, I set out to track you, then all of a sudden, there you go, whizzing by *The Gandy Dancer* again. I took off after you, followed you here. When Conner took this road, I knew a shortcut, took that, waited for your car to show up. I knew he couldn't have gone much farther. Actually, if he did, he would've found a really deep ravine just around the corner over there. But he decided to stop here, instead." Bert shook his head, as though pondering what might have happened. "Lucky for you, he did. Also lucky he didn't look behind him, 'cause I didn't have time to be fancy about tracking you guys. He seemed pretty much concentrated on you two, wasn't careful enough like he should've been." Bert made this comment as though passing judgment on the work of a fellow professional.

A thought struck Lori. "Have you ever followed *me,* Bert?" she asked.

Bert arched his eyebrows slightly, the only emotion he had displayed so far. "You *caught* that?" He clucked his tongue. "Must be losing my touch," he said, disappointed.

"What is your connection with Stewart," inquired Milliken, whose face had returned to its normal color.

"We served time together at Whitestone," Bert said. "Stewart did a lot of huge favors for me. Somehow, he was able to get messages to the outside, to family members, friends. I didn't know how he did that, *nobody* did. Well, maybe a few knew, but they never told the rest of us. We really didn't care, just so they could send messages, keep contact for us with the outside." Bert paused, chewed his gum, thinking. "You have no idea how much that means when you're in prison. I had a wife, pregnant, a sick mother, and I could keep in touch with them. No charge. I didn't have any money, Stewart never charged me. So I owed him *big.*"

Bert paused, as though collecting his thoughts, retrieving memories. "Stewart got nailed for something he did, and before he got sent to Ambrose, he asked me to keep track of you, find out what you were doing, and report back to him. He knew I was from this area and was the best man for the job. I've been doing that for the past two and a half years or so." A trace of hostility passed across his plain features, as his eyes darted to Lori, then Milliken. "I had to tell him some pretty bad things in that time," Bert added.

Lori blushed. Milliken looked away.

Bert continued. "I saw Stewart about a week ago at a Federal jail in New York City. He's there waiting for a re-sentencing hearing, which should come up any day now. He asked me pick up an envelope from Axel Thomas and hold it for him. I explained all this to Axel, but he wouldn't give it to me without hearing directly from Stewart. I guess that never happened."

"But I did see him take a phone call at Axel Thomas's place," Lori interjected.

"That was from his office," Bert clarified, pointing toward Milliken. "A secretary trying to warn you that Conner was on the way. Axel decided then to turn the envelope over to you, then told me about it. Since I didn't threaten him or anything, and you did, he must have figured I was one of the good guys, I guess. That's when I took off after you."

Lori marveled at this man's account. Milliken smiled broadly. "We owe you our lives, Bert," he said.

Bert looked at them sharply. "I should also point out that Stewart hired me full-time to make sure that envelope ended up in *my* hands." A threatening undertone added force to Bert's words. He shifted his rifle to a ready position, his body stiffened.

Lori felt a shiver, but Milliken responded with an analytical look, as though he were about to cross-examine a witness.

"You said, he *hired* you?" he asked.

"That's right," Bert confirmed. "Promised me a big reward, too."

"Oh, really?" Milliken said. "How big a reward?"

Bert initially regarded the question with suspicion. Finally, he shrugged. "Guess it don't matter telling you. He said he'd give me ten thousand dollars, cash. I know he's good for it, too. Always kept his word in prison."

Lori and Milliken exchanged looks. Milliken turned to Bert, smiling. "Ten thousand dollars, eh?" he repeated. "Well, Bert, I think I can make you a better offer . . ."

One week later, at a hotel room in New York City, Stewart Lawrence sat at the edge of his bed, staring blankly out the window. Street noises floated up to his room from the outside, an amorphous buzz of irrelevant sounds pattering his eardrums. He heard nothing. Motionless, stunned, he kept his vision locked on the window, as though it could rescue him from his tortured thoughts. But he was beyond rescuing, now. Prison had done that, purging his soul of all hope, leaving him with nothing but a faint glimmer that continued to burn in some private corner of his mind. And now, even the glimmer had been snuffed out. His soul smoldered in complete darkness.

Stewart replayed the previous week in his thoughts, recounting each devastating piece of news. Lori Armstrong, unreachable; or, adamantly opposed to communicating with him, which amounted to the same thing. Refused to return his calls, advised others to warn him: *stay away!* Axel Thomas, reachable, but not communicating. Same message: don't bother me. And his most trusted former prisoner-friend, Bert: vanished from the face of the earth. All of them, inaccessible. Probably forever.

Finally, he reached toward the phone and dialed a number he knew would produce a response. Three rings. A familiar voice sounded.

Stewart cleared his throat, uttered a single phrase, then hung up. Then he picked up his jacket and walked out of his room, the words he spoke still lingering in his thoughts:

The Three Musketeers Ride!

Chapter Forty-One

August, 1979

Dennis Bower lifted his New York Mets baseball cap from his damp head and mopped his brow with a soggy handkerchief. *Miserable, hot, stinking day,* he thought, turning another page of the newspaper in his lap. *Who wants to shop in ninety-two degree weather, especially for shoes?* he wondered, gazing across a nearly empty parking lot. *Who wants to WEAR shoes in weather like this?* He ruffled another page past eyes stinging from sweat, then closed the business section and placed it next to his chair, which sat in front of his shoe store. Heat radiated from the nearly empty parking lot, cloaking distant shops behind a translucent film of blurry waves. Hat off, paper down, faced swiped with white cloth, then fanned with the sports section. He wondered if the next day offered any relief. *Gotta be better than this,* he reasoned. Merciless heat, poor business, time that crawled on its belly, one boring minute after another—*what could be worse?* Then his sweaty gaze settled on a peculiar sight, which had baffled him all day.

A car, a blue Pontiac, parked four spaces from where he sat. He noticed it when he opened his store in the morning. He knew that often people met at this shopping center, took off in another car to shop elsewhere, then return. But this car had been there all day. Didn't make sense. It couldn't belong to an employee, either; they parked in the back. Bower couldn't figure it out.

Three o'clock slunk along, another hour drenched in humidity and dripping perspiration. Bower remained perched before his shoe store, with nothing else to do but suffer, work on a crossword puzzle, and occasionally let hot eyes roam over the shimmering pavement. Every glance up from the paper merely confirmed his judgment about another depressing business day. He never saw anything interesting. Then, unexpectedly, he spied something mighty peculiar. A car floated into the border of his desultory gaze, a white Plymouth. Just stayed there for a few minutes, parked about ten spaces away from the Pontiac. No other cars around it, just sat there, by itself.

A number of men emerged from the Plymouth. They trotted toward the Pontiac, carrying grocery bags. The containers appeared heavy. One of the men opened the trunk, they tossed a few bags inside, then climbed into the Pontiac. *Why did they tote those heavy bags that distance? Why didn't they just park next to that car?* he wondered. Bower observed this spectacle with pencil in hand. *Got nothing better to do,* he thought. He jotted down the license number of the Pontiac, as the men climbed in and drove away.

A lady ambled up to him. "Are you open today?" she asked.

"Oh, yes!" Bower said, getting up. He'd do anything to break the monotony. Even wait on a customer.

One hour later and a dozen attempts to fit shoes too small on feet too large, his customer left the store, wearing the pair she had bought. White pumps, straining to contain the bulk jammed inside, leaving no room even for a few wriggling toes. The customer was always right. Still, Bower felt relieved he didn't have to provide insurance against leather fatigue. He reckoned the life expectancy of those shoes in weeks, depending on how often she wore them. She seemed satisfied, and that pleased him. He walked her to the door, bade her farewell, and caught sight of a police cruiser stopped by the white Plymouth. Two policemen were examining the car intently.

Bower casually approached them. "What's up, officers?"

"We think this car might be stolen," one of them said.

"Really?" Bower said, his interest piqued. "Well, you know, that's funny, 'cause about an hour ago, I saw three or four guys park this thing here, carry a bunch of heavy shopping bags about ten spaces away to a car parked in front of my store, get inside, and take off. That really looked odd to me, so I took the license number of the car they left in. A Pontiac."

The two New York City policemen halted immediately. They looked at him sternly, as though a felon had suddenly materialized before their eyes.

Bower flinched, felt uncomfortable. His next utterance took them by even more surprise. "Do you think . . . that might be, um, *important?*" he asked.

November, 1979

"That's a Roger, Sky King. What's the view from up there?"

"Nothing to note, Ground Hog."

"Beam me up, Scotty. Let me take a look. Life's a drag down here."

"Negative, Ground Hog. Transporter's on the fritz. Maybe next time."

"Promises, promises."

"Plus, it's mighty crowded up here."

"It's always about you, isn't it?"

A quiet chuckle. "Sky King out."

"Ten-Four."

Click!

Detective Ralph Beamis placed his radio receiver down, acutely aware that their conversation was being recorded, standard operating procedure, and would become part of official police records. He didn't care. Occasional wisecracks helped break the tedium of what had become three months' round-the-clock surveillance of a blue Pontiac sedan, by helicopters and unmarked police cars. Plus his record showed a career track steeped in professionalism, studded with accomplishments. So if he sneaked in a little frivolity now and then, so what? He never claimed to be Mr. Spock, just a solid, dependable professional, performing his duty.

Professionalism. His thoughts lingered on that concept. The guys they had been tracking reeked of professionalism; cold, calculating, almost military-style expertise, which employed weapons but no firing, not yet. He wondered if the phrase, *radical professionalism,* lurked somewhere in manuals outlining police procedures. If not, he wanted to contribute this term and apply it not to law enforcement officers, but instead to the group of twisted intellects who had robbed forty-three banks over the course of the last thirty months. *Radical professionals, that's what they are,* he thought. Polite ones, too, by all descriptions. They hadn't shot anyone. Not yet, at least.

Beamis had been a member of the original task force created specifically to track down and capture *The Three Musketeers.* Consisting of agents and officers from the FBI, Nassau County, Suffolk County, and New York City, their group had grown to thirty-five officials, all dedicated to halting the most prolific gang of bank robbers in the annals of criminal justice. By this point, everyone realized that stopping this rampage would not only relieve a great many banks from future distress, but would make history as well.

So far, nothing had worked. At an earlier stage of the investigation, two dozen banks that officials pegged as likely targets, based on the Musketeers' habits, had been staked out for a period of two months. Expensive, time-consuming, totally ineffectual, this operation whimpered to a frustrating close. Then police attempted to track their cars, which the task force had learned comprised only of stolen Plymouths. Still no luck. The Plymouths never turned up until after the robberies, and totally clean, as well; no fingerprints, no articles carelessly left behind, no evidence. Nothing. The task force had even determined that shopping centers constituted transfer points after robberies. Still, police never made it in time to nab the gang. Or, they got the location wrong. Or something else maddeningly inexplicable tripped them up.

Beamis shook his head in amazement as he pondered this history. Uncounted hours of bleary-eyed scrutiny aimed at city maps sprouting colored pins, which stabbed locations of robbed banks, had failed to reveal clear patterns. Their maps permitted a few educated guesses, perhaps; but nothing that burst with clarity, offered undisputed direction. For several months, colored pins danced before his closed eyes when Beamis retired at night, taunting his exasperated imagination to squeeze out answers. *Either we're all incompetent fools, or they're bloody geniuses,* he thought. He didn't have to be defensive about his own work to conclude the latter was true. *The Three Musketeers,* or however many existed in the group, stood out as criminal geniuses.

Thus, it took a completely adventitious event to supply the task force with its best lead yet: a blue Pontiac, which police secretly equipped with an electronic homing device, sitting before him across the street. Unfortunately, the shoe store owner's description of the car's inhabitants proved virtually useless: three or four men, he believed, one tall, two shorter. The fourth, if he existed, struck no recollection. All carried kraft supermarket bags. All wore shirts, jeans; couldn't remember the color; tan, maybe. That was it. Still, better than nothing, especially since police now had positively identified the third vehicle, definitely not a stolen car. Its owner had to be someone connected to *The Three Musketeers.* Although the Pontiac's three previous excursions amounted to nothing, police kept their vigilance. They continued to wait. And watch.

Their patience was about to be rewarded.

Bank robbery number forty-four.

Anything magical about that number? Or ominous, maybe? Stewart Lawrence didn't know. He mentally thumbed through each line of the same meticulous rules that had guided all their previous successful ventures. Bank layout studied; customer flow examined; traffic patterns analyzed; notes jotted down; a few photographs taken, scrutinized; points of view exchanged, all ramifications thoroughly discussed. No misgivings snagged anyone's attention, nothing gnawed at their confidence to conduct this operation. Each member retained veto power; none had exercised it for this job. Looked perfectly achievable; routine, even. Stewart had demanded strict adherence to their manual of operations, and none questioned his leadership. All had achieved their financial goals except the recently acquired fourth member. But an additional robbery or two would satisfy him, after which the Musketeers agreed to disband their business and retire.

Peter Radius conducted a last equipment check. "We can do this forever," he said with a smug grin. "We're invincible, this plan works *every* time."

"The minute we start believing that, we're dead," Stewart cautioned. "Just do what we've always done. Don't get too cocky." He turned to Terrence Daly. "Are the cars ready?"

"Cleaned, vacuumed, washed, you name it," Terrence replied, peering down the barrel of his shotgun. He snapped it shut and buried it into a special compartment sewn into his clothing.

"Gabe, are you all set?" Stewart asked.

The fourth member of their business, a stocky forty-year-old, responded with a thumbs-up sign. Stewart circled each member, like a master sergeant checking his troops' state of readiness before embarking on a mission into enemy territory. Finally satisfied, he faced them as a group.

"Okay, let's go," he ordered. The four men filed out of their rented house and walked toward their car, a blue Pontiac sedan. It was two o'clock.

At that precise moment, a hugely sophisticated surveillance apparatus sprang to life, locked on their every move, enveloped them like a gigantic, electronic spider web. Instructions crackled across a myriad of points in the invisible network that surrounded them, waiting to snare *The Three Musketeers.*

"What if we don't get much on this hit?" Peter inquired.

"We could consider another, but I still think we should retire," Stewart said. "We don't want to push our luck."

"We can keep this up forever," Peter said again.

"I told you, stop talking like that," Stewart said.

Subjects traveling east on Hempstead Avenue. Copy that, Sky King. Click. Red Rover, check. Click. Got them, Ground Hog. Following through.

"You know I'd really like to increase my total pot a little bit," the newest member said. "But I'll leave that decision to you guys. You'll get no fuss from me, but could we at least talk about it after this hit?"

"Just drive," Stewart said.

Subjects turned south on Elmont Road. Click. Speed check? Normal. Proceed.

"Alabama," Gabe blurted. "I've always wanted to live in Alabama. You know that's the heart of the old south."

Three pairs of eyes trained on the driver. "Trust me, Gabe," Terrence said. "We've all been there. You don't want to go there for any reason."

Gabe seemed puzzled. "Why not?" he asked.

"We'll tell you later," Peter said. "Just believe me when I say that hell has a lot of chambers, and that's the worst one."

"No, it isn't," Stewart corrected. "But it comes close."

Subjects turned east on Southern State Parkway, appear headed east toward Valley Stream. Click. Copy that. Subjects observe speed limits carefully. Keep safe distance. Copy that. Click.

Gabe pulled into a shopping center parking lot that hosted a plethora of department stores, assorted factory outlets, and novelty shops. A sea of cars greeted their view. Perfect camouflage. He wheeled their Pontiac next to a delivery van, about a dozen spaces from number two car, a stolen gray and green Plymouth they had left at the lot a few minutes before the start of business hours. The four men got out of their legally owned car, walked toward the stolen Plymouth and climbed inside, with Gabe behind the wheel. He pulled out of the lot and headed toward another road leading them closer to their target. It was two-thirty, p.m.

Pontiac located exactly ten spaces from stolen vehicle. Positive ID's obtained on all subjects. Cameras functioning well, close-up obtained on driver. All now wearing gloves.

"How crowded was that A & P parking lot when you guys cased it?" Stewart inquired, peering out the window, as though the weather might have changed in the last two minutes. It hadn't.

"Crowded," Terrence replied. "Plus, they're having some sort of late fall sale at that department store next to it. I even picked up one of their ads."

"Maybe if we get a chance, we can stop for a minute and buy another bunch of white socks," Peter cracked. "I haven't gotten any new ones since, oh, hit number twenty-two, I think."

"You mean, you haven't *changed* your socks since that time," Terrence pointed out. Gabe chuckled.

"That's enough, you guys," Stewart said. He checked his watch. "Our timing is exactly correct," he commented, mostly to himself. Stewart insisted they rehearse their route at least twice before each robbery.

This job required three run-throughs, and the last excursion included purchasing several bags filled with groceries, which supplied them with containers they needed for stuffing cash once inside the bank. They pulled into the parking lot six spaces away from their number one car, another stolen Plymouth, white, with blue trim. A quick trot, master key again applied, four men plunged inside, Plymouth driven away.

Subjects appear headed toward Nassau County Bank, Valley Stream branch. Alert all units. Click. All units ALERTED and READY. Click.

Fifteen minutes traveling time elapsed. Talking ceased, concentration focused. Gabe wheeled their Plymouth into a space on a side road two blocks from the bank, the maximum distance their rules permitted. Stewart got out and plunked change into the meter. Discipline galvanized their moves with military precision, as though a common intellect had penetrated each mind, commanding their actions with whip-cracking efficiency. Gabe remained behind the wheel, while his three companions arranged their attire and weapons, stuffing ski masks beneath army-style fatigue caps. All wore identical clothing. Dark shirts beneath blue jackets, blue jeans, white socks, and sneakers, which made individual identification difficult.

A last minute check. A & P grocery bags, ready. Change of clothes, ready. Weapons, ready.

Let's go.

Stewart, Terrence, and Peter clipped on dark, one-way sunglasses and walked briskly toward Nassau County Bank, Valley Stream branch. One corner turned; then another. Bank stood before them, big, marble facade looming over main street. Slack time for this bank: between two-thirty and three o'clock. Few customers. Not many pedestrians. No cops. Looked just right. Two-forty-five, p.m. Time allowed for hit: five minutes. Departure time: two-fifty, p.m. *Exactly.*

Front of the bank . . . Sunglasses off . . . Ski masks pulled over faces . . . Shot guns whipped out . . . *NOW!*

Stewart, Terrence, and Peter burst into the lobby. Terrence sprinted toward the left, covered the manager, bank officials by desks. Peter dashed toward the teller windows. Lawrence skipped to the side of main entrance. Stop watch started. *Click!* Split-second scan. Seven employees, three behind desks, three by teller windows, one by drive-through booth. Three customers. No problem.

"This is a holdup!" Peter shouted. "Keep your hands and feet still! Make no sounds! Do exactly what we tell you, and no one will get hurt!" Looked at customers. "You, you, and you! On the floor, face down. *Don't move!*"

Shotguns raised, pointed. Stunned looks, instant compliance.

To the tellers: "Scoop the cash into the bags. FAST!"

"TWO!" shouted Stewart. Two minutes left.

Frenzied motions. Arms whipped into registers, jerking fingers grappled wads of currency, heaved it into the shopping bag.

THREE!

Dash toward the drive-in booth . . . "Throw it into the bag, lady! Do it fast!"

Shocked, frozen.

"Come on! Come on!"

Hand plunged into register, fumbling, clumsy movements, money grasped, thrown into bag . . .

"Lift it out, dump it! The whole thing!"

FOUR!

Metal insert of cash register emptied, last step completed. Terrence, Peter, backed away carefully, shotgun barrels roaming the bank interior, muzzles gliding across terrified victims . . .

By the door now, next to Stewart. Shotguns plunged into special holsters, handguns drawn. Stopwatch clicked. Four and a half minutes.

The three men spun around, passed through the entrance, emerged from the bank, turned right. They walked toward the car, normal pace, no hurry. Ski masks still on, handguns stuffed into pockets. One man carried a shopping bag. Peter.

"Excellent! Excellent!" Stewart muttered. "With thirty seconds to spare."

"Looks like a huge take, too," Terrence said.

They walked fifteen steps. Then, for the first and only time in their history, The Three Musketeers heard these words:

"FREEZE! POLICE OFFICERS!"

A dozen uniformed figures burst from parked cars, doorways to adjacent stores, two alleys, and dashed toward them. Twelve policemen surrounded three men, pistols raised, pointed at their chests from every angle. The Musketeers had no weapons in hand; they had put them away after leaving the bank. One of their rules.

An A & P bag filled with cash plopped to the sidewalk. Three pairs of hands raised. An expletive crept from one of the Musketeer's lips. Another whispered *Mother of God* under his breath. The third Musketeer simply lowered his head and stared at the ground.

The Three Musketeers' stunning career had come to an end, along with that of its brilliant leader, Stewart Lawrence.

Or, so it seemed.

Chapter Forty-Two

June, 1993, FBI Academy, Quantico, Virginia

Agent Kenneth Benton paused in his lecture and let his eyes roam over the classroom. Respectful silence and a phalanx of alert faces greeted his view. Benton threw a quick glance over their heads to the back of the room, caught Ted Simon's attentive gaze, then looked back at his students. Finally, the twenty-five year FBI veteran raised his chalk and scratched a few more words on the blackboard.

"*Rule number fourteen!*" he announced. "*Any* gang member is allowed to call off a job for *any* reason, even for something as flimsy as a bad feeling. Bad vibes, no job, no explanation necessary, *period*. In fact, the Musketeers factored this into their planning. Initially, they figured that one out of three or even half of their planned hits might have to be aborted. For instance, one time a police car cruised by a bank they were about to rob, for no special reason, just making rounds. The Musketeers noticed this and aborted the hit immediately. An unexpected traffic jam on a highway needed for their escape route stopped another heist. A few police officers picking up their checks at a bank put a halt to another. They stuck to their rules strictly, *no deviations.*"

A smile touched the corners of his mouth. "In fact, strict adherence to their own carefully worked out procedures is what got them caught. If The Three Musketeers had been more flexible, they wouldn't have parked so far from car number three to transfer their loot and clothes. Ironic, when you think about it. The rules that produced such spectacular success for them for the first forty-three bank robberies finally proved their undoing in robbery number forty-four." Agent Benton shook his head, amazement clinging to his features. "Which was supposed to have been their *last* job before they retired! A fact I still find incredible, even after teaching this course over the years."

A hand raised from a young man seated in the front row. "Mr. Benton, you explained that the police wanted to catch them in the act *before* making arrests, which I understand. But didn't that strategy risk everyone's lives in the bank while the robbery was being carried out? I know the Musketeers never shot anyone, but certainly the risk was always there, wasn't it?"

A gentle stirring in the classroom acknowledged the degree of interest in this question. Benton nodded as well, confirming the point advanced by his questioner.

"Thank God, the worst possible scenario never played out," he said, a bit uncomfortably.

Another hand. "I assume police called them The Three Musketeers because there were three of them who entered the bank?"

Benton grinned. "That's a good guess, but actually, police used the same name they used to refer to themselves," he said. "On one of their early hits, Lawrence blurted out something like, *'Go, Musketeers!'* before they dashed out the bank and made their getaway. Authorities couldn't come up with a better name than that. Could you?"

Expressions of merriment twittered through the room. "No sir, I guess I couldn't."

Ted Simon sat in the back row, smiling at this question and the inadequate answer that followed. Although he enjoyed Benton's lecture series, he agreed to attend on the condition that his old friend would not reveal his identity. Today's topic, entitled, *"The Three Musketeers: Rules of Engagement,"* captivated everyone in the classroom, Simon especially. Still, his thoughts remained haunted by a disturbing possibility that the last chapter on Stewart Lawrence, The Three Musketeers' legendary leader, had not yet been written. In the middle of an extended explanation of rule sixteen, Simon reached into his left pocket, pulled out a newspaper article, glanced at it, then gently folded the paper and put it away.

"Rule Number Nineteen," Benton continued, after making short work of two previous items among the list of edicts that studded The Three Musketeers' field manual of bank robbing operations, *"after* the hit, change clothes while driving *from* car number one *to* car number two . . ."

And on he went, darting from one end of the blackboard to another, stabbing the air with his forefinger for emphasis. He concluded with a sweeping peroration on criminal techniques, a review that dazzled his audience and inspired an appreciative applause.

"Any final questions?" he asked, eyes scanning the classroom. Several hands sprang toward the ceiling. Benton nodded toward one of them.

"Mr. Benton, how would you characterize the significance of catching this gang, putting an end to their string of robberies?"

A sense of intellectual satisfaction gushed from the lips of Kenneth Benton, Adjunct professor, FBI Training School. *"My characterization?"* He shook his head as if in self-denial, but obviously relishing the moment. "How about the characterization of those *who actually took part* in the special task force created to capture The Three Musketeers? Allow me to quote the words of one of these individuals: 'Willie Sutton'—you all have heard of Willie Sutton, I assume . . ."

Good-natured chortles rumbled through the classroom.

"Willie Sutton," he continued, "was a *rank amateur* next to these guys, especially compared to their leader, *Stewart Lawrence.*" Benton took a breath, captured every expression in his classroom with one intense look. "These arrests," he continued, "constitute the *most important* ones in the history of bank robbery in the United States." A pause. *"Ever!"* He turned to the questioner. "Does that answer your question?"

"Yes sir. Thank you."

Benton checked his watch. "Our time is exhausted, ladies and gentlemen. We'll continue on these themes in my final lecture tomorrow. Thank you."

Scattered expressions of appreciation, a few last comments advanced by lingering enthusiasts, and the classroom emptied. Simon remained seated. Benton walked over to him after the last student had filed out of the room.

"Great job, Ken," Simon commented. "I really appreciated your invitation. Tremendous lecture. Excellent technique."

"Whose technique are you referring to, mine or Lawrence's?" the FBI agent said with a grin, accepting Simon's handshake. Small talk cluttered the next few minutes before Benton had to leave for his next class. Then, over his shoulder, as a parting question. "By the way, do you have any idea whatever happened to Lawrence?"

"No . . . No idea at all," Simon answered. "Haven't heard from him. Which, I might add, is fine with me."

"See you tomorrow."

"Yes, tomorrow."

Simon left the classroom, walked down several long hallways, and exited the building. He strode toward his vehicle, enjoying the crisp breeze that whipped across his face from a cool, fall afternoon. Once inside his Jeep Cherokee, he reached for the newspaper article that had bedeviled his concentration during Benton's lecture. For the sixth or seventh time, he reviewed its contents:

FBI REMAINS BAFFLED

A spokesman for the Federal Bureau of Investigation reported today that the agency still has no leads to the identity of what they dubbed "The Wednesday Bandit." This bank robber, aged between fifty and sixty, height about six feet, had robbed thirteen banks in as many weeks, all but the last one on Wednesday. His thirteenth robbery took place on Thursday, at a bank within what appeared his region of activities, which covered southern New Hampshire, eastern Vermont, and northwestern Massachusetts. The lone gunman reportedly carried a single revolver, wore dark one-way sunglasses, a baseball cap, and a London Fog type raincoat. On some occasions he wore a tan jacket and dungarees. He spoke few words quietly, politely, but in a firm voice, and vanished after each robbery without a trace. Police speculate that he might have worked with a partner who drove the car. The "Wednesday Bandit" has not struck for several months now, after having absconded with approximately one half million dollars worth of cash. "It's as though the perpetrator had reached a preset limit," commented one official, "then decided to stop." The FBI continues to investigate but is no closer to a solution . . .

Simon could not read this without sensing that ghosts from Stewart Lawrence's past lurked between the lines of this press account. Stewart's first release from prison had been on a Wednesday; his second, after serving twelve years of an eighteen year sentence, occurred on a Thursday. Identical techniques, right age category, physical description, and so forth. Plus, Simon had been informed by FBI agents over the years that M.O.'s never change, and the recidivism rate for bank robbers hovers at a depressing *ninety percent*. Still, a coincidence? Simon didn't know. He didn't *want* to know.

He started his engine, thoughts in turmoil. *Has to be a coincidence,* Simon convinced himself. Nearly two decades of Stewart Lawrence's life had been spent in prison. That must have purged him of his bank robbing habits. Simon glanced at the article one last time before stuffing it into his pocket. He shook his head. *This guy couldn't be Stewart,* he thought. *Could it?*

The moment of truth had arrived.

Stewart Lawrence balanced two coffee mugs, planted his foot near the base of a sliding glass door to his log cabin retreat in New Hampshire, and gingerly eased it open. Keeping one eye on the mugs and another on a pitcher of cream he had somehow managed to grapple with an available pinkie, he walked carefully to a picnic table on his deck. He placed the containers down and took a seat. Two gorgeous sights instantly captured his vision: clumps of fog glimmering against invading cracks of morning light that streaked over distant mountains; and Lori Armstrong, who glowed with even more radiant beauty. Stewart took a sip of the steaming liquid. Tasted wonderful.

"So how's the Wednesday Bandit?" Lori asked, an impish look tweaking her features.

"Retired," Stewart proclaimed. "Seriously, permanently, unalterably retired. And the last job took place on a Thursday, remember?"

"The same day you were last let out of prison . . ."

"That's right," Stewart confirmed. He took another sip of coffee. "You said you wanted cream, right?"

"Is that your first, *official* question?" Lori asked.

"I thought I would start out small, then work my way up to the important stuff."

"I owe it to you, I guess," Lori said, letting her gaze drift toward the mountains. "I promised I would bring you up to date after the thirteenth bank, tell you everything." A wistful mood crept from her low voice. She spoke as though she were alone, to remind herself of obligations she had made.

"And I promised to quit the business, not to push my luck any longer," Stewart said, repeating his part of the deal they made four months ago, after Lori's phone call to him. "I'm pushing sixty! That's close enough to retirement age. By the way, how did you learn to drive like that?"

"After Madison died, I changed jobs, became a truck driver."

"*A truck driver?*" Stewart exclaimed. "I never heard of such a thing. Ladies driving trucks."

"Yeah, we can vote, too," Lori remarked with a smile.

"How did Madison die? Heart attack?"

Lori nodded.

Another sip of coffee, a worried glance to the side, inspired by a troubling question that leaped to the front of Stewart's thoughts. "Tell me, did he happen to be on top of you when that blessed event took place?"

"No!" Lori said vehemently. "He was in the hospital, with tubes sticking out from every part of his body. I was by Jeremy's bed when he died, because he asked for me. I don't think my being there helped him, though."

"Why not?"

Lori gave him a mischievous grin. "When he was barely conscious, I leaned over and whispered in his ear that I was the one who took his bonds many years ago. His eyes flared, I mean, like, *really* lit up, then closed. He jerked one last time, and he was gone. It's quite possible I had something to do with his timely demise."

A chortle erupted from Stewart's throat, which he tried to masquerade as a cough, with no success. "Seems quite possible to me, too," he remarked, cradling his coffee mug for stability. He clucked his tongue. "What a pity."

"Yes, a real pity," Lori agreed. She tossed him a coquettish look. "Was *that* your first, official question?"

"No, but give me time, I'm getting there."

Both heads turned, snatched soothing glimpses from their spectacular view, which offered continual solace to thoughts groping for proper expressions, for the least awkward ways to advance questions. Stewart looked at Lori again, felt as though he were ogling forbidden fruit, savoring its beckoning contours, but never quite daring to reach out and grasp it.

He cleared his throat. "Would you like some sugar for your coffee? Do you still love me?" he asked. He knew Lori took sugar with her coffee.

Lori smiled. "Yes," she said.

"Yes, you want sugar for your coffee, or yes, you still love me?"

"Yes to both," Lori stated firmly.

Stewart started to get up. "Okay, I'll get the sugar."

"Oh, for crying out loud, Stewart, sit down!" Lori said with a giggle. "Were *those* your first, official questions?"

"Yes to both," Stewart said. Again, his eyes floated to the mountains. Lori followed suit. Finally, "Lori, whatever happened to those bonds?" Stewart asked.

For the first time since they had renewed their acquaintance, Stewart saw pain touch Lori's worry lines, now accented by the passage of over twenty years.

She sighed, resignedly. "Milliken ended up with them all, or most of them," Lori said. "After Bert killed Conner and confronted us, Milliken promised him fifty thousand dollars cash if he would forget about you, let us both go, and disappear. Bert pressed for more, but Milliken stood firm, as though that was all he could offer, and I played along. Milliken cashed in the bonds, gave Bert his cut, and we never saw him again. When I asked for my half of what was left, Milliken just laughed in my face, told me to get lost. He said no one would ever believe my story. It was too self-incriminating. He also said no one would doubt his word. He had me where he wanted me. I trusted him, and he cheated me. More than anyone else, in fact. But there was nothing I could do about it."

Stewart whistled softly. "What happened then?"

Lori shrugged. "I went back to work for Jeremy, until he died, of course. His son took over the business. And—would you believe this?—he started to hit on me, too. Like father, like son. I'm old enough to be his mother!" Lori appealed for a sympathetic reaction from Stewart, and got it. "Anyway, I quit, went to school, started driving trucks. I bumped into Ted Simon once, quite by accident, really. Delivered a load to his factory, saw him, chatted politely, then he told me you had just gotten paroled. I decided to look you up, and you know the rest."

Lori took a sip of her coffee. "Needs sugar," she commented.

Stewart's thoughts wandered. He spoke as though in a trance. *"The perfect crime,"* he mused, thinking out loud.

"What?"

"Milliken committed the perfect crime. He got away with almost a half million dollars without putting himself at risk, not on purpose, anyway, and with no chance of being caught, ever. The perfect crime."

Lori just nodded, sipping her unsweetened coffee. She settled her soft eyes on Stewart. "Do you love me, Stewart?" she asked earnestly.

"Madly!" Stewart responded. "I never stopped loving you, Lori. Not for a moment. Even when you hurt me."

Lori considered this answer. "When you first had Madison's bonds, would you have shared them with me?"

"Yes," Stewart stated firmly. "Would you have done the same with me?"

"Yes," Lori said in a strong voice. "Though I think we both went crazy for a while . . ."

"That's far behind us, now." Stewart said.

The two gazed at each other with adoring eyes. The mountains receded into the background.

"I guess honesty isn't as bad as I thought it would be," Lori ventured.

Stewart got up, took Lori's hand, gently raised her from her chair, and embraced her warmly. He gave her a long, passionate kiss. "Why don't we make a habit of it, darling," he suggested. "And get married, while we're at it."

"That *would* make an honest woman of me," Lori agreed. She reached up, hungrily sought his eager lips. Another ardent kiss.

Then they again let their eyes rest on the mountains, arms wrapped around each other, like two young lovers dreaming about their future, hearts filled with longing and hope.

AFTERWORD
By
Bruce G. Siminoff

This book is based on a true story. The person depicted as Stewart Lawrence was an employee of my father's company during the time period indicated. All the names, locations, and most dates have been changed somewhat, while additional camouflage has been inserted in order to conceal, and, in some cases, protect identities of those involved. But the principal outlines, Lawrence's gambling, bank robbing, and prison experiences conform to history. On less weighty matters, the implements he used in his initial robberies—the jacket, sunglasses, and chrome-plated pistol, for example—he had indeed taken from my apartment. Other matters I prefer not to clarify, although curious readers should have little trouble isolating particular facts that are now part of the historical record.

Individuals familiar with my involvement have occasionally inquired why I tried to help Stewart, particularly during his stay at that notorious facility referred to here as Jackson County Jail. Several reasons stand out. Stewart was, of course, a friend and a valuable employee. I genuinely felt that encouragement on my part could indeed turn him around, rehabilitate him, in the best sense of that term. Further, the wretched, inhumane treatment he and other prisoners received at Jackson County Jail constituted a turning point in my attitude toward his confinement. Only a stone heart could ignore that den of evil.

The despicable officials in charge of Jackson County Jail couldn't even abide by their *own* corrupt rules on the exploitation of helpless prisoners. After Boss Hogg's underlings absconded with all of the food I brought for Stewart and his fellow cell mates, instead of just taking their usual "cut," I decided at that moment to try to help. It wasn't just the sandwiches and blueberry tarts; to me, their cavalier attitude issued from the depths of depravity. What would they do next? As indicated in those chapters, the course of action I chose posed great dangers: to me, to

Stewart, to others caught in the warden's nefarious web. Stewart constantly warned me to be careful. And he was right. Jackson County Jail cast a long shadow across my future. For a considerable period of time, I slept with a loaded pistol beneath my pillow, and I instructed my wife what to do in case a vengeful guard succeeded in snuffing out my life.

A question remains whether Stewart ever could have been diverted from the criminal path he embarked on immediately after his first release from prison. In short, did he experience a "turning point" during his prison experiences? I have frequently pondered this matter and remain unsure. Without question, his continued incarceration, after he served what should have been no more than thirty-six months of his original sentence, embittered him, probably irretrievably. Worse, Stewart didn't learn the reason for his extended jail time, which resulted mainly from the death of his original sentencing judge and the subsequent administrative failure to follow up, until he arrived in Judge Walton's chambers for his re-sentencing hearing. Nonetheless, before that point, Stewart continued to break regulations *while he was still in prison.* His escapades at Whitestone, for instance, indicated his willingness to push the rules at a minimum security facility to their limits. And even at his re-sentencing trial, in his emotional, tear-filled testimony, he failed to mention those infractions that resulted in his transfer from Whitestone to the maximum security prison in Georgia. That was Stewart. He had a peculiar way of looking at himself and those around him.

Which raises another intriguing question, to me, at least. Did Stewart ever lie to me? The answer is yes and no. Naturally, he was *not* about to tell me that he had "borrowed" what he needed from my apartment for his first, solo bank-robbing excursion. However, I have no doubt that Stewart placed special trust in me, especially after I decided to help him during his harrowing stay at Jackson County Jail. He confided in me from that point to the end of his first term in prison. That is how I found out about the prisoners' secret communication center at Whitestone, for instance (which may still be there, as far as I know), along with a host of other matters.* To take another example, at Ambrose, Stewart told me frankly he was seriously considering robbing banks after his release, a prospect that horrified me. As described in that chapter, I did my best to dissuade him, obviously, to no avail. The fact remains, he was simply

---

* Inmates today don't face the hurdles Stewart and his companions had to face during the early seventies. Currently, telephones are supplied to prisoners with far fewer restrictions on their use. Thus, the infraction that resulted in Stewart's transfer to a maximum security facility no longer is an issue.

being honest with me. Finally, he promised that he never would lie to authorities and somehow try to implicate me or others not involved in his crimes. He kept his word on that, and on other matters as well.

I believe these considerations leave one with mixed reactions to Stewart Lawrence. Without question, he was an individual for whom the term "criminal genius" was coined. Comparisons to other notorious perpetrators I found particularly apt, especially to Willie Sutton. Stewart's gang's exploits continued to be used for instructional purposes at universities in special courses on such topics. How important was he as a *historical* figure? The words of an official involved in his capture summarize the answer to this question most succinctly and were closely paraphrased in the last chapter. They bear repeating here: These arrests [of The Three Musketeers] were "the most significant in the field of bank robberies, ever."

Such was the legacy of Stewart Lawrence. Should he read this book, I still wish him well.